WARRIORS

WARRIORS

Book One: *Into the Wild*

Book Two: *Fire and Ice*

Book Three: *Forest of Secrets*

Book Four: *Rising Storm*

Book Five: *A Dangerous Path*

Book Six: *The Darkest Hour*

THE NEW PROPHECY

Book One: *Midnight*

Book Two: *Moonrise*

Book Three: *Dawn*

Book Four: *Starlight*

Book Five: *Twilight*

Book Six: *Sunset*

POWER OF THREE

Book One: *The Sight*

Book Two: *Dark River*

Book Three: *Outcast*

Book Four: *Eclipse*

Book Five: *Long Shadows*

Book Six: *Sunrise*

OMEN OF THE STARS

Book One: *The Fourth Apprentice*

Book Two: *Fading Echoes*

Book Three: *Night Whispers*

Book Four: *Sign of the Moon*

Book Five: *The Forgotten Warrior*

Book Six: *The Last Hope*

EXPLORE THE WARRIORS WORLD

WARRIORS

ENTER the CLANS

INCLUDES

**WARRIORS FIELD GUIDE:
SECRETS OF THE CLANS**

AND

WARRIORS: CODE OF THE CLANS

ERIN HUNTER

HARPER

An Imprint of HarperCollinsPublishers

Library of Congress catalog card number: 2006036237, 2008045061

ISBN 978-0-06-210239-3

Typography by Hilary Zarycky

16 17 18   PC/RRDC   10 9

❖

First Edition

CONTENTS

WARRIORS
FIELD GUIDE

SECRETS of the CLANS

Special thanks to
Tui Sutherland

For Cyd, because she loves cats, and for Rebekah,
because I'm sure she will, too

SECRETS of the CLANS

CONTENTS

THUNDER, WIND, RIVER, SHADOW, AND STAR:

The Clans

The story of the beginning of the warrior Clans
has been passed down by cats of all Clans, from elder to warrior,
from warrior to apprentice, from queen to kit. The story
is never the same twice, and parts grow uncertain,
or they become suddenly clear in the telling. There are some cats
who walk dimly, their names and deeds lost in the sweet fog
of the elders' den, for the warrior Clans have roamed
the forest for moons beyond counting....

HISTORY OF THE GLANS

Many moons ago, the forest was a wilderness, untamed by territories. In the north lay sweeping moorland; in the south was dense woodland. On the edge of the trees, a tumbling river flowed out of a dark ravine.

Cats came into the forest. They were drawn by the soft rustlings of small creatures, shadows under the water, and the sudden commotion of birds' wings in the trees. These were not warrior cats. They lived in small groups, not yet Clans. There were no borders set down. And they fought constantly, fearful that prey might run out and that their overlapping territories were being threatened. It was a lawless, bloody time for the forest, and many cats died.

One night, when the moon was full, the cats agreed to meet at a clearing in the forest surrounded by four great oak trees. They argued over stolen prey. Claws flashed; challenging yowls rang across the forest. A terrible battle followed, and soon the ground was wet with spilled blood.

Many cats died that night. Exhausted by their wounds, the survivors slept where they had fought. When they woke they were bathed in moonlight. All around them they saw the spirits of their slain kin, no longer torn and bloodied but shining like fallen stars. They huddled on the ground, and, as the spirits spoke, they saw terrible visions of the future. They saw the forest drowned in blood, their kits stalked by death at every pawstep. And they knew that the fighting had to end.

"Unite or die," said the spirits.

From among the living cats, a black female was the first to speak. She rose from the ground on stiff, battle-wearied legs. "My name is Shadow," she mewed. "How should we unite, unless we have a leader? I can hunt in the depths of the darkest night. Let Shadow rule the forest!"

"And you would lead us into darkness too!" meowed a silvery gray tom with green eyes. "I am River! I move through the forest along secret paths and hidden places. It is River, not Shadow, who should unite the forest!"

"The forest is more than River and Shadow," growled a wiry brown female. "Wind alone reaches its distant corners. I am as fast as the wind that blows from the high moors. *I* should be the ruler."

The largest surviving cat was called Thunder. He was a fiery orange tom with amber eyes and large white paws. "What good is any of that compared to my strength and skill at hunting? If any cat was born to rule, it is I."

A furious yowling broke out under the four great oaks, watched in silence by the spirit-cats. Dark clouds suddenly blew across the moon, and the living cats trembled in fear. On the top of a high rock, they saw a tabby cat, one of the fallen, her fur shining though there was no light in the sky. Her eyes flashed angrily at the cats on the ground.

"You are all as foolish as ducks!" she meowed. "Can't you think beyond yourselves for one moment? Think of your kits!"

The four cats—Shadow, River, Wind, and Thunder—looked up at the tabby, but none of them spoke.

"The forest is big enough to feed all your families and many more," she meowed. "You must find other cats like you, choose a home in the forest, and set down borders."

At that moment, the moon broke free of the clouds, revealing a circle of starlit spirit-cats around the edge of the clearing. A white tom stepped forward. "If you do this," he meowed, "we will reward you with eight more lives, so that you may lead your Clans for many moons to come."

Next to speak was a slender tortoiseshell. She stepped forward and stood beside the white tom. "We will watch over you from Silverpelt," she promised, and lifted her eyes to the crowded path of stars that swept across the night sky. "We will visit you in your dreams and guide you on your journeys."

"Once a month," meowed the white tom, "at the full moon, you will gather together here, between the four great oak trees, for a night of truce. You will see us above you in Silverpelt and know we are watching. And if blood is spilled on those nights, you will know we are angry."

"You will be warriors!" yowled the tabby from the high rock.

Thunder, River, Wind, and Shadow bowed their heads.

"From now on, you will live by a warrior code. Your hearts will be filled with courage and nobility, and if you must fight, it will be not for greed, but for honor and justice."

There was a long silence. Finally Thunder nodded his broad orange head. "This is wise advice. I believe we can choose our territories and lay down borders fairly, in peace."

One by one, the other cats murmured their agreement. Then they returned to their homes and sought out cats like themselves, with similar strengths and abilities. River found cats willing to fish for their prey. Shadow gathered nighttime hunters with clever minds and sharp claws. Thunder found hunters who could track prey through the thickest undergrowth. To Wind came the fastest runners and cats who loved the open moors. Then they divided the forest so each Clan had enough prey to survive, and all the cats could live in safety. And when the leaders returned to the four great oaks for the first night of the full-moon truce, their starry ancestors gave them eight more lives, as they had promised.

There was not always peace between the Clans, but that was to be expected—cats are born with claws and teeth for a reason. Still, as long as they lived by the warrior code, their fallen ancestors would watch over them and guide them through their lives.

And so the age of the warrior Clans began.

THUNDERCLAN

FIRESTAR ON THUNDERCLAN

I am Firestar. Welcome to ThunderClan—the
Clan of courage and loyalty. I was not a forest-born cat, but
ThunderClan welcomed me, and once I proved myself
as a warrior, they grew to respect me. I have risen to become
their leader and I would lay down all nine of my lives
for my Clan, just as my Clanmates would lay down their lives
for me and for each other. There is no other Clan in
the forest so true or so brave. I respect and admire the other
Clans, but my heart is here, with ThunderClan—
the Clan of heroes, the Clan of compassion,
the Clan of destiny.

Clan character: In peace, respectful of other Clans. In battle, fierce, courageous, and loyal. ThunderClan cats speak out for what is right and are not afraid to challenge the warrior code.

Prey: Mice, voles, squirrels, the occasional rabbit, and birds such as starlings, magpies, wood pigeons, and thrushes.

Hunting skills: Excellent stalking techniques. They keep upwind of their prey, creeping across the forest floor unseen and unheard.

THUNDERCLAN FOREST TERRITORY

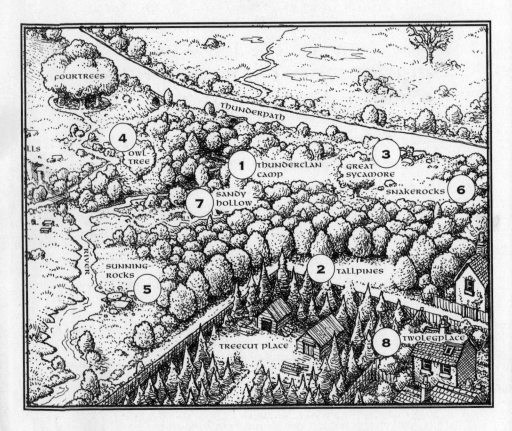

(1) ThunderClan camp: Sheltered at the foot of a sandy ravine and well protected by thornbushes, this camp is hard to attack and easy to defend.

(2) Tallpines: Watch out for the Twoleg tree-eater! It makes the ground rumble and leaves deep gullies that fill with muddy water.

(3) Great Sycamore: Its branches are thick and strong all the way to the ends. Young apprentices learn to climb here and dare one another to climb higher.

(4) Owl-Tree: Halfway up the trunk is a hole that is home to a tawny owl that flies out at night. Legend has it that an early ThunderClan apprentice learned the secrets of night hunting from one such owl. Every night, as the moon rose, he would wait at the foot of the Owl-Tree. When the owl swooped out, he followed, like the owl's shadow cast by the moon on the ground. Eventually this bold young apprentice became a great leader known as Owlstar. In the hunt, he was as silent and deadly as the tawny owl.

(5) Sunningrocks: A warm spot in the sunshine. Keep a sharp eye out for prey darting between the cracks! Many moons ago, when the river was much wider than it is now, Sunningrocks was an island. Only RiverClan cats could swim out to it. Then the water dropped, and Sunningrocks became part of the forest shore, so ThunderClan claimed it. They did not allow RiverClan cats to cross their territory to reach it. Since then, many battles have been fought between the two Clans over these smooth, sun-warmed stones.

(6) Snakerocks: Beware poisonous adders! Chervil grows abundantly here. The caves beneath the rocks provide shelter for dangerous animals, like foxes, badgers—and even dogs.

(7) Sandy hollow: A training hollow surrounded by trees. Warrior apprentices are unlikely to hurt themselves on the soft ground.

(8) Twolegplace: A maze of small Thunderpaths and Twoleg dens (see *Other Animals, Twolegs*). There are two different kinds of cats in Twolegplace: loners and kittypets (see *Cats Outside the Clans, Rogues and Loners,* and *Kittypets*).

BRIGHTHEART SPEAKS:
The Death of Swiftpaw

It wasn't fair that only Cloudpaw got to be a warrior. We were just as good and we tried so hard, but Bluestar ignored us and treated us like dopey kits.

Swiftpaw said we should do something so brave that Bluestar would have to make us warriors too. None of us knew what had been eating the prey around Snakerocks, but Swiftpaw figured if we went out there, we'd find a trail to follow. It made sense, you know? We'd follow the trail, find out who was stealing our prey, and then come back to tell Bluestar. And then we'd be warriors!

Swiftpaw knew a way out through the ferns behind the elders' den, so we sneaked out just before dawn and headed for Snakerocks. My paws trembled as we raced through the leaves. I knew my mentor, Whitestorm, would be angry with me—apprentices are not supposed to leave the camp without permission. But he'd be impressed when I helped save the Clan!

The smell near Snakerocks was strange—fierce and dark. I slowed down, but Swiftpaw kept running.

"Swiftpaw!" I hissed as he scrambled over a fallen tree. "Be careful!"

"Don't worry!" he called back. "There's nothing here!"

Just as he said that, a huge shape flew out of the cave and

fastened slavering jaws around Swiftpaw's throat. It was a dog—the largest I'd ever seen. I wanted to run away more than I've ever wanted anything, but I couldn't leave Swiftpaw behind.

Swiftpaw wrenched himself around, snarling and twisting, but the dog shook him like he was a squirrel, and then threw him to the other side of the clearing. I ran over and saw that he was bleeding, but he managed to stand, turn, and fight. The dog came toward us, its head low, its teeth bared and gleaming. I crouched, waiting until it was a mouse-length away, and then I lashed out and raked my claws across its face. It jumped back with a yelp, and for a moment I thought, *We'll be okay. It's just one dog, and there're two of us.*

And then I saw the others.

There were at least six dogs ranged across the clearing, all of them four times our size or bigger. They growled so loud it felt like the earth was shaking. *"Pack, pack,"* they snarled. *"Kill, kill."*

And then they sprang. I darted forward, jumped up, and sank my claws into soft underbelly. As I clung on, scratching and biting, I could hear Swiftpaw—spitting, hissing, and yowling in rage and

defiance. The world turned upside down, and the air was knocked out of me. I remember dust, a forest of legs, flying fur, blood. At one point I saw Swiftpaw break free from the pack and climb a tree. I prayed to StarClan that he would make it, but huge paws brought him crashing to the ground. Then blood filled my eyes, and I saw no more. I could still hear, though—and in among the growling and snarling, there were yelps too. I don't know when the end came for Swiftpaw. I only remember him fighting like all of LionClan. That's how I will always remember him.

Then I was shaken loose. I felt light as air. I slammed against rock, and everything went dark.

I woke up in Cinderpelt's cave three sunrises later. Fireheart and Cloudtail had found me and brought me home. Cinderpelt said I had nightmares, calling out *"pack"* and *"kill"* in my sleep, but I can't remember any of them now.

The first thing I remember was the feeling of Cloudtail's warm white fur pressed against mine. When I moved, he woke up instantly, as if he'd been waiting the whole time for me to awaken.

I knew something was wrong right away. It wasn't just the pain— my face felt frozen, and I couldn't see anything on one side. I had lost an eye! When I saw what the dogs had done to me, I wished I had died fighting beside Swiftpaw. And when Bluestar gave me my warrior name, Lostface, I no longer knew who I was.

I would not have survived that dark time if it weren't for Cloudtail. He gave me another destiny, and I knew that no matter what I looked like, I would be all right. As long as Cloudtail loved me, I was no longer Lostface, but Brightheart.

Thunderclan forest camp

Welcome to ThunderClan's forest camp! I'm Sandstorm, a ThunderClan warrior. Firestar has asked me to show you around. Watch out, though. Some of the elders might be cranky if we disturb them while they're having a nap.

Can you see the camp entrance? Well hidden, isn't it? Those brambles protect us from predators, but they don't stop the sunshine from warming up the camp.

Follow me down the ravine. Bluestar says it used to be a

river a long time ago, but I can't imagine that. It's so dry and sandy now. Keep your head down—we're going through this tunnel in the gorse. See the path under your paws? Hundreds of ThunderClan cats have been this way over many generations. Watch out for the prickles!

And here we are! No, Squirrelpaw, this is my guest. They didn't sneak up behind me. Yes, I know you're standing guard. I'm sure the whole camp knows we're here now.

Over this way is the nursery. See the thick bramble walls? The nursery is the strongest part of the Clan camp. Can you hear the kits mewing and playing inside? Queens and warriors will fight like TigerClan to protect them.

Notice the clump of ferns beside the tree stump? That's where the apprentices sleep. It's supposed to be lined with moss, but it looks like a certain apprentice has kicked up a bit of a mess. After guard duty, I promise you she will be cleaning it up. Poor Squirrelpaw! She has always been such a restless sleeper.

Warriors sleep under that bush—you can see the entrance tunnel there. As a senior warrior, I sleep in the center of the group, where it's warmest. I remember being a young warrior, though. It can get cold on the edge during leaf-bare!

This fallen tree is the elders' den. Go ahead, poke your nose inside. Oh, sorry, Dappletail! I'm giving a tour. No, they are not spying for ShadowClan! Don't you have an apprentice to torment, Dappletail?

Quickly, while she's gone, put your paws on the den floor. Don't the grass and moss feel soft? The apprentices keep it fresh. Nobody wants grumpy elders . . . well, no grumpier than usual.

Let's cross the clearing to that tall, smooth boulder over there. This is Highrock, and it's where our leader stands to make announcements to the whole Clan and to lead ceremonies. Can you picture it? You'd listen, wouldn't you?

Around here is Firestar's den. Hello? Firestar? He must be out on patrol. Peek through the lichen hanging over the entrance. This is where he sleeps. Before him it was Bluestar, and after him, who knows? Firepaw was a pudgy little kittypet when I first met him. Who could ever have dreamed he'd be our leader?

Before you go, let me show you the medicine cat's den. Come inside. I love the smell of the herbs. Leafpaw! That's my other daughter—she's in training to be a medicine cat, and she's very clever. She sleeps at this end of the fern tunnel. Her mentor, Cinderpelt, sleeps in that hole in the rock over there. Leafpaw! There you are. Always sorting herbs! She's so dedicated and hardworking. It makes me very proud.

What's that? You think your sister would rather be hunting than on guard duty? All right, I'll have a word with Firestar and see if she can come to the Gathering tonight—that should cheer her up.

And that's our camp! I should really be off hunting now. Watch your fur on the way out. And don't tell anyone you were here!

THUNDERCLAN LAKE TERRITORY

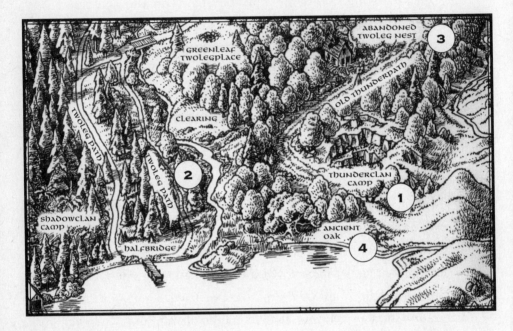

(1) ThunderClan camp: This symmetrical stone hollow, enclosed by towering cliffs of sheer stone left behind by Twolegs, was the obvious choice for ThunderClan's new camp.

(2) Twoleg paths: Twolegs mark their paths with shiny blue markers!

(3) Abandoned Twoleg nest: A good place for prey and an excellent source of herbs (see *Medicine, Catmint,* and *Borage Leaves*). It has an ominous, empty feeling and seems ready to fall down at any moment.

(4) Ancient Oak: In an old rabbit burrow below the twisting roots, Brambleclaw, Mistyfoot, Crowfeather, Tawnypelt, and Squirrelpaw sheltered on their first trip around the lake, scouting for new Clan territories and camps. Also known as Sky Oak.

thunderclan lake camp

hi! I'm Squirrelflight. I'm going to show you our new camp by the lake! It's perfect, and you know what? *I found it!*

I'll show you how I did it. Let's creep through these thornbushes here . . . okay, stop! Careful! You nearly did what I did, didn't you? Only I was running really fast after a vole. And suddenly—WHOMP! I took off through the air! And then I landed in a pile of brambles! Here, lie on your belly and peek over the edge of the cliff. See that bush down there? That's where I landed. Ouch!

But actually, I was lucky. If I'd tripped over that side instead, I would have had much farther to fall. These walls around the camp are tall and stone and hard to climb. Here, slide along this wall. Completely smooth, right? Isn't that weird? We think Twolegs were here a long time ago, slicing stone off the walls with their monsters. Don't ask me why! Twolegs are so mouse-brained.

Luckily they've gone away, and now there are lots of bushes and trees growing up over this hollow to protect us. The stone walls keep out the wind, although we have to watch our step near the edge. Brambleclaw keeps lecturing me about that. You'd think I was a newborn kit the way he talks to me!

All right, duck your head and squeeze through this thorn barrier. Intimidating, isn't it? If you were a ShadowClan cat, you'd probably turn tail rather than attack, wouldn't you?

Behold our beautiful camp! Isn't it amazing? Isn't it perfect? Did I mention that I found it? You've come at a good time—it's sunhigh, so lots of cats are sleeping. Look at grumpy old Mousefur over there, snoring away. The cat next to her with his nose in the air is Longtail. He's blind, but he can probably smell you; that's why he looks anxious. Don't be offended. Not every cat smells as great as ThunderClan.

Jump up on these rocks here—watch your claws; the rocks can be slippery. Now we're standing on the Highledge. You can see the whole camp! Firestar makes his announcements from up here. He puffs out his chest like this, and he struts forward like this, and then he opens his mouth and yowls: "Let all those cats old enough to catch their own prey join—"

Uh-oh. I think I did that a bit louder than I meant to. Here come Cloudtail, Dustpelt, and Brambleclaw. Quick, into Firestar's den! Oh, come on, move your fur, it's just a cave. In, in, in!

Isn't it cool in here? It's so dim and shady. Firestar sleeps back here on this bed of ferns and moss. It looks soft and springy. I

don't know how he keeps it so neat all the time. Doesn't it make you want to jump on it and roll around? Oops! I thought it would hold up better than that. Do you think he'll notice? Maybe we should get out of here.

See the caves where the apprentices and the elders sleep? The warriors—like me!—sleep under that big thornbush over there. Under the biggest bramble thicket is the nursery. Want to visit my friend Sorreltail? She has the cutest kits in the world. Come on, let's go over and stick our noses in.

Hello, Sorreltail. Hi, kittens! Oh, Sorreltail does look sleepy. Sorry, we'll let you get back to napping.

Across the camp is the medicine cat's den. Hurry, Brambleclaw is coming with his extra-grumpy face on. What cute kits! I don't want any of my own yet, though. I want to do a lot more warrior stuff first. Although it does look comfortable in the nursery.

You can't see the den here because it's hidden by this curtain of hanging bramble tendrils. But slip through it and—see? Look at this great cave! Hey, Leafpool, how's it going? My sister is our medicine cat. The smell in here always makes me sneeze. *Achoo!* Oops, sorry, Leafpool . . . were those supposed to be stacked like that? Look, this is my friend. I wanted to show how nice it is in here. It almost makes you want to get sick. The sand is really soft, and there's a little pool in the back for water. Leafpool stores her herbs in these cracks in the wall, or, I guess, out here in a pile where any cat can step on them. What? I didn't do it on purpose!

Uh-oh—hear that yowling? That's our bossy tabby friend looking for me. Perhaps you'd better go. Tell you what, I'll jump on him, and you make a dash for the tunnel. Then you *might* want to keep running as far and as fast as you can. Brambleclaw can be very serious about scaring off trespassers. Okay, ready? All right, go! Run! Quick as you can!

SIGNIFICANT LEADERS

Only some leaders and medicine cats are remembered by the Clans. Their names cast long shadows over the history of the forest; their deeds—good or evil—are told and retold by each generation until they pass from history into legend. Of the others, the ones whose names and deeds have been forgotten or, in some cases, banished from living memory, only StarClan knows.

THUNDERSTAR

Large orange tom the color of autumn leaves,
  with amber eyes and big white paws.

Strong, courageous, and determined.
Founder of ThunderClan—worked with
  Wind, Shadow, and River to develop
  the warrior code. According to legend it
  was Thunderstar who insisted on its more compassionate
  elements.

Deputies: Lightningtail, Owleyes (later Owlstar)
Apprentices: Unknown

OWLSTAR

Dark gray cat with large, unblinking amber eyes.
ThunderClan's second leader was a legendary hunter, who
  learned the ways of the tawny owl to stalk prey by night in
  silence.

Deputies: Unknown

Apprentices: Unknown

SUNSTAR

Tom with yellow tabby stripes, green eyes, and long fur.

Fair minded, even tempered, wise.

Held his Clan together through dangerous leaf-bare.

Fought to keep Sunningrocks away from RiverClan.

Deputies: Tawnyspots, Bluefur (later Bluestar)

Apprentice: Lionpaw (Lionheart)

BLUESTAR

Blue-gray she-cat with piercing blue eyes and silver hairs tipping muzzle and tail.

Wise, kind, beloved, and strong.

Brought a kittypet named Rusty to join ThunderClan. Rusty (renamed Firepaw, and later Fireheart) grew to become one of the most essential, valued, and respected cats in all the forest.

Deputies: Redtail, Lionheart, Tigerclaw, Fireheart (later Firestar)

Apprentices: Frostpaw (Frostfur), Runningpaw (Runningwind), Firepaw (Fireheart)

FIRESTAR

Tom with bright green eyes and flame-colored pelt.

Brave, intelligent, loyal—a natural leader.

Has an unusually strong connection with StarClan, and is the subject of StarClan's prophecy, "Fire alone can save our Clan" (see *Prophecies and Omens*).

Brought WindClan back from exile after they were driven out by
    ShadowClan.
Uncovered Tigerclaw's treachery in time to stop him killing
    Bluestar.
Saved Clan from terrible fire in camp.
Discovered Tigerstar's scheme to unleash a pack of dogs to the
    camp, and organized plan to save Clan.
Led the Clans of the forest against BloodClan.
Kept Clan together through the Twoleg destruction and brought
    them safely to new lake home.
Deputies: Whitestorm, Graystripe, Brambleclaw
Apprentices: Cinderpaw (Cinderpelt), Cloudpaw (Cloudtail),
    Bramblepaw (Brambleclaw)

❖

SIGNIFICANT MEDICINE CATS

CLOUDSPOTS

Long-furred black tom with white ears, white chest, and two
    white paws.
Inquiring, curious, and thoughtful, though sometimes appeared
    shy and reserved.
Very interested in the theory of medicine—not quite so keen on
    dealing with sickly kits.
Discovered the difference between greencough and whitecough,
    and identified catnip as a possible cure. (See *Beyond the
    Territories, How the Moonstone Was Discovered.*)

FEATHERWHISKER

Pale, silvery gray tom with bright
   amber eyes, unusually long feathery
   whiskers, and a sweeping plume of a
   tail.
Sunstar's medicine cat and also his brother.
Gentle, sweet-natured, and kind mentor—
   passed on his compassion and
   deep connection with StarClan to his
   apprentice, Spottedleaf.
Worked tirelessly to save Clanmates during greencough
   epidemic, which ultimately killed him.

SPOTTEDLEAF

Beautiful dark tortoiseshell she-cat with amber eyes, white paws,
   black-tipped tail, and distinctive dappled coat.
Skilled interpreter of StarClan's mysterious messages.
Received StarClan prophecy that led Bluestar to bring Firepaw
   into Clan.
Walks dreams of ThunderClan cats, especially Firestar's.

YELLOWFANG

Ornery gray she-cat with bright orange
   eyes and broad, flattened face.
Gifted healer—could be bad-tempered
   and difficult.
Helped rescue ThunderClan kits from
   ShadowClan.

Became ThunderClan's medicine cat after Spottedleaf was killed.
Died as lived—fighting to save Clan.

CINDERPELT

Fluffy gray she-cat with enormous blue eyes.

Bright and energetic with boundless enthusiasm.

Quick learner—could have been agile warrior, were it not for injury.

Rescued two ShadowClan cats and nursed them back to health against orders.

Nursed Bluestar back to health when she contracted greencough.

Saved Brightpaw's life after the apprentice was mauled by the pack of dogs.

Died fighting to save Sorreltail.

LEAFPOOL

Small, light brown tabby with amber eyes, white paws, and white chest.

Quiet and soft-spoken—the opposite of her sister Squirrelflight!

Through their deep connection, she and her sister are able to share each other's feelings and dreams.

Found Moonpool—the place in Clans' new lake home where they can communicate with StarClan.

Saved RiverClan from deadly Twoleg poison by helping Hawkfrost, and helped Mothwing cure the cats.

Nursed Clan back to health after badger attack.

According to StarClan, Leafpool faces a destiny unlike any medicine cat before her.

WINDCLAN

TALLSTAR ON WINDCLAN

*Welcome. I am Tallstar, and this is WindClan—
a Clan that has known great suffering, but always survives.
We are the fleet-footed warriors of the moor, the fastest Clan in the
forest. We have struggled through terrible hardship, but we never give up. I
know the other Clans sometimes see us as weak . . . but the truth is,
they could not last a moon in the broad, open spaces we live in,
chasing rabbits for our prey. We are the closest Clan to StarClan,
spiritually and physically, and we always know our warrior ancestors are
watching over us. That is what makes us strong. No matter what trials
we must endure, WindClan will last forever.*

Clan character: Fiercely loyal, tough, fast-running, and easily offended cats. They are nervous and quick to flee, due to the lack of cover on the open moor. They take pride in being the closest Clan to the Moonstone. (See *Beyond the Territories, How the Moonstone Was Discovered.*) Of all the Clans, they have the deepest knowledge of Twolegs from seeing them on the nearby farms.

Prey: Mainly rabbits.

Hunting skills: Fast, lean, and swift. Their short, smooth pelts of browns and grays blend in with the rocks and grasses.

WINDCLAN FOREST
TERRITORY

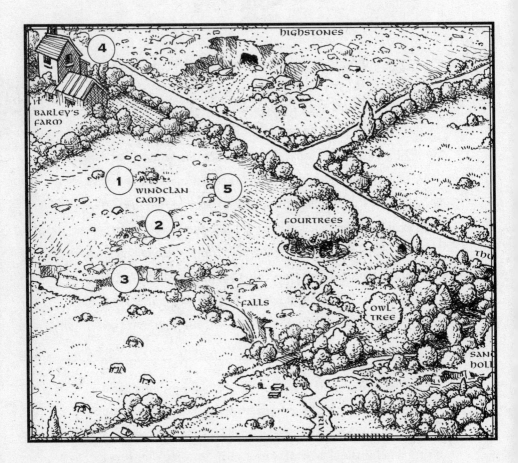

(1) **WindClan camp:** Tucked into a natural dip in the sandy
moor, this camp is sheltered from the wind but has proved
vulnerable to attack.

(2) **Abandoned badger set:** WindClan apprentices used to come
here to learn the scent of badger. Now a great spot for hunting
rabbits!

(3) The gorge: WindClan elders boast that they leaped all the way across in their youth, but apprentices are strictly forbidden to go too close.

(4) Twoleg farm: Cows, sheep, dogs, Twolegs, and two loner cats

named Barley and Ravenpaw (see *Cats Outside the Clans, Rogues and Loners*) live here. WindClan sheltered in the barn on their way home from exile.

(5) Outlook Rock: This large, flat, gray stone slopes steeply above the level moors. From here, you can spot movement far across the grassland, especially a slow-moving or brightly colored cat from another Clan. WindClan apprentices are assigned to Outlook Rock to test their alertness and guard-duty skills.

WINDCLAN FOREST CAMP

Welcome to our camp! I'm Onewhisker, a warrior in WindClan, the greatest Clan in the forest.

You couldn't see our camp as you came this way, could you? That's because it's hidden in the only sheltered spot on the moor. It's a sandy hollow in the ground, surrounded by a tangle of gorse. The elders say that our first leader, Windstar, reached down from StarClan and scooped out a pawful of sand to make a hollow for us to live in.

Press through the prickly branches here and you'll be able to see the center of the camp. Breathe deeply. Don't you love the fresh air? It's so full of life and energy. I don't know how those other Clan cats live where they do. If I couldn't see the sky all day and all night, I'd go mad!

That's why the warriors sleep out here, under the stars, where our warrior ancestors can see us. It gives us a special connection to StarClan. We've had to deal with a lot of trouble and danger, but when I see them up there before I close my eyes, I know they're watching out for us.

Elders and kits can't sleep out in the open, though, so we've built dens for them along the edge of the gorse wall. And the leader has a den back behind the Tallrock, too, but he doesn't usually sleep there. Tallstar likes to sleep out in the open with us. What's the Tallrock? Oh, it's that large boulder over there from where Tallstar makes announcements and conducts ceremonies.

Hear that? It's an apprentice calling from Outlook Rock. That means there are trespassers in our territory! I'd better go chase them out.

Thanks for visiting!

RAID ON THE CAMP!

It was the darkest of nights. Heavy clouds flitted in front of a claw moon, blackening the sky. There were no StarClan ancestors watching over the WindClan camp that night.

At the camp entrance were two young warriors, Thrushwing and Stoneclaw. They had received their warrior names that night and were proudly standing guard.

Stoneclaw stood up, his ears pricked. What was that? A rustle in the gorse. A whisper of paws in the grass. A gleam of eyes in the darkness. What was that beyond the bushes? Should he sound the alarm?

Too late! A shadow appeared before him, and sharp claws slashed his throat. Thrushwing turned to see her brother lying on the ground, the life bleeding out of him. She shrieked a warning to the Clan, but the air was knocked out of her lungs by the weight of a large cat, and her voice died. Pinned to the ground, she felt the large cat's teeth stab at her neck as enemy cats poured past her into the clearing, moving swiftly, melting into the shadows.

Onewhisker was woken by Thrushwing's call. Beside him, Tornear and Deadfoot scrambled to their paws, and all three rushed into battle, sounding the WindClan warrior yowl.

"ShadowClan!" hissed Mudclaw from Tallrock. "I can smell their stink!" He launched himself off the boulder into the thick of the fighting, barreling into a hefty white tom.

"You're in no condition to fight!" Ashfoot growled at Morningflower, shoving the pregnant queen back into the nursery.

"But I want to fight!"

"Stay here and protect my son. I will fight."

Morningflower curled around the trembling gray shape of Eaglekit and licked the top of his head as comfortingly as she could. Ashfoot's enraged howls came from outside the tangle of branches.

Another WindClan warrior howled in fear, his belly sliced

open by a ShadowClan claw. Thrushwing had rejoined the battle and, in spite of an injured leg, fought like TigerClan to avenge the death of her brother. The bodies of two elders slumped next to a fallen apprentice. Deadfoot pounded over to Tallstar, his lame paw sending stabs of pain through him.

"They're going to kill us all!" he yowled. "We have to escape!"

"And abandon our camp?" Mudclaw hissed. "I'd rather die fighting than let these crow-food-eaters drive us out."

"Deadfoot's right," Tallstar meowed, his tail lashing furiously. "We've lost too many already. If we lose any more, there will be no more WindClan."

"Let's go, now," Deadfoot panted.

Tallstar ordered Onewhisker to fetch Morningflower and Eaglekit from the nursery. Then, the WindClan warriors and apprentices circled the queen and the two surviving elders and fought their way to the edge of the clearing. Morningflower was first to break through the gorse wall and run into the darkness, Ashfoot's kit bumping against her legs in terror. Thrushwing was next, supported by Onewhisker. One by one, the rest of WindClan followed, tearing through the gorse, their blood spattering the ground, until only Tallstar remained.

"This isn't the last of WindClan, Brokenstar," spat Tallstar.

"Wherever you run, I will find you," the enormous ShadowClan tabby hissed back at him.

And with that, Tallstar disappeared into the bushes, and WindClan left their home and fled into the night.

WINDCLAN LAKE TERRITORY

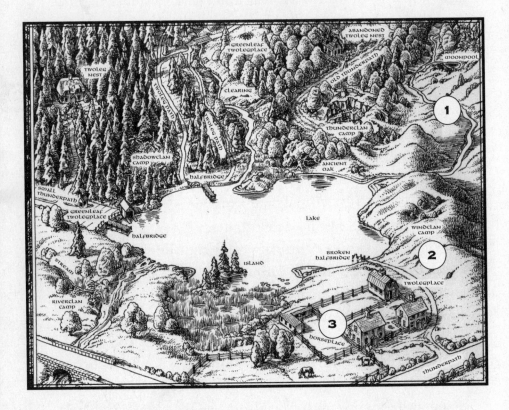

(1) Moonpool stream: This tumbling stream leads along the edge of the WindClan border and up into the hills to the Moonpool (see *Beyond the Territories, the Moonpool*).

(2) WindClan camp: A shallow scoop in the ground, open to the sky. Unlike other cats, WindClan warriors prefer to sleep out in the open; in really bad weather, they retreat into underground burrows left by foxes and badgers.

(3) Horseplace: Hear that thundering? It's the pounding of horses' hooves! Stay on this side of the fence!

WINDCLAN LAKE CAMP

Can't you keep up? It must be true what they say about WindClan cats being faster than other cats! Come on, hurry!

Now, rest here and look down. See where my tail is pointing? That's our camp. It doesn't look protected, does it? You don't see any trees or rocks around it. But don't get any ideas! See how many heads are lifted down there? Half the warriors in our camp are watching you, sharpening their claws. No cat comes over these hills without being seen!

You might as well know that I'm Crowfeather and I brought WindClan to this place.

Let's go. Quickly! Follow me down—if you can keep up!

Now you are inside. Keep quiet and look only where I tell you.

This giant boulder is Tallrock, where Onestar makes his speeches. Yes, I know there are plenty of other boulders, but this is the biggest. Stop asking mouse-brained questions! Stop asking *any* questions!

This gorse bush against the boulder is the nursery. Move along—you'll scare the kits! Now, see this boulder? See the large crack in it? Smells like mouse bile, doesn't it? Our medicine cat, Barkface, is treating a tick problem in the camp. WindClan cats must have picked them up on the journey—all that hanging around among trees and swamps. *Blech!* Anyway, Barkface keeps his supplies in here. Any sick cat can sleep there too. If you ask me, fresh air is the best medicine. But what do I know?

See the tunnel under this gorse bush in the corner? It leads to an old badger set. You wouldn't catch me sleeping inside. It still stinks of badger. I sleep under the sky, near my warrior ancestors. Don't stick your nose in there! Rushtail might claw it off. It's the elders' den now.

So, that's the camp. You can tell Onestar I did as he asked. Now leave! Head straight up the hill and keep going until you see a bunch of large galumphing creatures with hooves. Horses, they're called. Past there is RiverClan territory—maybe they'll share their secrets with you next.

And remember . . . I'll be watching you go!

Significant Leaders

WINDSTAR

Wiry brown she-cat with yellow eyes.

Proud, wily, stubborn, and fastest cat in the forest.

Founder of WindClan—worked with Thunder,
   Shadow, and River to develop warrior code.

Many of her descendants run with Clan today,
   including current deputy, Ashfoot, and
   Ashfoot's son Crowfeather.

Deputies: Gorsefur (later Gorsestar)

Apprentices: Unknown

GORSESTAR

Thin gray tabby cat.

Remembered for his bravery and devotion to Windstar, his mate.

Deputies: Unknown

Apprentices: Unknown

TALLSTAR

Black-and-white tom with long tail and amber eyes.

One of the wisest and longest-lived WindClan leaders.

Unusually close to
    ThunderClan and
    particularly their
    leader Firestar.
Watched over Clan as
    they were forced
    out of home by
    ShadowClan.

One of first cats to argue for leaving the forest, according to the
    prophecy. (See *Prophecies and Omens.*) Frail and on last life,
    he led Clan to new home.
On his deathbed, Tallstar changed his deputy from Mudclaw to
    Onewhisker—a wise choice in the long run.
Deputies: Deadfoot, Mudclaw, Onewhisker (later Onestar)
Apprentice: Morningpaw (Morningflower)

ONESTAR

Small, mottled-brown tabby tom.
Loyal, devoted, strong, and compassionate.
Guided Clan through time of terrible tension after Tallstar made
    him leader in Mudclaw's place.
Survived rebellion against him.
First leader to receive nine lives at the Moonpool.
Took warriors to save ThunderClan when the badgers attacked.
Deputy: Ashfoot
Apprentices: Whitepaw (Whitetail), Gorsepaw

SIGNIFICANT MEDICINE CATS

MOTHFLIGHT

Soft white fur and stormy green eyes.

First WindClan medicine cat.

Loyal and true to her Clan, her restlessness, curiosity, and
dreaminess were at first deemed unwarriorlike.

These qualities gave her a new destiny, leading her to the
Moonstone.

THRUSHPELT

Stone-gray she-cat with flecks of darker brown fur.

Warrior for several moons before becoming medicine cat.

Interpreted signs with immense confidence.

Expert herb finder.

Temperamental and quick to fight.

Took care of Clan through a sick-rabbit epidemic.

BARKFACE

Brown tom with stumpy tail.

Reliable, practical, and efficient.

Long, dependable service.

Received prophecy foretelling death at Gorge after WindClan
returned home. (See *Prophecies and Omens*.)

RIVERCLAN

LEOPARDSTAR ON RIVERCLAN

*There is a Clan unlike any other—a Clan
with all the strength, brilliance, and beauty of water.
Welcome to RiverClan. I am Leopardstar, the leader here.
Can you hear the river? In its flowing current you can
see what makes us the greatest Clan in the forest. Nothing can
stand against the force of water, just as nothing can defeat
RiverClan warriors when we rise up together. But when trouble
comes, RiverClan knows how to weave through the dangers,
adapting to the changed world, just as the river flows
around rocks and over waterfalls. We are grace.
We are power. We are RiverClan.*

Clan character: Contented, sleek, well fed. Long fur and glossy coats. They love beautiful things and often collect rocks, shells, and feathers for their dens. They do not fear water.

Prey: Mainly fish but also water voles, shrews, and mice.

Hunting skills: Strong swimmers, moving silent and scentless through water. They scoop fish out of the water from the bank—a skill most cats in the other Clans cannot master.

(1) RiverClan camp: This well-drained island is circled by gently rustling reeds instead of thorns, but the other Clans' hatred of water means that it has never been attacked.

(2) The gorge: See *WindClan Forest Territory*.

(3) The river: It is a source of prey and protection to RiverClan, yet it is as changeable as the moon. Sometimes it is quiet, gentle, and murmuring, but sometimes it froths and roars like a Twoleg monster.

(4) Twoleg bridge: A safe way to cross the river and get to Fourtrees when the water is high.

RIVERCLAN FOREST CAMP

hi, I'm Feathertail. You'll have to get your paws wet if you want to see our camp. It's on an island! Don't be afraid of crossing; just listen to the murmur of the river—it's very soothing.

Under these long, trailing branches, that's right. They are willow trees. You should see them in leaf-bare after a frost. They sparkle like frozen raindrops!

All right, shake your paws, duck your head, and follow me through the reeds. The whole camp is surrounded by reeds, murmuring in the breeze. I love the sound they make, under the burble of the water. Look! It's our camp!

Here, in this central clearing, we lie in the sun and share tongues. In the mornings, I lie here and dry my fur after an early patrol. It's my favorite spot in the whole camp.

Here's the warriors' den, in this tangle of reeds. It's next to the nursery to protect the kits. Poke your head inside—it's all right; all the warriors are on patrol.

Look up at the roof of the den. See how we've woven feathers into the branches? And along the edges are sparkling rocks and shells from the river. They make the den shimmer, don't they? I love to lie in here, watching the lights and colors. It's just as beautiful in the nursery.

See how close the river comes to the nursery? Here, it's shallow and safe, but once before I was born, the river rose up suddenly and swept away the floor of the nursery and two kits—my mentor's kits. Now the walls are stronger. We like to have the kits living near water. They inherit our love of it and learn to swim quickly. Oh, look, they are practicing now!

You are doing wonderfully, kittens! Soon you'll be swimming faster than I can!

Across the clearing are the other dens, including Mudfur's— he's our medicine cat. Peek inside. You'll see that he makes small caves in the earth for the herbs. Now the kits can't scatter them when they run through his den chasing frogs.

On the other side of the island, a couple of rocks stick out of the river when the water isn't too high. They soak up the warmth of the sun. My favorite days begin with hunting with my brother, Stormfur, and end in the sun on those rocks. But you have to be fast. There is space for only a couple of cats, and if senior warriors or elders want them, you're out of luck. Our whole Clan could fit on Sunningrocks, where we used to bask. There was even room left for chasing prey and play-fighting. But I won't get into that now!

Uh-oh, it looks like rain. I'm going to curl up in the warriors' den and listen to the raindrops on the roof.

You should probably go too. But thank you for visiting!

FLOOD!

It was the coldest leaf-bare many cats could remember. The river turned to ice, trapping frosted reeds and cutting off RiverClan warriors from the fish. Prey on land was scarce.

With spring came the relentless *drip-drip* of melting ice. Cats grumbled about the soggy ground and the puddles in camp. But the worst was yet to come.

A young warrior, Silverstream, was on night watch. She listened to the roar of the river. It had been louder than usual for two days. The sun would be rising soon, and then she could nap. She stood up and stretched, padding off to patrol the boundary.

Sploosh! Silverstream jumped back. In the dark, she thought she had accidentally wandered off the island. No . . . the river must have risen. She padded over to her father's den.

"Crookedstar," she whispered. "There's something you should see."

The RiverClan leader followed his daughter to the camp entrance. The stream that separated them from the mainland had become a ribbon of dark, frothing water.

"The water is already moving fast," Silverstream meowed. "Should we evacuate the island?"

"It may go down again," Crookedstar meowed gruffly.

As the day went on, the water kept on rising, swirling through the reeds surrounding the camp. Mudfur moved his medicine cat supplies to a high rock, and the other cats watched the river nervously.

Leopardfur called Stonefur and Blackclaw to join her on patrol. "We'll see how far the floodwater reaches." The three warriors left the camp.

A yowl came from the end of the island.

Silverpaw and Shadepaw were scrabbling at the earth to try to block off a stream of water that had broken through the reeds. Loudbelly and Mistyfoot ran to help them.

"It's too strong!" Shadepaw yowled as the water burst into the camp.

Mistyfoot raced back toward the nursery. "Silverstream!" she yowled. "Help me!"

They scrambled inside to see brown water bubbling through the reeds and, in a corner, two kits mewled piteously, clawing at each other's fur. "My kits," Mistyfoot wailed, searching for the other two.

"They're gone!" Silverstream meowed above the sound of the rushing water. "But these two still need you!" She seized one kit in her jaws and backed out of the nursery.

Mistyfoot nudged the other kit. He opened his mouth and gave a small wail. She licked him, then picked him up and followed Silverstream to the river crossing.

The river gives us life, she thought, looking back at the flooded camp. *But now it's destroying us.* She placed a paw into the fast-moving water. *Oh, StarClan, how could you let this happen?*

Mudfur and Loudbelly stood downstream of the long line of cats, ready to catch them if they slipped or fell. No cat dared swim. The moment they lifted a paw off the pebble bed of the stream, the current tugged it away. Dark water swirled above their stomachs.

Crookedstar was last to cross. *We're no more powerful against this river than any other Clan,* he thought. *Everything that makes us RiverClan has been taken away from us.*

Mistyfoot and Silverstream scrambled out, the kits dangling from their jaws. The apprentices helped the elders ashore.

"Where do we go now?" Silverpaw meowed.

Crookedstar shook his fur. "The river is our home," he meowed. "StarClan will look after us." He nodded up the hill. "For now, we will rest in those bushes until Leopardfur's patrol returns."

Not long after they had settled in the shelter of the bushes, a yowl sounded from outside. Silverstream scented the air. ThunderClan! Graystripe!

She scrambled to her feet and pressed through the bushes to see the solid gray shape of the cat she loved best. Graystripe was sitting next to Fireheart. His eyes lit up when he saw her, and his tail flicked. Then she noticed the dripping bundles at the paws of Stonefur and Blackclaw.

Silverstream dashed to get Mistyfoot. "It's Fireheart and Graystripe," she panted. "They have your kits."

Silverstream had to compose herself before returning to Graystripe. She was so proud of him, and she was sure the other cats would sense it. She had to look as if he meant no more to her than any other cat.

Crookedstar listened to the story of the kits' rescue. *Is this how StarClan chooses to help us? By using enemy cats?* His throat was tight with injured pride that ThunderClan warriors could see the desperation of his Clan. But he knew that he could not refuse their help. It was a sign from StarClan. He would do whatever it took to save his Clan, and the river would be their home again soon.

RIVERCLAN LAKE TERRITORY

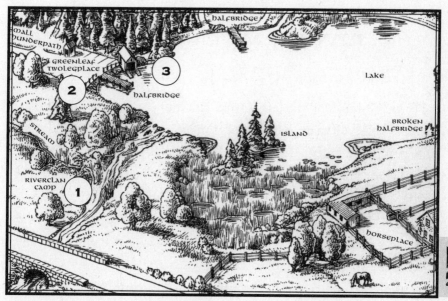

(1) RiverClan camp: Safely tucked away on a triangle of land between two streams, this camp is well sheltered from weather and enemy attack, with easy access to a constant source of prey.

(2) Greenleaf Twolegplace: A bees' nest of Twoleg activity during greenleaf! Twoleg kits jump into the lake with loud splashes and shrieks. Some of them can swim like RiverClan cats but more noisily.

(3) Halfbridge: A most peculiar bridge that ends halfway out in the water. It doesn't seem to go anywhere! Twolegs tie their "boats" to it.

RIVERCLAN LAKE CAMP

I know I'm biased—but RiverClan found the best lake home. Have you seen our camp? I'm Mistyfoot, by the way, the RiverClan deputy.

Before we go in, just look around you. The trees are lush, and the stream is full of fish. Back there is the lake. It's harder to catch fish in the lake than it was in the river, but we're learning. The biggest problem is the Twolegs. They love this place in greenleaf!

See where the smaller stream joins the main one? On the triangle of land between the streams is our camp. Can you swim across the stream like a RiverClan cat? Or will you splash through the shallows? You can also jump across on these pebble islands. Watch your step! Some of them are slippery!

Well done. You've made it. Now, look at all the vegetation! You can barely hear the noise of the Twolegs on the lake. See those

brambles? That is the nursery. Quite often there is a patch of sunshine outside the entrance. In those thickets are the dens of the elders and Leopardstar.

Smell that? Sort of sharp and sweet at the same time? That's how you know we're near the medicine cat's den. Come around this thornbush—watch out for the prickles. See how it overhangs the stream? The earth below was washed away, leaving a pool in the roots and a hole in the bank where Mothwing keeps her supplies. She sleeps on that mossy nest. Oh, hello, Willowpaw!

Organizing berries, I see. Is Mothwing with Dawnflower? She was complaining of bellyache this morning. We'll just poke our heads in, take a sniff, and then leave you in peace.

One day this place will be as beautiful as our old camp. We haven't found as many shells in the water, but the Twolegs leave a lot of shiny things behind that our kits like to play with. We check everything carefully before we bring it into the camp, though. So many Twoleg things are bad for us!

Well, that's our camp. Watch your paws crossing the stream, and keep an eye out for Twolegs!

LEOPARDSTAR SPEAKS:
A Deadly Alliance

How dare you judge me? Have you been leader of a Clan? Have you had the fate of so many cats in your paws? Have you faced fire, flood, poison, starvation, predators, and Twolegs, all within a few short seasons? Kits and elders were dying under my watch. And I was supposed to sit back and let it all happen?

I am a great leader. I make tough decisions and stick to them. I discipline bad behavior with fair, strict punishment. My warriors respect me and would follow me to the end of the river if I told them to.

And I recognize strength when I see it. Tell me this—why is it all right for Crookedstar to accept help from those bleeding-heart ThunderClan warriors, but wrong for RiverClan to ally itself with Tigerstar? He has a plan for the forest—a vision for all the Clans! If you met him, you'd understand. He knows how we have suffered and how to save us. WindClan and ThunderClan will join us soon, I am sure.

As one Clan, we will rule the forest. No cat will go hungry. There will always be prey somewhere—in the river, in the woods, or on the moors—and all cats will benefit.

Why waste our energy fighting one another when our common enemies are dogs, badgers, and Twolegs? With the combined strength of all our warriors, perhaps we could fight back against the Twoleg monsters! Think of what we could accomplish! Think of how powerful we would be!

Tigerstar believes in TigerClan so strongly. I can see the future spreading out before us as he talks. If I join him now, he and I will be joint leaders. Tallstar and Firestar will have to follow us. I know that Tigerstar is in charge now, but this was his idea. Once everything is settled, he will listen to me.

And if TigerClan is inevitable, as I believe it is, I would rather be the second-strongest cat in the whole forest than cast out of the Clan to wander alone. Tigerstar has been there. He knows what it is to be weak and alone. He told me about it, and I never want to be that cat.

The only thing that makes me nervous is the way he keeps talking about half-Clan cats. I had no idea that Stonefur was half ThunderClan when I made him my deputy. Neither did he, in fact. But now we know he is, he and his sister, Mistyfoot. And half-Clan cats cannot be trusted, Tigerstar says.

He has a point—remember what happened with Graystripe? I always suspected he was spying on us, waiting for a chance to tell ThunderClan our secrets. He betrayed us in the end. Divided loyalties are not what TigerClan needs if we want to survive all the troubles facing us.

I don't know what Tigerstar plans to do with our half-Clan cats, but I know something must be done. For now, I've allowed him to leave a few ShadowClan warriors in our camp to protect us. They're not like RiverClan cats. They're building a hill of prey bones down by the riverbank. It gives me nightmares. . . .

Significant Leaders

RIVERSTAR

Silvery gray, long-furred tom with green eyes.

Generous and warm-hearted with his own
Clan—uninterested in the troubles of other
Clans. (Would skip Gatherings if he could!)

Founder of RiverClan—worked with Thunder,
Shadow, and Wind to develop warrior code.

Thought to have suggested mentoring program of training
apprentices.

Deputies: Unknown

Apprentices: Unknown

CROOKEDSTAR

Huge light-colored tabby tom with green
eyes and twisted jaw.

Determined, strong, and willing to bend the
rules for safety of Clan.

Guided Clan through terrible leaf-bare and flood.

Accepted help from ThunderClan warriors to save Clan from
starving.

Offered shelter to ThunderClan when fire drove them from their
home.

Deputy: Leopardfur (later Leopardstar)

Apprentices: Graypaw (Graypool), Stonepaw (Stonefur)

LEOPARDSTAR

Spotted golden tabby she-cat.

Proud, hostile, and fierce. Single-minded about what is best for RiverClan. Showed bad judgment in turning over control of RiverClan to Tigerstar.

As deputy, she helped ThunderClan when they fled the fire in their camp.

Also led her Clan to their new lake home, where she quickly established a strong base.

Deputies: Stonefur, Mistyfoot, Hawkfrost (temporarily)

Apprentices: Whitepaw (Whiteclaw), Hawkpaw (Hawkfrost)

SIGNIFICANT MEDICINE CATS

DAPPLEPELT

Delicate tortoiseshell she-cat.

Brave, reckless, quick to act.

Saw being a medicine cat as a different type of warrior, fighting the invisible enemies of sickness and injury on behalf of her Clanmates.

Saved an entire litter of kits after the nursery was washed away by a flood. (See *Beyond the Territories, How the Moonstone Was Discovered.*)

BRAMBLEBERRY

Pretty white she-cat with black-spotted fur, blue eyes, and a strikingly pink nose.

Charming, quick-thinking, and good at getting her own way—
   Crookedstar would do anything she asked.

Cautious about interpreting StarClan's omens.

Came up with a clever way to hide medicinal herbs in fresh-kill so
   sick kits would eat them.

MUDFUR

Long-haired, light brown tom.

Patient, intelligent, and straightforward.

Interpreted moth's wing sign to choose his new apprentice, despite
   her non-Clan origins.

MOTHWING

Beautiful dappled-golden she-cat with large amber eyes in a
   triangular face, and a long pelt rippling with dark tabby stripes.

The daughter of a rogue cat, Sasha, and the former leader of
   ShadowClan, Tigerstar, Mothwing struggles for acceptance by
   her Clan.

Believes StarClan does not exist.

With Leafpool's help, healed her Clan when kits brought traces of
   Twoleg poison back to camp.

SHADOWCLAN

BLACKSTAR ON SHADOWCLAN

*Greetings. I am Blackstar. You must be brave indeed,
to approach the territory of ShadowClan. Few are welcome here,
in our world of secrets and darkness. We are a Clan of
cunning and cleverness, a Clan well suited to the shadows and
the cold north wind. No other Clan can walk the paths of night like
we do. Other Clans may be faster or stronger, but we are the
most dangerous warriors: fierce, proud, and independent. We are
ruthlessly willing to do what it takes to protect our great Clan.
There won't be any softhearted alliances here! ShadowClan
will always be the dark heart of the forest.*

Clan character: Battle-hungry, aggressive, ambitious, and greedy for territory. It is said that the cold wind that blows across the ShadowClan territory chills their hearts and makes them suspicious and untrusting.

Prey: Frogs, lizards, and snakes that live in ShadowClan's boggy, peaty territory. A secret food source is the Twoleg garbage dump on the far boundary, although they have to be careful not to eat infected rats or crow-food.

Hunting skills: ShadowClan cats hunt by night better than other Clan cats and are skilled at skulking unseen through the undergrowth.

shadowclan forest territory

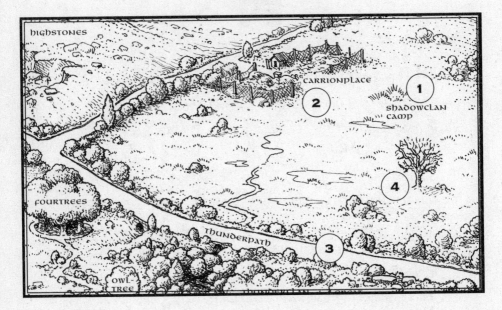

(1) **ShadowClan camp:** A dark, well-concealed hollow, the camp is hidden deep in the shadows and is surrounded by brambles as prickly and fierce as the hearts of ShadowClan warriors.

(2) **Carrionplace:** Yuck! Smell that? This is an evil place where rats and disease lurk.

(3) **Thunderpath tunnel:** The ability of ShadowClan cats to move freely across the most feared border of the Thunderpath has enhanced their reputation for mysterious strength and invincibility.

(4) **Burnt Sycamore:** An ancient tree destroyed by lightning many moons ago. Apprentices are often trained here to hunt at night and stalk noiselessly through the undergrowth.

SHADOWCLAN FOREST CAMP

My name is Boulder. Ah, I can see you've realized it's not a warrior name. Well, I used to be a loner in Twolegplace, and proud of it. I caught prey for myself. I could look after myself. Then I met a cat from ShadowClan. He told me about the forest. He wanted me to give up my freedom and join his Clanmates! I nearly clawed off his fur. I didn't need a leader or a Clan.

But he kept talking, and some of the things he said made sense. Like, what was I going to do when I was old and couldn't catch my own prey? I'd never thought about that before.

I agreed to visit his camp. Follow me, and you'll see what I saw on that day I first came to the forest. I've never left since.

I love the forest on this side of the Thunderpath. The soft carpet of pine needles under my paws. The fresh and sharp smell of the pines. The boggy soil is full of amazing smells; can you sense prey darting around under the leaves?

Through these brambles, that's right. This tiny path—here, where my paws are—leads to a hollow. I know it's not exactly grassy around here, but the ground is muddy and cool. Good for keeping fresh-kill fresh. Our leader sleeps over there, beneath the roots of that big oak tree. The warriors' den is over there, underneath the bramble bush. I know it looks prickly on the outside, but inside it's lined with pine needles and moss. I can tell you, it's a lot more comfortable than any place I found to stretch my paws in Twolegplace.

The smooth boulder at the edge of the clearing is where the leader speaks to us. Do you see that other rock propped against it, creating a sheltered half cave underneath? That's where the medicine cat lives. There are holes dug in the ground to keep the leaves and berries fresh, and sick cats can rest in the ferns that grow on the other side of the boulders. I never had another cat care about my injuries when I lived in Twolegplace.

The nursery's over there, in that hollow shielded by a thornbush. You can smell the scent of milk from here—a new litter was born yesterday. I don't spend much time with the tiniest kits—always worried I'll step on them or something— but I like watching them grow into strong apprentices and loyal warriors.

Why do you keep staring at the fresh-kill pile? Oh, I see

you've spotted a frog. I know they look pretty unappetizing—trust me, I was as reluctant as you to try them when I first came to the forest. But you should try them. Peel off the skin first—that's very chewy. Underneath, it tastes like if you mixed rabbits and fish together. Honestly! Well, okay, maybe leave it for one of the warriors. Look, I know the other Clans think ShadowClan cats are strange and dark-hearted, but we're loyal warriors, just like them. There's no need to fear us.

Not all of the time, anyway.

shadowclan lake
TERRITORY

(1) ShadowClan camp: Much closer to Twolegs than forest home, but the camp is still well hidden and should be difficult for enemies to attack.

(2) Twoleg nest: Home to two aggressive kittypets. Don't let them catch you out alone, or you're kittypet food!

(3) Twoleg path: Steer clear of these during greenleaf. Twolegs tramp up and down these paths all season long!

(4) Greenleaf Twolegplace: Another place haunted throughout greenleaf by Twolegs, who put up small dens and build terrifying little fires here. On the plus side, sometimes they leave behind food like we used to find at Carrionplace.

shadowclan lake camp

I never thought Blackstar would let you into the ShadowClan camp. He's a little prickly mostly. But we like having a cat in charge who says exactly what he thinks.

I'm Tawnypelt, and I found this place—you've heard about that?

I tell you, by the time we found the camp, I was getting worried. The territory looked right—pine trees everywhere, shadows, and darkness. But the tree branches were much higher than we were used to, and there wasn't much undergrowth.

It was getting dark when we came up this slope here. Did you see the pool down at the bottom? It's close to the camp so we can fetch water for the elders and kits without having to go all the way to the lake. Here, follow me up these boulders until we get to that top one—it's got the best view of the camp.

Great, isn't it? You can barely tell there are so many cats down there, hidden below the tangles of brambles. And look at all these low-hanging branches all around and above us. You won't catch us getting trampled by badgers like ThunderClan!

Not that we're cowards, mind you. Every ShadowClan cat, down to the tiniest kit, will fight to the death to defend our territory and our pride. We're the fiercest Clan in the forest, no matter what any other cat might say.

I wasn't born a ShadowClan cat—but I'm very glad I'm here now. I like being ferocious, and I like hunting in the dark. You won't find me lolling around in the sun like those RiverClan cats or crashing through the forest making as much noise as a ThunderClan cat.

But we can have fun too. Smokepaw and I like to climb trees near the lake and watch the Twolegs on the water. Their boats look like swan wings. The Twolegs make a lot of noise and splashing, and sometimes the boats tip over and they fall in! Then they get back up and fluff out their wings to try again. You've never seen anything so funny. I would never set paw on a boat—leave that to the RiverClan cats!

Anyway, slip on through these bramble bushes and you can see the camp. Like in the old camp, there is a clear progression of dens from one side to the other: nursery first, then the apprentices' den, then the warriors, the leader, and the elders at the end of the circle. That puts the kits and elders closest to the lowest-hanging branches and leaves the warriors facing the entrance, in case of trouble.

The medicine cat's den is in that far corner, beyond the leader's den. Littlecloud found a place where the branches aren't so bunched together—he needs to see the sky so he can read the signs from our warrior ancestors.

Blackstar makes his announcements from the branch that hangs over his den. You should see him swarm up that tree when he's angry!

So that's our camp. I'd let you poke your nose into the dens, but ShadowClan cats aren't friendly to strangers. Even though Blackstar said it would be okay, I think you should keep your stay as short as possible. And if I were you, I wouldn't linger on ShadowClan territory. Head this way, cross a stream, and you'll hit ThunderClan's part of the forest. You'll be perfectly safe there. They take in strays all the time, those softhearted geese.

Bye now!

SIGNIFICANT LEADERS

SHADOWSTAR

Black she-cat with green eyes and
thick fur.

A strategist, ferociously independent
(even untrusting of Clanmates),
bold in battle.

Founder of ShadowClan—worked with
Thunder, Wind, and River to develop warrior code (she
spent the rest of her life complaining about it).

First of founding leaders to die—losing ninth life in battle she
started with other Clans.

Deputies: Unknown

Apprentices: Unknown

RAGGEDSTAR

Large dark brown tabby. Fur ragged and patchy from fighting
as a kit.

Proud and cunning—failed to see his son Brokentail's
bloodthirsty nature until too late.

Defeated rats in violent battle near Carrionplace that kept
them from bothering ShadowClan for many moons.

Deputies: Foxheart, Cloudpelt, Brokentail (later Brokenstar)

Apprentices: Clawpaw (Clawface), Brokenpaw (Brokentail)

BROKENSTAR

Long-haired dark brown tabby with torn ears and a broad,
   flat face. Tail bent in middle like broken branch.

Cold, ambitious, heartless, murderous, and cruel.

Killed own father, Raggedstar.

Weakened Clan by focusing its energies on war, apprenticing kits
   too early, and forcing Clan to eat crow-food instead of prey.

Blinded and killed by own mother, Yellowfang.

Deputy: Blackfoot (later Blackstar)

Apprentices: Mosspaw, Volepaw (both died mysteriously before
   becoming warriors)

NIGHTSTAR

Elderly black tom.

Brave but frail.

Took over leadership when Brokenstar was driven into exile.

Struggled to rebuild broken Clan—StarClan did not grant him the
   nine lives of a leader.

Died from sickness from Carrionplace shortly after his deputy
   died, leaving Clan target for Tigerstar's ambitions.

Deputy: Cinderfur

Apprentice: Dawnpaw (Dawncloud)

TIGERSTAR

Large dark brown tabby tom with amber eyes and long front
   claws.

Ambitious, crafty, charismatic, and brilliant fighter.

Exiled by Bluestar after attempt on her life.

After period in exile, gained leadership of ShadowClan—
rebuilding it with exceptional efficiency.

Allied ShadowClan with RiverClan to make TigerClan.

Brought BloodClan into forest at cost of many cats' lives.

Killed by Blood, the leader of BloodClan.

Deputy: Blackfoot (later Blackstar)

Apprentice: Ravenpaw (while in ThunderClan)

BLACKSTAR

Large white tom with huge jet-black paws.

Arrogant and defensive. Tigerclaw brought him back to
ShadowClan from exile—he still feels a hint of gratitude and
loyalty toward the dangerous tabby.

Led Clan away from Twoleg devastation in the forest to new lake
home.

Deputy: Russetfur

Apprentice: Tallpaw (Tallpoppy)

SIGNIFICANT MEDICINE CATS

PEBBLEHEART

Dark gray tabby tom.

Selfless, caring, desperate to help his
Clanmates with any problem. Weakened
himself by working tirelessly.

Realized that rats at Carrionplace were a source of infection.
(Unfortunately he died from a rat-borne infection.)
(See *Beyond the Territories, How the Moonstone Was Discovered*.)

YELLOWFANG

(See *ThunderClan Medicine Cats, Yellowfang*.)

RUNNINGNOSE

Small gray-and-white tom with perpetual sniffle.
Nervous and quiet. Lived long enough to retire and become an elder.
Apprentice: Littlecloud

LITTLECLOUD

Undersize brown tabby tom with light blue eyes.
Compassionate and devoted to his calling.
Close friends with ThunderClan medicine cat Cinderpelt ever since she saved his life.
As a warrior, sought help from ThunderClan during time of terrible disease. Returned with remedy that saved ShadowClan.

YELLOWFANG SPEAKS:
A Thankless Kit

As soon as I found out I was going to have kits, I knew it was a punishment from StarClan. Medicine cats are not supposed to fall in love. My relationship with Raggedstar was wrong in every way, and I knew it.

But I never expected all of ShadowClan would be punished for my mistakes.

I kept my secret well. No cat knew that their medicine cat was carrying kits, although of course I told Raggedstar. He was so pleased. . . . That should have frightened me even more. The arrogance of thinking we could do whatever we wanted, without consequences . . .

It was a hard birth, a horrible birth. That was an omen too. I snuck out of camp that morning, knowing my kits were coming. I found a hollow in a dead tree, filled with damp leaves. There was a smell of toadstools and something rotting, but I didn't have the strength to drag myself any farther. And I hoped the stench would hide my scent while I gave birth, alone in the woods. I didn't want any ShadowClan cats to find me, not even Raggedstar. I just wanted it to be over.

I felt like I was lying in that dead tree for days. Everything hurt—my whole body, down to the tips of my fur and the ends of my claws. As a medicine cat, I should have been able to take care of myself, but I was too weak to do anything, even eat the herbs I'd brought.

Finally there were three small bundles next to me on the pile of leaves. Two of them were squirming; one was completely still. I prodded

it with my paw, but she had been born dead. Her eyes would never open.

I dragged the other two toward me. With all the strength I could manage, I began to lick them, trying to warm them and wake them up. One let out an angry wail the minute I touched him; the other only whimpered slightly and jerked her paws. I could see that the tom kit was a fighter right from the beginning. His lungs were so powerful, I was surprised it didn't bring the entire Clan running to find us. He battered his sister with his paws every time he moved, but she barely reacted.

I tried as long as I could, licking and licking her, but her breathing only got shallower and shallower, until finally it stopped altogether. Her tail twitched once and was still. I buried my nose in her fur, feeling grief crash down on me. It was a clear sign from StarClan. These kits should never have been born.

I turned my attention to my only surviving kit and saw the expression on his small, flat face. He was new to the world—couldn't yet see, could barely crawl to my belly to feed. And yet his face was already twisted with strong emotion. . . . Rage? Hatred? I'd never seen such a terrifying look on any cat, let alone a tiny newborn kit.

Fear flooded through me, making me cold. Maybe this kit wasn't meant to survive, either. A kit born with so much anger in him could mean only grave danger to the Clan, maybe to the whole forest.

But then he squirmed over to me and pressed his face into my fur. He was so small, so helpless. Perhaps I had misunderstood what I'd seen. He was only a little kit, after all—my kit, and the son of Raggedstar, the cat I loved. I couldn't keep him for myself, but I could watch him from across the clearing as he grew up. I could make sure he turned into a fine warrior. I licked the top of his head, and he let out a small purr. My heart seemed to expand to fill my whole chest.

I buried his sisters before we returned to camp, digging deep into the dirt so no cat would ever sniff them out. Then I slunk back through the undergrowth, my fur matted and stinking of toadstools, the kit dangling from my mouth. I stopped to clean myself in a pool near the camp entrance. By the time we entered the camp, no cat would be able to guess the ordeal I had been through.

Raggedstar spotted us the minute I pushed through the bramble tunnel. He barely even looked at me; his eyes were all for the kit, and they were full of hope and excitement. He came bounding across the clearing to follow me into the nursery.

Lizardstripe was there, of course, tending to her own two kits, born a few days earlier. Her pale brown tabby fur and white underbelly seemed to glow in the darkness of the nursery den. She looked at me with narrow, unfriendly eyes. I had never really liked or trusted Lizardstripe, but she was the only nursing queen at the moment. I had no choice.

I dropped the kit at her paws, and he let out another furious shriek.

"What," said Lizardstripe, "is *that*?"

"It's a kit," I said.

"It's *my* kit," Raggedstar said proudly, shouldering his way into the den.

"Oh, yes?" Lizardstripe said dryly. "What a miracle. If I'd known toms could have kits, I would have made Mudclaw have these brats of mine himself."

Raggedstar ignored her. The space seemed to get smaller with him in it, as if he drew all the light into himself. I wanted to press myself into his fur and tell him everything I'd been through and about the two tiny bodies out in the forest. But he still wasn't looking at me.

He crouched and sniffed at his son. The kit tried to lift his head and then swiped his paw through the air, connecting with Raggedstar's nose. Our leader jerked his head back in surprise.

"Look at that!" he cried delightedly. "He's a little warrior already!"

Lizardstripe's yellow gaze was making me uncomfortable. "His mother wishes to keep her identity secret," I said. "She cannot be a mother to this kit, and she hopes that you will take him in for her."

Lizardstripe lashed her tail. "What kind of mouse-brained nonsense is that?" she snapped. "Why should I have to put up with another mewling lump of fur? I didn't ask for these kits, either, but you don't see me dumping them on some other cat. It's not my job to take care of every unwanted kitten in the Clan."

Raggedstar snarled, and Lizardstripe shrank back in her nest. "He is *not* unwanted," Raggedstar spat. "He is my son, and I will always claim him as my own. You are being given a great honor, you unworthy cat. Who wouldn't want to be mother to the Clan leader's son—and perhaps the future leader of the Clan himself?"

Lizardstripe hissed softly. But she knew better than to argue with Raggedstar. And perhaps she saw the wisdom of his words. As the mother of Raggedstar's son—even if the Clan knew she wasn't his real mother—she would hold power in the Clan.

"All right, fine," she spat ungraciously. "Hand him over."

As I nestled my son into the curve of her belly, I felt a strong pang of uneasiness. What kind of life would he have, with an ambitious queen like Lizardstripe raising him? No cat would know I was his mother, not even the kit himself. I would never be able to sway him to be good, to follow the warrior code and believe in the wisdom of StarClan. I would just have to hope that he would turn out all right.

"His name is Brokenkit," I said, my voice faltering. Lizardstripe nodded, seeing the bend in his tail, like a broken branch. That's where every cat would think he'd gotten his name. But the truth is, I named him for the feeling in my chest as I left him there, as if my heart were breaking in two, as if my life had broken down the middle.

Most cats assumed that Raggedstar's deputy, Foxheart, was Brokenkit's mother. She was always a little secretive, and he let her get away with a lot. She never contradicted the rumors; it was to her advantage to let other cats think she was the secret mother of Raggedstar's kit. She died a few moons later, anyway, in a battle with rats near Carrionplace, shortly before Lizardstripe died of greencough. The next deputy, Cloudpelt, didn't last much longer than they did, and by then Brokentail was old enough for Raggedstar to make him deputy.

Raggedstar always thought his son would make a great leader. He was blind to all of Brokentail's faults—his cunning, his ruthlessness, his violent nature. Raggedstar didn't care for me anymore. His life was all about Brokentail from the moment he laid eyes on that kit.

My punishment stretched on as Brokentail clawed his way to power, and I realized what a monster I'd brought into the forest. But it was my mistake, and I had to live with it. And there was a part of me that still remembered him as a newborn kit—the tiny scrap of fur I nursed in the hollow of a dead tree.

When I had to kill him to protect my new adopted Clan, I knew I was finally at the end of my punishment. I had brought him into the world; I had to send him out, as painful as it was.

But by then I had found a truer son than Brokentail ever could have been. I only hope Fireheart will rise to be the great leader that Brokenstar never was and that, in some small way, I have helped to set him on that path.

Then, perhaps, StarClan will forgive me at last.

STARCLAN

Wait until it is dark and the night sky is full of stars. Can you hear them? Do they whisper to you of secret places and adventures? Follow the path of the moon through the forest. Feel the bracken crackle under your paws and the wind ruffle your fur. Mist curls around you and blurs the familiar shapes of the forest. Press through the ferns until you come out into a clearing.

Towering over you are four giant oaks, massive and dark, outlined by the moonlight. In the center of the clearing, on the Great Rock, I will be waiting for you.

I am Lionheart. I was a ThunderClan warrior. In a fierce battle, I died defending my Clan. Now I belong to StarClan, a Clan of the spirits of our warrior ancestors.

Yes, you are dreaming. We often walk in the dreams of those we watch. Don't be afraid. I know it looks like a land of mist and shadows, but I promise there is enough light to warm the darkest of hearts.

From here, we watch over the Clans we have left behind.

The saddest moments are when kits come to join us, whether through illness, predators, or unexpected disaster. But we love it when new kits are born, and my heart swells with pride every time a ThunderClan apprentice becomes a warrior.

Sometimes we can sense the destiny of these warriors. It is clearest with new leaders. When Firestar became leader of ThunderClan, I could see that he would lead the Clan through terrible times with courage and wisdom. When Tigerstar rose to power in ShadowClan, we all knew that darkness lay ahead.

Sadly, we cannot change what will happen to the cats we watch. I would have done anything to prevent the fire that swept through ThunderClan territory or to save my Clanmates from the dog pack. But the lives of warriors are filled with tragedy, and there's nothing we can do to stop it. All we can do is warn our descendants with signs and prophecies and hope that they listen.

The cats with the closest bond to StarClan usually become medicine cats. Spottedleaf had a particularly special connection to us; Firestar's daughter Leafpool does as well. Firestar himself often has prophetic dreams—he even had them when he was a kittypet. These cats meet us in their dreams. They can read the omens we paint in the sky or the leaves or the water. They know the meaning of a falling star or a strange cloud pattern. We need them to understand us, so they can keep our Clans safe.

There are sacred places too, which inhabit both the world of living cats and the world of dreams. Here leaders may come to receive visions and seek our guidance. We also grant them nine lives and their star name.

We most often speak to cats of our own Clans. Yet, sometimes, we reach out to cats of other Clans. I understand the other Clans better than I did when I was alive. I wish them well, even the cats I fought. We need all four Clans to survive.

Cats who have caused great pain in their lives wander a strange forest of darkness in death. We sense this distant place. Tigerstar, Brokenstar, Clawface, and Darkstripe are there, exiled from the Clan of their ancestors, of no comfort to one another.

There are other skies where other cats walk as well. The Tribe of Rushing Water have ancestors of their own, and while our questing cats were in the mountains, we could not see them clearly. They were in the territory of different spirits, where we couldn't go.

On the journey to the lake, we had trouble reaching our warriors. We had to travel ourselves, through unfamiliar sky paths, to find our new home. We could not have found it without them, and they could not have found it without us.

Are you wondering how we can be here, at Fourtrees, if the forest has been destroyed by Twolegs? Don't worry. Fourtrees will always be in our hearts. It is a part of StarClan too, wherever we are.

Now return to your den and your peaceful dreams. Thank you for visiting StarClan. Remember, keep your eyes and ears open, watch for anything unusual, and you too may see the signs we leave in the world around you.

SNOWFUR SPEAKS:
A Sad, Cold Death

My name is Snowfur, and I am now one of the warrior ancestors. I came to StarClan as a young warrior, killed by a Twoleg monster while I was chasing ShadowClan intruders out of our territory. I mourned along with my Clan, but not for my own life. I only wished I could have stayed until my son became a warrior. Of course, I watched his ceremony from the stars, a few moons later. Whitestorm was so excited, so brave, and I was so proud of him. I think he knew I was there with him during his vigil.

It was not long after that when we learned that my sister, Bluefur, was having kits. I wished we could just be happy for her, but she had broken the warrior code, and I knew it was going to bring her much sorrow. The father of the kits was not ThunderClan. He was the RiverClan deputy, Oakheart.

"A kit is coming to join us," Brambleberry, the former RiverClan medicine cat, meowed. "Half ThunderClan, half RiverClan."

"Half-Clan!" spat a ShadowClan warrior.

"It is an innocent kit," Brambleberry meowed with fierce anger in her voice.

The cats of StarClan were gathered at Fourtrees, which was blanketed by snow just like the whole forest in the world of our descendants. It was a bitter leaf-bare, and many cats were starving. More cats came to StarClan every day, and we were all feeling frustrated that there was nothing we could do to help.

"This kit did not have to die," hissed Moonflower. She was my and Bluefur's mother, but she did not approve of what my sister was doing. "It is Bluefur's fault for falling in love outside the Clan in the first place. And now she is dragging her three helpless kits out into the snow with her! Of course one of them is going to die. I'm amazed the other two will make it as far as RiverClan."

"But they will be safer there than they were in ThunderClan," meowed a RiverClan spirit. "RiverClan has more prey than any other Clan. If Oakheart will take them in, they have a better chance of survival than they did before."

"We don't know that," Moonflower meowed. "If she had kept them safely in our den, all three of them might have lived to be warriors."

"And what else lies along that path?" meowed Owlstar, one of the oldest ThunderClan spirits. "Study that future carefully, Moonflower."

"It is too dark to see it clearly," she protested.

"But we can guess," Owlstar murmured. "If Bluefur stays in the nursery with her kits, Thistleclaw will become deputy instead. He is an ambitious, violent cat, and we know it. He would lead his warriors to attack other Clans—the last thing this forest needs right now. Would you rather see more warriors coming to join us because of his bloody leadership?"

"So a kit's life is the price to be paid for the warriors whom Thistleclaw *might* lead into death," Moonflower growled. "I know that Bluefur believes Thistleclaw would be the wrong leader for ThunderClan. But how do we know that being deputy wouldn't make him a better cat?"

"We don't know," Brambleberry meowed. "And neither does Bluefur. She must make her choices based on what she thinks might happen. I don't agree with what she's doing . . . I would never endanger innocent kits . . . but I can see why she's doing it."

"It is for the good of the Clan," Owlstar meowed.

"But not for the good of the kit," Moonflower spat.

"We cannot change what will happen to Mosskit," Brambleberry meowed. "We can only make sure he is protected on his journey to StarClan."

"I will take care of him," I spoke up. The others all looked around at me. "I was a queen when I died," I pointed out. "My son, Whitepaw, had only recently left the nursery. I remember well how to care for kits . . . and I miss it. I would be a good mother to this kit."

Owlstar nodded. "I think Snowfur is right. She would be a good choice."

"I agree," Brambleberry meowed.

Moonflower nodded as well, her eyes soft and sad.

I slipped away from the group and followed the edge of the river down toward Sunningrocks. My paws skimmed the smooth pebbles like I was swimming over them. I could feel the cold blasts of wintry air in the forest world, although they could not pierce my thick white fur.

A few fox-lengths into the trees, I found Bluefur curled around three small gray shapes. She was lucky they all looked like her, I thought—if any had had Oakheart's coloring, some cat in ThunderClan might have suspected her secret by now. Two of the kits were squirming and protesting as Bluefur licked them. The third seemed to be sleeping in the snow. This was Mosskit.

Bluefur kept nudging him with her nose. Her eyes were pools of grief, and I could feel it with her. The snow buffeted her sides, where her ribs were showing through her thin gray fur, but she kept meowing: "Oh, Mosskit! What have I done? Mosskit, please wake up

Mosskit, don't leave. There's warmth and safety just on the other side of the river. Your father will look after you, I promise. Just a little bit farther, my tiny, brave son." She crouched closer to him, gathering him between her paws. "Mosskit, how could I do this to you?"

My heart ached for her, but it was too late. Mosskit had crossed over into my world. I ducked my head and whispered, "Mosskit, wake up."

The dark gray kit opened his eyes and looked at me. "Who are you?" he squeaked. "Why do you have stars in your fur?"

"Don't be scared," I murmured. "I'm Snowfur. I'm here to take care of you."

Mosskit shook himself and staggered toward me on tiny paws. His spirit nuzzled into my fur. Behind him, his body was still curled beside Bluefur, but Mosskit didn't notice.

"I'm cold," he protested. "I'm so cold. Cold all the way to the tip of my tail. My whiskers are frozen, look."

"I know," I meowed, licking the top of his head. "Come with me, and you will be warm."

Mosskit hesitated, looking up at me with wide green eyes. "What about my mother?"

"She'll be all right," I meowed. It was true. It would be hard for a long time, and she would never forget Mosskit, but she would push aside the memory and focus on her Clan. She would survive.

"But I want to be with her," Mosskit whimpered. "I want my mother and Mistykit and Stonekit."

"You will see them again," I promised. "You will watch over them from the stars until they come to join you."

He pressed his face into my fur and nodded. I looked back at my sister one more time, and then Mosskit and I walked away, following the moonlight back into the stars.

TERRITORIES

HIGHSTONES

BARLEY'S FARM

WINDCLAN CAMP

FOURTREES

FALLS

OWL-TREE

RIVER

SUNNING-ROCKS

RIVERCLAN CAMP

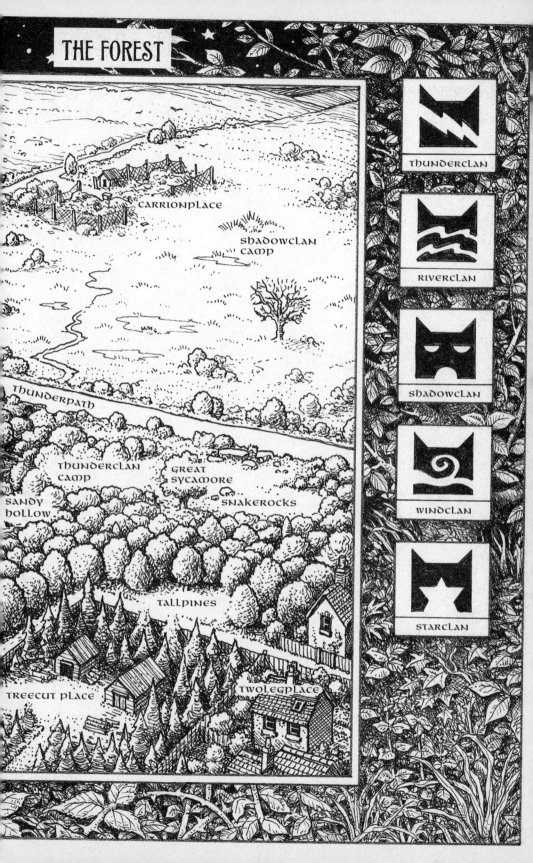

THE FOREST

CARRIONPLACE

SHADOWCLAN CAMP

THUNDERPATH

THUNDERCLAN CAMP

GREAT SYCAMORE

SANDY HOLLOW

SNAKEROCKS

TALLPINES

TREECUT PLACE

TWOLEGPLACE

THUNDERCLAN

RIVERCLAN

SHADOWCLAN

WINDCLAN

STARCLAN

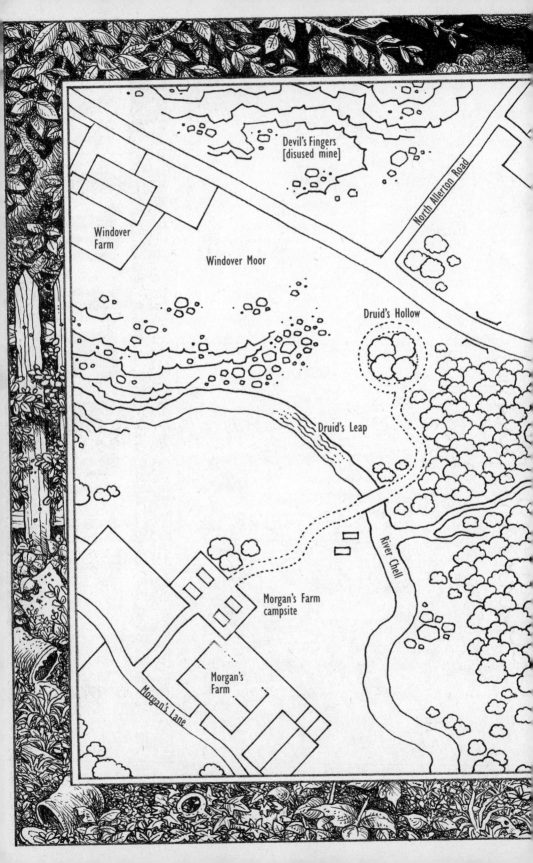

Devil's Fingers
[disused mine]

North Allerton Road

Windover
Farm

Windover Moor

Druid's Hollow

Druid's Leap

River Chell

Morgan's Farm
campsite

Morgan's
Farm

Morgan's Lane

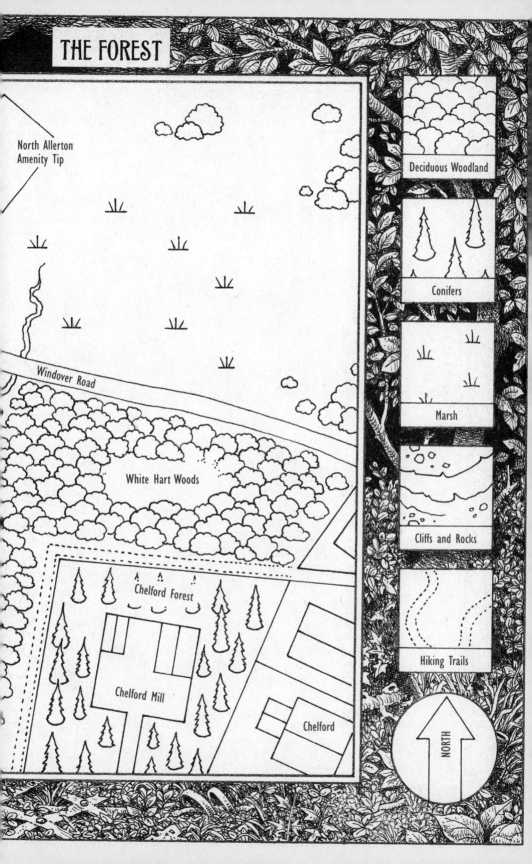

THE FOREST

North Allerton
Amenity Tip

Windover Road

White Hart Woods

Chelford Forest

Chelford Mill

Chelford

Deciduous Woodland

Conifers

Marsh

Cliffs and Rocks

Hiking Trails

NORTH

Hareview Campsite

Sanctuary
Cottage

Sadler Woods

Littlepine Road

Littlepine
Sailing
Center

Littlepine
Island

River Alba

Whitchurch Road

BEYOND THE TERRITORIES

FOURTREES

In a clearing at the center of the forest, where all four Clan territories converge, there is a space sacred to StarClan. Four great oaks stand at the corners of the clearing. At one end is a large boulder called the Great Rock, where the Clan leaders stand during Gatherings. Every month, at the full moon, cats from all four Clans gather here in peace for one night to share the news of the forest.

BLUEPAW SPEAKS:
My First Sight of Fourtrees

From the moment you take your first pawsteps outside the nursery, you long to go to Fourtrees. You long to meet cats from other Clans, to gaze up at Great Rock beneath StarClan. But you have to wait. Six moons, to be exact, until you're an apprentice.

My first Gathering was only two days after I received my apprentice name, Bluepaw. In my first training session, I caught a squirrel that was as big as me. My mentor, Stonepelt, was so impressed, he invited me to the Gathering, ahead of the older apprentices.

The moon was as round and yellow as my mother Moonflower's

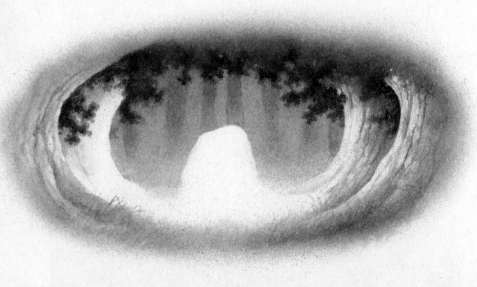

eyes. She ran beside me, her tail lifted proudly. We stopped at the top of a wooded slope. I gazed down into a wide clearing. At each corner of the clearing was a tree—four massive oaks that looked as old as the Highstones beyond.

The clearing was full of cats, meowing and murmuring. In the moonlight, their fur looked silver, and it rippled like the surface of the river. Their eyes flashed like leaping fish. In the center of the clearing stood the Great Rock. It seemed to grow out of the earth, like the peak of a mountain whose roots spread beneath the whole forest.

My fur tingled as I scrambled down into Fourtrees for the first time. I vowed that one day I'd be the one leading ThunderClan in a flurry of fur and claws into the clearing. I'd be the one who leaped onto the Great Rock with the other Clan leaders. One day, I would be Bluestar, leader of ThunderClan.

HIGHSTONES

Far to the north of WindClan's territory, across a dangerous Thunderpath, there is a range of mountains known to the cats as Highstones. Deep inside a cave in the mountain lies the Moonstone, a glowing rock turned to silver by the moonlight. This is where cats from all the Clans must go to communicate with StarClan. Leaders travel here to receive their nine lives and their warrior name. Medicine cats visit the Moonstone together once a month at the half-moon, to trade remedies and share tongues with StarClan.

HOW THE MOONSTONE
WAS DISCOVERED

Many moons ago, at the dawn of the forest, Clan leaders had no way of sharing tongues with their warrior ancestors. Spirits appeared to them in dreams, but they had no way of seeking guidance.

At this time, there was a WindClan cat named Mothflight. She had soft white fur and stormy green eyes. Her paws were swift, and her heart was true, but she was restless, easily distracted, and forgetful. She would return from hunting patrols with berries instead of prey. When asked what the berries were for, she would say she didn't know, but she thought they might be useful.

More than once, the WindClan deputy, Gorsefur, found Mothflight nosing at plants over the border in other Clans' territories. If she was caught by cats from another Clan, Gorsefur knew that WindClan would pay the price.

One morning, Windstar was leading a patrol along the edge of the Thunderpath. She felt the rumble of a Twoleg monster beneath her paws and glanced back at her warriors. Her breath caught in her throat.

Mothflight was crossing the Thunderpath, following a light blue feather as it drifted over into ShadowClan territory.

"Mothflight!"

The WindClan leader's yowl was drowned out by the monster's roar as Gorsefur dashed across the Thunderpath, shoving Mothflight to safety on the far side. Gravel spat into their faces as the monster rumbled past, trailing foul-smelling smoke.

"Stay here," Windstar hissed to the rest of the patrol, and sped across the Thunderpath. She was furious. Gorsefur was not just her deputy; he was the father of her kits.

"Mouse-brain!" Windstar growled at the white warrior. "Stargazing, feather-watching, hollow-headed mouse-brain! You could have been killed—you could *both* have been killed!"

Mothflight scuffled her paws in the dirt. "I'm sorry, Windstar," she meowed. "I felt like it was calling to me."

"The feather?" Windstar meowed. "Calling you where?"

Mothflight nodded at a ridge of jagged stone peaks in the distance, far beyond any Clan territory.

"Very well then," Windstar meowed. "Follow your feathers, stuff your head with clouds, eat nothing but berries as far as I care. If you cannot devote yourself to the warrior code, we cannot trust you in our Clan. You must go."

Mothflight's face fell. "But I belong to WindClan!"

"This is your punishment, Mothflight." Windstar's eyes were cold as the north wind.

Heavy with sorrow, Mothflight left her home. She walked all day, crossing out of ShadowClan territory, toward the teethlike rocks. As she climbed higher, the grass below her paws became bare, rocky soil, and the trees were replaced by boulders as large as the Great Rock at Fourtrees. The sun sank behind the ridge, turning the rocks to sharp black fangs.

Mothflight was licking her scratched paws when a thrush burst out of a bush, flying low to the ground. She tore after it, then came skidding to a halt around a large boulder. Mothflight barely noticed as the bird escaped into the orange sky. She was staring at the mountain in front of her, where a large, square hole yawned in the rock face.

Cautiously she padded up to the opening. It was completely dark inside, black and silent like a gaping mouth. Outside, the shadows were lengthening. She would be an easy target for night predators. She sniffed the black air inside the tunnel; it did not smell of other animals.

Mothflight padded into the mouth of the cave, feeling the cold stone under her paws. She crept forward, feeling the tunnel narrow and wind downward. Sometimes she became aware of other passages going off in other directions, but something drew her on. In the cold black air she felt dizzy and light, as if she were made of clouds. Her tail brushed the roof of the tunnel. But she traveled deeper into the mountain, unafraid.

She didn't know how long she had been walking when a new scent drifted into her nostrils. It smelled like fresh air and prey. Mothflight stopped. A silvery light was trickling into the darkness in front of her, revealing a glittering cavern. High in the roof, she saw a triangle of night sky and then the climbing moon. It poured its bright silver light through the hole onto a stone at the center of the cave.

The stone was three tail-lengths high, and it glittered like raindrops on cobwebs. Mothflight crept forward, her fur tingling. Following an instinct she didn't understand, she lay down, closed her eyes, and pressed her nose against the cold surface of the stone. Then she opened her eyes. The cave was filled with shimmering cats.

"Welcome, Mothflight. You have found the Moonstone," one of the spirits murmured. "It is a sacred place. You must take the knowledge of this place back to the forest cats."

"But I can't!" Mothflight blurted. "I've been exiled." She hung her head.

"You were exiled precisely for the strengths we need," meowed the spirit. "Your curiosity, your visions, your openness to the signs in the world. We choose you to be the first medicine cat."

Mothflight's heart filled with a strange, fierce joy. "What does that mean?"

"You will devote yourself to your Clan," meowed another spirit. "You will learn the ways of healing herbs. You will read the omens we send you to advise your leader on difficult questions and keep your Clan safe."

Mothflight shook her head. "Windstar will never let me return."

"Is that true, Windstar?"

Mothflight spun around to see the shadowy figure of her leader.

"You are dreaming, Windstar," whispered the spirit. "Welcome your new medicine cat. She will return to you."

Windstar's ears twitched, and her fur flattened. She looked into Mothflight's green eyes, nodded, and vanished into the air.

"These are the cats you must find," another voice meowed. Three cats appeared before her, each of them curled in a sleeping ball.

"Dapplepelt, from RiverClan," purred one starry cat, padding up to a delicate tortoiseshell.

"Pebbleheart, from ShadowClan," whispered another, prodding a dark gray tabby until he snarled in his sleep.

"And Cloudspots, from ThunderClan." The first spirit pointed his tail at a long-furred black cat with white ears, a white chest, and two white paws.

"Bring them here at the next half-moon," the spirit-cats meowed, "and we will teach you all how to be medicine cats."

As they faded away, leaving only the glitter of stars, Mothflight stretched and tucked herself into a comfortable ball. Tonight she would sleep beside the Moonstone. Tomorrow, she would return to the forest as the first medicine cat of the Clans.

THE MOONPOOL

When the warrior Clans arrived at their new home by the lake, they knew they needed to find a replacement for the Moonstone. Highstones was too far to travel, and the cats needed guidance from StarClan. The ThunderClan medicine cat apprentice, Leafpaw, was the one who found the Moonpool. This small pool high in the hills above WindClan is surrounded by stone walls and fed by a trickling waterfall. Ancient pawprints in the stone suggest that other cats came to this sacred place once, a long time ago. . . .

AN ANCIENT CAT SPEAKS

My name is Rock. Many generations past, my kin lived on the lakeshore. Now new cats have come here and walk in our pawprints. They have brought their own warrior ancestors with them. Their fur brushes mine as they learn the sky paths I have trodden for seasons.

They live in four Clans, unlike our three Tribes that scattered so long ago. They have a separate medicine cat and leader, unlike our healers, who were both. And they have found the Moonpool, the place of the ancestors. The pool is as round as the full moon.

I used to travel to the Moonpool with the two other healers. Then we followed the stream up to its source, high in the hills, and onward to a deep claw-slice in the hills. At the far end, we climbed a steep, rocky slope to a stream beyond.

We followed the stream up to a barrier of thornbushes. Once inside, we would stand for a short while, looking down at the hollow and listening to the sound of the water bubbling out of the sheer cliff beyond.

In the center of the hollow is the Moonpool.

We knew the path that spiraled down to it like the scent of our own Tribes. Then we closed our eyes, drank from the water's edge, and waited for the visions to appear. I remember the clear, cold taste of the water, like drinking silver moonlight.

It gives me joy to see new tribes traveling to the Moonpool. I hope it will bring them serenity, wisdom, and guidance for many moons to come.

THE ISLAND

In their new home by the lake, the Clans also needed a replacement for Fourtrees—a place to hold the peaceful monthly Gathering. At first they met by the Twoleg horseplace, but a better spot was soon found. The Island is just off the shore of RiverClan territory. It would be impossible for young cats and elders to swim to, but StarClan made a tree fall across the span of the water. Now the cats use the tree as a bridge to get to the Island every full moon. There they can meet in safety, on neutral, sacred ground.

DUSTPELT SPEAKS:
How StarClan Gave Us a New Gathering Place

When we first arrived at the lake, I remember looking down from the hill and seeing a dark shape on the near end, and I thought to myself, *Dustpelt, that's an island!* I said so to Ferncloud, although she doesn't remember it now.

Hawkfrost said it would be a perfect place for the RiverClan camp. Imagine! One Clan taking the whole Island! And anyway, how would their kits and elders manage the swim from the lakeshore? But StarClan had other plans. They wanted the Island to be the place of Gatherings, a neutral place for the Clans to meet, like Fourtrees.

A huge storm blew in. Mudclaw tried to snatch the leadership of WindClan away from Onewhisker, but we chased him off, down to the lakeshore. Then a bolt of fire struck a tree on the Island and brought it crashing down on the lakeside, crushing Mudclaw. Onewhisker was the rightful leader of WindClan, and to prove it, StarClan had sent us a way to get to the Island for Gatherings.

Now every full moon, the Gathering takes place in the clearing at the center of the Island, surrounded by bushes and trees. The leaders look down on all the Clans from the branches of a tree, with their deputies on the roots below.

It's a strong and safe place. And best of all, it belongs to all the Clans now.

SUN-DROWN-PLACE

Not far from the Clan's new lakeside home, there is a vast expanse of water known as the sun-drown-place. Here the sun sinks into the sea every night as if it were being swallowed up. The water is strangely salty and roars as it beats the shore. This is where Midnight the badger lives. This is where the questing cats were sent to learn that the Clans had to leave the forest and travel to a new home.

TAWNYPELT SPEAKS:
Journey's End

Icould barely lift my paws to follow the others. The air was filled with the smell of salt, and beneath the shrieking of strange birds I could hear a distant roaring sound. I thought the giant cats of LionClan were prowling out of sight.

Then we reached the top of a cliff, and there below us was a sandy slope stretching down to the water. I didn't know there was room in the world for so much water. We couldn't even see the end of it. It was frothing and roaring and leaping up onto the sand. The sun was a flame-red ball on the horizon; we watched it sink into the water, leaving the world dark.

Brambleclaw led the way along the cliff, which slanted closer to the water the farther we went. The edge of the cliff was jagged. I could see the frothing water through cracks in the rock. It was through one of these cracks that Brambleclaw fell, with Squirrelpaw and me tumbling after him.

The salty water got into our mouths and stung our eyes. It wanted to drag us away. But we swam to dry ground. This was the cave we'd been looking for.

Of course, Feathertail found a better way down, using a series of ledges along the cliff wall. That's how Midnight gets in and out. Who's Midnight? Oh, she's a badger. But we'll get to her story later. . . .

CEREMONIES

LEADERS

Clan leaders are the heart of the Clan; their personality affects how the Clan operates and how their warriors treat one another and the world around them. It is up to the Clan leaders to set a good example and guide their Clanmates along the path of the warrior code. They are responsible for calling Clan meetings, appointing warriors, mentors, and apprentices, and deciding Clan policy and strategy with the help of their deputy and any cats they choose to consult for advice (usually the medicine cat, the elders, or senior warriors).

When a cat becomes Clan leader, he or she must travel to the Moonstone (or after the Clans moved to the lake, the Moonpool) and share tongues with the warrior ancestors of StarClan. The Clan's medicine cat accompanies them on the journey but leaves them alone for the ceremony, in which the leader is granted eight extra lives and a new name with "star" at the end (Bluestar, Firestar, etc.).

This process can be surprising and painful, but it is important for leaders to be able to fight fiercely for their Clan and live long enough to pass along their wisdom and prepare a new leader. During the ceremony, each life is given to the new leader by a cat whose life was significant to the new leader in some way (see *Firestar's Nine Lives*).

When a leader loses a life, she or he blacks out for a short period of time, during which that cat visits StarClan and speaks with its warrior ancestors. On returning to consciousness, the leader must still recover from the injury or illness that felled him or her. Medicine cats can usually tell how many lives a leader has left, although the number is kept secret from rival Clans.

FIRESTAR'S NINE LIVES

LIONHEART The brave former ThunderClan
deputy gave Firestar a life with the gift of
courage, to defend his Clan in battle.

REDTAIL Firestar never met Bluestar's first
deputy, but he worked hard to uncover
the truth about Redtail's murder. For this
reason, Redtail gave him a life with the gift
of justice, to judge his Clanmates fairly.

SILVERSTREAM The beautiful RiverClan
tabby, the love of Graystripe's life, gave
Firestar the gift of loyalty to what he knows
to be right. This understanding would guide
him even beyond the reach of the warrior
code.

RUNNINGWIND The swift ThunderClan
warrior presented his life with the gift of
tireless energy, so Firestar could serve his
Clan to the utmost.

BRINDLEFACE With this life, Brindleface
gave Firestar the same desire to protect his

Clan that a mother has for her kits. He expected this to be a warm, nurturing feeling, but instead he felt it as the fiercest anger burning in his claws, ready to slash and kill to defend his Clanmates.

SWIFTPAW This young apprentice strayed from the Clan into the jaws of a dog pack. He gave Firestar the gift of mentoring.

YELLOWFANG Compassion was Yellowfang's gift, the compassion of a medicine cat for all those who need her help. It is an important gift for a leader, who must be mindful of cats weaker than himself.

SPOTTEDLEAF With her life, the young medicine cat gave Firestar love, signaling her approval of his love for Sandstorm.

BLUESTAR Firestar's leader and mentor gave him his last life, along with the gifts of nobility, certainty, and faith, so that he would be able to lead his Clan in the way of the warrior code for all nine of his lives.

DEPUTIES

"I say these words before the body of Redtail,
so that his spirit may hear and approve my choice.
Lionheart will be the new deputy
of ThunderClan."

A Clan's deputy is chosen by the leader, to assist in taking care of the Clan. To qualify, a warrior must have had an apprentice and must be strong and brave, with the qualities needed to take on leadership of the Clan if necessary.

The deputy presides over Clan meetings when the leader is absent, stands in for the leader at Gatherings if the leader is ill, organizes daily patrols, and oversees the training of apprentices. According to the warrior code, when a deputy dies or steps down, the leader must announce a new deputy before moonhigh.

Deputies stop being deputies if:

❖ the Clan leader dies, leaving the deputy to take over as leader.
❖ the deputy retires and becomes an elder.
❖ the deputy commits a crime against the warrior code and is demoted or driven from the Clan.
❖ the deputy dies or is killed in battle.

APPRENTICES

"By naming apprentices, we show that
ThunderClan will survive and remain strong.
Birchkit, from now on you will be known as Birchpaw. . . .
Ashfur, you are ready for an apprentice.
You will be Birchpaw's mentor."

Before a cat can become a warrior, he or she must be trained to fight and hunt and defend the Clan. At the age of six moons, kits leave the nursery and become apprentices. At this point they change the second half of their name from "kit" to "paw" to symbolize the path their paws are now on. The Clan leader assigns each apprentice a mentor—an older warrior to guide the apprentice on the path to being a warrior. Apprentices are responsible for chores around the camp, such as tending to the elders, in addition to their training. If they work hard, listen to their mentors, and live by the warrior code, soon they will earn their warrior name, and hopefully, one day, the chance to be a mentor themselves.

BIRCHPAW SPEAKS:
A New Apprentice

I can't believe I'm finally an apprentice. I've been dreaming of this for moons! It's true my mother, Ferncloud, wouldn't have minded keeping me in the nursery a while longer. She still licks me as if I were a tiny kit sometimes. But I know she misses Larchkit and Hollykit, who died when the forest ran out of prey, and she worries about me, so I let her.

I'm lucky to have Ashfur as my mentor. He's smart and patient and lets me practice everything instead of just showing me how to do it.

I love hunting patrols the best. We can't eat anything until we've brought back enough food for the elders, but it's so exciting to jump on a mouse, or chase a squirrel, or sneak up on a starling. I've heard stories about apprentices who ate while they were supposed to be hunting and how much trouble they got in. That's not going to happen to me!

I can't wait for my first Gathering, when we are allowed to talk in peace with cats from other Clans. I hope to see Toadkit, Marshkit, and Applekit there. They're ShadowClan cats, but we became friends on the journey from the forest. Maybe I'll tell them that the thrush I nearly caught was actually an eagle. They'd be so impressed!

WARRIORS

*"Brackenpaw, you warned the Clan today,
and you fought bravely in the battle," Bluestar meowed.
"It is time for you to become a warrior."*

Warriors are the lifeblood of the Clan. They patrol the borders, keep the fresh-kill pile supplied, and defend their Clanmates against attacks from enemy cats or predators. They fight to protect the Clan for as long as they are able and are often called upon to mentor apprentices, passing on the skills they were taught. During the warrior naming ceremony, an apprentice gives up the "paw" half of his or her name and earns a real warrior name—such as Fireheart, Sandstorm, or Brambleclaw.

BRACKENFUR SPEAKS:
A New Warrior

I remember the day I became a warrior. I was stretching outside the apprentices' den when Fireheart asked if I wanted to go hunting with him. I don't know where my own mentor was—Graystripe seemed very busy in those days.

When I smelled the WindClan and ShadowClan cats, I knew our camp was in danger because of Brokentail. Back when I was a kit and he was leader of ShadowClan, he stole me and my brother and sisters from ThunderClan. He was driven out and exiled from ShadowClan, but then he led a rogue attack on the ThunderClan camp. Now he was a ThunderClan prisoner, and the other Clans didn't like it one bit. That's why they were coming to attack us.

Fireheart sent me back to camp to warn Bluestar and Tigerclaw. I knew they were coming for Brokentail, so I planted myself outside his den and fought as hard as I could. It was strange fighting to defend such an evil cat. But I knew Bluestar wanted us to defend him. That's what loyalty to the Clan is all about.

After we drove off the invaders, Bluestar made me a warrior. The whole Clan called out my warrior name, Brackenfur. I felt their support and love, and I was so proud of my actions and my choices.

That's what I thought about during my silent vigil. After the ceremony, I wasn't allowed to speak to any cat until dawn. I guarded the camp alone, though I was tired from the battle. I looked up at the twinkling lights of Silverpelt and felt StarClan watching me. It was comforting to know that even when my Clanmates left this life, they'd watch over me, until the day I joined StarClan as well.

When Firestar gave me Whitepaw to mentor, he talked about how I'd learned about strength and friendship from Graystripe and how he hoped I'd pass on that loyalty and determination to her. Whitepaw is eager to learn and excited. I take her on boundary patrol whenever I can, renewing the scent markings and checking for signs of trespassers. We hunt for food for the elders and the queens, and I'm teaching her to climb trees and jump as high as she can to catch flying birds.

Soon, she will become a warrior. I can't wait to see her eyes shine as Firestar says her warrior name and to share in her happiness with the rest of the Clan.

FIGHTING TECHNIQUES

One of the most important skills a mentor must teach an apprentice is how to fight. Warriors are often called upon to defend the borders or protect the Clan from attack, whether by enemy Clans or predators like badgers and foxes. Even medicine cats must learn enough fighting technique to be useful in battle.

Back kick Explosive surprise move to catch opponent from behind. Judge opponent's distance from you carefully; then lash out with your back legs, taking your weight on your front paws.

Belly rake A fight-stopper. Slice with unsheathed claws across soft flesh of opponent's belly. If you're pinned down, the belly rake quickly puts you back in control.

Front paw blow Frontal attack. Bring your front paw down hard on your opponent's head. Claws sheathed.

Front paw strike Frontal attack. Slice downward with your front paw at the body or face of your opponent. Claws unsheathed.

Killing bite A death blow to the back of the neck. Quick and silent and sometimes considered dishonorable. Used only as a last resort.

Leap-and-hold Ideal for a small cat facing a large opponent. Spring onto opponent's back and grip with unsheathed claws. Now you are beyond the range of your opponent's paws and in position to inflict severe body wounds. A group of apprentices can defeat a large and dangerous warrior in this way. It was deployed to great effect against BloodClan's deputy, Bone. Watch for the drop-and-roll countermove, and try to jump free before you get squashed.

Partner fighting Warriors who have trained and fought together will often instinctively fall into a paired defensive position, each protecting the other's back while fending off an opponent on either side. Slashing, clawing, and leaping together, battle pairs can be a whirlwind of danger for attackers.

Play dead Effective in a tight situation, such as when you are pinned. Stop struggling and go limp. When your opponent relaxes his grip, thinking you are defeated, push yourself up explosively. This will throw off an unwary opponent and put you in an attacking position.

Scruff shake Secure a strong teeth grip in the scruff of your opponent's neck; then shake violently until he or she is too rattled to fight back. Most effective against rats, which are small enough to throw. A strong throw will stun or kill them.

Teeth grip Target your opponent's extremities— the legs, tail, scruff, or ears—and sink in your teeth and hold. This move is similar to the leap-and-hold except your claws remain free to fight.

Upright lock Final, crushing move on already weakened opponent. Rear up on back legs and bring full weight down on opponent. If opponent does same, wrestle and flip him under you. This move makes you vulnerable to the belly rake, so requires great strength and speed.

ELDERS

"Goldenflower, is it your wish to give up
the name of warrior and go to join the elders?"
"It is."
"Your Clan honors you and all the service
you have given us. I call upon StarClan to give
you many seasons of rest."

The life of a warrior is difficult and dangerous, and many die young—in battle, of disease, or from a natural disaster. Those cats lucky enough to live a long life may eventually retire from their warrior duties to become elders. These elderly cats are viewed with the deepest respect by the rest of the Clan. Many moons of experience make them an invaluable source of advice for the Clan leader, and they keep alive Clan history by passing down the old stories.

GOLDENFLOWER SPEAKS:
A New Role to Play

As a young apprentice, I dreamed of being a warrior, and I wondered what it would be like to have kits. But I never thought about becoming an elder. Now I know I am lucky to have made it this far.

All the cats treat elders with respect. Even apprentices listen to me; I can't say they always did when I was a warrior. We elders spend our days peacefully, for the most part—discussing the goings-on in the forest, telling stories about the old days, or just snoozing in the sun.

Don't get me wrong. I still have plenty of fight left. I'd be ready to hunt or defend the camp in an instant. When I was a queen nursing Swiftkit, an elder named Rosetail died defending us from a ShadowClan attack. I would do the same for our nursery kits today.

There is one sad duty we elders perform. When a cat dies, all Clan cats gather for a final vigil. We share tongues and groom our Clanmate one last time. That night certain cats lie beside the body in mourning—its family, mentor, apprentice, and littermates. At dawn, we elders are the ones who take the body out of the camp for burial.

So it has always been. I've served my Clan for a long time, and it's nice to finally have some peace and quiet. I hope I get to stick around and enjoy it for many moons to come.

BREAKING THE WARRIOR CODE

❖

CLOUDTAIL SPEAKS:
Tempted by the Kittypet Life

I didn't mean to break the warrior code. I just didn't understand it. Parts of it seemed stupid to me, so I figured I should just follow the smart parts. And Fireheart never stopped to explain *why* I had to follow these rules. He was too busy pointing out the things I did wrong instead of the things I did right. I was faster than Brightpaw, stronger than Thornpaw, and smarter than Swiftpaw and Ashpaw put together. I was determined to show the Clan that I could be a great warrior, even though I was born a kittypet.

One day, I caught a pigeon just before it took off. Instead of praising my skill, Fireheart scolded me like a wayward kit. He said I didn't respect my prey.

I was fed up with Fireheart's lectures, so I ran off. He could have chased me, but he didn't. I ran until I smelled the Thunderpath, and I knew I had reached Twolegplace. I thought about visiting my mother, but I was too worked up, so I decided to explore.

I saw a plump black-and-white tom sunning himself on top of a fence, and a long-haired gray cat chasing a butterfly in circles. It looked more fun than hunting for elders or sparring with Fireheart, so on I went.

I was just passing a pale green fence when a gate opened. It nearly scared my whiskers off! A Twoleg female stood over me, and when she saw me, she crouched down and made this odd cooing noise. I flattened my ears and hissed, and to my surprise, the Twoleg went back through the fence, leaving the gate open. Had I scared her off? I poked my nose inside to see. The grass was short, with flowery bushes around the edges. I watched the Twoleg climb some steps and go through the door of her nest. Then, the door opened again, and the Twoleg set something down on the steps. I waited until she had gone back inside; then I crept forward to investigate. It smelled delicious, like fish, only heartier and less slimy. It was pink and sitting on top of a hard white leaf. Next to it was another leaf, filled with something white that brought back memories of the nursery. I realized it was milk.

Before I knew it, I'd eaten and drunk it all. I was hungry! And besides, I couldn't take it back to the elders. I wasn't hurting anyone. I knew the warrior code said that we shouldn't let ourselves live like kittypets. But I didn't see why we should reject free food. It left more in the forest for everyone else, right? And it was so easy.

I started going nearly every day, whenever I could slip off. Soon the Twoleg let me come inside, where I saw a Twoleg male clomping about. They had a small, yippy white dog. It tried to play with me at first, but it wasn't dangerous. It was barely smart enough to walk.

Mostly I got hard brown pellets to eat, instead of the yummy pink stuff, but they didn't taste bad. I didn't even mind the stale water.

Sometimes I wondered why my mother had sent me away from this life. But I didn't mean to stay. I still wanted to be a warrior. I just thought I could have both. Well, I learned the hard way that I was wrong.

When the Twolegs caught me and put me in a wire web inside the belly of a monster, I thought that ThunderClan would be pleased to see the last of the kittypets. But I still wanted them to know that I had been taken against my will. Deep down, I was a ThunderClan cat. I wanted my warrior ceremony. I wanted to be admired as a great hunter and fighter. I wanted to go to Gatherings. And I'll tell you a secret . . . I was already a little bit in love with Brightpaw.

Fireheart said StarClan led him to me, but I think it was luck that I ran into his friend Ravenpaw near the Twolegs' new nest. Either way, when I saw Fireheart through the window, it felt like all of LionClan had come to rescue me. I was so happy that ThunderClan wanted me back.

Fireheart was angry, of course. But Sandstorm was nice about it. Ashpaw was excited to see me again, and the elders loved hearing the story of my capture; I couldn't help exaggerating a bit. I loved the way they thought I had been on some heroic quest instead of misbehaving.

After all that, I knew better than to go near Twolegs again. And I realized there were parts of the warrior code that I might not understand but that were there for a reason. Seeing my Clanmates listen to my story so eagerly made me want to be a warrior, like Fireheart, who really was a hero.

More than anything, I wanted to be a loyal ThunderClan warrior.

CROWFEATHER SPEAKS:
A Forbidden Love

Have you ever loved another cat so much it made your heart ache and your fur tremble?

Feathertail understood me, and she listened to me. Her eyes were the clear blue of her river home. She died saving us all from Sharpclaw. After that, I wanted only to serve my Clan to the limits of my strength, and then to join Feathertail in StarClan.

But then I met Leafpaw. She was patient and kind. Her voice was like water flowing over pebbles, and her scent had hints of wildflowers in it.

What was happening to me? How could I fall in love with anyone—let alone a ThunderClan cat—let alone a ThunderClan medicine cat? I know the warrior code! I've always been a loyal WindClan cat. I knew that if I let myself fall for her, it could endanger my Clan. If my loyalties were divided, how could I be a true warrior? How could I defend WindClan against a ThunderClan attack, knowing that I might hurt her or someone Leafpaw loves?

And medicine cats are especially forbidden to fall in love. She cannot be thinking of me instead of her Clanmates—they depend on her too much. And StarClan might have trouble reaching her if her thoughts were all wound up in me. I knew they would be very angry with us. I wished I could fall in love with a WindClan she-cat—I wished I could feel this way without breaking the warrior code. But

there is no cat in WindClan like Leafpaw.

I thought that when we reached the lake and went our separate ways I'd be able to forget her. But first she came to our camp to bring watermint to our sick cats, Morningflower and Darkfoot. And the way I felt when I saw her—it made me angry to realize how little I could control my feelings. Onewhisker asked me to escort her home. I went as fast as I could; if I spoke to her, my secret might come spilling out. As I left her camp, Leafpaw thanked me in this sweet, natural way, as if I hadn't been behaving like a badger with its fur clawed off. I had to get out of there before every cat could see what I was trying so hard to fight.

After Leafpaw found the Moonpool, she brought me a message from Feathertail. She said I should stop grieving and open my eyes to the living. What did that mean? Could Feathertail approve of my love for Leafpaw? Wasn't she angry?

It was raining the night everything changed. Onewhisker was planning to travel to the Moonpool to receive his nine lives. I'd noticed Mudclaw's whispers and looks, but I never thought he'd try anything so reckless as attack to Onewhisker—and bring other Clans to help him too!

As the battle was breaking up, Brambleclaw sent me chasing after two ShadowClan cats who made a run for it. We tore across the moors and into the ThunderClan woods. Branches whipped at my face, and rain sliced through my fur, but I ran on, determined to catch the traitors and punish them for all the wrongs done to my Clan.

I heard yowling ahead of me, and I crashed through some bushes, and there she was. The two ShadowClan warriors had fallen to their deaths, but Leafpaw was clinging desperately to the edge of a cliff, her claws scrabbling on the slick, wet rock. Her wild amber eyes met mine, and she called for help. I was frozen. . . . All I could think of was how I had failed Feathertail, how she had died because I couldn't save her.

But I saved Leafpaw. She brought me back. She helped me shake off the memories as I reached forward and pulled her to safety. We lay there on the ground, gasping for breath, and I knew in that moment that I couldn't fight my feelings anymore. I loved Leafpaw, and I told her so.

From the look in her eyes, I knew she felt the same way. She said everything I'd been feeling—that this couldn't happen, that she was a medicine cat. But I could see her heart blazing in the depths of her eyes. I could see how much she cared for me too. I'd seen the same look in Feathertail's eyes . . . but this was different. This was more dangerous, more forbidden. There was a feeling like lightning prickling along my fur every time I looked at Leafpaw. And now I knew she felt it too.

I decided at that moment that we would find a way to be together. The future was terrifying, but we would face it together . . . our pelts brushing, our tails twined. Our hearts in love, forever.

prophecies and omens

StarClan's messages are not always clear. Perhaps the hardest part of a medicine cat's job is reading the omens that are hidden in the natural world. Do they truly come from StarClan? What do they mean? How can they guide our pawsteps?

It is easy to misread their meanings or to manipulate how they are read. For instance, RiverClan's medicine cat, Mudfur, found a moth's wing lying outside his den, which he took to be a sign that Mothwing should be his apprentice, even though she was the daughter of a rogue cat and Tigerstar. However, as Leafpool later discovered, Mothwing's brother Hawkfrost actually left the moth's wing there on purpose, intending to trick Mudfur into believing it was a sign. His plan succeeded, paving the way for Hawkfrost to blackmail his sister into manipulating future signs to his benefit as well.

Some cats see signs everywhere; others doubt that StarClan is behind them. If our spirit ancestors can walk in our dreams and speak with us, why would they need to use such cryptic messages?

But there have been some undeniable omens. Before the battle with BloodClan, Firestar saw instead of his own reflection the face of a lion in a pool. He realized this was a reference to the lion and tiger prophecy (see *Major Prophecies*) and that only by combining the four Clans into LionClan could he save the forest.

As WindClan returned from their exile, the WindClan medicine cat, Barkface, saw the dawn clouds stained with blood. He interpreted that the day would bring an unnecessary death. It was true. On their way back to the ThunderClan camp, Fireheart and Graystripe were attacked by a RiverClan patrol, and a warrior named Whiteclaw fell to his death over the edge of the Gorge.

Prophecies, on the other hand, are proclamations from StarClan that foretell huge events in the future of the Clans. Although they may seem ominous and hard to understand, they mark significant turning points in the span of Clan history.

MAJOR PROPHECIES

✦

BLUESTAR SPEAKS:
Fire Alone Can Save Our Clan

Spottedleaf received this message from StarClan on the night of the battle at Sunningrocks. It was my first defeat as ThunderClan's leader. Morale was low, and there were stirrings of trouble from ShadowClan. ThunderClan needed more warriors, and I needed a sign from StarClan. But what we got didn't make sense.

"Fire alone can save our Clan."

But fire is feared by all the Clans. How could it save us?

A few days later, I was leading a patrol along the edge of the woods near Twolegplace. Tigerclaw had gone on ahead with Ravenpaw, and I was turning to ask Redtail a question when I spotted a cat sitting on a fence, looking out at the forest. From the way he held himself, I thought he must be a Clan cat. He looked proud and restless and curious, ready to charge into battle. A ray of sunshine broke through the clouds and touched his orange pelt. It lit up like a blaze of flame. In the next instant, the clouds closed in, and the fire dimmed; the cat began washing his paws with quick, delicate strokes. I realized he was just a kittypet—the prophecy must have muddled my brain. A kittypet would be about as much use to us as fire!

Still, I kept thinking about him, and I wasn't surprised when we ran into him again on a patrol. Lionheart and I saw him hunting a mouse. He had excellent form and sharp eyes. When Graypaw attacked him, rather than running like a regular kittypet, he turned to defend himself.

Maybe there was something to my theory after all. . . .

That's why I invited him to join the Clan. That's why I named him Firepaw—part of me was hoping that he was a cat of prophecy and destiny.

And I was right.

When I died and joined StarClan, I knew that Fireheart had saved ThunderClan many times over and would do so again as leader. He is living fire: he has the warmth of fire to protect his Clan and the ferocity of fire to defend it.

FIRESTAR SPEAKS:

Four Will Become Two, Lion and Tiger Will Meet in Battle, and Blood Will Rule the Forest

This prophecy came to me during my leadership ceremony. I had received my nine lives and my Clan leader name. Then, even as StarClan welcomed me, I saw a hill of bones spattered with blood. I heard Bluestar whisper, "Something terrible is coming, Firestar. Four will become two. Lion and tiger will meet in battle, and blood will rule the forest."

The meaning of the prophecy revealed itself to me gradually. Four will become two—that meant the forest Clans. RiverClan joined ShadowClan under Tigerstar's leadership, calling themselves TigerClan. ThunderClan joined WindClan to make LionClan . . . two Clans where there used to be four. Then lion and tiger would meet in battle.

I had no way of knowing about BloodClan, of course, until Tigerstar revealed his alliance with Scourge. That's when I discovered our real enemy. LionClan and TigerClan had to unite to drive out Scourge, or else Blood really would rule the forest.

Luckily I had something Scourge did not—faith in StarClan. With my nine lives and my warrior ancestors fighting beside me, I defeated BloodClan.

In the end, peace, not blood, ruled the forest.

BRAMBLECLAW SPEAKS:

Darkness, Air, Water, and Sky Will Come Together and Shake the Forest to Its Roots

This prophecy came to me, Brambleclaw, not to a medicine cat or a leader. Bluestar, the former ThunderClan leader, told me in a dream that I had to meet with three other cats at the new moon and listen to midnight.

Have you ever heard anything more peculiar? Who were these cats, where were we supposed to meet, and how could midnight tell us anything?

I learned the full prophecy later, after much traveling and danger. "Darkness, air, water, and sky will come together and shake the forest to its roots. Nothing will be as it is now, nor as it has been before."

Can you guess what this meant? It meant that four cats from each Clan would come together. ShadowClan was darkness, WindClan was air, RiverClan was water, and ThunderClan was sky. We did shake the forest to its roots, but we had no choice. The Twolegs were destroying our home with their monsters. There was no safe way for cats to live in the forest anymore. Tawnypelt, Crowpaw, Feathertail, and I were chosen to lead our Clanmates to a new home.

That's what StarClan meant when they said, "Nothing will be as it is now, nor as it has been before." From the moment we set paw outside the forest, with the cats of all four Clans following us, I knew that wherever we went and wherever we settled, nothing could ever be the same.

LEAFPOOL SPEAKS:
Before There Is Peace, Blood Will Spill Blood, and the Lake Will Run Red

This prophecy came to me on our first night in the new camp, in a dream. I am Leafpool, the ThunderClan medicine cat. In my dream, I was gazing at the stars reflected on the lake when the water turned bloodred. Then I heard a voice whisper, *"Before there is peace, blood will spill blood, and the lake will run red."*

I knew it meant that there would be bloodshed before there could be peace. But what could I do about it? And when would it happen?

When Mudclaw and Hawkfrost rose up against Onewhisker, I wondered if that was the event in the prophecy. Later, I thought it might be the badger attack. But the prophecy kept returning to my dreams.

I knew that Brambleclaw was meeting his father, Tigerstar, in his dreams, and, of course, I was afraid of where that might lead. So when I heard that Firestar was in mortal danger, I thought he had been betrayed by Brambleclaw. I blamed myself for not having warned my father in time.

But I was wrong.

Brambleclaw's brother, Hawkfrost, had set a trap for Firestar. Brambleclaw had fought and killed Hawkfrost to protect his leader. That's what the prophecy meant by "blood will spill blood"—the death of Hawkfrost at the paws of his brother.

As Hawkfrost's blood spilled into the lake, turning the water red, I knew that I could never fight a cat of my own blood. I couldn't imagine how Brambleclaw must be feeling.

At least now, I thought, there can finally be peace.

MEDICINE

MEDICINE CATS

*"Leafpaw, do you promise to uphold
the ways of a medicine cat, to stand apart from the rivalry
between Clan and Clan, and to protect all cats equally,
even at the cost of your life?"
"I do."
"Then by the powers of StarClan I give you
your true name as a medicine cat. Leafpaw, from this
moment you will be known as Leafpool."*

N
o Clan could survive without a medicine cat's knowledge of healing herbs and compassion for the sick. In addition, these cats have a spiritual responsibility. Their unusually strong connection to StarClan allows them to receive and interpret visions that can guide the Clan through dark times.

Most medicine cats are born to their destiny. From a young age, these special kits are drawn to the medicine cat den. They are fascinated by the herbs and often have strange dreams of their

own. A medicine cat can spot which kit would make a good apprentice. If the kit agrees, he or she is brought to the sacred space (the Moonstone or the Moonpool) and initiated into the ranks of medicine cats through a secret ceremony.

The life of a medicine cat is not easy, but it is very rewarding. Although medicine cats cannot have a mate or kits, they are beloved and respected by the whole Clan. They devote their lives to protecting their Clanmates in a way that ordinary warriors cannot. And they know that there is a special place waiting for them in StarClan.

LEAFPOOL SPEAKS:
Not Just About Herbs

I knew I wanted to be a medicine cat from the time I was a small kit. I watched Cinderpelt taking care of sick cats and checking on my mother in the nursery. *I* wanted to be that gentle, kind, and intelligent. I wanted to know how to heal and how to read the signs from StarClan. I couldn't imagine anything more important.

I knew that medicine cats can never have kits. But I didn't think about what that would mean for me. I didn't ever expect to fall in love.

Cinderpelt let me help her in her den even before I was an apprentice. My sister was disappointed that we didn't get to train together as apprentices, but she understood how important this was to me.

Cinderpelt took me to the Moonstone for the initiation ceremony when I became an apprentice. It's a secret ritual involving the medicine cats of all the Clans and also StarClan—I've never felt closer to StarClan than I did then. . . . It was amazing. There's another ritual when we earn our full medicine cat names. I really wish I could tell you about it, but I have not the words. In truth, my experience of these ceremonies is not that of every medicine cat, and for this reason we are forbidden to talk about it. Perhaps it's true that there are some secrets that should never be told.

That's the best and also the scariest thing about being a medicine cat. Knowing all the herbs and helping my sick Clanmates is wonderful too, but more than that, I know that StarClan is depending on me. I am the one who has to bring their messages to the Clan. I have to understand what they want us to do or else terrible things could befall us. I am my Clan's guardian, in a way.

My friend Mothwing is RiverClan's medicine cat, but she doesn't believe in StarClan. It makes me sad for her—she's missing the most important part of this life. And for a while StarClan had no way to communicate with her, which placed the whole Clan in danger. But now she has Willowpaw, her apprentice. StarClan can speak to her, and so the line of wisdom passed down from our ancestors can continue unbroken.

We get a lot of respect in our Clans, but there is a lot of responsibility too. If I make a mistake, a cat could die. This is why you too have to be careful with your own cat friends. I'm showing you this list of our medicines, but you mustn't try using them yourself. You are not a medicine cat. Out in the forest, we have to use whatever we find, but kittypets have something called a veterinarian to look after them. My friend Cody told me about this. The veterinarian is like a Twoleg medicine cat, as far as I can tell. They heal cats, but they have many more medicines to work with than we do. Don't try giving any sick cats these herbs—either come find me, or take them to the veterinarian. Trust me, they'll thank you for it!

❖

IMPORTANT MEDICINES
AND THEIR USES

BORAGE LEAVES To be chewed and eaten. The plant can be distinguished by its small blue or pink star-shaped flowers and hairy leaves. Great for nursing queens as it helps increase their supply of milk. Also brings down fever.

BURDOCK ROOT A tall-stemmed, sharp-smelling thistle with dark leaves. A medicine cat must dig up the roots, wash off the dirt, and chew them into a pulp, which can be applied to rat bites. Cures infection.

CATMINT (also known as catnip) A delicious-smelling, leafy plant that's hard to find in the wild; often found growing in Twoleg gardens. The best remedy for greencough.

CHERVIL A sweet-smelling plant with large, spreading, fernlike leaves and small white flowers. The juice of the leaves can be used for infected wounds, and chewing the roots helps with bellyache.

COBWEB Spiderwebs can be found all over the forest; be careful not to bring along the spider when you take the web! Medicine cats wrap it around an injury to soak up the blood and keep the wound clean. Stops bleeding.

COLTSFOOT A flowering plant, a bit like a dandelion, with yellow or white flowers. The leaves can be chewed into a pulp, which is eaten to help shortness of breath.

COMFREY Identifiable by its large leaves and small bell-shaped flowers, which can be pink, white, or purple. The fat black roots of this plant can be chewed into a poultice to mend broken bones or soothe wounds.

DOCK A plant similar to sorrel. The leaf can be chewed up and applied to soothe scratches.

DRIED OAK LEAF Collected in the autumn and stored in a dry place. Stops infections.

FEVERFEW A small bush with flowers like daisies. The leaves can be eaten to cool down body temperature, particularly for cats with fever or chills.

GOLDENROD A tall plant with bright yellow flowers. A poultice of this is terrific for healing wounds.

HONEY A sweet, golden liquid created by bees. Difficult to collect without getting stung, but great for soothing infections or the throats of cats who have breathed smoke.

HORSETAIL A tall plant with bristly stems that grows in marshy areas. The leaves can be used to treat infected wounds. Usually chewed up and applied as a poultice.

JUNIPER BERRIES A bush with spiky dark green leaves and purple berries. The berries soothe bellyaches and help cats who are having trouble breathing.

LAVENDER A small purple flowering plant. Cures fever.

MARIGOLD A bright orange or yellow flower that grows low to the ground. The petals or leaves can be chewed into a pulp and applied as a poultice to wounds. Stops infection.

MOUSE BILE A bad-smelling liquid that is the only remedy for ticks. Dab a little moss soaked in bile on a tick and it'll fall right off. Wash paws thoroughly in running water afterward.

POPPY SEED Small black seeds shaken from a dried poppy flower, these are fed to cats to help them sleep. Soothes cats suffering from shock and distress. Not recommended for nursing queens.

STINGING NETTLE The spiny green seeds can be administered to a cat who's swallowed poison, while the leaves can be applied to a wound to bring down swelling.

TANSY A strong-smelling plant with round yellow flowers. Good for curing coughs, but must be eaten in small doses.

THYME This herb can be eaten to calm anxiety and frayed nerves.

WATERMINT A leafy green plant found in streams or damp earth. Usually chewed into a pulp and then fed to a cat suffering bellyache.

WILD GARLIC Rolling in a patch of wild garlic can help prevent infection, especially for dangerous wounds like rat bites.

YARROW A flowering plant whose leaves can be made into a poultice and applied to wounds or scratches to expel poison.

NOTE:

DEATHBERRIES Red berries that can be fatally poisonous to kits and elders. They are NOT a medicine. Known to Twolegs as yew berries. BEWARE!

❧ ❧ ❧

CATS OUTSIDE THE CLANS

BLOODCLAN

Clan character: Not so much a Clan as a loosely organized group of cats who have come together for their mutual protection in hostile and crowded living conditions. These cats have no warrior code, no belief in StarClan, no ceremonies, and no formal training for young cats. Their leader rules by strength and fear.

Habitat: Twolegplace.

Leader: Scourge is a small black cat with icy blue eyes and a high-pitched voice. He wears a collar studded with the teeth of the dogs and cats he has killed, and attached to his claws are dog's teeth. Cruel, calculating, and deadly, Scourge murdered Tigerstar with one blow.

Deputy: Scourge does not have an official deputy, but the closest cat to him is Bone, a large, muscular, black-and-white tom with green eyes. He does all of Scourge's dirty work and reinforces the black cat's leadership with violence and brutality. He also wears a collar studded with teeth.

Notable history: Came to the forest after being offered a deal by Tigerstar, recently made leader of ShadowClan. In return for helping him drive out the other Clans, BloodClan would be allowed hunting rights in the forest. Firestar told Scourge about Tigerstar's past, how he had tried over and over to control the whole forest and failed every time, and how he lied, betrayed, and murdered to satisfy his endless greed for power. Scourge refused to fight on Tigerstar's behalf, and when Tigerstar insisted, Scourge killed him, ripping all nine lives from him with a single blow. With Tigerstar dead, the forest Clans united against BloodClan and drove them out, back to Twolegplace. Scourge himself was killed by Firestar, leader of ThunderClan and Tigerstar's chief opponent.

BARLEY SPEAKS:
Flight from BloodClan

I never questioned my life with BloodClan until I met Fuzz. I thought all cats lived in terror, afraid of being punished by one of Scourge's minions. I thought every cat had to find his food by scrabbling through Twoleg trash. I thought all cats slept in dark, cold alleys and dreaded the day they got too sick or too old to take care of themselves.

My mother taught me and my littermates how to scrounge for food and how to fight. She loved us, but she had to be harsh, or we would never learn to survive. When we were twelve moons old, she threw us out of her den. She had no choice. Scourge had decreed that all cats must fend for themselves. I think he was afraid that strong families might challenge him. As long as we were isolated from one another, we had to rely on Scourge.

I knew my two brothers would seek out Bone and try to become part of Scourge's guard. They admired strength and power, and they wanted some for themselves.

Although it was against the rules, my sister and I stayed together. Violet was a tiny cat, pale orange with thin darker orange stripes. Her paws were small and white and always seemed too delicate for the hard Thunderpaths we ran across or the dirty garbage heaps we had to dig through. We found a hollow below a bush in a Twoleg park where we both could live.

It wasn't a great den. Rain seeped through the branches and into the ground until we were shivering and soaked. And there were always Twolegs around, often with dogs, who sniffed loudly at the entrance to our den.

Violet was terrified of both the Twolegs and the dogs, and I was terrified that Bone would find out we were living together. I convinced her that she should stay inside the den all the time. It was safer, and I could hunt for both of us. I think she was relieved. She could still go out at night, when the park was empty, and stretch her legs in the moonlight.

Bone caught me a few times with an extra mouse in my teeth. When he snarled at me, I would give him both mice and tell him they were an offering for Scourge. He liked that, although he must have known I was lying, just as I knew that those mice would disappear into his own mouth the moment I walked away.

Once I ran into my brothers as they patrolled the dump where Scourge made his den. At first I nearly didn't recognize them. Their eyes were now cold and hard. And around their necks were collars studded with teeth. I stopped and stared at them as they strutted up to me.

"Jumper?" I meowed. "Hoot?"

"Those aren't our names anymore," Hoot sneered. "I am Snake."

"And I am Ice," hissed Jumper. "And don't even think about hunting here."

I hurried away. I'd had my ears battered enough by Scourge's guards. In fact, my ribs were aching and my back leg was bleeding from a beating I had received the morning I met Fuzz. Bone and one of his guards had decided to demonstrate fighting skills on me for a pair of terrified kits.

When I got away, I limped onto a small Thunderpath, looking for prey that lived on the edge of the forest. A Twoleg monster came out of nowhere. I shot up the nearest tree and over a fence so fast that I tumbled off and landed with a thud in the grass.

"Mrrrow!" a voice exclaimed. "That was some jump!"

My whole body tensed to run, but I was too winded to scramble back up. I lay there as the strange cat padded closer. I could tell from his scent that he wasn't BloodClan. He smelled of milk and Twolegs. There was the bright blue collar around his neck, with a small silver bell that jingled as he moved. He was plumper than BloodClan cats, and his long gray fur was feathery and well-groomed. He looked at me as if the moon had fallen into his yard.

"My name is Fuzz!" He jumped back into a play-crouch. "What's yours?"

"Er—Barley," I meowed.

"Hello, Erbarley!" Fuzz meowed.

"No, just Barley," I meowed.

"All right, Justbarley," Fuzz meowed.

I began to get the idea that this wasn't the brightest cat I'd ever met.

"You should let my Twolegs take a look at that leg."

"Oh, no!" I couldn't think of anything more alarming.

"Don't worry," Fuzz purred. "They do this all the time. It's their job." He let out a yowl loud enough to wake a sleeping badger on the far side of the forest. The door to the Twoleg nest swung open, and a tree-tall Twoleg male stepped out into the garden.

I must have blacked out. When I awoke, I was nestled in something soft, surrounded by warmth. I opened my eyes slowly.

Fuzz's face was a mouse-length from my own, peering at me with his giant green eyes.

"You're awake!" he meowed, sounding delighted and amazed. "Have some milk!"

I twisted around to sniff at my leg. It was wrapped in a soft white web of stuff and felt much better. I tried to stand and realized I could put my weight on it with only a little pain.

Suddenly I remembered Violet. I glanced up at the window. The sky outside was dark.

"How long have I been here?" I asked Fuzz.

"All day," Fuzz meowed cheerfully.

"I have to get back to my sister," I meowed, scrambling to my feet. "She'll be so worried."

"Well, eat something before you go," Fuzz urged me. I swiped my tongue around the saucer, licking up the scraps of tuna that were left. The flavor was dazzling. Fuzz led me through a flap in the door. Then I was back out in the yard, scrambling over the fence and hurrying back to the park.

The moon was high in the sky when I reached our den.

"Violet?" I called, crawling into the darkness below the branches. "Violet?"

Bone's scent hit my nose just before he spoke from the shadows. "Your sister is not here."

I froze, all my muscles turning to stone. "W-where is she?" I stammered.

"She came looking for you." The black-and-white cat stood and stretched his long, muscular legs. His eyes gleamed in the fragments of moonlight. "What an interesting setup you have here, Barley. You and your sister, living in this den. Isn't that *against the rules?*"

"I'm just taking care of her," I meowed. "We're no threat to Scourge."

"That is for Scourge to decide," Bone hissed. "Come." He stalked out of the bush, brushing past the thorns as if he didn't feel them. I hurried after him, my heart sinking as we approached the trash heap where Scourge held court.

The small black cat was perched atop a mound of discarded Twoleg things. The teeth on his collar and claws glinted like the freezing chips of ice that were his eyes. Cats were gathered all around the mound, waiting for something to happen. Below Scourge, in a cleared circle of dirt, my sister was sitting with her shoulders hunched. Her eyes were huge and terrified.

"Violet," I cried, springing forward, but Bone whirled around and slammed his paw into my head so I was knocked aside, my vision spinning. I crouched for a moment, shaking my head.

"This is what we do with cats who break the rules," Scourge hissed in his eerily high-pitched voice. He flicked his tail at the shadows to his left. My brothers emerged into the moonlight, their teeth bared in furious snarls.

"No!" I yowled. "Leave her alone! Fight me, if you must! She's done no harm!"

"It's true," Scourge snarled. "You are the one who broke the rules. You are the one who must be punished." He swiped his tongue over his paw, making us all wait for a long, horrible moment. Then he looked down at me with a sinister twitch of his whiskers. "And what better punishment could there be than for you to watch your sister die right in front of you."

"No!" I wailed, but before I could move, Bone leaped on me and pinned me down. I could only struggle futilely, my claws scrabbling at the ground, as Snake and Ice stalked up to Violet. There was a flash of claws and a shriek of pain from Violet. And then my poor little sister was lying on the ground, blood spilling out of her, her paws twitching feebly. I stared in horror as Snake and Ice licked the blood off their paws and slunk back into the shadows. Scourge nodded, looking pleased, and then he melted away into the darkness, with all his followers disappearing behind him. Bone lifted his paws and looked down at me with disgust in his eyes.

"Don't ever try to fight BloodClan again," he snarled. "We always win."

Then he too vanished into the darkness.

I crawled over to Violet, my breathing coming in ragged gasps. She was so still, so small. I nosed her face gently and suddenly her eyes opened.

"Barley." She coughed. "Help me."

She was alive! I frantically tried to stop the blood spilling out of the long slice in her stomach, but I didn't know anything about healing another cat.

Then I remembered Fuzz and the Twoleg. It was risky, but it was the only thing I could think of to do.

I closed my mouth gently around the scruff of Violet's neck and dragged her out of the dump. She kept letting out little yips of pain, but she didn't struggle. I dragged her all the way down the small Thunderpath to the gate in the Twoleg fence where Fuzz lived. And then I laid her down on the path and started yowling with all my heart.

Fuzz shot out the cat door a few moments later, his face as brightly confused as ever. He sprang up to the top of the gate and teetered precariously, gawking at me and Violet.

"Who's *that*?" he exclaimed. "She's the most beautiful cat I've ever seen! Why is she so sad? Oh, my whiskers, is she bleeding too?

What on earth is wrong with your Twolegs? Why don't they take better care of you?"

"Fuzz, I need your help," I panted. "I need your Twoleg to take care of Violet for me."

"Where are you going?" Fuzz asked, all wide-eyed innocence. Until he said that, I hadn't really thought about it. I knew I couldn't stay anywhere near BloodClan. She would be safe only here in this Twoleg nest—and she would be safe only if I was far away. Then perhaps Scourge and Bone would forget about us.

"The far side of the forest," I meowed. "Please will you take care of her?"

"Sure," Fuzz meowed. "She doesn't look like she eats much tuna. Maybe she'll share hers with me." He tilted his head at Violet.

The door opened behind him, spilling yellow light into the garden. I bent my head to whisper in Violet's ear.

"You'll be safe now," I meowed. "Remember, I love you."

She blinked up at me. "I love you too, Barley."

"I'll always be your brother," I meowed. "However far apart we are."

"Bye, Justbarley!" Fuzz meowed.

I dashed across the Thunderpath and up a tree. From there, I watched as the Twoleg swung open the gate and saw Violet. He made a sad, shocked sound, then leaned over to gently pick her up. From the way he cradled her as they went back inside, I could tell that he would take care of her. I didn't know why I felt so sure we could trust him, but I did.

Fuzz scampered after them. His long, fluffy tail whisking through the door was the last I saw of the Twoleg nest before I turned and ran swiftly toward the woods.

I traveled quickly through the trees. I could smell other cats around me, but I was afraid they would be like BloodClan, so I didn't stop. I crossed a stream and ran through a clearing guarded by four tall oak trees. I scrambled up a rocky slope and found myself on an open moor, where I ran even faster, as if my life depended on it. I wanted to put as much distance as I could between myself and BloodClan.

Finally, as the sun was rising over the distant hills, I came to a large Twoleg nest. It smelled of hay and mice and sunshine. I could tell after a short exploration that Twolegs came here often but didn't stay long. Something about it felt safe and friendly. Nothing could have been more different from the dark alleys and cold puddles of Twolegplace.

I dug my way into a pile of hay and curled up, breathing in the sweet warmth.

I would be safe here. Safe and free to live my own life. Maybe one day I'd go back and look for Violet—or maybe she'd be happy living with Fuzz and his Twolegs. Maybe she'd get plump on tuna and sleep on the bed with the Twolegs, purring contentedly. The important thing was we'd escaped from BloodClan.

Scourge couldn't hurt us anymore.

THE TRIBE OF RUSHING WATER

Tribe character: Smaller and leaner than forest cats. They smear their fur with mud for camouflage against the rocks. Tribe cats are born as either cave-guards or prey-hunters and are known as *to-bes* while training. Their warrior ancestors belong to the Tribe of Endless Hunting, cats who appear in whispers in the leaves and the pattern of water over stones. Their most sacred place is the Cave of Pointed Stones, where the Healer may interpret signs in the way rain drips from the roof and in the shadows of the stalagmites and stalactites cast by moonlight.

Habitat: The mountains.

Camp: A rocky path leads behind a waterfall into a huge cave, as broad as the waterfall and screened from the outside world by the rushing water. The cave burrows under the mountain. Narrow passages lead off on either side, one to the Cave of the Pointed Stones, one to the nursery. Cats sleep in hollows on the cave floor lined with moss and eagle or heron feathers. A trickle of water runs down a mossy rock into a small, clear pool, providing fresh drinking water.

Leader (known as Healer): Teller of the Pointed Stones, called *Stoneteller*, is a wise old brown tabby cat who serves as both leader and medicine cat. He is responsible for reading the signs in the Cave of Pointed Stones, and he guides his Tribe according to the messages from the Tribe of Endless Hunting.

STONETELLER SPEAKS:
The Coming of the Silver Cat

There are strangers in our cave tonight.

They are returning to their home in the forest, but they must not linger there long. They say that a terrible danger is destroying their home. Soon all the forest cats must go on a journey to no cat knows where. . . .

We are struggling with a terrible danger too. I cannot tell the strangers about it. I fear they would leave the mountains if they knew. And yet one of them must save us from Sharptooth.

I have read the ripple of shadows on the rock wall, the drops of water in the moonlight. I have seen bright gray fur flash in the pool. The signs are clear. A silver cat, not from this Tribe, will come to save us from Sharptooth—that is what the Tribe of Endless Hunting has promised.

The six cats arrived wet and shivering in our cave. They are scrawny, tired, and suspicious, and one of them is badly injured. I have heard them whispering about us—they don't realize how good our hearing is. They can see that we are afraid of something.

I believe the silver cat must be the one called Stormfur. His fur gleams with the dark silver of the moon when it is just a claw in the sky.

The dark tabby, the one called Brambleclaw, is their leader, although the small black cat and the tortoiseshell don't hesitate to challenge him. Nor does the ginger she-cat named Squirrelpaw, yet

I can see her respect for him in every ripple of her fur. There is something about those two—a destiny longer, darker, and more fraught with danger than I care to look at. But it does not affect my Tribe.

Once the strangers dried off, I saw there was another silver cat in the group—Stormfur's sister, Feathertail. Could the prophecy refer to her instead? No, it must be Stormfur. He has a proud courage about him, a strength in those shoulders that would defeat any of my cave-guards.

Whatever he is going to do to save us, I hope it will be soon. My Tribe has lost so many cats already. And it is not only the lives of the dead cats that Sharptooth has taken. He has taken the pride, the joy, the fierce will to live of all my Tribe. We are but a shadow of a Tribe now, haunted by the flashing claws and teeth of a mindless killer.

I beseech you, Tribe of Endless Hunting. Guide the silver cat's paws to save us from Sharptooth, so that we may have peace again.

ROGUES AND LONERS

A rogue is a Clan cat who has been banished for crimes against the warrior code. These cats are usually hostile and live as outlaws on Clan territory or on the outskirts. Loners are cats who choose to live neither in Clans nor with Twolegs. They live and hunt alone. Loners can be friendly and even helpful to the Clan cats.

BARLEY: A black-and-white tom who left BloodClan to live as a loner in the forest. (See *Barley Speaks: Flight from BloodClan.*) His home is a warm barn north of WindClan territory. Warriors often pass through his farm on their way to Highstones, and so most of the Clans know of him. The Twolegs who run the farm don't mind him living there, since he keeps down the rodent population.

Barley bravely came to the aid of Bluestar during a rat attack when she was leading four ThunderClan cats back to the forest from Mothermouth. Later, he offered his barn as shelter for WindClan while they journeyed home to their camp. When BloodClan came to the forest, he was able to give Firestar insight into their weaknesses, which helped LionClan win the battle.

RAVENPAW: A small black loner, originally a ThunderClan apprentice. His mentor was the ThunderClan deputy Tigerclaw. During a battle at Sunningrocks, Ravenpaw saw Tigerclaw kill the ThunderClan deputy, Redtail. This

knowledge put Ravenpaw's life at risk. With the help of
Firepaw, he fled the ThunderClan camp to the safety of
Barley's barn. He is happy here; the loner lifestyle suits him
better than Clan life.

SASHA: A tawny-colored rogue. She fell in love with Tigerstar
while he was recruiting BloodClan. She bore him two kittens,
Mothwing and Hawkfrost, and brought them to RiverClan for
a better life, as she wasn't interested in raising kits by herself.
Later, she tried unsuccessfully to convince them to rejoin her
instead of traveling to the Clans' new home.

PURDY: An elderly, mottled brown tabby tom who met the
questing Clan cats on their way to the sun-drown-place.
Purdy did his best to help the cats find their way through the
confusing tangle of Thunderpaths and Twoleg nests, although
it might not have been by the shortest route! He tried to
warn the young cats of the danger in the mountains, but it
was their destiny to go that way, no matter what he said.

SMOKY, DAISY, AND FLOSS: These three cats live as
loners in a barn near the horseplace. They do not hunt prey,
since they are fed by the Twolegs. This, in the opinion of
many Clan cats, makes them as useless as kittypets.

Smoky is a muscular gray-and-white tom, who is distant
but not unfriendly. He met the Clan cats on their way to
the first Gathering. He is the father of Daisy's kits: Berrykit,
Hazelkit, and Mousekit.

Daisy is a creamy brown she-cat with blue eyes. She
brought her kits to join ThunderClan.

Floss is a small gray-and-white she-cat, whose kits were
taken away by the Nofurs (their name for Twolegs).

DAISY SPEAKS:
My Only Hope

"Your kits! Where have they gone?"

The barn suddenly seemed a large, forbidding space, with a thousand different places for kits to get hurt. I scrabbled through a stack of hay next to my friend Floss. She had recently had kits—but her kits had vanished.

"Their eyes were still closed! They couldn't even walk!"

Floss was lying on her side in a patch of sunshine. She blinked large, sad eyes at me.

"It's the Nofurs," she explained. "They take our kits after they're born. They took my first litter too."

"Why would they do that?"

"Maybe they think three cats in one barn are enough?" Floss meowed. "Maybe there are other barns that need cats."

I curled my tail over my stomach as if I could already protect the little lives inside. I thought there might be three of them, from the way they kicked and wriggled.

"But—you never see them again?" I meowed softly.

"One moment they're here." She lifted a paw and licked it. "The next, they're gone."

I studied her face carefully. I think she was more heartbroken than she was letting on. "Then I'll have to leave," I meowed. "I'll take my kits far away from the Nofurs."

"Where will you go?" Floss asked. "And how will you survive, all on your own with a family of hungry mouths?"

She was right. I wasn't used to being on my own. I wouldn't know how to feed myself or my kits. And I would miss the friendship of Floss and Smoky.

"What about those new cats?" I remembered. "The ones who moved to the lake?"

"Strange creatures. Why not find a nice warm barn to live in?" meowed Floss. "It must be cold and wet out there."

It was true; I hated being cold and wet. But some of those wild cats had looked friendly. There was that white tom who had nodded to me, and the orange leader who had warm green eyes.

Floss narrowed her eyes. "We don't know anything about those cats, except that there are a lot of them," she meowed.

But I was sure they would help me. I could carry my kits there, if I needed to. I knew Smoky wouldn't try to stop me. He had always cared more about Floss than me. Perhaps out there I could find a cat to care about me the way Smoky and Floss care about each other. And he'd take care of my kits too.

I knew there were scary things outside the barn, but I was sure that the wild cats would protect me and my kits, so that I could see them grow up. I knew what I was going to call them too: Mouse, Berry, and Hazel. They're going to be fine, strong cats, and I will be there for every pawstep.

❖

KITTYPETS

Cats that live with Twolegs are called kittypets. They wear collars and are usually timid, soft, and scared of Clan cats. They are fed by their Twolegs, and so have no need to hunt. They have only a vague sense of territory beyond their Twolegs' garden.

> **SMUDGE:** Friendly, plump, and contented black-and-white tom. He lived next door to Firestar, whom he knew as Rusty. He sees none of the appeal of the forest or Clan life.

> **PRINCESS:** Firestar's sister. A light brown tabby with a white chest and white paws. She is intrigued by the forest and gave up her son, Cloudkit, to be raised as a ThunderClan cat. Yet she finds it terrifying too; she could never leave her Twolegs to chase mice in the forest! Cloudkit had some trouble adjusting to the warrior code at first, and he has never believed in StarClan, but he is still a brave, loyal ThunderClan warrior.

> **CODY:** Sweet, plucky, tabby kittypet with blue eyes. Cody ran away from her Twolegs, intending only to have a bit of fun before returning home. She was caught by the construction crew tearing down the forest and thrown into a cage with the wild cats. Here, she befriended Leafpaw, and after they were rescued, Cody went with her to ThunderClan. Although she was willing to help the Clan in their hour of need, the precarious, violent life of the warrior cats was not for her, and she returned to her housefolk. She will never forget her friend Leafpaw.

JACQUES AND SUSAN: Jacques is a huge black-and-white tom with a torn ear. Susan is a small tabby she-cat. They live in a Twoleg nest in ShadowClan's lake territory. Both of them are hostile and dangerous, with no warrior code to guide their actions. When the warrior cats moved into their territory, they showed their displeasure by targeting young or weak cats. ThunderClan helped ShadowClan teach them a lesson.

MILLIE: A light gray tabby she-cat. Millie befriended Graystripe when he was captured by Twolegs. When he decided to leave in search of his Clan, she chose to leave her housefolk and go with him. Although she was raised as a kittypet, Graystripe has trained her to fight, and she is committed to becoming a true ThunderClan warrior.

OTHER ANIMALS

FOXES

Russet-red fur, bushy tails, sharp teeth, and pointed
noses. Look a bit like dogs.

Live in dens, often in sandy ground hidden by
undergrowth.

Live alone or with their cubs.

Mean, suspicious, and hostile, they don't eat cats,
but they will kill for pleasure and not just for prey.

They hunt mostly at night and have a strong and unpleasant
smell.

BADGERS

Large, with short black fur and a white stripe
down their long, pointed muzzles.

Small, beady eyes, powerful shoulders, and
sharp claws.

Live in either caves or sets, which are tunnels
underground, bushes, or tree roots.

Live alone or with their kits and have a very
distinctive smell.

Badgers sometimes prey on young cat kits. Can trample their
victims with enormous paws or deliver a deadly bite.

Have tremendously powerful jaws that make it nearly impossible
to escape their grip.

Midnight: An exceptional badger at the sun-drown-place. She
has no hostility for cats. She has a special connection with
StarClan and can speak both Cat and Fox. It was Midnight
who passed on the message that the Clans must leave the
forest.

DOGS

Size varies from that of a kit to a
pony. Fur can be long or short,
white, brown, black, gray, or
a mix. Can have pointy or flat
noses, droopy or sharp ears.
Make loud, angry noises and love
chasing cats.

Live mostly in Twoleg nests or barns.
Wild dogs might sleep anywhere;
one pack in recent Clan history made their home in the
caves below Snakerocks.

Loud, fast, and sharp-toothed. Many dogs seem to be devoted
to their Twolegs and are seen only in Twoleg company.
There is a theory that most dogs are too dim-witted to be
truly dangerous. Packs of dogs are always to be feared.
(See *ThunderClan, Brightheart Speaks: The Death of
Swiftpaw.*)

BIRDS OF PREY

Winged predators with hooked beaks and sharp, curving talons,
these include hawks, eagles, falcons, and owls.

Nest in hollows or branches of trees, or on the ledges of cliffs.

Extremely sharp vision for spotting prey from a distance. Hawks
and eagles are daytime hunters; owls hunt at night. They
swoop down from the sky to carry off prey, which includes
kits. This was the fate of Snowkit, Speckletail's deaf son,
when a hawk attacked the camp after a forest fire had
burned away its protective cover. The Tribe of Rushing Water
have developed clever ways to hunt these birds.

HORSES/SHEEP/COWS

Four-legged farm creatures.

Horses are tall and swift with flowing manes and tails
and giant, pounding hooves.

Sheep look like fluffy white clouds dotted across a
green field.

Cows can be black and white or brown,
and their hooves are to be avoided.

Live in large fenced fields and sometimes
hay-filled Twoleg barns.

Mostly harmless. However, take caution
passing through their fields. A galloping horse or
stampeding herd of cows would trample a cat
without even noticing.

RATS

Brown-furred and beady-eyed rodents, with long, naked tails and
sharp front teeth. Not much bigger than kits.

Live in garbage dumps like Carrionplace in ShadowClan territory
or anywhere they can scavenge Twoleg food.

Live and travel in packs. Individually they pose no threat to
cats, but their numbers are often overwhelming, and bites
can cause infection. A single rat contaminated the whole of
ShadowClan during Nightstar's brief time as leader.

TWOLEGS

Tall, smooth-skinned creatures with some fur on their heads.
Walk on two legs.

Live in large, boxy nests with hard roofs and floors, often
surrounded by tidy gardens and fences.

Also known as Nofurs or Upwalkers. Twolegs ride around in
monsters and seem to like dogs. They are to be avoided
if possible, as they are capable of doing something
unpredictable at any moment, such as tearing down a tree,
starting a fire, or locking up a cat for no reason.

MYTHOLOGY

Every Clan has its legends—the great adventures
of its warrior ancestors, passed down through the generations.
But all the Clans share the stories of the ancient, giant, gold-pelted
cats who once ruled the forest. LionClan had flowing manes,
like the rays of the sun. LeopardClan were swift; they had black spots
on their pelts like racing pawprints. TigerClan were flame-
colored night hunters, with black stripes like shadows flickering
across their fur and the darkness of night in their souls. The giant
cats are gone now, but they have passed down special talents to their
descendants, the warrior cats.

HOW LEOPARDCLAN WON THE RIVER

In a time when the forest was young and untouched by Twolegs, the three Clans of mighty cats came together for a Gathering during the frosts of leaf-bare.

The leader of LionClan, a proud cat named Goldenstar, stepped forward.

"There is a wild boar loose in the forest," he roared.

"There are many wild boar loose in the forest," responded Swiftstar, the LeopardClan leader, with a dismissive flick of his tail.

"Not like this one," growled Goldenstar. "He is as large as a horse. He has tusks as thick as sycamore branches and a fleece of black hair as sharp as thorns. He killed one of our apprentices."

"I know of this boar too," rumbled the TigerClan leader, Shadestar, twitching her ears. "We call him Rage. A TigerClan hunting party met him in the woods two days ago, but he escaped us. He fights with the strength of ten warriors and can kill with a single blow of his fierce tusks."

"Ha!" A voice rose from the crowd of warriors, which parted to reveal a LeopardClan warrior named Fleetfoot. "Such a beast would be no match for a LeopardClan warrior," she boasted. "We would outrun it, outsmart it, and kill it."

"Oh, yes?" Shadestar snarled. "Then why don't you do as you say and kill Rage?"

"Show us that your deeds can match your words," growled Goldenstar.

"With pleasure," Fleetfoot responded proudly.

"And in exchange," Swiftstar quickly added, "LeopardClan may claim the river as our hunting grounds."

"Hmm," meowed Shadestar, narrowing her eyes.

"Very well," Goldenstar agreed. "If Fleetfoot kills this beast, LeopardClan may claim the river for one moon, during which no other Clan will hunt there."

Swiftstar bowed his head in agreement. He leaped down from the Great Rock and swept out of the clearing, with his LeopardClan warriors pouring after him.

Shadestar turned to Goldenstar as the spotted cats disappeared from sight. "There is something we didn't tell Fleetfoot."

"I know," meowed Goldenstar. "She will find it out soon

enough. Rest assured, we will not have to give up the river and its hunting grounds."

The hunt began that night. Fleetfoot tracked the boar by its scent until she found him under a tall oak tree, nosing the ground underneath it. She leaped at him with a ferocious yowl, and the boar, startled, turned and ran. Fleetfoot chased Rage through the forest, leaping fallen trees, dodging bushes, staying close on his heels.

At last they burst out into an open patch of ground, and before the boar could stop himself, he went hurtling off a cliff. Fleetfoot leaped after him into the torrent of the river below. She found him thrashing around and wrapped her claws around his back, pinning him under the water until she thought she would burst for want of air.

As the sun rose over the gorge, Fleetfoot and Rage washed up on the shore of the river. The wild boar was dead.

Fleetfoot staggered to her feet, dripping wet and trying to catch her breath. Then she saw something that made her fur prickle all along her spine. Standing on the bank of the river was the boar's mate—an even bigger, fiercer beast who rarely left her den, as Goldenstar and Shadestar knew. This she-boar was named Fury.

Fleetfoot and Fury fought on the bank of the river for two nights and two days. Finally, exhausted, Fleetfoot drove the she-boar out onto the stepping-stones, where Fury lost her footing, fell into the river, and drowned.

Goldenstar and Shadestar were ashamed of their treachery. The young LeopardClan warrior had saved them all from two terrible enemies. So, they gave LeopardClan sole hunting rights to the river forever.

And that is how LeopardClan won the river.

HOW SNAKES CAME TO THE FOREST

There once lived a brave LionClan warrior called Sunpelt. Sunpelt had heard stories of the giant snake called Mouthclaw, who lived in a dark cave by Snakerocks. She was the only snake in the entire forest. She had killed many great warriors from all the Clans. Her sharp-fanged jaws could swallow a living cat whole, and she spat deadly venom.

Cats from all Clans were forbidden to go to Snakerocks. The leaders were afraid to lose any more warriors to Mouthclaw. But Sunpelt wanted to prove what a great warrior he was. He thought that by killing Mouthclaw, he would earn the respect of the forest.

One morning he left the camp before sunup and journeyed to Snakerocks. He stood outside Mouthclaw's cave and called, "Come out and fight!" Then he angered her further by kicking stones into her cave with his back legs.

Mouthclaw slithered out of her cave, her tongue flickering like lightning. She was ten fox-lengths long and as thick as a badger with a bellyful of cubs. Her eyes were evil red slits, and her scales glittered in the dawn light.

She bared her fangs with pleasure, for LionClan warriors were one of her favorite meals. And then she lunged. But the young warrior was too quick. He leaped from rock to rock, while Mouthclaw spat poison and threw up clouds of dust with her lashing tail. The fight went on all day, but she could never get close enough for the kill.

Finally Mouthclaw could fight no more.

"I have been living in these rocks for a thousand moons," she hissed. "Spare my life, and I shall grant you one wish."

The brave warrior thought for a moment. Then he roared, "I wish that you would shrink to the length of a cat's tail. If you were that small, then I would allow you to remain living at Snakerocks."

"And that is all you ask of me?" hissed Mouthclaw with an evil glint in her eyes.

"That is all," said Sunpelt. He knew a tiny snake would be no danger to the giant cats of the forest. He would be a hero.

Mouthclaw began to writhe and slither, back and forth. A great cloud of dust rose up, and when it settled, Sunpelt leaped backward in horror.

A thousand snakes, each the length of a cat's tail, covered the ground, spitting poison. Now instead of one giant snake at Snakerocks, there were many, each of them deadly and fierce.

Sunpelt could not believe what he had done. Horrified and guilt-stricken, he raced back to camp and confessed all to his leader.

At first Goldenstar was angry. "This was a dangerous thing you did," he growled. "You should know better than to bargain with snakes. They are cunning and will outwit us every time."

"I know," Sunpelt admitted, hanging his head.

"However," Goldenstar meowed, "you have done a great service for the forest. These smaller snakes may be dangerous, but none can be as dangerous as Mouthclaw. Now no warrior has to fear being swallowed or bitten by her deadly fangs."

"That is true," Sunpelt meowed, his spirit rising.

Goldenstar forgave his brave warrior. After all, Sunpelt was not the first cat—or the last—to be tricked by a snake in the grass.

HOW TIGERCLAN GOT THEIR STRIPES

When the big cats first walked the forest, TigerClan and LionClan both had pure gold coats, but only LionClan cats had a mane of long hair like the rays of the sun. The TigerClan cats were jealous of these golden manes, and they were jealous of LeopardClan's ability to run faster than any other cats. Jealousy made them bitter, and they started hunting at night and keeping to the shadows during the daytime.

One TigerClan warrior, Thorntooth, was more bitter than the rest. He started attacking the other Clans at night, stealing their kits and raiding their fresh-kill pile. Shadestar, the TigerClan

leader, knew what Thorntooth was doing, but she did nothing to stop him, because her own heart was black with envy.

Then a day came when Thorntooth sneaked back to camp with a small lion cub dangling from his jaws and mewling sadly.

Shadestar took one look at the kit and flew into a rage.

"That's Petalkit!" she roared. "You've stolen Goldenstar's only daughter!"

"Yes, I have," Thorntooth replied smugly, dropping the she-cat on the ground. Petalkit let out a wail and buried her nose in her paws.

"What have you done?" Shadestar snarled. "This will mean war. LionClan will not rest until they rescue this kit. They will slaughter us all if they have to."

"We can fight them," Thorntooth growled angrily.

"And let TigerClan warriors die? For what?" Shadestar hissed. "For nothing. We're giving Goldenstar's daughter back immediately."

Shadestar called a Gathering that night and gave Petalkit back to Goldenstar before LionClan could attack. Here was proof that Thorntooth was behind the night raids. Goldenstar and Swiftstar demanded that Shadestar put a stop to her warrior's dishonorable behavior.

"But it's not fair!" Thorntooth protested. "TigerClan has nothing special. We are plain orange cats with no great skills. We should have something to set us apart like LionClan and LeopardClan have!"

"Enough!" Goldenstar snarled. "Shadestar, your Clan must be punished. For the next moon, TigerClan shall not be seen in daylight. The light of the sun shall not touch your pelts. You may not speak to cats of other Clans. For one whole moon, you forfeit your Clan's honor. If you stop your raids, you may rejoin the Clans at the next Gathering."

So TigerClan walked only by night for a moon and stayed away from the other Clans. When the full moon came around again, they stepped into the Gathering under the moonlight. All the other cats gasped.

"Your pelts!" Swiftstar meowed.

TigerClan had spent so long walking in the shadows that their brightly colored pelts were sliced through with jet-black stripes. Thorntooth was pleased, because now TigerClan was marked out like the other Clans.

From that day on, all TigerClan cats were born with stripes.

GLOSSARY

Catspeak: Humanspeak

Crow-food: rotting food

Fox dung: an insult; stronger offense than mouse-brain

Fresh-kill: recently killed prey

Gathering: a meeting that the Clans hold in peace at every full moon

Greencough: severe chest infection, which can be fatal in elders and young kits

Greenleaf: summer

Greenleaf Twolegplace: a place where humans visit only in the summer (a campsite, resort, etc.)

Halfbridge: a dock

Horseplace: fields and stables near the lake where half-tamed cats live

Housefolk: a house cat's word for its humans

Kittypet: a house cat

Leaf-bare: winter

Leaf-fall: fall/autumn

Loner: cat that lives peacefully on its own in one place but doesn't defend its territory

Monster: usually refers to human machines such as cars and bulldozers

Moonhigh: the time of night when the moon is at its highest—often midnight

Mouse-brained: not very smart

Mouse dung: an insult; stronger than mouse-brain, but less offensive than fox dung

Newleaf: spring

Nofurs: another word for humans

One moon: one month (half-moon = two weeks, quarter-moon = one week)

Rogue: a potentially hostile cat who lives outside the Clans and never spends too long in one place

Sharing tongues: term used to describe cats grooming each other

Silverpelt: the Milky Way

Sun-drown-place: the sea to the west, where the sun sets

Sunhigh: noon

Thunderpath: a road

Tree-eater: bulldozer

Twoleg nest: a human house

Twolegplace: a human town

Twolegs: the Clans' word for humans

Upwalkers: another word for humans

Whitecough: mild chest infection

WARRIORS

CODE OF THE CLANS

For Mr. Pugh, with love

Special thanks to Victoria Holmes

CODE of the CLANS

CONTENTS

The Dawn
of the Clans

✦

Many moons ago, a community of cats settled in dense woodland close to the edge of a moor. Some were kittypets intrigued by the idea of exploring beyond their housefolk's backyard; others had been born and raised in the wild, by cats who knew how to catch their own prey and find shelter in the cold nights of leaf-bare.

The woodland, with the river running fast and deep at the edge of the trees, proved to be good territory for the cats. There was enough shelter for every cat, enough prey to feed them all, and the freedom to hunt among the trees, on the open moor, and along the fish-filled river.

The cats began to settle according to their preferences for hunting and prey. The fish-eaters kept mostly to the banks of the river, making their dens among the reeds and twisted willow roots; the mouse-pouncers stayed under the densest trees, perfecting their leaps among the tangled undergrowth; the rabbit-chasers, faster and leaner than the other cats, kept to the open moor; the squirrel-stalkers settled in the sparser woodland, where they learned to climb trees and hunt among the branches; and the cats who had a taste for snakes and lizards, and the cunning to catch them on marshy ground, settled among brittle grass stalks and rattling pine trees on the farthest edge of the territory.

There were no borders at first, and within each hunting ground the cats lived separately, meeting only as they went in pursuit of the same prey. Occasionally cats clashed over a piece of fresh-kill or a good place for a den, but battles between large numbers of cats were unheard of.

Then a time came when prey was scarce, and there were too many mouths to feed and bodies to shelter in each hunting ground. Battles broke out, just a few cats at first, but more and more until hunting ground took on hunting ground, fighting for survival, not just for themselves, but for the cats who lived alongside them. After one dreadful battle, when the ground beneath the four great oak trees turned red with blood, the spirits of the dead cats came back to plead for peace with the strongest cats from each hunting ground: Wind, River, Thunder, Shadow, and Sky.

The five vowed to their fallen companions that they would find a way to put an end to the fighting, to live in their separate hunting grounds in communities that would preserve each territory for generations of cats to come.

THE TIME OF THE
CLANS HAD BEGUN...

THE WARRIOR CODE

1. Defend your Clan, even with your life. You may have friendships with cats from other Clans, but your loyalty must remain to your Clan.

2. Do not hunt or trespass on another Clan's territory.

3. Elders and kits must be fed before apprentices and warriors.

4. Prey is killed only to be eaten. Give thanks to StarClan for its life.

5. A kit must be at least six moons old to become an apprentice.

6. Newly appointed warriors will keep a silent vigil for one night after receiving their warrior name.

7. A cat cannot be made deputy without having mentored at least one apprentice.

8. The deputy will become Clan leader when the leader dies or retires.

9. After the death or retirement of the deputy, the new deputy must be chosen before moonhigh.

10. A gathering of all Clans is held at the full moon during a truce that lasts for the night. There shall be no fighting among Clans at this time.

11. Boundaries must be checked and marked daily. Challenge all trespassing cats.

12. No warrior may neglect a kit in pain or in danger, even if that kit is from a different Clan.

13. The word of the Clan leader is the warrior code.

14. An honorable warrior does not need to kill other cats to win his or her battles, unless they are outside the warrior code or it is necessary for self-defense.

15. A warrior rejects the soft life of a kittypet.

welcome to the warrior code

❋

hello! Firestar told me you'd be visiting today. Come in.
Watch out for the brambles at the entrance; they've grown
faster than ever with the warm rain we've had this moon. Sorry,
did that one catch on your pelt? I have some marigold leaves if it's
cut you. No? Good. My name is Leafpool, by the way, and I'm
ThunderClan's medicine cat—but I expect you knew that, didn't
you? I forget how well-known our Clan has become, even among
loners and kittypets.

Sit down, please, and make yourself comfortable. We have a
lot to talk about!

Firestar said that you wanted to learn about the warrior code. I can see how it would fascinate you, born and raised outside the Clans. Does it seem as if our lives are governed by strict, ancient rules? Your life must feel free as air in comparison; you can hunt when you like, eat what you catch, and choose friends and enemies wherever you please without having loyalties and responsibilities forced upon you. I can see by the glint in your eyes that you sometimes pity us for the code that binds us like bramble tendrils to our Clanmates, our territories, and our long-dead ancestors. But the warrior code isn't like that. If you're born to it, raised in its nurturing paws, it feels as obvious as breathing.

You hunt just for yourself, yes? But what would happen if you got injured or sick? In the Clans, the strongest cats, the warriors, hunt for all of us. And when it is their turn to have graying muzzles and trembling paws, new warriors will catch prey for them until they walk with StarClan and hunt like young cats once more.

You think the Clans hate one another and fight all the time. It's true, we live in close quarters with the other Clans, and that can lead to tension, but we also unite against common enemies— you heard about the badger attack, yes? We would have been destroyed if WindClan hadn't come to help us. And when we had to leave the forest, four Clans succeeded in making the Great Journey where one alone would have starved or frozen to death.

Being part of a Clan means knowing that you'll never be alone. The life of the Clan surrounds you and stretches into the distance as far as your imagination can see. You follow in the paw steps of Clanmates born moons before you and those who are younger will follow your paw steps in moons to come. You will always be part of your Clan, even when you walk among your ancestors in the stars.

You're still uncertain, aren't you? No matter. Wait until you hear how each part of the code came about. No, I am not going to tell you stories. Relax your mind and together we will travel back through the ages, through many generations of cats. Just as grass grows even on the bare cliffs around the hollow, each code arose from the Clans' daily lives as a way of ensuring that every cat was safe, nurtured, and fed from its very first breath. You will see that while the warrior code is still a force for good, for protection and balance among the Clans, many cats have challenged it—for it can bring terrible conflict to individual lives.

Are you ready? Let us begin with the first code. . . .

CODE ONE

> **DEFEND YOUR CLAN, EVEN WITH YOUR LIFE. YOU MAY HAVE FRIENDSHIPS WITH CATS FROM OTHER CLANS, BUT YOUR LOYALTY MUST REMAIN TO YOUR CLAN.**

It's hard to imagine a time when cats were allowed to have friendships with cats in other Clans. I know better than most cats the agony of loving a cat from a different Clan— and of knowing that I had to return to my own Clanmates because they needed me, and because I wanted to remain loyal to the warrior code. Come with me, and let me show you the sad fate of Ryewhisker and Cloudberry. Though it breaks my heart, you will see why this terrible piece of the code came to be. As every cat must learn, the strength of the entire Clan depends on the loyalty of each one of its members.

The Beginning of the Warrior Code

"**R**ace you to the hawthorn bush!"

"Not fair, Ryewhisker! You know you'll win!" protested Cloudberry.

Ryewhisker turned to look back at the dark gray she-cat. Cloudberry was slender for a RiverClan cat, but her fur was thick and sleek.

"I'll give you a head start," he offered. Cloudberry tipped her head on one side, her blue eyes sparkling. "Or . . . or I'll close my eyes, or run backward, or carry a stone in my mouth. . . . "

"Bee-brain," she purred. She padded up to him and rubbed her head against his cheek. "I'll race you to the hawthorn if you race me across the river."

Ryewhisker backed away, shaking his head. "No way! You can't tell me it's natural to get your fur wet! I tried it once, don't you remember?"

"You fell off a stepping-stone! Hardly a proper way to start swimming!"

Ryewhisker reached out with his tail to touch Cloudberry's flank. "Do you think our kits will be able to run fast and swim?" he meowed softly.

Cloudberry stared at him in astonishment. "How did you know? I . . . I was going to tell you, I promise, but I wasn't sure how you'd feel. I thought you might want WindClan kits. . . . "

Ryewhisker let out a frustrated *mrrrow*. "They will be WindClan kits! And RiverClan kits! They will be ours, and that's all that matters! Do your Clanmates know?"

The she-cat began to roll some small stones restlessly beneath

her paw. "Not yet. I wanted to tell you first."

"You're worried about what your father will say, aren't you?" Ryewhisker guessed.

Cloudberry looked up at him, her eyes pleading. "Emberstar is a good leader. You can't blame him for wanting more RiverClan kits. We need more warriors after that bout of greencough in leaf-bare."

"But they *will* be RiverClan kits!" Ryewhisker reminded her. He flicked his tail impatiently. "I'll let you teach them to swim as soon as they open their eyes!"

"Then you'll let me raise them in RiverClan?" Cloudberry queried.

Ryewhisker blinked. He hadn't thought that far ahead. "Well, yes," he meowed. "I'll come stay with you when they're born, of course. Your father has never minded me staying in your camp. And you can bring them to WindClan when they're old enough to walk that far."

Cloudberry nodded, but her eyes were still troubled. Ryewhisker pressed his muzzle against her ear. "It'll be fine," he promised. "Every cat knows that Emberstar's closest friend is Thistletail, in ThunderClan. If any cat understands that friendships don't stop at the border of a territory, it's Emberstar."

"But what about the stolen fish?" Cloudberry asked. Last moon, RiverClan had accused WindClan of stealing fish from the river and had sent a patrol to Duststar, WindClan's leader, to warn him to keep away. Duststar had insisted his Clan would never eat fish, but Ryewhisker knew the RiverClan cats were still suspicious.

"We didn't take those fish," he told Cloudberry. "Maybe these kits will bring our Clans together again."

Cloudberry relaxed against him and Ryewhisker closed his eyes, imagining tiny lives stirring within her, dark gray like their mother or brown tabby like him, swift-pawed and strong swimmers. These kits would bring peace between the two Clans, he was sure of it.

"WindClan! Retreat!"

Ryewhisker shook his head to clear the blood from his eyes as Stonetail yowled the order. The big gray tom was standing on a tree stump, wild-eyed as he called to his Clanmates to leave the battleground. Ryewhisker leaped back, freeing the RiverClan warrior from beneath his paws. This fight was all RiverClan's fault! They had accused WindClan twice more of stealing fish and threatened to tell the other Clans that the cats on the moor were thieves and trespassers. As if any WindClan warriors would get their paws wet chasing that slimy prey! Duststar had decided that the only way to stop the complaints was to teach RiverClan that WindClan cats were strong enough to catch their own prey—and well-enough fed not to need anyone else's.

"Retreat!" Stonetail yowled again.

"Mouse-hearted cowards!" spat a RiverClan warrior behind them.

"If you're going to steal

our fish, you should make sure you're strong enough to fight us for it!" hissed another.

Ryewhisker felt the fur stand up along his spine, and his paws tingled with the urge to spin around and claw their ears. When would these dumb cats realize that WindClan was not stealing their precious fish? The reeds closed around them as they headed back toward the Twoleg bridge, and for a moment Ryewhisker could hear nothing except his Clanmates' panting and the rattling of the brittle stalks.

"Stop right there!" screeched a voice up ahead.

Ryewhisker collided with Hawkfur's haunches as the black warrior halted in front of him. Peering past his Clanmate, he saw a ginger-and-white RiverClan warrior glaring at Stonetail, blocking his way.

"You didn't think we'd let you go so easily, did you?" growled the RiverClan cat.

Stonetail didn't flinch. "We'll continue to fight if we have to," he replied. "Is that what you want?"

The RiverClan warrior bared his teeth. "This fight is far from over!" He sprang at Stonetail, who rolled onto his back, scrabbling at his attacker's belly with his hind paws. The reeds clattered together and more RiverClan warriors rushed forward, leaping onto the WindClan cats. A stocky gray tabby sank its claws into Ryewhisker's shoulder and dragged him onto the ground. Ryewhisker ripped himself free, blood soaking into his fur, and jumped at the warrior with all four paws stretched out. The warrior crouched low and sprang up to meet him, knocking him out of the air and grappling with him as they fell side by side, lying half in and half out of the reeds.

Ryewhisker found himself being smothered by thick gray fur. He wrenched his head up to draw breath—and stared straight into the startled blue eyes of Cloudberry. As he watched, a dark shadow reared up behind her, claws glinting in the sun, and plunged down onto her neck.

"No!" screeched Ryewhisker, leaping up so violently that the attacker, Ryewhisker's Clanmate Hawkfur, tumbled off into the reeds.

"Ryewhisker, you can't do this!" called the gray she-cat, who was struggling to her paws. "We have to fight our own battles!"

Ryewhisker glanced at her over his shoulder. "You think I'm going to let our kits be harmed by my own Clanmate?"

Hawkfur stared at him in disbelief. "Kits?" he echoed.

The brown tabby met his gaze. "Cloudberry is expecting my kits. I cannot let you hurt her."

"Look out!" screeched Cloudberry.

There was a thunder of paws, abruptly cut off as a broad-shouldered RiverClan warrior leaped into the air. Then a soft thud as Ryewhisker's legs folded under the weight of his attacker and he slumped to the ground, his eyes already closed. Blood pooled out from his shoulder, dark and shiny on the wet ground. The gray tabby scrambled off him, shaking his pelt.

Cloudberry didn't move, just stared at the limp brown body. "Oh, Ryewhisker, what have you done?" she whispered.

"Is every Clan here?" Duststar called from on top of the huge gray rock. All around him, trees murmured softly in the night breeze, casting blurred shadows across the moonlit hollow. Duststar had asked the other leaders to meet him here because the hollow lay at the center of the Clans, yet it belonged to none since the battle that had separated the Clans for the very first time. The elders who could recall that battle stayed away from the hollow, convinced that the bloodstains would never be washed out of the grass. Duststar had chosen the night of the full moon because it would enable cats to travel safely—and offer none the temptation of darkness to launch an unsuspected attack.

"We are here," replied Birchstar, leader of SkyClan. He sprang onto the rock to join Duststar, his strong haunches powering him up. The other leaders, unwilling to be left at the foot of the rock, scrambled up, too: Emberstar from RiverClan, Hollystar from ShadowClan, and Whitestar from ThunderClan, whose pelt glowed as bright as the moon in the half-light. The rest of the cats stayed on the ground, a patrol from each Clan, gazing somberly up at the leaders with their tails tucked over their paws.

"If you're going to blame my Clan for the death of your warrior—" Emberstar began, raising his hackles.

Duststar shook his head. "No, Emberstar, that's not why I asked you all to come here. Ryewhisker's death is a tragedy we can ill afford after such a hard leaf-bare, but it would not have happened if he had not been . . . attached . . . to Cloudberry." He looked down at the RiverClan cats, but Cloudberry was not among them. She was probably too close to having her kits.

"From now on, cats must be loyal only to their own Clanmates. Friendships with cats from another territory must be put aside for the sake of their Clan. We cannot allow our warriors to be distracted in battle or to fight for anything other than what is best for their own Clan. Are we agreed?"

Whitestar stood up. "Clan above all else. It makes sense to me."

Hollystar and Birchstar nodded. Emberstar meowed, "Well said, Duststar. My Clan is sorry for the loss of your warrior. But from now on, each Clan stands—and fights—alone."

"If we have less contact across borders, how will we let one another know about something that could be important, such as the arrival of foxes or Twoleg interference?" asked Hollystar, her blue eyes like tiny pieces of sky.

"We could meet here every full moon, when the forest is light enough to walk easily, and come in peace to share our news," Birchstar suggested.

"A truce?" Duststar meowed.

There was a shocked murmuring among the cats of all Clans.

"We cannot promise peace when ThunderClan steals our prey!" hissed an elderly WindClan warrior.

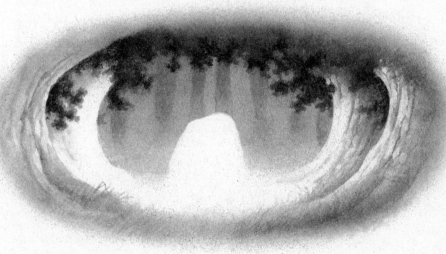

"And we cannot promise peace while WindClan attacks our border patrols!" meowed a ThunderClan warrior with a torn ear.

"And which of the Clans can trust ShadowClan?" asked another cat.

A great yowling broke out among all the cats.

"Enough!" Duststar growled. He stretched to his full height and stared down at the cats in the hollow. "Birchstar, I see more clearly than ever that your suggestion is wise. Though I doubt any peace will hold even for one night, let us try it and see what it brings."

"That's all I ask," Birchstar meowed.

"Cats of all the Clans!" Duststar continued. "From now on you must defend your Clan, even with your life. You may have friendships with cats from other Clans, but your loyalty must remain to your Clan, as one day you may meet cats you have befriended in battle. This will be our code, the law of warriors, and it is up to each one of us to carry it in our hearts. Until the next full moon, may StarClan guide your path."

He jumped down from the rock and, with a flick of his tail, led the WindClan cats out of the hollow, toward the moon-washed moor.

CODE TWO

DO NOT HUNT OR TRESPASS ON ANOTHER CLAN'S TERRITORY.

---

*We take it for granted now that each Clan lives in the
territory best suited to provide food for its particular hunting skills.
But come with me to the time before borders were fixed, when
cats took food from other territories if their own ran short. You will
see that this code was needed, because if anything
is likely to cause trouble, it's theft of precious fresh-kill.*

Finders Keepers

Three seasons had passed since the leaders of the Clans
decided to meet in peace each full moon, and the truce
had held. Stonestar, the WindClan leader, stood on the Great
Rock and surveyed the cats filing into the moonlit hollow. Their
pelts stood out sharply against the snow, apart from Whitestar
of ThunderClan, who was only visible when he looked up and
Stonestar caught a glimpse of his dark eyes.

Whitestar, Emberstar, Birchstar, and Brindlestar, the new
leader of ShadowClan, joined him on the rock. The leaders
nodded to one another before standing in a line to look down on
the cats below.

As the oldest leader, Emberstar was usually the first to speak, but Brindlestar didn't give him a chance. "I have a complaint against ThunderClan!" she declared.

Whitestar faced her, his tail twitching. "We aren't the ones stealing prey!" he hissed. "You can't complain because our patrols drive you out every time."

"It's not stealing!" Brindlestar snapped. "What are we meant to eat, if we can't find prey in our own territory?"

"Each Clan lives in the place where it is best suited to hunting," Birchstar pointed out.

"Yeah, since when did ShadowClan start hunting in undergrowth and through brambles?" challenged Vinetail, ThunderClan's deputy.

"Since we started starving in our own territory," growled Lakestorm, the ShadowClan deputy.

Stonestar stepped forward. "ShadowClan should keep to its own prey," he meowed firmly. "No Clan has prey to spare, especially not during leaf-bare."

"Then what are we supposed to eat?" yowled Lakestorm. His voice cut through the icy air, and for a moment the hollow fell silent. Then a creaking sound began. . . .

Stonestar peered up, trying to see where the noise was coming from. In the clearing, the cats huddled together in their Clans, too scared to flee.

Crashhhhhh!

A huge branch ripped away from one of the giant oaks and plunged onto the cats, sending flurries of snowflakes into the air. Stonestar watched in horror as the cats vanished in a swirling cloud of snow and twigs.

"SkyClan! SkyClan! Is every cat all right?" Birchstar ran to the edge of the rock and peered down, calling to her Clanmates.

Whitestar and Brindlestar joined her, yowling into the cloud.

"Wait!" Whitestar ordered. Pushing his way through the other leaders, he turned to face them. "One at a time, or no cat will hear you. Birchstar, you go first." He stepped back, and only his trembling paws showed how terrified he was for the safety of his own Clan.

"SkyClan cats! Can you hear me?" Birchstar yowled.

There was a muffled sound, then a speckled gray head popped up at the edge of the hollow. It was Rainsplash, the deputy. "We're all here, Birchstar!" he called.

Stonestar stepped forward. The ground seemed a long way down, a mess of churned snow divided by a huge black branch bristling with twigs. "WindClan? Are you there?"

Mudpuddle, the brown-and-white deputy, scrambled up from the far side of the clearing. "All safe, Stonestar!" he reported, and Stonestar let out his breath in relief.

Emberstar quickly established that the RiverClan cats had been too far back to be hit by the falling branch. That left ThunderClan and ShadowClan. The branch had toppled right into the center of the Gathering, directly onto the two quarreling Clans.

Brindlestar walked to the edge of the rock. "ShadowClan, are you all right?"

The leaders waited in silence. Heartbeats passed, broken only by the faint plop of snow sliding from the trees. Then, "We're all okay, Brindlestar!" A bundle of twigs rattled together at one side of the branch, and Lakestorm pushed his way out. Once he was free, he turned to help his Clanmates out behind him.

Brindlestar narrowed her eyes, checking each member of her patrol. She nodded. "Lakestorm's right," she murmured. "ShadowClan is safe."

Now it was Whitestar's turn. Stonestar held his breath again. There was no way that branch could have fallen into the hollow without crushing several cats. It was too big, too heavy. It had carved too great a slice through the clearing. . . .

"We're fine, too!" Before Whitestar could speak, Vinetail's voice rang out as he wriggled free from a heap of snow. The rest of the ThunderClan cats tumbled out around him, shaking cold, wet clumps from their pelts and out of their ears.

"How can this be?" Whitestar whispered. "That branch fell on top of ThunderClan and ShadowClan; there was no room between them!"

Stonestar looked once more at the massive chunk of tree, then at the two groups of cats standing on either side, unhurt and exclaiming at their good luck.

"It's a sign from StarClan," Stonestar meowed, loud enough for his fellow leaders to hear but not the cats below. "StarClan is telling us that even when Clans are close together, they are separate, far enough apart for a tree to fall without touching them. Borders may be invisible and thin as a whisker, but they are strong as oak, and they cannot be crossed. Not for friendship, not for prey, not for anything."

Whitestar was nodding. "It's a sign," he said.

Brindlestar was staring in disbelief at the cats of her Clan. They were dazed and shocked but without injuries. Then she looked down at the fallen branch. "StarClan has spared my cats for a reason," she mewed.

"Find food in your territory," Stonestar urged. "Use the skills that only you and your Clanmates have—your cunning, stealth, ability to walk through the darkest nights. The prey is there, and you're the only Clan that can find it."

"You are right. StarClan must not wish us to take inferior food from inferior Clans." Brindlestar glanced at Whitestar, who wisely did not respond.

"Then it's decided," Emberstar meowed. "Another rule has been added to the warrior code. We must not hunt or trespass on another Clan's territory."

"Agreed," the other leaders mewed in unison. They dipped their heads to one another. "Until the next Gathering, may StarClan walk your path."

Hunting Fish!

*Not all cats obey the code all the time.
For where there are young cats and a set
of rules to break, there is always
mischief brewing. . . .*

"**O**uch! You're stepping on my foot!"

"Sorry!" puffed Dappletail. "I thought it was a pebble."

"Since when do pebbles have fur?" demanded White-eye, shaking her paw. She turned so that starlight glowed in her remaining eye; the other had been clawed out by a badger when she was an apprentice, blinding her.

Dappletail wriggled up beside her—on the side where White-eye could see. "Are we at the river?" she mewed.

White-eye shifted to make room under the ferns. "Yup. Look!"

Ahead of them, the ground was covered with small gray stones, sloping down to the thick black water that flowed swiftly by, sparkling with reflected stars.

"It's kind of spooky at night," Dappletail whispered, shrinking back against White-eye's sturdy shoulder.

White-eye gave her a nudge. "We'll be fine," she assured her. There was no way she was going back to the camp now. This was the biggest adventure she'd ever had! In fact, it was probably the biggest adventure any ThunderClan cat had had. They didn't *need* to take RiverClan's prey—it was greenleaf, and the woods were thrumming with juicy birds and squirrels—but White-eye wanted to know what fish tasted like, and why RiverClan was so snooty about its prey being the best of all the Clans'.

Dappletail jumped onto a flattened rock at the edge of the river and peered into the water. "I don't see any fish," she whispered. "Do you think they've gone to sleep?"

White-eye huffed impatiently as she squeezed onto the rock beside her. "Fish don't sleep!"

"They must," Dappletail argued. "Otherwise they'd be really tired."

"Well, maybe some of them are awake." White-eye wriggled forward until her front legs dangled over the water.

Dappletail eyed her dubiously. "Is that how RiverClan cats catch fish? You look like you're about to fall in."

"Look!" White-eye strained her neck out, her whiskers quivering with the effort. "There's something over there!" She tensed her hindquarters, and before Dappletail could say anything, she leaped off the rock with her front paws outstretched and plummeted into the water with an enormous splash.

Dappletail sprang back, blinking as drops flew into her eyes. She shook her head and stared at the river. The current flowed as swiftly as ever, but now it was carrying White-eye, gasping and scrabbling to keep her head above the surface.

"White-eye!" Dappletail wailed. "Come back!"

"I'm . . . trying . . . " came the muffled reply. There was another splash and White-eye's head bobbed under a wave as the water swept her around a rock.

Dappletail stood on the shore, her tail bristling with shock. "Help!" she yowled.

White-eye reappeared farther downstream. "Don't . . . tell anyone . . . we're . . . here," she spluttered. "Get . . . into . . . trouble. . . . "

"But you're drowning!" Dappletail shrieked. "Help!"

Somewhere in the forest an owl hooted, but there were no sounds of cats coming to help. Dappletail looked at the swift black river, took a deep breath, and ran into the waves. The water was so cold she couldn't breathe. Waves slapped around her, cutting her off from either shore and filling her ears with a deafening hiss.

Swimming's just like running, but in water, right?

She untangled her legs and tried to move them as if she were walking on grass, but as soon as she hauled herself upright in the water she sank and had to scrabble back to the surface, gasping for air. This was the worst idea White-eye had ever had!

"What in the name of StarClan is going on?"

An angry voice sounded above Dappletail's head, and she floundered around to see who was speaking. A brown-and-white tom was standing on a rock on the RiverClan side of the river, his eyes huge as moons.

"Help!" Dappletail yowled, before a wave filled her mouth and made her cough.

Another cat appeared beside the first one. "Owlfur, it's clearly not out for a nighttime swim. You'd better go fish it out before it drowns."

The brown-and-white tom slid into the water and his small head began bobbing steadily toward Dappletail. She kept her mouth shut and flailed with her paws, trying to stay in the same place. She winced as the tom clamped his jaws tightly in the scruff of her neck, and she felt herself being dragged through the water toward the shore. Her paws scraped against stones and she staggered out with most of the river streaming from her fur.

"My Clanmate!" she coughed. She twitched her tail downriver. "She's still in there!"

"Mouse-brains!" hissed the second cat. He braced his thick-pelted gray shoulders and headed for the river. "Owlfur, you stay here and make sure this feather-head doesn't try to follow me." He broke into a run and disappeared into the river, his pace staying the same even when he started swimming.

"You're from ThunderClan, aren't you?" Owlfur mewed disapprovingly.

Dappletail nodded, her whiskers heavy with drops.

"Let me guess. You were trying to steal our fish."

Dappletail's head drooped even lower. "S-sorry," she muttered.

The brown-and-white tom hissed, then raised his head. "Looks like Hailstar found your Clanmate," he meowed.

Hailstar? Oh, great. We've been rescued by the leader of RiverClan.

"Dappletail! Look!"

Noisy splashing behind her made Dappletail turn around. White-eye was stumbling out of the water with Hailstar shoving her from behind. Her pelt was slicked to her sides and her ears looked huge against her wet head, but his eyes shone as she dropped a twitching silver fish onto the stones.

"I caught a fish!"

Hailstar rolled his eyes. "You squashed it against a rock," he corrected. "And it wasn't yours to catch in the first place." His eyes narrowed. "You're trespassing and stealing. What do you say about that?"

"Hey! Are those our missing ThunderClan warriors?"

There was a shout from across the river. On the far shore, Pinestar and his deputy, Sunfall, were standing at the edge of the water, their fur frosted by starlight.

"We caught some unusual prey tonight," Hailstar called back. "Why not come across and see if it suits your appetite better?"

The ThunderClan cats ran along the shore and jumped across the stepping-stones, clearly visible in the low greenleaf river. Dappletail glanced sideways at White-eye as they waited for their Clan leader to arrive.

"I am never, ever listening to you again!" she hissed.

The four older cats stood in a line in front of Dappletail and White-eye and surveyed them.

"Just how many rules of the warrior code did you want to break tonight?" Pinestar began. "Trespassing, stealing prey, catching food for yourself . . . "

"I wanted to see what fish tasted like," White-eye mumbled.

Pinestar leaned closer to her. "We are from ThunderClan," he growled. "We. Don't. Eat. Fish."

Owlfur stepped forward. "Wait, I have an idea. Since these mouse-brains seem so determined to be RiverClan cats, why not let them eat their fresh-kill? After all, White-eye caught it."

Dappletail looked up in surprise. Weren't they going to be punished?

Pinestar's eyes gleamed. "What a good idea, Owlfur. White-eye, Dappletail, eat up. Don't waste a scrap, or that would be very insulting to your hosts."

White-eye didn't wait to be asked again. She opened her mouth wide and sank her jaws into the fish just behind its head. Feeling very uncomfortable with the other cats watching, Dappletail crouched by the tail of the fish and took a bite.

Yuck!

Both cats sprang back, their lips curling. Wet, cold, slimy, tasting of stones and weeds and mud . . .

Hailstar cocked his head on one side. "What's the matter?"

"It's disgusting!" White-eye spluttered.

Sunfall looked shocked. "You can't say that when RiverClan is so generously letting you eat your catch."

Dappletail forced herself to swallow and concentrated very hard on not being sick. "Please don't make us eat any more," she meowed.

Pinestar looked at them both. "The warrior code exists for a reason. ThunderClan cats don't eat fish, don't catch fish, don't swim, don't have anything to do with the river at all. RiverClan cats don't eat squirrels, so they don't live in the woods. ShadowClan cats don't eat rabbits, so they don't live on the moor."

Hailstar spoke up. "I think nearly being drowned is enough of a lesson for now. Go back to your Clan and leave the fish to us."

White-eye nodded hard. "No more fishing," she promised.

"No more adventures ever," Dappletail meowed. ThunderClan cats ate ThunderClan fresh-kill; as far as she cared, RiverClan cats could have all the fish in the world.

CODE THREE

*Caring for the weaker members of the Clan lies at
the heart of the way we live. We are taught to respect elders who
fought for the Clan in the past and kits who can't yet hunt for
themselves. However, moons ago, when the blood of warriors flowed
thick and fast over Sunningrocks, if you had asked a warrior
what he or she fought for, the warlike answer would have shocked
you. All that would change thanks to a visionary warrior
called Splashheart, who went on to lead RiverClan and bring
peace to the forest. Let me take you back. . . .*

A Mystical Battle

The shape was little more than a flicker beneath the surface of
the water, a trembling shadow cast on the stones crisscrossed
with waving green fronds. Splashheart kept absolutely still, waiting
for the fish to come closer. Another flicker, less than a tail-length
away, and Splashheart shot out one paw, his unsheathed claws
slicing through the cold water. When he felt his pad brush against
the fat, slick body, he curled his paw and swiped it toward him. The
fish flew out of the water, scattering silver droplets, and landed on

the bank beside him, where he finished it off with a swift blow.

"Good catch," said a voice behind him. It was Reedshine, the dark orange she-cat who had mentored him until two sunrises ago, when he received his warrior name.

"Thanks," Splashheart purred. "Want to share?"

Reedshine padded closer and sniffed at the fish before taking a bite. Splashheart bent down and took a mouthful from the other side of the fish. This was only his second catch as a warrior, and it tasted as good as the first.

On the other side of the river, Sunningrocks loomed, casting a heavy black shadow onto the water. These smooth gray rocks quickly grew warm in the sun, making them perfect to lie on and share tongues or just watch the river sliding past below. Some of RiverClan's elders could remember when the river flowed on the other side of Sunningrocks, cutting off RiverClan from ThunderClan's wooded territory. But then a great flood came one leaf-fall and the river burst its banks to surround the rocks, until they resembled a bleak gray island. When the floodwater went away, the river had carved a new course on RiverClan's side of the rocks. Before the next sunrise, ThunderClan had claimed Sunningrocks as its own, swarming across the dried-out riverbed to set scent markers along the new riverbank. The Clans had fought over them many times since, and at the moment the scent markers lay on the far side of the rocks, keeping ThunderClan firmly out.

Splashheart narrowed his eyes. There was a cat creeping along the far riverbank, head and tail low. The cat was half hidden by the shadow from the rocks, but it was a leaner, sleeker-furred shape than RiverClan cats, who grew plump and thick-pelted thanks to their watery prey. *ThunderClan!*

"ThunderClan intruders on Sunningrocks!" he yowled.

"I'll fetch help!" Reedshine told him. "Stay on this side of the river until I get back." She plunged into the reeds, her orange pelt quickly vanishing among the rattling brown stalks.

Splashheart's fur stood on end and his paws tingled. His first battle as a warrior!

"This is our territory now, fish-fur!" snarled a cat from the other side of the river.

"Never!" Splashheart hissed. He sank his claws into the edge of the bank, ready to leap into the water and start the battle on his own.

"Splashheart, wait!" Darkstar burst out from the reeds behind him.

Splashheart whirled around to face his leader. "We can't let them get away with this!" he protested.

The small brown she-cat met his gaze. "We won't," she promised grimly. Dry stalks rattled behind her and suddenly the bank was thronging with cats, warriors and apprentices, their fur fluffed up and their claws gleaming in the sun.

"RiverClan, attack!" yowled Darkstar, plunging into the river.

Splashheart scanned the rocks. Thank StarClan, they didn't seem to be outnumbered. Blackbee and Eeltail were chasing after a ThunderClan she-cat who was streaking for the cover of the ferns at the bottom of the rocks; Reedshine held another warrior in a paw lock, hissing a warning into his face. Darkstar had satisfied herself with a quick slash of claws across a dark brown cat's ears before standing back to let him run away, yowling.

As the warriors' screeches faded among quivering ferns, Splashheart heard a scraping noise from behind a tumble of boulders. He gathered his haunches beneath him and sprang onto the top of the nearest boulder. A pair of terrified amber eyes stared up at him from the other side.

"Don't hurt me!" bleated the small black-and-white cat—an apprentice, by the look of him.

"Then stay off our territory!" hissed Splashheart.

The ThunderClan cat didn't move. Instead, he curled his lip in a snarl. "Are you sure you want to threaten me, fish-fur?" he challenged.

Too late, Splashheart heard the scrape of claws on the rocks above him and felt a rush of air as two sleek-furred shapes landed, one at each flank. In a heartbeat, his face was thrust down against the rock. "Care to threaten us as well?" growled a voice in his ear, and the massive paw pressed harder on his neck.

"Get off him and fight a cat your own size!" screeched a voice from the riverbank. Splashheart caught a glimpse of dark orange fur leaping toward the boulders. Reedshine! She crashed straight into the warrior holding Splashheart down, and both cats plummeted into the narrow gap where the ThunderClan apprentice was crouching. The young cat jumped on top of Reedshine and began pummeling her belly with his forepaws; as Splashheart scrambled to his feet, he saw bright red streaks blossom in Reedshine's soft fur. He tried to jump down after her but the other ThunderClan warrior swiped his hind paws from underneath him and rolled him over.

The warrior loomed over him, her green eyes blazing. "StarClan changed the course of the river!" she hissed. "Sunningrocks belongs to ThunderClan now!"

"Never!" Splashheart spat, but the warrior pressed her paw against his throat and the sky began to go dark and fuzzy.

Suddenly there was a thud as two heavy bodies collided above Splashheart, and the weight on his throat lifted. He gulped down air, almost stopping when it felt like swallowing thorns.

"Don't just lie there, Splashheart," hissed Darkstar, who

crouched on the rock beside him. "Get down to the shore with the others, quick." Splashheart sprang down to the stones at the edge of the water. The rest of the RiverClan warriors were huddled together, some of them belly-deep in water.

There was a scuffle behind him and Splashheart turned to see Darkstar half carrying Reedshine down the bank. The dark orange warrior left a trail of dark red smears behind her, and her eyes were half-closed. Splashheart raced over.

"Reedshine, wake up!" He looked at Darkstar. "We have to get her back to camp, now!"

Darkstar opened her mouth to let Reedshine sink gracelessly onto the stones. The leader's eyes were black with rage. "We will take her back," she promised. "But first, we will reclaim what is rightfully ours!" She raised her voice at the end so every RiverClan cat heard. They lifted their heads and stared at Darkstar in astonishment.

"But the battle is lost!" Eeltail spat. He jerked his muzzle toward the top of the rocks, where several ThunderClan warriors stood in triumph, their tails kinked high above their backs as they jeered at the defeated cats.

"It is only lost when we stop fighting!" replied Darkstar. She jumped onto the riverbank so all the cats could see her. "Our elders, and our elders' kin, and their kin before them, fought to keep Sunningrocks in our territory. Many of them lost their lives, giving up their last breath for stones that belong to us. Can we give up where they did not, turn tail and flee when they kept fighting so that their kits could hunt and play and bask on these rocks? Will you fight with me now, in honor of all our elders and all our unborn kits?"

"We will fight!" roared the RiverClan cats. In that moment, Splashheart saw the rocks swarming with starry shapes of cats who had gone before him, his Clanmates from long ago battling over and over to keep Sunningrocks as their own. Now he would join them, set his paws where their paws once stood, and feel their battles echo around him as he proved himself worthy to walk among them.

With a single yowl, the RiverClan cats surged up the riverbank and onto the boulders. The ThunderClan warriors stood in a line on the far side of the summit, staring at them in astonishment.

"The battle is over," snarled one of them, a broad-shouldered tabby with amber eyes.

Darkstar faced him boldly, the fur standing up along her spine. "How can that be, when we are not beaten?" she challenged.

With a screech, the tabby sprang at her, but Darkstar sidestepped, spun around, and sank her claws into his back as he crashed to the floor. The RiverClan warriors leaped forward to meet the other ThunderClan cats, and Splashheart felt his teeth sink into short white fur. He didn't let go until he dragged the cat to the edge of the rocks.

"Go!" he ordered, releasing the cat's scruff at last. Without looking back, the warrior scrambled down the boulders and disappeared into the ferns at the edge of ThunderClan's territory.

"Good work," murmured a voice beside Splashheart. He had plunged back into the throng of cats, and for a moment he couldn't tell which cat was speaking to him.

"Watch out for that black-and-white tom over there," the voice continued, and Splashheart saw a ThunderClan warrior stalking toward Eeltail, who was holding down a spitting she-cat.

"Thanks!" he gasped and crossed the open ground in three quick strides, landing squarely on the black-and-white cat. Eeltail turned at the noise and lifted his paw so that the she-cat could flee; then he joined Splashheart and together they chased the black-and-white tom after his frightened Clanmate.

When the two cats had gone, Splashheart realized that the sounds of battle had grown quieter, muffled as if he were underwater.

"The battle has been won," whispered the voice. "Sunningrocks is safe."

Splashheart turned his head—the only part of his body he seemed able to move—and saw a faint, glimmering cat standing beside him. Her fur was the color of floodwater, almost black with streaks of pale gray, and her tail was so long the tip rested on the rock. RiverClan scent hung around her, but he'd never seen her before.

"Who are you?"

The cat dipped her head. "My name is Aspentail," she replied. "I am kin of your elders and of your elders' elders. I fought for these rocks once, and I will fight for them again, for as many moons as it takes, until ThunderClan learns that Sunningrocks belongs to RiverClan."

"I will fight with you," Splashheart vowed. Aspentail nodded and started to fade so that Splashheart could see the gray of the rock through her fur.

"Splashheart? Who are you talking to?"

Blackbee was standing behind him, looking puzzled. "Didn't you realize?" she demanded. "We won! Those fox-hearted ThunderClan cats won't set paw on Sunningrocks now."

"Not for this moon, at least," Splashheart whispered. "But if they do, we'll fight them again. Aspentail, too."

"What was that?" mewed Blackbee. "Are you okay, Splashheart? You're not wounded, are you?"

"No, no, I'm fine," Splashheart promised.

"Cats of RiverClan!" Darkstar was summoning her warriors

to the center of the summit. "Sunningrocks belongs to us once more! And in honor of our elders and their kin before them, who never stopped fighting to defend our borders, we will catch fish on our way home and feed it to the oldest and youngest cats of the Clan. This victory is for them!"

Some of the warriors looked surprised, but Splashheart nodded. He would catch the plumpest fish he could find in memory of Aspentail and take it straight to the elders' den. And if he ever became leader of his Clan, he would make it part of the warrior code that elders and kits should be fed first, in honor of all they had done, and all they would do, for his Clanmates to come.

* * *

A Dark Path Chosen

As you have seen, Clan cats are part of something bigger than ourselves, and that ensures we are as strong as our strongest warrior when trouble comes. But come see what can happen if this part of the warrior code is ignored.

Longtail winced as a cold drop of water splashed onto his neck. "The den is leaking again," he complained to Darkstripe, who was curled up beside him.

Darkstripe opened one yellow eye. "Better tell Redtail," he murmured. "He'll have to organize a cat to fix it before we drown in our sleep."

Longtail slid out of his nest, shivering as the bead of water rolled down his back, and pushed his way into the clearing. Leaf-fall was giving way to leaf-bare, and the sky was flat and gray like water. Longtail picked his way over to the cleft in the rock where he could hear Redtail, the ThunderClan deputy, speaking quietly with Bluestar. His words were punctuated with coughs that racked the warrior's body and left him breathless: The Clan was fighting off greencough, and Redtail had only just emerged from the medicine cat's den where he had been treated.

"We need to send out a hunting patrol," he wheezed to Bluestar. "The fresh-kill pile was ruined by the rain last night, and the sick cats won't get better if they're weak with hunger."

"Very well, but only send out healthy cats," Bluestar warned. "Which means you stay here, Redtail."

The deputy started to argue but was interrupted by another bout of coughing.

"Longtail!"

A tortoiseshell-and-white she-cat, her pelt dappled like a glade in greenleaf, was calling him from the shelter of a clump of ferns. Longtail changed direction to join her.

"What's up, Spottedleaf?"

"Has Redtail organized any hunting patrols yet?" The medicine cat's eyes were dark with worry. "I can't help sick cats when they're so hungry. I know hunting is hard in this weather, but we have to find them something to eat." Her bones shifted under her pelt as she moved, and Longtail guessed that Spottedleaf had been giving up her own share of fresh-kill to the cats she was trying to heal.

"I think he's just about to send one out," he told her.

"Good. Let's hope they come back quickly. Poppydawn is hardly strong enough to eat the catmint."

Longtail peered past her into the ferns, where he could just make out the dark red fur of the sick elder. Poppydawn told good stories and was popular with all the kits in the Clan because she let them chase her tail, which was as thick as a fox's.

Redtail nodded to Longtail, flicking drops of water from his feathered ears. "Are you free to go on a hunting patrol?"

"Yes," Longtail replied.

"Good. Take Darkstripe with you. Try Snakerocks—there might be some prey sheltering there. You shouldn't find any snakes at this time of year, but don't go too deep into the caves."

At least Darkstripe won't order me around, Longtail thought as he squeezed back into the warriors' den. In spite of the leaky roof,

Darkstripe had gone back to sleep. Longtail prodded him with his paw.

"Wake up! We've got to go on a patrol."

Darkstripe raised his head and stared at him blearily. "In this weather? You must be crazy! Did you tell Redtail that the roof needs fixing?"

"I didn't get a chance," Longtail confessed. "Come on, it's just us. Redtail suggested we try Snakerocks."

"Great," Darkstripe grumbled, heaving himself to his paws. "I can either drown or get bitten for the sake of my Clan."

"It's not raining that hard," Longtail pointed out as they headed for the tunnel that led out of the camp. "It's mostly just water being shaken from the trees."

"Is that supposed to make me feel better?" Darkstripe muttered, but he sprang gracefully up the rocks that littered the side of the ravine and reached the top before Longtail.

The rain kept Twolegs and their dogs out of the woods, so

the warriors had a clear run all the way to Snakerocks. Longtail shivered. Even if the snakes had gone for the cold season, this place still made him nervous. Darkstripe skirted the edge of the trees, sniffing at the dead bracken.

"I'm starving," he meowed. "We'd better catch something. I haven't found anything good on the fresh-kill pile for days."

Longtail headed for the pile of rocks, telling himself that he wouldn't go into any caves at all, not even a little way. His whiskers trembled as he picked up the scent of squirrel at the foot of the rocks. The trail led behind the stones and a little way into a clump of brambles. Crouching low, Longtail stepped paw by paw under the thorns. There was a patch of gray fur just visible through the tendrils. He gathered his haunches under him, wriggled to get his balance, then sprang. Blasting his way through the brambles, he landed squarely on the squirrel. Muttering a prayer to StarClan, and spitting out leaves, Longtail backed out of the thicket, dragging his fresh-kill.

"Good catch!"

Darkstripe was standing right behind him, making Longtail jump. The black-striped warrior padded forward, sniffing appreciatively. The squirrel's fluffy gray fur rippled under his breath. Darkstripe glanced over his shoulder. "This won't taste nearly as good once we've hauled it back to the camp."

Longtail shrugged. "We should catch something else quickly; then it will still be fresh."

"But it won't be as fresh as it is now." Darkstripe looked back at the squirrel. "And we'll hunt much better after a decent meal."

"The warrior code says we can't eat until the elders and kits have been fed," Longtail reminded him. His pelt was starting to prickle as if ants were crawling through it.

"How will any cat know?" Darkstripe murmured. He narrowed

his eyes until they were tiny amber slits. "You won't tell, will you?" His voice was barely a whisper; Longtail could hardly hear him.

"I . . . I . . ."

Darkstripe opened his jaws and sank his teeth into the squirrel, without taking his eyes off Longtail. He chewed slowly, releasing the tempting smell of warm, plump meat.

We're as hungry as the rest of the Clan, and we need our strength to hunt. It makes no sense to let the warriors starve when they have to look after every other cat. I caught this squirrel easily; we'll catch plenty more.

Longtail bent his head and bit into the fresh-kill. Above him, a cold wind rattled the trees, and the rocks loomed gray and silent against the heavy sky.

Pelting rain made the sides of the ravine slippery, and the cats picked their way carefully down with their catch gripped in their mouths. Longtail had been lucky with the squirrel; prey had been much harder to find after that, and all they brought were two mice and an old, tough-looking blackbird. Neither cat looked each other in the eye as they dragged their fresh-kill over the muddy ground to the gorse tunnel. Darkstripe hung back, forcing Longtail to go first. The thorns seemed sharper against his pelt than before, and a feather from the blackbird had worked its way into his throat, making him choke and splutter through his mouthful. He pushed his way into the clearing and looked around, expecting to see a row of hungry cats waiting by the fresh-kill pile.

The clearing was empty, the ground shiny and bouncing with raindrops. Darkstripe joined Longtail and they stood side by side with their catch by their front paws. Before either of them could speak, a wail rose from the ferns around Spottedleaf's den.

"Poppydawn! No! Don't leave me!"

It was Rosetail, her daughter.

"It is her time to join StarClan. Our warrior ancestors are waiting for her." That was Spottedleaf, her voice muffled by grief.

Longtail looked at Darkstripe, feeling a wave of panic rise inside him. "We're too late! Poppydawn is dead! Spottedleaf said she needed to eat in order to fight the sickness, but we didn't come back in time! We should never have eaten that squirrel!"

"Shut up!" Darkstripe hissed. "What's the matter with you? Poppydawn was going to die anyway. We should let the old, useless cats go if it means the warriors survive. The Clan depends on us now, not them."

"We killed her. . . . "

"We did not! Greencough killed her. She was old and weak. We are the important cats; we should eat first. Do you want to do what's best for your Clan?"

"Of course . . . "

"Then you'll keep your mouth shut and let your Clanmates be grateful for what we brought back. There's one fewer mouth to feed now. Why spoil everything by trying to blame yourself for Poppydawn?"

But Poppydawn might still be alive if we had come back earlier—if we had come back with the squirrel.

Darkstripe was peering at Longstripe as if he could read his thoughts. "You'll keep quiet, won't you?" he hissed, and this time there was a hint of menace behind his eyes. "After all, I saw you eat that squirrel. I'll tell them what you did, how you insisted on stealing prey from the elders, how you refused to let me bring it back to the camp."

A hard, cold lump froze inside Longtail. "There's nothing to tell," he growled back. "We were sent to hunt for prey, and that's what we've done. No other warrior could have done better."

As he bent his head to pick up the blackbird and carry it to the fresh-kill pile, a waft of warm air ruffled his fur and a familiar scent brushed over him. Longtail lifted his head in horror.

Poppydawn! I'm so sorry!

Too late, came the silent reply. *Too late.*

CODE
3

CODE FOUR

> **PREY IS KILLED ONLY TO BE EATEN.**
> **GIVE THANKS TO STARCLAN FOR ITS LIFE.**

When you eat, whom do you thank for your food?
It was the clear-sighted leadership of Lilystar of ShadowClan,
moons ago, that taught us to respect our prey and helped us
to see how much we owe to our warrior ancestors for training us
and bringing us to a place where we can live like this.

Mouse Games

"Over here, Fallowkit!" Driftkit dodged around a fallen branch and poked his head over the top to call to his sister.

Fallowkit popped up and shoved the mouse they were playing with toward him. Its limp body rolled over, leaving a faint mark on the boggy ground. The snow had only just melted and the ShadowClan camp was so wet, the kits' mother, Splashnose, spent every night licking the mud out of their belly fur. Driftkit scrambled onto the branch and launched himself off, landing flat on the mouse. It felt squishy under his paws, and it smelled of dirt and snowmelt.

Driftkit knew he was going to be the best ShadowClan warrior ever! He'd scratch out those scrawny WindClan cats' eyes, he'd chase the fat RiverClan cats until their legs fell off, he'd creep up on the ThunderClan cats and claw their ears. . . .

"Driftkit! What in the name of StarClan are you doing to that mouse?"

Driftkit fell off the mouse in surprise. A ginger-and-white she-cat with a bright orange tail was stalking toward him. "I was just practicing being a warrior, Sunnytail," Driftkit stammered to the ShadowClan deputy.

Sunnytail stared down at the mouse. "That's not fit to eat now! Does Splashnose know what you're doing?"

Fallowkit padded up, her light brown fur standing on end. "She's in the nursery. She told us to go outside and play."

Sunnytail shook her head. "This was the last piece of fresh-kill we had. Now the Clan will have to go hungry until the next hunting patrol."

"Sorry," Driftkit muttered. He wished a giant hole would open up in front of him so he could jump in and not be yelled at anymore. He was just having fun. He'd been stuck inside the den for moons because of the snow, and his legs felt as if they could run all the way to the Thunderpath that the warriors talked about.

The branches around the nursery rustled and a dusty-brown tabby with a white streak on her muzzle appeared. "What's the matter?" she called.

"Driftkit and Fallowkit have been playing with the last piece of fresh-kill, Splashnose," Sunnytail replied.

"I'm sure they didn't know it was the last piece . . ." Splashnose began.

"They must have known!" Sunnytail argued. "There would have been nothing left!"

"Is this true?" A pale gray cat padded up, her tail kinked

questioningly over her back. She looked from her deputy to Driftkit. "Did you take the last of our food?"

Driftkit tried to make a hole appear in front of his paws by staring at the ground really hard. Just his luck that Lilystar had overheard. "I guess," he whispered to the ShadowClan leader.

"It wasn't his fault," Splashnose put in, but Lilystar hushed her with a flick of her tail. When she spoke, her tone was unexpectedly gentle.

"Driftkit, you should not have taken that mouse to play with. Prey is too scarce to be wasted. That mouse did not die to become a toy, but to keep us alive after a long leaf-bare. Do you understand?"

Driftkit nodded without looking up. Beside him, Fallowkit squeaked, "Yes, Lilystar."

Suddenly a shadow swept over the clearing, and there was a strange rushing sound above Driftkit's head.

"Owl! Run!" screeched Splashnose, and the cats bolted for safety.

Driftkit was too terrified to move. He stared up at the huge white bird, which swooped closer and closer. He could see every feather on its chest, its sharp hooked talons, the ring of yellow around each eye as it glared down at him. He gulped, waiting to be swept up into the air.

The owl folded its wings at the last moment and dropped with its talons outstretched. Nearer, nearer . . . then it was pulling itself back up into the air with its mighty wings. Driftkit opened his eyes. He was still on the ground. The mouse had vanished; when he looked up, he could see its battered body dangling from the owl's claws, getting smaller and smaller as the bird disappeared over the trees.

I survived!

Splashnose raced up to Driftkit. "Are you all right, precious?" she gasped, sniffing him all over.

Driftkit shrugged away. Fierce warriors didn't get fussed over by their moms whenever they won a battle. "I'm fine," he muttered.

Lilystar pricked her ears to follow the path of the owl. "It is a sign," she declared. "StarClan gives our prey to us, and StarClan can take it away. We should give thanks to our warrior ancestors that we are able to eat at all. They provide every mouthful as well as our ability to hunt and feed ourselves. From the next Gathering, there will be an addition to the warrior code. Prey must be killed only to be eaten, and we must give thanks to StarClan for its life. This is the way of the warrior."

CODE
4

CODE FIVE

A KIT MUST BE AT LEAST SIX MOONS OLD
TO BECOME AN APPRENTICE.

*It seems so obvious now that kits should not be allowed
to fight until they are properly trained and strong enough to
take on full-grown warriors. But it was not always like this.
It took the love of a mother cat to put a stop to
the destruction of fragile lives.*

The Queens Unite

"Attack! Jump! Swipe! Roll! No, *roll.*"
Daisytail winced as Specklepaw scrambled to his
feet and shook his head, panting. He looked dazed, and there was
a bead of blood welling at the tip of one ear. His mentor, Slatepelt,
nudged him toward the other apprentice in the training circle,
Adderpaw.

"Try again," Slatepelt instructed gently.

Daisytail couldn't watch as Specklepaw launched himself
at his rival. It seemed like only a moon ago that his freckled,
pale brown head had nuzzled into her belly searching for milk.
Adderpaw had been training for several moons longer and he
looked full-grown next to Specklepaw, whose head barely reached

his shoulder. There was a thud behind Daisytail, and she bit her tongue to stop herself from wailing out loud.

"Did you see that?" Specklepaw called. "Did you, Mom? Did you? I pushed Adderpaw right over!"

Daisytail turned around and forced herself to purr approvingly. She could tell from the look exchanged by Adderpaw and Slatepelt that the older apprentice had deliberately let the little cat win. "Well done, nutkin," she called. A tuft of fur on Specklepaw's head was sticking up, and she longed to go over and lick it flat. "You'll be a warrior before you know it!" *Before my milk has dried up*, she added silently.

Slatepelt nodded to her. "He's learning fast. Which is good, because it looks like we'll be fighting ShadowClan again soon. They've been seen stealing rabbits in broad daylight, and Hazelstar won't let them get away with it."

Daisytail didn't answer. Her kit was too small to take part in a real battle. He couldn't even take on his own Clanmates, who would never try to rip his pelt, tear his eyes, claw his ears into shreds . . .

"Daisytail? Are you okay?" A dark brown face was peering anxiously out of the entrance to the nursery. Hawkfoot's three kits were half a moon younger than Specklepaw: They would be made apprentices any day now and kept bouncing around their nest practicing their battle moves.

"There's going to be another battle with ShadowClan," Daisytail burst out. "I can't let Specklepaw fight, I just can't!"

"You don't have a choice," Hawkfoot pointed out. "He's an apprentice now; this is what he's being trained for."

Daisytail lifted her head. "And if your kits are apprentices by then, will you let them go? Knowing they'll face blood-hungry ShadowClan warriors?"

Hawkfoot prodded a bramble tendril with her forepaw. "It's our duty to provide the Clan with new warriors," she mewed.

"And is it our duty to see those warriors die before they're full-grown?" Daisytail challenged. She turned and stalked away from the nursery.

"Where are you going?"

"To put a stop to this once and for all."

A bright orange sun stretched its paws over the edge of the moor, turning the sky above to pink and cream. Dew sparkled like starlight in the shadows cast by rocks and gorse bushes. On one of the rocks, Hazelstar stood to address his warriors. They stretched in a line on either side of him, facing the ShadowClan border, marked by a line of stunted trees.

"Warriors of WindClan!" Hazelstar cried. There was an indignant murmur from farther along the line, and Hazelstar's whiskers twitched. "And apprentices! ShadowClan has stolen from us one too many times! We will teach them that WindClan's borders are strong, they will be defended with claw and tooth, and our prey protected for our Clan alone."

The cats yowled in support, and the grass flickered with the shadows of lashing tails.

Like an echo, a yowl came from the trees on the other side of the border. The grass beneath the trees stirred, and a line of ShadowClan warriors stepped out. A white-furred cat with hard green eyes stood in the center. "Are you sure about that, Hazelstar?" he sneered. "Some of your warriors look awfully small."

His gaze swept over the smallest WindClan apprentices, who suddenly looked even tinier beside their Clanmates.

"I'd say we're evenly matched, Blizzardstar," Hazelstar replied calmly. He glanced toward the cats at the end of the ShadowClan line, some of whom still had a fuzz of kit fur around their ears.

Blizzardstar curled his lip. "We'll put that to the test, shall we?" he snarled. "ShadowClan, attack!"

"STOP!" Daisytail leaped onto the rock she had been hiding behind. Hawkfoot scrambled up beside her. "We won't let you fight!"

Blizzardstar stared at the queens in astonishment. "Are all your cats this scared of combat, Hazelstar?"

CODE 5

"It's not fear," called a cat from the ShadowClan line. She stepped into the open, her amber eyes reflecting the sun.

"Oakleaf? What in the name of StarClan are you doing?" Blizzardstar demanded.

Daisytail jumped down from the rock and padded into the open space between the battle lines. The grass felt cool and springy beneath her paws; she would not let it turn red with her own kit's blood. "We're stopping this battle," she announced. To her relief, her voice didn't give away how much she was trembling inside. "Some of these apprentices are barely weaned from their mothers' milk. They are too young to die, too young to fight, too young to be treated like full-grown warriors."

The ShadowClan queen walked out to join her. "Daisytail came to see me with her Clanmate Hawkfoot two sunrises ago. She told me that she didn't want to let her kit go into battle when he was too small to fight his own Clanmates, and she asked me if I would let my kit die like this, too." When Blizzardstar let out a questioning grunt, she turned and explained, "I met Daisytail once at a Gathering, when we had both just learned we were expecting kits. She remembered me and knew I would not want my kit to fight any more than she did."

Hazelstar turned to Daisytail. "What are you saying?" he queried, looking baffled. "That we should never fight again? Do you really think that is how the Clans could live?"

Daisytail shook her head. "No. I know battle is part of our life. It's what warriors train for. But they should only be asked to fight when they are old enough to stand a chance of winning. What is the point of training kits so young that they'll be lost in their first conflict?"

Out of the corner of her eye, she saw Specklepaw duck behind Adderpaw. Embarrassment prickled from every hair on his pelt, and he refused to meet her gaze. Inwardly Daisytail gave an amused purr. One day, he'd understand—he'd still be alive to know why his mother did this.

Oakleaf trotted across the grass and stood side by side with Daisytail and Hawkfoot. "We are united, Blizzardstar," she told him. She nodded toward the line, and several other she-cats padded out. Daisytail dipped her head to greet them; some of these queens were too old to have kits as young as hers, but they all felt the same: The youngest cats should not be expected to fight. The grass whispered softly as WindClan she-cats joined them, falling in beside their ShadowClan rivals.

Daisytail held her breath and looked from Hazelstar to Blizzardstar and back again. The leaders could still order their warriors into battle. All that would happen would be that she would be forced to watch her kit fall beneath the paws of a giant ShadowClan warrior, never to get up again.

"Hazelstar? Our queens have spoken." Blizzardstar stepped out from his battle line, looking hard at his rival leader. "Should we ignore them and fight?"

The ginger tom paused, letting his gaze rest on the group of she-cats before glancing at his tiny warriors. Then he faced

Blizzardstar again. "What sense is there in losing the future of our Clans, when if we let them grow stronger, battles will be more easily won?"

Daisytail almost purred out loud. Hazelstar had managed to make this sound like a threat to ShadowClan rather than a decision to decrease his battle line.

Blizzardstar nodded. "If you are going to remove your youngest cats, then so must I. ShadowClan cannot be accused of being unfair in battle."

"I would never suggest such a thing," Hazelstar murmured. He turned to Daisytail. "How do you propose that we make sure all Clans keep their youngest cats from battle?" he asked.

Daisytail gulped. Was she really being consulted by the leader of her Clan? She thought rapidly. "I think there should be an addition to the warrior code. That kits must be"—she looked up and down the battle line, judging which cats looked big enough to take on a fully trained warrior—"six moons old before they are allowed to train as apprentices."

Oakleaf brushed the tip of her tail against Daisytail's shoulder. "Until then, they must live within the camp, where the queens can be responsible for their safety."

Hazelstar nodded. "That makes sense to me. Thank you, Daisytail. And thank you, Oakleaf." He dipped his head to the ShadowClan queen. "Blizzardstar, are we agreed?"

The ShadowClan leader bowed his head. "We are. We will take this to the Gathering at the next full moon."

Daisytail gazed at Specklepaw, who looked ready to burst with frustration. *There will be other battles, my little warrior. But not yet. Not until you are ready.*

The Smallest Warrior

Only a leader that walks the blackest of paths
would break the code that protects kits. Brokenstar
of ShadowClan was such a leader.

The WindClan warrior sprang with his claws unsheathed, and the little black-and-white cat fell to the ground without making a sound. A trickle of blood crept from his ear, which was crumpled in the dust. Flintfang shook off the warrior trying to sink her teeth into his tail and bounded over to his unmoving Clanmate.

"Get off him, you mangy worm!" Flintfang snarled. Then he bent down to grasp Badgerpaw's scruff between his teeth. The apprentice's fur was still soft and fluffy, and it tickled Flintfang's nose. Blinking to stop the sneeze, Flintfang lifted the tiny limp body into the air and carried it to the edge of the WindClan camp. Behind him, screeches and thuds echoed around the shallow dip in the ground where WindClan had once made its home. Now all the dens were trampled and ruined, and the ground was sticky with blood. Brokenstar was right: This battle would force WindClan to leave the moor, and ShadowClan hunters would be able to take over the territory to feed their growing Clan.

But not Badgerpaw. His breathing was quick and shallow and a strange smell came from him, sour like blood and crow-food. There was nothing any cat could do to help him. Flintfang shook his head angrily. He had trained his apprentice in every battle skill he knew and made sure he could duck and roll and slash as well as any of the other apprentices. But Badgerpaw was only three moons old; he was too small to take on a full-grown WindClan warrior, his legs too short to reach the easily wounded parts of belly, eyes, and ears. What could a mentor do when he was expected to train a kit? The warrior code said that a warrior must be at least six moons old, but that didn't worry Flintfang as much as he feared Brokenstar. Flintfang had failed his leader— and Brokenstar would make sure every cat in the Clan knew. He turned away, ready to abandon his apprentice and teach that fox-faced WindClan warrior a lesson he wouldn't forget.

Badgerpaw's eyes flickered. "Flintfang? Is that you?"

Flintfang's heart sank. "Yes, it's me."

"Was . . . was I good enough?" Badgerpaw rasped in a tiny voice. His paws shifted in the dust and a bead of blood appeared at the corner of his lip. "I tried to remember everything you taught me."

Flintfang stared at the battered little body. Badgerpaw hadn't stood a chance from the moment the first battle yowl split the air.

"I hope Brokenstar is proud of me," Badgerpaw went on. His eyes were clouding over and starting to close. "And my mom."

Flintfang felt something stir inside him. What was he going to tell Fernshade? That her kit was always going to die in this battle because he was too small, too weak?

"Fernshade will be very proud of you," he meowed.

Badgerpaw opened his eyes with an effort and

looked straight at Flintfang. "Are you proud of me?"

Flintfang crouched beside Badgerpaw and stroked the apprentice's eyelids with the tip of his tail to close them again. "You fought brilliantly," he murmured.

"Will you be all right without me?" Badgerpaw asked fretfully. He moved his head and the trickle of blood coming from his ear thickened, spilling out faster.

"We'll do our best," Flintfang replied gravely. "And we'll always remember you and how brave you were."

Was it his imagination, or did the tiny black-and-white chest swell with pride?

"Do . . . do you think StarClan will make me a warrior now?"

Flintfang swallowed hard; there seemed to be a stone wedged in his throat. "I'm sure they will."

"What will my name be?" Badgerpaw wondered, his voice growing even fainter.

"I expect they'll let you choose your own name," Flintfang replied. The lump in his throat was growing, making it hard to speak.

"I'd like to be called Badgerfang. Like you, because you were such a great mentor."

Flintfang leaned forward and rested his muzzle on top of his apprentice's head. "That is a great honor. Badgerfang is a very good name for a warrior." He could feel Badgerpaw's breaths coming quicker now, his flank hardly rising at all as he fought for air. "You will watch over us from StarClan for all the moons to come." Badgerpaw let out a tiny sigh, and his flank stilled.

Flintfang straightened up. "This was not your time to die. For as long as I live, I will honor the warrior code and not train another kit who should still be at his mother's belly. Go now, little one, and walk with warriors."

CODE SIX

*Being a warrior isn't just about catching prey and fighting
other Clans, you know. It's about being part of a tradition that
stretches back longer than any cat can remember, and one
that will last for all the moons to come. It was a RiverClan medicine
cat who learned that the time when every cat realizes this most
is when they are first given their warrior name and become
responsible for the safety and survival of their Clan.*

A Night of Listening

"**M**eadowpelt! Meadowpelt, we need you!"
Meadowpelt put down the willow stick he was
shredding and wove his way between the pale yellow stalks that
shielded his den from the rest of the camp. It was greenleaf, and
for once the ground underpaw was dry and dusty rather than
pooling with water.

Several other RiverClan cats were in the clearing, looking
anxious as their Clanmates crackled nearer. Suddenly the

reeds rattled together and a small black tom burst out. "Snaketooth is hurt!" he yowled.

"What happened, Molewhisker?" Troutstar demanded. Just then, two more cats appeared with a third propped between them, his dark brown head lolling and one of his hind legs trailing uselessly behind.

Troutstar glanced over his shoulder. "Meadowpelt, take over."

Meadowpelt ran forward to take a look at his latest patient. This wasn't the first injury he'd treated among these young warriors in the last moon. Molewhisker had ripped out one of his claws trying to jump across the river, and Lightningpelt, a light brown tabby with a distinctive white streak down her back, had nearly poked out her own eye chasing through the thickest part of the reeds. Every day, the warriors seemed to come up with yet another competition to discover who was the strongest, fastest . . . *or most mouse-brained*, Meadowpelt thought crossly.

Lightningpelt and Nettlepad laid Snaketooth on the ground in the middle of the clearing. Meadowpelt studied the twisted leg, noticing the way the snapped bone jutted out beneath the skin. There was a chance Snaketooth would never walk without a limp.

"What was it this time?" Meadowpelt sighed.

"Climbing one of the Great Oaks," Snaketooth muttered through gritted teeth. "I won."

"You should have seen him!" Lightningpelt burst out. "He practically climbed onto a cloud!"

"If I had seen him, I wouldn't have let him do something so utterly mouse-brained," Meadowpelt growled. "When will you learn to stop showing off and start putting your Clan first? At this rate there'll be no warriors left by leaf-bare." Lifting his head, he looked around and spotted Oatpaw, whom he was thinking of taking as his apprentice. "Oatpaw, fetch me some poppy seeds, will you?"

Oatpaw ducked his head and ran to the den, quickly returning with several tiny black seeds stuck to his forepaw.

"Lick these up," Meadowpelt told Snaketooth. He turned back to Oatpaw. "Help me carry him to my den. He'll need to stay there tonight."

Moonlight filtered through the reeds, striping the floor of the medicine cat's den with sharp, thin shadows. Meadowpelt checked that the reeds on Snaketooth's splint were bound tightly enough, and then padded heavily across the clearing to his nest.

The reeds slid apart and Molewhisker, Lightningpelt, and Nettlepad squeezed into the tiny space beside their sleeping friend. "We wanted to see if he was okay," Molewhisker explained in a loud whisper.

"That's up to StarClan now," Meadowpelt replied. "I've done as much as I can. Now go to your own dens and let him sleep."

It was too late. Snaketooth stirred and lifted his head a little way off the pillow of moss. "Hey, guys!" he croaked.

Nettlepad bent over him. "How's your leg? It looked really gross!"

Meadowpelt flicked his tail. "You can stay for a few moments, but no more, understand?"

The three healthy warriors looked at the medicine cat and nodded solemnly. With a grunt, Meadowpelt threaded his way between the reeds that circled his nest and settled down. Tired as he was—and getting a little deaf in his old age, he had to admit— he could still hear the warriors whispering to Snaketooth.

"You've got to get better real soon!"

"We're jumping into the gorge on the full moon, remember?"

"Yeah, I dared you, so if you don't do it, I win!" That was Nettlepad, his voice rising with excitement.

"Hush!" Lightningpelt hissed. "Don't let every cat hear you! You know what the old ones are like—they never want us to have fun."

"They just wish they were young enough to jump into the gorge. But I bet they were never brave enough to try. Not like us!" Molewhisker sounded as if he thought he could grow wings and glide safely into the river as it thundered and foamed through the steep-sided canyon at the edge of their territory.

"Look, he's gone to sleep," whispered Lightningpelt. "Come on, let's leave him."

Meadowpelt listened to them padding away, bristling at their foolishness. His mind filled with shadows, and sleep was a long time coming.

"Troutstar? May I speak with you?" It was the following day, with hot, merciless sunshine bouncing off the reeds and the surface of the river.

The RiverClan leader opened his eyes from his doze. He was curled on a flat stone by the shore, his gray fur blending into the sun-bleached rock. "Is Snaketooth all right?" he asked anxiously.

Meadowpelt grunted. "You mean apart from having no sense at all? He'll live. But whether he'll be able to hunt and fight again, I'm not sure."

Troutstar shook his head. "I don't know why those warriors keep doing such ridiculous things."

"That's why I wanted to talk to you. I want to go to the Moonstone to ask StarClan for advice."

The gray cat looked at him in surprise. "Do you really think StarClan needs to be involved?"

Meadowpelt nodded. "Yes, I do. We have raised a whole generation of warriors who only want to amuse themselves. There aren't enough apprentices for them all to be mentors, so they're wasting time making up stupid, dangerous games. They've all been hurt, but it hasn't stopped them. Did you know they're planning to jump into the gorge on the full moon?"

Troutstar's tail bristled. "No, I didn't know that. Meadowpelt, if you think StarClan can help, then you must go. May StarClan be waiting for you with answers."

It was past nightfall by the time Meadowpelt reached the entrance to Mothermouth. The Highstones jabbed angrily into the sky, black against dove-gray. Meadowpelt let his mind empty as he felt his way down the long, dark tunnel. At the bottom, the flattened-egg moon made the Moonstone glow brightly enough to light up the chamber. Meadowpelt lay down at the foot of the Moonstone and pressed his muzzle against the sharp, cold rock.

"StarClan, please show me how to make my Clanmates understand that the Clan depends on them for its survival, and that they can't play like kits now that they are warriors."

He closed his eyes, and at once the scents of the riverbank brushed against his fur. He could hear the water rolling past, whispering against the stones, and the reeds rattling together as they were bent over by the breeze. When he opened his eyes, he found that he was lying in the center of the RiverClan camp with cats stirring softly around him, preparing for the night. With a shock, Meadowpelt realized that he didn't recognize any of them—no, it was more that he couldn't see them clearly enough, as if their faces were always in shadow and their scents too mixed by the breeze to distinguish one cat from another. Even their voices sounded muffled, almost familiar but not quite. He lay still with his chin on his paws and listened.

"We tracked that fox to the border, so hopefully it will stay away," one voice reported.

"I'm on dawn patrol tomorrow, so I'll look out for any new scents," came the reply.

"The elders are convinced it will come back once more," meowed another voice. "They said that foxes will check out a place twice before deciding whether or not to settle. I think we should take their advice and be prepared to chase it out again."

"I promised I'd take all the apprentices for a fishing lesson tomorrow. Could you do a hunting patrol in my place?"

"Sure. With those kits due any day, we're going to need a full fresh-kill pile. Have you seen how much the queens eat when they're nursing?"

There was a *mrrow* of amusement from the other cats, and Meadowpelt purred, too. Whoever these cats were, they were the kind of warriors RiverClan could be proud of: brave, loyal, hardworking, and aware of how much the whole Clan depended on them, from the frailest elder to the tiniest kit.

Warm dawn light roused Meadowpelt and he sat up, blinking, in the sunlit cavern. Was that it? He'd spent a night in his own Clan, listening to unidentified cats talk about their lives? *How is that supposed to help?*

There was the faintest echo inside his head: *A night in his own Clan, listening . . . But how does that provide me with answers for our mouse-brained warriors?*

Silence pressed on his ears. What was he going to tell Troutstar?

A night of listening . . .

To cats who cared about their Clan, who understood their duties and took pride in doing them well.

Is that what the warriors need?

Meadowpelt burst into the dazzling air and started to run down the rock-strewn hill. StarClan had given him the answer!

"One night? To think about being a warrior?" Troutstar sounded unconvinced, and Meadowpelt was starting to wonder if this wasn't such a great idea after all. Knowing the current RiverClan cats, they'd just come up with a bunch of games to play in the dark.

But Meadowpelt kept his doubts to himself. The full moon was only a day away, and with any luck a sleepless night would at least make the warriors too tired to carry out their mouse-brained scheme of jumping into the gorge.

The young cats looked startled when Troutstar explained what they had to do: spend one night in silent vigil, watching over the camp while their Clanmates slept. "And make sure you listen, as well!" he added sternly.

The sun was already sliding behind the outline of the Twoleg barns beyond the willow trees, so the Clan started to prepare for the night. Molewhisker, Lightningpelt, and Nettlepad stayed in the middle of the clearing, looking uncertain about what they were supposed to be doing. Meadowpelt couldn't blame them; he wasn't sure anymore that he'd understood StarClan.

Meadowpelt slid into his nest and gave in to a wave of black sleep.

"Fox! Wake up! Fox attack!"

Meadowpelt was on his feet and racing into the clearing before he had fully opened his eyes. The camp was bathed in cold white light and cats were plunging out of the reeds, hissing in alarm. Nettlepad stood in the middle of the clearing with his fur bristling.

"We heard a fox!" he gasped. "Creeping up on the nursery. Molewhisker and Lightningpelt have chased it away."

Troutstar nodded to a couple of senior warriors. "Go after them. Make sure they don't try to confront the fox. We just need it to leave the territory."

A white she-cat with splashes of ginger on her fur padded up to Nettlepad. A pair of tiny kits bundled along beside her. "You saved our lives!" she exclaimed. "Thank you!"

"I didn't even hear that mangy ol' fox creeping up on us!" squeaked one of the kits.

"Yeah, even though you've got really big ears!" taunted his littermate.

"Have not!"

"Have so! You look like a rabbit!"

Meadowpelt padded over to Nettlepad, who was looking rather uncomfortable at being the center of attention. "Sunspots is right; you saved her life and her kits'. You should be very proud."

Nettlepad shuffled his paws. "It's because we were being quiet, like you said. We'd never have heard that fox if we'd been in our dens."

Meadowpelt narrowed his eyes. "Or jumping into the gorge. Or climbing the Great Oaks at Fourtrees. Or chasing one another through the reeds, scaring off prey."

Nettlepad hung his head. "Yeah, I guess that was pretty mouse-brained."

Just then, Lightningpelt and Molewhisker hurtled back into the clearing, followed by the senior warriors. "We chased that fox all the way to the border!" Molewhisker panted, his eyes shining with triumph.

CODE 6

"It won't come back here in a hurry!" Lightningpelt declared.

"Don't be so sure," rasped Fernleaf, one of the elders. "Foxes have a habit of coming back once more before they decide whether or not to settle. You need to be ready to chase it off again."

Molewhisker straightened up. "No problem," he promised.

Lightningpelt spotted a row of apprentices peering out of their den. "Hey there! I know some great fishing techniques! Would you like me to show you them today?"

Nettlepad nodded. "She's really good, honestly. I'll do your hunting patrol for you, Lightningpelt."

"Thanks, that would be really helpful."

Meadowpelt stared. His vision was unfolding around him, faces and scents falling into place like raindrops. A night of listening had turned these cats into warriors that RiverClan could be proud of.

"Thank you, Meadowpelt," murmured a voice beside him. It was Troutstar.

Meadowpelt shrugged. "Thank StarClan," he mewed gruffly.

"At the Gathering tomorrow night, I'll suggest we add a new

part to the warrior code: that all new warriors must spend one night in silent vigil so they understand how much their Clan needs them now," Troutstar went on.

Meadowpelt nodded, and inside a small worm of pride stretched and swelled satisfyingly. *Yes, make it part of the warrior code, so that all cats have a night of listening. . . .*

❖

Squirrelflight's Words of Wisdom

*One day even you might have to sit vigil.
Here are a few tips from Squirrelflight to help you pass the
night—if you're a ThunderClan warrior, that is!*

A vigil is the proudest and scariest night of any warrior's life. It was for me! Having to spend a whole night awake guarding the Clan, trying not to doze off, jumping at every leaf fall in case it's an enemy attack, it's enough to send any cat running back to the nursery. So, I'm going to give you some tips on how to get through a vigil. That way you'll be prepared when it's your turn.

First, don't lie near the warriors' den; the noise of all that snoring will make you want to nod off. Or deafen you. If you feel sleepy, jump onto the Highledge—quietly, obviously, so you don't wake Firestar. I know, I know, we're not supposed to go up there, but it will give you a surge of energy and keep you going. When I kept my warrior's vigil, back in the old forest, I climbed onto the Highrock in the middle of the night and it was *amazing*. The camp looked so tiny!

And I thought about how brilliant it would feel to summon all the cats just by calling them together. . . . Don't look at me like that; you know I'd never have done something like that. Honestly.

Even if you don't go up to the Highledge, make sure you stand up and stretch every so often, otherwise you'll feel like you've turned into a lump of stone. A little game of mouse-chase won't offend the ancestors if it gets really cold. Just don't send it flying too close to the nursery, like I did, or you'll wake every kit. They can hear a game going on even when they're fast asleep! Trust me, the queens won't thank you for that.

If you hear or see anything suspicious, call out, "Who's there?" Even if it's just a cat coming back from the dirtplace, better to be safe than sorry. After all, tonight you're in charge! The safety of the whole Clan depends on you! Sorry, I'm really not trying to worry you. Let's hope nothing does happen, because after all you're not supposed to make any noise during the vigil. Unless there is a raid, in which case you must wake Firestar first, then the warriors. Don't investigate anything on your own; it's too risky. Obviously you're allowed to call for help if you need it. And you can drink if you get thirsty, but you mustn't eat. Your old mentor will come and tell you when the vigil is over, once the sun is up.

So, does all that sound okay? I haven't scared you, have I?

Good luck! May StarClan watch over you!

CODE
6

CODE SEVEN

> ### A CAT CANNOT BE MADE DEPUTY WITHOUT HAVING MENTORED AT LEAST ONE APPRENTICE.

Our skills and our knowledge will live forever,
thanks to our mentors, who teach the next generation of Clan cats
the way of the warrior. But it took a great leader to see
that it was not only the apprentice who gained valuable knowledge
from the mentor. Being entrusted with an apprentice teaches the
mentor how to lead and gain loyalty and respect. For what is a
deputy or leader if not a mentor to the whole Clan?

Second in Command

"STarClan, hear me as I make my choice. Acorntail will be the new deputy of WindClan."

Featherstar stretched out and rested her muzzle lightly on top of Acorntail's head. Acorntail closed his eyes, swallowing his grief for Pebblefur, the cat who had once been his mentor, and whose death from a strange, agonizing lump in his belly had shocked the Clan.

"Acorntail! Acorntail!" called the cats behind him, but to Acorntail, they sounded flat and disappointed. It was obvious they didn't want him to be their deputy.

"Good luck, Acorntail," murmured a voice in his ear. It was Morningcloud, the dark gray she-cat who had made no secret of her surprise when Acorntail was picked for deputy instead of her.

"Thanks," Acorntail meowed. Behind her, he could see her apprentice Quickpaw glaring at him, his pale ginger face screwed up with indignation. Acorntail wondered if all young cats rewarded their mentors with such fierce loyalty. He hadn't yet had an apprentice of his own, so he didn't know what it would be like to train a new warrior and to watch him or her develop from bumbling kit to strong, skillful fighting cat.

Morningcloud padded back to Quickpaw, and Acorntail heard the young cat hiss, "It should have been you!"

The she-cat quieted him with a flick of her tail. "Maybe one day," she murmured softly.

"Acorntail, you need to sort out the patrols for today," Featherstar prompted. Her tone was almost apologetic, as if she didn't want to remind him of his duties.

"Oh, yes, of course," Acorntail stammered. "Gorseclaw, Sheeptail, and Cloversplash, you can go on hunting patrol."

Cloversplash, a lightly built dark brown she-cat with a white flash on her nose shaped exactly like a cloverleaf, stopped him. "We went on hunting patrol this morning. We should have a training session with our apprentices now."

Acorntail felt as if the three apprentices attached to these warriors were looking at him with a mixture of scorn and pity. He ducked his head. "Oh, yes, of course, training. Well, maybe you could take the evening hunting patrol?"

CODE
7

"Sure," mewed Thistlepaw, Sheeptail's apprentice. "We're always in the mood for chasing rabbits all over the place after fighting all afternoon."

Acorntail's fur prickled with embarrassment. Why didn't he think of that? Why was he being such a flea-brain?

"Right, okay. Morningcloud, could you and Quickpaw do a hunting patrol instead?"

Morningcloud put her head on one side. "On our own?" she questioned.

"Er, no. I'll come with you," Acorntail decided hastily. He glanced at Featherstar, who gave a tiny nod. Acorntail felt lower than a worm's belly. *Why did Featherstar make me her deputy when I'm so useless?*

"You'll do fine, Acorntail," Featherstar told him. She sounded tired and strained, and Acorntail realized how much she must still be grieving for Pebblefur, who had died only three sunrises ago. They were in her den, a shallow scoop in the sandy earth shielded by a wall of gorse. Sunhigh had just passed, and the hunting patrol was due to leave.

"Prey is running well at the moment. You'll catch plenty with Morningcloud and Quickpaw."

Acorntail heard the dismissal in her tone. He backed out of the den. Morningcloud and Quickpaw were waiting for him in the center of the camp. Quickpaw still looked hostile, but the she-cat's expression was impossible to read. Morningcloud just nodded and let Acorntail lead the way up the slope and out onto the moor.

Acorntail quickly detected the musky tang of rabbit and hurtled off. For the first time since being made deputy, he felt sure of what he was doing, confident in the swiftness of his paws and the prospect of a good piece of fresh-kill for the Clan. The rabbit tried to outrun him but he drew steadily alongside, pounced from running full speed, and brought it down with a muffled snap of neck bones. He lifted his head and looked around. Morningcloud was racing after a young rabbit, her tail bouncing as she tore across the warm grass, and Quickpaw was sniffing the ground as if he had picked up the scent of a plover's nest. Eggs laid in a scoop of earth were a rare treat for the cats as plovers defended their unhatched young fiercely, but Quickpaw already had a reputation not just for tracking the nests but for carrying the eggs undamaged back to camp, tucked under his chin. Acorntail felt a little pebble of worry in his stomach dissolve. His Clan was the best by far, and it was an honor to be their deputy.

He stiffened. There was another scent on the air, not rabbit or freshly laid eggs, but feline. The breeze was carrying it from the direction of Fourtrees and the border with ThunderClan. What did those mangy tree-dwellers want now? They were far too slow and fat to catch WindClan's prey, so why would they even try?

His fur bristling, Acorntail shoved his rabbit under a gorse bush and trotted toward the border. The scent grew stronger. As he crested a rise close to the edge of WindClan territory, he saw three ThunderClan cats walking along the border, barely a whisker-length from trespassing.

"Did you want something?" he growled.

The biggest ThunderClan cat shook his head. "Just doing a patrol," he replied indifferently.

Acorntail looked closer. The smallest cat, which looked like an apprentice, had a tuft of dusky-brown fur stuck on his nose. There was only one type of prey that had fur like that.

"Have you been stealing rabbits?" Acorntail hissed.

The apprentice's eyes stretched wide—in guilty horror, Acorntail was sure—but the big warrior just curled his lip. "As if we'd waste our energy chasing your scrawny prey."

Acorntail opened his jaws; he could clearly taste the scent

of fresh-killed rabbit clinging to these cats. Before he could say anything, Morningcloud and Quickpaw hurtled up from farther along the border.

"We found a dead rabbit!" Quickpaw panted.

"With ThunderClan scent on it," Morningcloud added. She skidded to a stop and narrowed her eyes at the rival patrol.

Acorntail flattened his ears. "So you did steal our prey!"

"It was dead already," growled the ThunderClan warrior. "We know better than to waste good fresh-kill—unlike your Clan."

"It did look old and it smelled funny," Quickpaw meowed before Acorntail could silence him. "It could have been dead for days. Yuck, you just ate crow-food!"

"That's not the point!" Acorntail hissed. *What kind of deputy lets the first rival patrol he meets get away with trespassing and theft?* "These cats have stolen our prey! They must be taught a lesson! WindClan, attack!"

He sprang at the big ThunderClan warrior, claws unsheathed. To his surprise, the warrior didn't try to jump away or fight back. Instead, he stared past Acorntail with a glimmer of amusement in his eyes. Acorntail thudded to the ground and looked over his shoulder.

Morningcloud and Quickpaw were standing close together, watching him.

"Attack!" yowled Acorntail.

"Don't be such a mouse-brain," Morningcloud retorted. "I'm not putting my apprentice in danger for the sake of crow-food. If they want to eat rotten prey that will give them bellyache, that's up to them."

"But they trespassed!" Acorntail protested, starting to feel like the day couldn't get any worse.

"Actually we didn't," the other ThunderClan warrior put in helpfully. "The rabbit was on our side of the border."

Acorntail looked questioningly at Morningcloud. She nodded.

"Why didn't you tell me?" Acorntail demanded.

"We were going to," Morningcloud replied. "You didn't give us a chance."

"And now I think you'll find you're trespassing on our territory," the first ThunderClan warrior pointed out.

Acorntail walked stiffly back across the border. "Morningcloud, Quickpaw, we're going back to the camp," he announced. "Featherstar needs to be told that a rabbit has died on ThunderClan's territory."

Morningcloud looked faintly surprised, but to his relief, she didn't argue.

"Which means it belonged to us anyway!" called the ThunderClan warrior as they headed back up the hill. "You should pick your battles more carefully."

I don't know enough to be a deputy, Acorntail thought miserably. *I'm going to tell Featherstar I can't do this.*

"You've made a mistake. You'll have to choose another cat to be deputy."

Featherstar regarded him from her nest, her blue eyes glowing in the half-light behind the gorse bushes. "When you became an apprentice, did you know all the fighting moves and how to hunt prey?"

"Of course not," Acorntail replied, puzzled.

"And when you became a warrior, did you know how to lead patrols, how to find the best places to hunt, and where our rivals were most likely to try to cross our border?"

Acorntail shook his head.

"Then why do you expect to know everything about being a deputy on your very first day? Every cat knows you have things to learn, but once you have, you'll be as good as Pebblefur."

Never.

"Think back to when you were an apprentice," Featherstar went on. "Remember what it was like to learn new things every day, knowing they would all lead to making you a warrior of WindClan?"

"But that was different," Acorntail argued. "I didn't have responsibility for the whole Clan then."

"And you don't now," Featherstar pointed out. "I'm still the leader." She put her head to one side. "Why do you feel that you're not worthy of giving orders to your Clanmates, Acorntail?"

"Because I don't know how to! Look at what happened today: Morningcloud would never have given the order to attack. She'd have found out all the information first, and then made sure that her apprentice wasn't in danger if a fight started. She'd make a much better deputy than me."

"But I chose you," Featherstar meowed. She was silent for a while, and Acorntail tried not to fidget. Then she lifted her head and looked straight at him. "I'm sorry. I should have given you an apprentice first. You would have gotten used to giving orders, and you would understand how protective mentors feel about sending young cats into battle."

She sounded so flat and defeated that Acorntail felt a rush of concern for her. She had lost her last deputy, now making her life even more difficult.

"It's not too late," he meowed firmly. "Give me an apprentice now, and I can learn. Cherryfeather's kits are nearly six moons old; let me have Pricklekit."

Featherstar held his gaze. "If I do that, will you stay as my deputy?"

Acorntail nodded. "I'll be the best deputy I can be. Pebblefur would have wanted me to do that."

"And you'll be as good a mentor to your apprentice as he was to you," Featherstar assured him. She went on, "I think I'll suggest an addition to the warrior code at the next Gathering, that a warrior cannot be made deputy unless he has had an apprentice."

Acorntail winced, and she added quickly, "Not because I regret choosing you, Acorntail, but because you're right. Training an apprentice teaches a cat how to give orders, how to protect the less-experienced fighters, and establishes bonds of loyalty that can survive the worst battles.

"Now, go sort out the dawn patrols for tomorrow. And then you might like to visit the nursery to see how your future apprentice is faring!"

CODE
7

CODE EIGHT

> ## THE DEPUTY WILL BECOME CLAN LEADER WHEN THE LEADER DIES OR RETIRES.

*At the dawn of the Clans, new Clan leaders were chosen
from the kin of the previous leader: often their kits, but sometimes
their littermates or their kits' kits. Leaders were well respected
enough that their kin was respected, too, by the whole Clan, and it
seemed the easiest way to choose a new head of the Clan. But not all
cats follow their kin in skills and temperament, and as you will see,
not every new leader was well suited or well received.*

Follow My Leader

The air stilled until the trees were silent, and the only sound was the splash of water over stones. The brown tabby cat lay in the shelter of thick ferns, his breathing so shallow that his flank barely stirred.

"Robinwing?" he rasped.

"Yes, I'm here, Beechstar." Robinwing leaned closer, refusing to flinch away from the stench of death that already clung to the old cat's fur. "Your Clan is safe."

The tip of Beechstar's tail twitched. "They won't be safe for long. RiverClan will not be content with my death. SkyClan must attack again before they do. Take the battle into their territory this time. And make sure we win."

"Hush, Father," urged Mothpelt. "Get some rest, and we'll take you back to the camp tomorrow."

"This is my final rest," Beechstar whispered. "My ninth life is slipping away; my warrior ancestors are already waiting for me." His milky blue gaze focused on a point past them; Robinwing instinctively turned to look, but there was nothing except trees and bracken. "I come, my friends. Wait just one moment longer." With an effort, Beechstar dragged his gaze back to the black-and-brown cat beside him. "Lead our Clan well, Mothpelt. Make me proud as I watch you from StarClan."

"Father, no!" Mothpelt yowled, but the leader's eyes were closing now and his legs relaxed as he surrendered his final life.

Robinwing exchanged an agonized glance with a third cat watching the tragic scene: Maplewhisker, SkyClan's deputy. He knew she shared his concerns about Mothpelt as a leader. They had shared the nursery with him, trained side by side to become warriors, and seen him struggle to mentor a succession of apprentices.

CODE
8

Maplewhisker fell in beside Robinwing as they walked back to the camp to fetch the elders who would bury Beechstar. "No cat can doubt his loyalty to SkyClan and to the memory of his father," she pointed out, even though Robinwing hadn't said a word. "And he fought as bravely as any of us yesterday, especially after his father fell."

Robinwing didn't reply. He wanted to give Mothpelt a chance to show he could lead SkyClan—for the sake of his Clanmates. They were still at war with RiverClan over the territory on the SkyClan side of the river, and he needed to be at least as strong and wise as his father.

"He will need our support," Maplewhisker went on.

Robinwing glanced sideways at her. "Even if we don't agree with him?"

Maplewhisker flicked her ears. "He is our leader now. StarClan will guide his paws."

"Let all cats old enough to catch their own prey gather to hear me!"

It was raining hard, and Mothpelt had to raise his voice to be heard above the thundering of water through the trees. His father had been buried the day before, and he would be going to the Moonstone to receive his nine lives and his new name that night.

"Cats of SkyClan! My father's last wish was that we take the battle to RiverClan's side of the river and prove once and for all that SkyClan cannot be beaten!" Mothpelt declared.

There were yowls of support from the cats huddled below the branch where he balanced. Robinwing kept quiet. He was wondering what the river looked like after all the rain.

Mothpelt leaped down from the branch and ran to the entrance of the camp, his tail waving. "I will lead my warriors into battle, to honor my father who was the greatest leader SkyClan has ever known!"

And who would know better than to set out before checking the height of the river, Robinwing thought.

The warriors streamed out of the camp, apprentices racing to keep up without tripping over branches brought down by the weight of sodden leaves. Storms this late in greenleaf were dangerous because water wasn't the only thing to fall from the sky. Robinwing dropped back to give his own apprentice a shove over a slippery tree trunk. Rubblepaw's fur was slicked to his sides, black with rain and streaked with mud and scraps of moss.

Rubblepaw looked up at Robinwing and blinked raindrops

from his eyes. "I feel like I'm going to drown before I get to the river!" he spluttered.

And I'm afraid you'll drown when you get there. "You're doing great. Just follow the warriors," Robinwing told him. Picking up his pace, he squeezed past the other cats until he was at the front, next to Maplewhisker.

"What do you think the river's like today?" he asked as quietly as he could between panting for breath.

She gave a tiny shake of her head. "We'll see when we get there."

Suddenly they burst out of the trees and their paws crunched on pebbles that sloped steeply down to the edge of the water. Robinwing stopped and stared in horror. The river was swollen to twice its size; the shore was no more than a narrow strip of pebbles, barely a fox-length wide, and the crossing stones were marked only by flashes of white water where the waves broke over the top.

"SkyClan, attack!" yowled Mothpelt, rushing toward the river.

Robinwing glanced at Maplewhisker, who looked as horrified as he felt. RiverClan wouldn't need to fight them; they could just sit on the far bank and watch the floodwater carry the SkyClan cats away. Beechstar would not have wanted his Clan to die like this!

"Mothpelt, stop!" Robinwing screeched. He flung himself across the stones and brought his Clan leader crashing down, careful to keep his claws sheathed.

"What in the name of StarClan . . . ?" spat Mothpelt. "Robinwing, let me go! Since when were you such a coward?"

Robinwing let his leader stand up, but positioned himself between Mothpelt and the river. Behind the leader, the SkyClan cats lined up, their expressions ranging from angry to bewildered to relieved. "I won't let you cross the river," Robinwing meowed. "It's too dangerous."

"Get out of my way," Mothpelt growled. "Or have you turned traitor and joined RiverClan?"

"I am as loyal to SkyClan as I ever was," Robinwing replied, keeping his voice even. "Too loyal to watch my Clanmates drown before they have a chance to fight. We can fight this battle another day."

"No! This battle will be fought now, before the memory of my father fades in our hearts. His death must be avenged!"

"Not if it means other SkyClan cats die!" Robinwing protested, but Mothpelt was already pushing past him and plunging into the water. Almost at once, a wave broke over his head and he disappeared, but then he bobbed up farther into the river, his ears twitching as he struck out for the first crossing stone. White water spat in his face but he screwed up his eyes and clung to the rock with his claws until he could drag himself onto it and stand belly-deep in churning foam.

"Come on!" he yowled. "All those SkyClan cats who wish to avenge our leader's death, follow me!"

Robinwing watched helplessly as at least half of his fellow warriors and their apprentices ran past him and splashed into the river.

"No!" he yowled, watching as they floundered in the icy water.

Robinwing turned to face Maplewhisker, reading in her eyes that she was torn between loyalty to her leader and fear for her Clanmates in the swollen river. "It looks like Mothpelt is all right for now, as long as he stays on that rock," Robinwing meowed. "We'll have to get the others out before they go under."

The cats who hadn't rushed into the river were creeping forward, their eyes huge as they watched their Clanmates struggle. Rubblepaw came up to Robinwing. "We have to help them!" he gasped.

"Yes, we do," Robinwing agreed. "Maplewhisker, do you agree?"

She nodded. "Warriors and apprentices of SkyClan!" she called, addressing the cats on the shore. "Our Clanmates are in danger from the flooded river. No cat must go into the water without having two other cats in a chain behind. No apprentices must go near the water. Rescue the cats closest to the shore first; don't take unnecessary risks." She glanced at Robinwing. "Do you think that will work?"

"Definitely." He touched her shoulder with the tip of his tail, wanting to know how proud he was of her right now. "I'll form a chain with Rubblepaw and Spiderpelt. You stay on the shore and watch out for cats who need help most quickly." He watched her run along the shore, encouraging cats to join into chains. Then he flicked his tail at Spiderpelt. "Come on. You take my tail, and Rubblepaw will take yours."

"Ready?" Robinwing called, and the other cats nodded. Taking a deep breath, he jumped over a wave and landed up to his chin in icy cold water. He flailed his legs, pulling himself toward the middle of the river. On either side of him, other warriors did the same, their necks strained to keep their muzzles above the surface. A red-brown shape bobbed on the other side of a wave. Robinwing held his breath as the wave swept over his head, then struck out toward the shape. It was Squirrelfur. His eyes were closed and he looked exhausted as he battled to stay afloat.

"Don't struggle," Robinwing panted before biting deep into Squirrelfur's scruff. At once, he felt his tail being tugged, and he was pulled back toward the shore, dragging Squirrelfur with him. Maplewhisker was standing belly-deep at the edge of the river; she grabbed Squirrelfur's scruff on the other side and nodded to

Robinwing that she had a firm hold on him. Robinwing plunged back into the river.

One more warrior and two apprentices soon stood shivering on the bank, with Rubblepaw glaring sideways at them as if he held them responsible for his mentor risking his life to save them.

"You've done enough," Maplewhisker urged Robinwing as he crouched on the stones, coughing up river water. He shook his head.

"I have to fetch Mothpelt," he gulped. The leader was still clinging to the crossing stone, watching silent and wide-eyed as his Clanmates were rescued from the angry river. Robinwing knew he would be too cold and exhausted to make it back to the shore without help.

"Promise me one thing," he meowed. Maplewhisker looked puzzled. "Promise me you'll be the new leader of SkyClan."

"I can't do that!" Maplewhisker protested.

"You have to. And with the support of your Clanmates, you will," Robinwing told her. He flicked his tail at the cats around them, staggering onto dry ground with grateful glances at their deputy for organizing the rescue patrol.

"I'll support you," Spiderpelt offered.

"And me," Rubblepaw put in.

"Our Clanmates aren't mouse-brained," Robinwing murmured. "They respected you as their deputy, and they'll respect you as our leader. And they'll respect Mothpelt as a warrior."

Maplewhisker looked once more at her sodden Clanmates, then nodded. "And I'm not mouse-brained enough to think that my Clan doesn't need me. If Mothpelt agrees, then I'll lead SkyClan."

"In that case, we'd better fetch him," Robinwing meowed. He glanced at Spiderpelt and Rubblepaw. "Ready?"

"Lead on," Spiderpelt meowed, and Robinwing plunged back into the waves. SkyClan would be safe under Maplestar's leadership. And Robinwing would suggest that a new rule be introduced to the warrior code: that deputies replaced leaders when they lost their ninth life, as the cats most used to leadership and dealing with rival Clans.

Too Late for Regrets:
Tallstar Explains

In StarClan there is plenty of time for fallen leaders to think over the decisions they made when they ruled their living Clanmates, and there is no escaping judgment as they watch over the consequences. Listen as Tallstar, the fallen WindClan leader, talks to Bluestar about one such decision, still hoping that it was the right one.

Bluestar? May I speak with you, my friend? My thoughts trouble me and keep me from sleeping.

You think I made a mistake, don't you? You may shake your head, but I can tell by your eyes that you're afraid of what I have done. Would you have let Mudclaw take over your Clan? Why? Because it was the only way to fulfill the warrior code and the expectations of all your Clanmates? But my vision, Bluestar, I cannot forget my vision. I dreamed of a hillside stained with blood, of cats wailing

for their kits and of warriors who had to watch their life drain out onto the grass. I could not tell who was fighting whom, just that every cat in WindClan had suffered a loss from an unjust battle. And looking down on it all from the crest of the hill was Mudclaw—Mudstar, now, leader of WindClan—because I had let him remain as my deputy. How could I let that happen?

I know my Clanmates assumed my reasoning was muddled because my final life was slipping away. Even your Clanmates Firestar and Brambleclaw looked at me with pity as they pretended to support my change of heart. I didn't have enough breath, enough words left to explain what I had just seen behind my closed eyes. I died knowing that my Clan might hate me for changing everything so late—and knowing that I had no choice. Onewhisker would have been as good a deputy as Mudclaw, and he will make a great leader.

I know you think that I'm an arrogant old cat who has made everything much, much worse by giving my Clan a leader they were not prepared for. But it was the only way to save them!

I know that WindClan will be safe under Onewhisker. He will have to prove his strength one day; every leader does. And if I was wrong, if I should have let Mudclaw succeed me because he was my deputy first, then it's too late. What's done is done. I didn't come to StarClan to regret my last decision as leader of WindClan. Whatever happens, it cannot be worse than the fate WindClan would have suffered if Mudclaw had remained.

CODE NINE

AFTER THE DEATH OR RETIREMENT
OF THE DEPUTY, THE NEW DEPUTY MUST BE
CHOSEN BEFORE MOONHIGH.

*It may seem callous to cats like you that a new deputy
is named over the body of the old one. Would you prefer to grieve
for one cat before passing your loyalties to another?
As you are about to see, dwelling in the past is not a luxury
warrior cats have; we must face the future.
The time for mourning will come.*

A Sign from StarClan

Redscar studied the spluttering, hunched cat in front of him and shook his head. "You can't go to the Moonstone today, Brightwhisker. You wouldn't make it as far as the Thunderpath."

Brightwhisker paused to gulp in air, then protested, "But I have to go! I have to receive my nine lives and my new name from StarClan!"

"StarClan will be perfectly aware of how sick you are," Redscar pointed out. "They won't want you to exhaust yourself so soon. Your Clan needs you whole and well. They have already accepted you as their leader."

The brown-and-white she-cat's eyes clouded. "They mourn for Snowstar as much as I do. I wish I was still his deputy."

"Snowstar will be mourned for many moons, but that can't stop us from doing our duty. And yours," Redscar added, "is to get rid of this whitecough so you can be fit and strong to lead your Clan."

"Are you sure it's whitecough? Could it be greencough, like Snowstar had?"

"It's whitecough, definitely," Redscar meowed. "Now, lie down and rest."

"But I need to appoint a deputy, too," Brightwhisker protested, lapsing into a fit of coughing.

"It can wait until you can do it without coughing in his or her face. I'll bring you some tansy to soothe your chest and a poppy seed to help you sleep."

When he returned, Brightwhisker was curled in her nest, her flank rising and falling evenly. She didn't stir, so he decided not to wake her. He left the tansy leaves and the poppy seed beside a clump of moss soaked with water. Stretching the stiffness from his legs one paw at a time, he picked his way across the rutted, half-frozen clearing and headed for his nest of crow feathers and dry bracken. Darkness claimed him as soon as he closed his eyes.

"Redscar! Redscar! Come quickly!"

Redscar shot out of his nest and pushed his way into the open. Flowerstem was staring at him as if all the foxes of the forest were on her tail. "I can't wake Brightwhisker!" she wailed.

Every hair on Redscar's pelt stood on end. He'd left her only one poppy seed, barely enough for a whole night's sleep.

"Come see," Flowerstem pleaded, but Redscar was already pushing past her, heading for the leader's den. It was dark inside, and Redscar had to blink and wait impatiently for his eyes to adjust. Slowly he made out Brightwhisker's sleeping shape. She didn't seem to have moved since he last checked on her.

Oh, StarClan, don't let her be dead!

Redscar pushed his nose into her neck fur, but there was no sign of the telltale throb of life beneath the skin, and her fur was as cold as frost.

"Redscar?" Flowerstem was standing in the entrance to the den.

He turned to her and shook his head. Another leader had died, before she'd had a chance to receive her nine lives.

"Oh, no!" Flowerstem wailed.

A tortoiseshell head appeared behind her. "What's wrong?"

"Oh, Mossfire!" Flowerstem turned to face her littermate. "Brightwhisker's dead!"

Redscar padded out of the den, his paws heavy as stone. "She must have developed greencough in the night. She died in her sleep."

Mossfire stared at him. "But . . . she never chose a deputy! Who will be our leader now?"

Redscar knew he had to help his Clan find a way out of this terrible darkness. "I'll call the cats together," he meowed.

He chose to stay on the ground rather than stand on the fallen log that the leaders had used to address the Clan. Brightwhisker had taken her place there only once, to greet her Clan for the first time since Snowstar's death; a fit of coughing had stopped her, and Redscar had ordered her back to her den. *I should have known it was greencough! There must have been something else I could have done.*

Like let her appoint a deputy? a small voice inside him challenged.

Redscar pushed it away. "Cats of ShadowClan, Brightwhisker is dead. There will be time to grieve for her, but first we must choose a new leader. Are there any cats who wish to volunteer?"

His Clanmates shifted restlessly and there were worried murmurs, but no cat spoke out until Jumpfoot stepped forward. His muscles rippled under his black pelt, and his green eyes were somber. "I will lead ShadowClan, if my Clanmates wish it."

There were several yowls of approval, but some murmurs of disagreement. "We think Mossfire should be leader," called one of the queens. "Jumpfoot is too quick to go into battle. We want peace for our kits."

Mossfire walked forward to stand beside Jumpfoot. She dipped her head to Redscar. "My Clanmates honor me, and I would be willing to be their leader."

"Not all of them want you," snarled Jumpfoot. "Who'd want a Clan full of cowards, too frightened to defend their borders?"

"Not rushing into every battle doesn't make me a coward," Mossfire retorted. "I can fight as well as you any day."

"Prove it," Jumpfoot challenged.

"This is no way to choose a leader!" Flowerstem cried.

Jumpfoot glared at her. "We'll fight, and whichever cat StarClan favors will be victorious."

Flowerstem looked pleadingly at Redscar, but he felt frozen. What was happening to his Clan?

Jumpfoot and Mossfire started circling each other; the other cats moved back to give them more room. Mossfire struck first, with an easy swipe that Jumpfoot sprang away from with a contemptuous hiss. "You'll have to do better than that!"

"Very well," spat Mossfire, and she leaped at him, front legs outstretched, claws glinting in the frosty sun. She raked a set of scratches into Jumpfoot's flank, leaving scarlet beads of blood.

With a yowl, Jumpfoot spun around and slashed at her face, then sank his claws into her shoulder and rolled her onto the ground, pummeling at her with his hind legs.

Redscar turned away. He could not believe StarClan wanted two warriors to fight like this in order to lead their Clan. He winced as he heard Mossfire gasp with pain and the sound of ripping fur as she retaliated. There was a thud as Jumpfoot went down and a gasp from the watching cats. Then another, softer thud as Mossfire crumpled beside him.

"Mossfire! No!" That was Flowerstem.

The stench of blood told Redscar what he would see. He turned around. The two cats were lying still as their lives ebbed away from blows struck too close, too hard. Redscar felt numb. He had failed, again.

Three elders were already shuffling forward to rearrange the bodies for their Clanmates' vigil. It would last all night, and then what? ShadowClan still had no leader. The cats were silent, moving slowly as if their limbs had frozen, none quite meeting another's eye. *The blood of these cats stains all our paws.*

Flowerstem alone seemed to have her voice; she wove among the stunned cats, comforting them, sending them to the fresh-kill pile to eat: "We have to keep up our strength. There is still sickness in the air; no more cats must die." Quietly she asked two of the senior warriors to take out hunting patrols with all the apprentices. "There is no need for them to spend all day looking at these fallen warriors. Keep them busy, but battle training would not be appropriate, I think." Her Clanmates nodded and led the younger cats silently out of the clearing.

Then Flowerstem approached Redscar. Her eyes looked dull with shock, but she spoke calmly. "Is there anything I can do for you, Redscar? Fetch herbs or water?"

Redscar shook his head. There was nothing any cat could do. "I'll be in my den," he told her and headed for the thicket of hawthorn that screened his nest and his store of herbs. He stumbled into his nest, feeling many seasons older than he had when he last lay down, and closed his eyes.

"Redscar? Redscar, wake up."

He opened his eyes. He was lying in a clearing among beech trees, their branches black and sharp against the snow-colored sky. The grass beneath him was crisp and cold; he jumped up, shivering.

"Redscar, you must find a new leader for ShadowClan."

"Snowstar?"

The gray cat nodded. "I have been watching my Clan, and I grieve for every one of my cats. Most of all, for Brightwhisker, who would have been a great leader, and for Jumpfoot and Mossfire who let ambition cloud their senses and sharpen their claws. You must put this right, my friend."

"What can I do?" Redscar wailed.

"You will choose a new leader," Snowstar meowed. "And that cat must choose a deputy at once. A Clan must never be left like this again, a headless creature that wades into blood because it cannot see. At the next Gathering, the new leader must introduce a new rule for the warrior code: Deputies must be replaced by moonhigh, so a leader will never be alone for more than half a day. Now tell me, who would you choose as your next leader?"

Redscar started to protest that he couldn't, wouldn't, choose, but the look in Snowstar's eyes silenced him. "Flowerstem," he meowed. "She watched her sister die in front of her, but her only thoughts were to make the Clan feel safe and keep them occupied before tonight's vigil."

"A wise choice. So tell the Clan."

Redscar stared at him. "Why should they listen to me? I've done nothing for them, nothing."

Snowstar narrowed his eyes. "You're their medicine cat. They will listen to you, if you use the right words." The beech trees were looking paler now, blurring against the white clouds. Snowstar was fading, too. "Go now, Redscar," he called. "Appoint Flowerstem as the new leader of ShadowClan!"

Redscar blinked and he was back in his nest with a crow feather tickling his ear. He shook his head irritably. The Clan was in turmoil. They must think their warrior ancestors had given up on them.

No words, but maybe an action?

He padded into the clearing. The camp was quiet and deserted, apart from the bodies of Mossfire and Jumpfoot lying in the shelter of some dry bracken. He slipped out of the camp and trotted to a place where an oak tree grew on ground that was less marshy than the rest of the territory. Mossfire and Jumpfoot would be buried near here. At the foot of the tree, sheltered from the wind, grew a bunch of delicate white flowers, the color of snow and the shape of raindrops.

Checking there were no cats around, he nipped one of the snowdrops off at the base of its stalk. Laying it on the ground, he pulled off the smooth white petals, leaving just the stem. Then he curled it up and pushed it into a clump of moss that he dug up from underneath a tree root. Picking up the moss in his teeth, he headed back for the camp. No cat would question a medicine cat fetching moss; it was used for bedding as well as to carry water.

When he returned to the camp, there were more cats around. The hunting patrols had come back with a fair haul of fresh-kill, and pale sunlight had tempted their Clanmates out to eat. Redscar nodded to one or two as he crossed the clearing. As he passed the fallen log used by the leaders to address the Clan, he relaxed his grip on the moss and felt the snowdrop stalk spring out. Quick as lightning, he dropped the moss and kicked it with his paw so that it rolled underneath a hawthorn, out of sight.

"Look!" he cried, gazing down at the pale green stem lying at his paws. It was as slim as a whisker, still quivering from where it had uncurled. "Did any cat bring this into the camp?"

His Clanmates gathered around. "It's a snowdrop stalk. They only grow by the oak tree, right?" meowed one of the apprentices.

Redscar lifted his head and faced them. His paws were shaking but he sank his claws into the earth to keep them still. "It's a sign from StarClan," he announced. "They want us to know their choice for the new ShadowClan leader."

"Who?" gasped a she-cat plump with kits.

Redscar touched the stalk with his paw. "Flowerstem."

There was a gasp, then murmurs of agreement.

The ginger-and-white she-cat was pushed to the front of the cats. She looked dazed. "I don't know what to say," she began.

"Just say you will lead us, as StarClan wishes," meowed Redscar.

Flowerstem looked down at the snowdrop stalk, then over her shoulder at her motionless sister. "To honor Mossfire's memory and Jumpfoot's, yes, I will." She dipped her head as joyful yowls rose around her.

Maybe StarClan had needed Redscar's help to send this sign, but it was what Snowstar wanted. And he would tell Flowerstar to choose her deputy before the moon reached its height, in front of the bodies of her fallen Clanmates, and Brightwhisker, so that their spirits could hear and approve her choice.

"Thank you, Snowstar," he whispered.

CODE TEN

A GATHERING OF ALL CLANS IS HELD AT THE FULL MOON DURING A TRUCE THAT LASTS FOR THE NIGHT. THERE SHALL BE NO FIGHTING AMONG CLANS AT THIS TIME.

Even though the Gatherings started with the very beginning of the warrior code, the full-moon truce did not become part of the code until much later. Now the truce is respected by every cat, whether it is because they value the chance to exchange news in peace with their close neighbors, or because they are afraid of what their warrior ancestors might do if they break the code. Come with me to Fourtrees long ago, when the ancestors first looked down on the full-moon gathering and bound the Clan cats to the full-moon truce.

The Vanishing Moon

The four giant oaks cast thick shadows across the moon-washed clearing as Finchstar crouched at the top of the slope. Behind him, his Clanmates waited, the air clouded with their breath. Several cats dotted the hollow already, circling to keep warm as they exchanged cautious greetings with warriors from rival Clans.

"Come on, ThunderClan!" Finchstar called. He stood up and began to run down the slope, stretching his tail up so his Clanmates could follow.

"Good," muttered Daisyheart, his deputy, as she bounded beside him. "If I'd stayed still much longer I'd have turned into an icicle."

Frost crackled under Finchstar's paws as he jumped onto the flat stretch of grass. Two WindClan elders nodded to him and a RiverClan warrior called a greeting as he wove his way through the cats to the Great Rock.

"How's the prey running, Finchstar?" SkyClan's leader, Hawkstar, asked as he leaped onto the top of the smooth silver boulder.

"Fast," he replied. "It doesn't like being out in this weather any more than we do!"

"Our rabbits run so quickly, they're nothing but muscle and bone when we catch them," Dovestar, the WindClan leader, put in. "So tough to chew!"

The RiverClan leader, Reedstar, said nothing. He was sitting on the far side of the rock, as far from Hawkstar as he could get without falling off. Their Clans had been at war over a strip of shoreline for almost three seasons; one battle had led to the death of SkyClan's former leader, Dewstar, and his Clanmates were far from forgiving their rivals across the water.

Finchstar looked down at the clearing. "ShadowClan not here yet? It's not like Ripplestar to be late."

Dovestar lifted his haunches off the stone and settled down again with his tail curled up. "I'll stick to this rock if we don't start soon. It's colder than ice."

Reedstar shifted, sending his shadow flickering over the

edge of the boulder, crisp in the moonlight. "Maybe the frost has delayed them?"

The tip of Hawkstar's tail twitched. "Something's wrong," he murmured. "My pelt's been itching all day."

"Fleas," muttered Reedstar.

Finchstar glared at him. It was full moon, the one night they were supposed to put their rivalry aside and share news for the good of all the Clans.

There was a hiss like wind at the edge of the clearing. Finchstar pricked his ears and stared into the moon shadows. Was that a branch waving in the breeze, or something more?

Why does Fourtrees suddenly feel unsafe?

"ShadowClan! Attack!"

The shadows exploded, spitting and yowling. The cats in the clearing whirled to face them, but before they could brace themselves, ShadowClan warriors fell on them, claws and fangs bared. Within a heartbeat, the hollow thrashed and rippled like a river full of salmon. The leaders of the Clans stood on the edge of Great Rock, staring down in horror. Then Reedstar leaped down, quickly followed by Hawkstar and Dovestar. Finchstar heard them screech orders to their senior warriors, splitting them into battle groups to defend the elders and apprentices who had come to the Gathering.

A ginger-and-white face flashed up at Finchstar from the turmoil at the foot of the rock.

"Help us, Finchstar!" Daisyheart wailed, before she whipped around to claw a ShadowClan warrior over his ears.

Finchstar bunched his haunches, ready to jump down, when a shadow fell across him. He looked up. Ripplestar stood beside him on the Great Rock, his yellow eyes glowing as they watched the battle.

CODE
10

"I bet you never thought I'd do it," he meowed, so quietly Finchstar could hardly hear him over the screeches and yowls from below.

"Do what? Attack four Clans when they came in peace to a Gathering, with elders among them?" Finchstar hissed. "No, Ripplestar. I never thought you'd be as cowardly as that."

The black-and-orange cat lashed his tail. "Hardly the actions of a coward, to take on all four Clans at once!"

Slipping his claws free, Finchstar sprang at Ripplestar, bringing him down on top of the rock with a muffled thud. The ShadowClan leader squirmed around until he was lying on his back, then raked Finchstar's belly with his hind paws. Finchstar sank his claws deeper into the loose fur around Ripplestar's neck, feeling the slender bones underneath.

"Call off your cats!" he spat. "This attack is wrong!"

Ripplestar scrabbled to his feet and glared at Finchstar. "I wouldn't call an easy victory wrong," he gloated. "Look at your precious cats now."

Finchstar risked a sideways look. The battle was slowing; many cats were slumped on the silver grass, bleeding and motionless. ShadowClan warriors paced among them, ready to lash out if any cat stirred.

"No!" Finchstar yowled. "You can't do this!"

He jumped at Ripplestar but his hind paws skidded on the icy rock, and the ShadowClan leader stepped easily out of the way.

"So you keep telling me," Ripplestar observed. "But I seem to have done it anyway! Looks like I don't have to listen to you, Finchstar."

For a heartbeat, the hollow glowed bright white, outlining every leaf, every blade of grass, every whisker. Then the air cracked, and the two cats on the rock flung themselves down, clinging to the stone as it trembled beneath them. Finchstar pressed his face into the cold surface and waited for the roll of thunder to fade away. A storm in leaf-bare? But there were no clouds. The moon was out. . . .

"Finchstar!" His name was barely a whisper, drowned by another clap of thunder slamming into the forest.

Finchstar forced himself to lift his head. His eyes were still dazzled by the first flash of lightning and he had to blink to see clearly. The clearing was much darker than before, so dark he couldn't see Ripplestar. The moon had vanished. The sky was covered with thick black clouds.

Finchstar shook his head, waiting for his eyes to adjust. He could make out the trees now and the shape of the Great Rock beneath him. But still no Ripplestar.

"Help . . . me. . . ."

A scratching sound came from the edge of the rock. Finchstar saw Ripplestar's yellow eyes staring over the top and his black-and-orange paws.

"Hold on!" Finchstar yowled. He hurled himself across the stone, reaching out with his front paws to grab Ripplestar's scruff and haul him to safety.

He was a mouse-length away when the sky burst open again, filling the air with blazing white light and letting out a roar that sounded like every tree in the forest was falling at once. Finchstar crashed down onto the rock and pressed his paws into his ears, trying to block the explosion of noise that bounced around the hollow. He heard a thin, terrified wail as Ripplestar lost his grip and plunged to the ground.

The clearing was silent. The cats still on their paws were staring at something Finchstar couldn't see, at the foot of Great

CODE
10

Rock. Then a heavily scarred gray warrior rushed forward.

"Ripplestar! No!"

Finchstar bowed his head. The ShadowClan leader must have been on his ninth life. He was young to die as a leader, but perhaps his battle-hungry career had used up the rest of his lives too quickly.

"Murderer!"

The gray warrior—Marshscar, the ShadowClan deputy, Finchstar suddenly realized—was glaring up at him.

"Come down here and let me avenge our leader's death!" Marshscar snarled.

"I didn't kill Ripplestar!" Finchstar told him, feeling the fur rise along his spine.

"Then who did?" the gray cat challenged.

Finchstar looked up at the bubbling clouds that hid the full moon. The truce had been broken the moment Ripplestar told his warriors to attack the unsuspecting Clans. Then the moon disappeared and a storm came, bringing thunder and lightning that shook the forest to its roots.

"StarClan killed him," Finchstar announced. His paws trembled. Would his warrior ancestors forgive him for accusing them of cold-blooded murder? But the sky stayed quiet.

"StarClan has punished ShadowClan for breaking the truce and attacking on the night of a full moon," Finchstar went on. "There is no clearer message they could send."

A pale brown tabby from RiverClan stepped forward. "StarClan, forgive us all for fighting!" he yowled.

"From now on, the full moon will be honored by every Clan!" Dovestar called.

Finchstar stepped to the edge of the rock and raised his voice so every cat could hear him. There would be time afterward to tend to the wounded and carry them home. For now, he had to make sure this would never happen again.

"There will be a new rule in the warrior code!" he declared. "There will be no fighting at the time of the new moon. The truce is sacred and will be protected for every Gathering."

StarClan, forgive us.

CODE ELEVEN

BOUNDARIES MUST BE CHECKED
AND MARKED DAILY. CHALLENGE ALL
TRESPASSING CATS.

*Not all parts of the warrior code come from
tragedy and conflict. Some, like this one, were needed to
clear up a long-running misunderstanding and avoid
the need for blood to be spilled.*

Poppycloud's Rule

The air was so still, Poppycloud could hear herself breathing. She waited with one paw raised, knowing the dried leaves would crackle loud as thunder as soon as she set it down. It was leaf-fall, and in SkyClan, with all its trees and little undergrowth, moving silently was almost impossible. The hair along her spine prickled as she strained to listen.

"Can you hear anything, Poppycloud? Can you, can you?"

Bracken rustled behind her and she turned, resigned, as a small black-and-white cat exploded from the brittle stems.

"Yes, Mottlepaw, I can hear something," she meowed.

The apprentice stopped dead and stared at her. "Really? What?"

"*You!*"

Mottlepaw's tail drooped. "But I tried to be quiet, like you showed me."

Poppycloud walked over to him and touched the tip of his ear with her nose. "I think we need to practice some more."

Mottlepaw wriggled free and padded up to the border. "Why does Rowanstar make us come this way when he knows ThunderClan doesn't like it?"

Poppycloud shrugged and nudged a piece of leaf off her tortoiseshell fur. "I think he likes to know if anything happens in our territory. If we just stuck to the best hunting areas, we'd never visit some places."

"Like this one." Mottlepaw's voice was muffled as he stuck his head into a clump of long grass. "I can't smell any birds *anywhere!*"

"That's because you're in ThunderClan territory!" came a snarl.

Poppycloud spun around. A broad-shouldered brown tom stood a fox-length away, his lip curled to reveal sharp yellow teeth.

"What a surprise!" he hissed. "SkyClan cats lurking on the border again. What's wrong with your own territory?"

Poppycloud felt her hackles raise. "Nothing!" she retorted. "We have every right to go anywhere inside our borders."

"Which your apprentice isn't," the ThunderClan warrior growled.

Mottlepaw pulled back from the clump of grass and stood with his head down, trembling.

CODE
11

"Mottlepaw, come over here," Poppycloud ordered. The black-and-white apprentice shot toward her, swerving around the ThunderClan tom, who hissed as he went past.

"It was a mistake," Poppycloud pointed out. "We weren't trying to steal your prey."

Ferns parted and another cat joined the brown warrior. She fixed her startlingly green gaze on Poppycloud. "Why are there always SkyClan cats snooping around here? Is your own Clan so bad that you want to join ours?"

"Never!" Poppycloud retorted. "We prefer not to chew through mouthfuls of fur when we're eating our prey!"

The brown tom tipped his head to one side. "Oh, and feathers are so much tastier, are they?"

"Come on, Oatwhisker," urged the she-cat. "We're wasting our time. If these dumb cats want to spy on us, they won't learn much from the bushes around here. I don't think I've even been to this part of the territory before."

Oatwhisker narrowed his eyes at Poppycloud. "Don't think this is over. I'm going to tell Lionstar I caught SkyClan cats hanging around the border yet again, and I wouldn't want to be in your pelts if he thinks you're planning an attack."

He stalked out of the clearing with his green-eyed Clanmate. As soon as they had vanished, Poppycloud turned to Mottlepaw. "How many times do I have to tell you? You can't go into another Clan's territory!"

Mottlepaw sniffed. "I wasn't doing anything wrong," he complained. "Anyway, it's so hard to tell where our territory turns into ThunderClan's. It's not like there's a river in the way!"

Poppycloud opened her jaws to taste the air. Mottlepaw was right: The scents of the different Clans were very faint here, so she couldn't blame her apprentice for straying too far. "Come on," she meowed. "We'd better go and tell Rowanstar what happened, in case ThunderClan makes a fuss."

"He won't be angry with me, will he?" Mottlepaw whimpered. "I already had to put mouse bile on the elders' ticks after I scared Morningmist's kits with my tiger roar."

"I'll tell him it was an honest mistake," Poppycloud promised. "Just try not to get into any more trouble on the way back."

"Tell Rowanstar that we wish to speak with him."

A buzz of curiosity ran through the camp.

"Who's that?"

"ThunderClan cats!"

"What do they want?"

"Have they come to get me?"

Poppycloud looked down at Mottlepaw, who was staring at her with his blue eyes stretched wide. "I'm sure they haven't come to get you," she meowed. "But I'm glad we told Rowanstar what happened on the border."

Oddfoot, a brown tabby who was born with one of his paws twisted inward, led the visitors into the clearing. A massive tom with long ginger hair padded beside him, flanked by the green-eyed gray tabby Poppycloud had met on the border and a dark brown tom who looked as if he expected to be jumped on at any moment. Poppycloud drew in her breath sharply: This must be serious if Lionstar had come himself.

Nightmask, the SkyClan deputy, met them in the center of the camp. "Lionstar, Greeneyes," he greeted them with a nod of his head. Poppycloud stared at the gray tabby with new interest; she hadn't realized this was the recently appointed ThunderClan deputy.

"You are, of course, welcome to speak with Rowanstar. Will he know what this is about?"

CODE 11

Greeneyes curled her lip. "It's about your warriors spying on us!" she hissed.

Lionstar flicked his tail, warning her to stay quiet. "I am concerned that there are always SkyClan cats on the edge of our territory, and I want to know what they're doing there."

"I think you'll find they're on the edge of our territory," came a deep voice. Rowanstar, his black-and-brown coat gleaming in the weak sunlight, padded out of his den. "So there shouldn't be any problem."

"But there's nothing there!" Lionstar argued. "Nothing but the start of ThunderClan's territory."

Rowanstar glanced at Poppycloud. "From what I hear, it's not always easy to tell where your territory begins. Perhaps if you visited your border more often, your scent would be clearer."

Lionstar's hackles raised, swelling him to nearly twice his size. Mottlepaw shrank behind Poppycloud with a whimper.

"ThunderClan should not have to patrol its boundaries to make sure SkyClan isn't trespassing!" Lionstar growled.

"If you patrolled more often, there would be less danger of us crossing the border!" Rowanstar flashed back.

Greeneyes stepped forward. "The warrior code says nothing about it being a Clan's responsibility to keep cats out! It should be obvious that other Clans aren't allowed across the border."

"Well, maybe the code should say something!"

All eyes turned on Poppycloud. She snapped her mouth shut, feeling as if her pelt were on fire. *Did I really just say that in front of the leaders of two Clans?*

"Yay! Go, Poppycloud!" Mottlepaw cheered behind her. Poppycloud silenced him with a glare.

Rowanstar put his head to one side. "That's an interesting

theory, Poppycloud. Go on."

Poppycloud felt a small nose nudge her from behind. She shot a fierce glance at her apprentice before padding into the clearing. Every cat watched her. Greeneyes looked scornful;  this made Poppycloud square her shoulders and tilt her chin defiantly toward the ThunderClan deputy.

"I . . . I just think all the quarreling about SkyClan being on the ThunderClan border would be cleared up if every Clan did the same as Rowanstar wants us to do: have regular patrols around the entire territory. That way, the scents of each Clan would be left behind more frequently, not just in the places where the cats hunt most often, and boundaries would be more clearly marked. Any cats that crossed over the border could be punished, because it wouldn't be a mistake."

Rowanstar nodded. "And if both ThunderClan and SkyClan patrols regularly went along our shared border, then neither Clan could be accused of spying or trying to trespass." He flicked his tail at Poppycloud. "That's a great idea."

Lionstar hissed. "So you think the warrior code should tell us how to defend our territories, do you? What kind of leader would be mouse-brained enough to need instructions like that?"

"The kind of leader who thinks that a patrol walking along their own boundaries is planning an attack," Rowanstar meowed smoothly.

"Well, I think it's a ridiculous idea," sniffed Greeneyes. "The Clans have lived in these territories for more moons than any cat can remember, and we've never needed the warrior code to tell us how to protect our borders. Clearly some cats are more mouse-brained than others."

Slanting her eyes at Poppycloud, she turned away with a huff.

Lionstar started to turn and follow his deputy, but Rowanstar called out, "Wait!" When Lionstar faced him again, the SkyClan leader announced, "I shall put forward Poppycloud's idea at the next Gathering. We should let the other leaders decide—not because I think any Clan cat needs to be reminded that their territories should be well defended, but because it will stop needless suspicion over border patrols."

Lionstar stretched one forepaw and let his claws slide out. "You do realize that if the other leaders agree to this ridiculous rule, then I'll be allowed to tear the fur off any of your apprentices who just happen to cross our border?"

From the corner of her eye, Poppycloud saw Mottlepaw back into the brambles that surrounded the apprentices' den, until only his white patches could be seen.

Rowanstar didn't flinch. "And we'd punish any ThunderClan cats who trespassed," he meowed. "The situation will be clear and fair—like the boundaries."

Lionstar spun around and started to stalk toward the entrance. "Until the next Gathering, Rowanstar. We'll see what the other Clans think of your idea then."

"Indeed we will," Rowanstar murmured as the ThunderClan cats were swallowed up by the bracken.

Poppycloud watched until the fronds of bracken stopped trembling. *If this becomes part of the warrior code, I will live forever!* She shook her head to chase away such huge dreams and looked for Mottlepaw. Adding rules to the warrior code was kit's play compared with trying to keep her apprentice in line. But he was a quick learner and would one day make a warrior to be proud of.

Not that I could be any prouder of him than I am already, as his mother as well as his mentor. With a soft purr of amusement, she went in search of her unruly son.

✤

Who Goes There? Whitestorm Teaches Border Tactics

Once the borders were fixed, cats of neighboring Clans started to meet frequently across their borders when on patrol. It became apparent that cats of all Clans must know how to handle disputes. Here's Whitestorm training a group of ThunderClan apprentices in border tactics.

Is every cat here? Firepaw, Graypaw, Ravenpaw, Sandpaw, and Dustpaw? Dustpaw, stop trying to push Firepaw into the brambles. I'm not blind; I can see what you're doing. Firepaw, go to the other end of the line. Sandpaw, he does *not* have fleas! Stand still, all of you.

As Lionheart told you, we're going to practice border defense today. You can be the patrol, and I'll be a deputy from another Clan who's crossed the boundary. Who'd like to lead the patrol? Don't look so terrified, Ravenpaw. I won't make you be the leader if you don't want to be. Graypaw, why don't you have first turn? If you could just pick up that stick in your mouth and use it to draw a line across the sand, we'll call that the border. Sandpaw, it doesn't matter that the line is wobbly. Boundaries aren't whisker-straight, are they? So, you're on that side, walking along on a dawn patrol. Off you go, patrol!

Did you really need to yawn like that, Graypaw? Oh, I see, it's because it's the dawn patrol, and you're tired. Well, let's pretend you all had a really good night's sleep and are full of energy. Now, what should you be doing?

Yes, sniffing, tasting the air—what for? That's right, Sandpaw. ThunderClan border marks. And what else? Yes, Firepaw. The border marks of the other Clan. But only where the two borders meet. Beside the river and the Thunderpath, it would be bad news to find any scents of RiverClan or ShadowClan, because it would mean they'd crossed over from their side. So keep sniffing.

Maybe not that much, Sandpaw. Have a good sneeze and you should get the sand out of your nose. So, border marks, border marks. Can you smell both sets? Good. But what's this? A cat from another Clan has ignored the marks and stepped over your border?

No, Ravenpaw, I didn't mean we were actually being invaded. The cat from the other Clan is me. See how I just stepped over the line in the sand? What are you going to do about it? Wha . . . whoa! Stop treading on my ears!

Well, yes, Dustpaw, launching an attack and knocking me back across the border is one option. But is it wise to take on a cat twice your size? Or a trained warrior with more experience than you? The purpose of a patrol is to assess the situation and report back to your Clan leader. You won't be able to do that if your pelt is clawed to shreds at the farthest part of the territory from the camp. Any other ideas?

How about asking what I'm doing? I might have a valid reason for crossing the border, especially if I'm alone. That's right, Graystripe: *What do you want?* is a good way to start. Don't be too hostile: Remember, you are in the stronger position, because this is your territory and you have the right to defend it. Unless I have a very good explanation for crossing your border, I don't have any rights at all. What do you think my reply might be?

Yes, Ravenpaw, I might need your help. My Clan might have been invaded, we might have serious trouble with prey, or we might have sickness that needs your herbs. All these reasons would mean that I am *weak*, so you can allow me into your territory but never out of sight.

If I am hostile, then meet me with hostility—which isn't the same as aggression, Dustpaw. You've started with a strong challenge—What do you want?—and now you need to give me some sort of warning. Ravenpaw, what would you say?

Hmmm. If you're going to threaten to claw a cat's ears, you should try not to look so terrified at the prospect. Firepaw, would you like to try? Ah, yes, I like that you indicated the rest of your patrol. It's always good to let the enemy know they're outnumbered. Sandpaw, *put that fire ant down.* No, I don't care that Firepaw might not know what it is. Now is not the right time to show him—and he certainly doesn't need to get bitten by one.

So, you've challenged the trespasser, warned me that there's a whole patrol here that can take me to your Clan leader if that's what I wish; what next? That's right, Graypaw, let me—the intruder— speak. If I can't give you a convincing explanation for what I'm doing on your territory, if I don't ask to be taken to Bluestar at once, then chase me off with no more questions. Don't provoke a full-scale war—chasing means chasing, not catching and clawing. Just make it clear that you will defend your boundaries from any kind of invasion, even one paw across the border. A good warrior is always ready to fight, but only if it's absolutely necessary: A good warrior will seek a peaceful, claws-sheathed solution first.

You will all make good warriors one day. Don't look so doubtful, Ravenpaw. You need to find only a little more courage to be as good as your denmates. Your hunting skills are excellent—Dustpaw, you'd do well to watch him. Who knows? You might even lead this Clan one day!

Now, back to camp, all of you, and leave this old warrior to enjoy the sun in peace.

CODE TWELVE

> ## NO WARRIOR MAY NEGLECT A KIT IN PAIN OR IN DANGER, EVEN IF THAT KIT IS FROM A DIFFERENT CLAN.

The strength of a Clan does not depend only on the strength of its warriors. We also need to raise healthy kits to follow in the paw steps of their Clanmates. For this reason, kits are protected by all the cats in the forest, wherever their Clan loyalties lie. But it was not always so. As you will see, it sometimes takes a tragedy to teach the simplest of lessons.

A Loss for All Clans

Graywing stood on the flattened rock overlooking the river and closed her eyes, letting the fine mist spray her face. Heavy newleaf rains had swollen the water to a fast black torrent that spat and tumbled out of the gorge. Today the rain had stopped, sending Graywing and most of the RiverClan cats out of the camp to stretch their cramped legs and see which parts of the territory were underwater.

"Don't fall in!" warned a voice behind Graywing. "All this damp weather is bound to bring coughs and stiff joints, so we need our medicine cat!"

Graywing turned to see a sleek tortoiseshell she-cat padding over the stones toward her. "Don't worry, Brindleclaw. I have no intention of going for a swim today."

A ginger tom slid out of the reeds behind Brindleclaw. He scowled at the flooded river. "We'll be living off voles for a while," he predicted. "We can't risk any of our warriors trying to catch fish in that."

Brindleclaw nodded. "I'll warn the hunting patrols to stay well clear of the river until the level has gone down. Perhaps you could take a patrol into the fields, Foxwhisker?"

The ginger warrior grunted in agreement.

Graywing jumped down from the rock. "I need to see if my supply of mallow has survived the floods. I'll see you back at the camp."

Brindleclaw opened her mouth to reply, then stopped, staring straight past Graywing with a look of horror in her eyes. Graywing spun around. Three tiny fluffy shapes were clinging to the side of the gorge on the WindClan side, their hind legs dangling over the foaming water below.

"Great StarClan!" snarled Foxwhisker. "What on earth do those kits think they're doing?"

Brindleclaw was already running along the bank toward the mouth of the gorge. "It doesn't matter what they're doing!" she called over her shoulder. "They're going to fall!"

As she spoke, one of the kits lost its grip on the rocks and fell like a ripe apple into the river. There was a high-pitched squeal from one of its denmates, and another bundle plunged down into the water. Graywing felt as if her paws were frozen to the ground; the only thing she could do was watch as the third kit fell. It was impossible to see where they landed; any little splashes were swallowed up in the foam as the river burst out of the narrow canyon.

"Come on!" Brindleclaw yowled. "We have to help them!" She reached the end of the open river and raced down the shore to where the water exploded out of the gorge.

"Stop!" Graywing screeched. Her paws suddenly let go of their grip on the stones and she tore after Brindleclaw with Foxwhisker on her heels. "You can't go in!"

Brindleclaw stared at her. "What do you mean? Those kits will drown if we don't get them out!"

Graywing felt a pain in her chest as if she had just swallowed a boulder. "They're probably dead already," she forced herself to say. "We can't risk our own lives trying to save them. Besides, they are WindClan kits. They are not ours to save."

Beside them, there was a tiny squeak from the waves, and a paw the size of a blackberry shot above the surface before disappearing again.

"They're not dead!" Brindleclaw gasped. She bunched her haunches, ready to leap into the water, but Graywing took hold of her scruff with her teeth.

"I can't let you do this!" she choked through thick tortoiseshell fur. "StarClan made me medicine cat to serve RiverClan, not risk my Clanmates' lives to help other Clans."

Brindleclaw wrenched herself free and glared at Graywing. "How can you watch those kits drown without doing anything? What kind of a medicine cat are you?"

"One that is loyal to her Clan above all else," Graywing murmured. The pain in her chest swelled until she couldn't breathe, and her vision blurred.

"Graywing is right," meowed Foxwhisker. "It would have been madness to risk the life of a RiverClan warrior to save cats from another Clan. Come on, Brindleclaw."

The two warriors crunched away over the stones. Graywing

CODE
12.

let her legs crumple beneath her until she was slumped on the pebbles, feeling them hard and cold through her pelt. The only thing she could think of was the pitiful cry from the river as the kit had been swept away.

Ivystar, the RiverClan leader, was shocked to hear about the WindClan kits, but agreed that Graywing had been right not to let Brindleclaw jump in. She studied her medicine cat closely as Graywing stood before her with her head bowed. "It wasn't your fault those kits fell in," Ivystar murmured. "I'm sure they were told over and over to stay away from the gorge."

Graywing shook her head. "Their poor mother. Such a terrible loss for their Clan."

"And it could have been a terrible loss for RiverClan, too, if Brindleclaw had gone in after them," Ivystar pointed out. "Now go get some rest. I'll tell the patrols to keep an eye out for your mallow plants."

Graywing walked slowly to her den. Two RiverClan kits, Wildkit and Minnowkit, bounced around her.

"Did you really see those kits drown?"

"Were they all wet and horrid looking?"

"Did their eyes fall out?"

"Wildkit! Minnowkit! Stop asking such horrible questions!" their mother scolded from the nursery. "Come back here at once!"

Graywing didn't look up. She padded to her nest and curled up with her nose under her tail. *It's not my fault that those kits died.*

So why do I feel so guilty?

When Graywing opened her eyes, moonlight flooded her den and the camp was still and quiet. She sat up, shocked that she'd slept for so long. The reeds that shielded her den rattled, and she heard a soft murmur from the clearing. Wondering if a cat had been taken ill, Graywing slipped out of her nest and pushed her way through the reeds. Three cats stood in the center of the camp, their fur frosted by the dazzling white light.

"Who are you?" Graywing stammered. These weren't RiverClan warriors, and she didn't recognize them from Gatherings. She wondered how they had managed to get all the way into the camp without being challenged.

The tallest of the strangers, hard-muscled beneath his brown tabby coat, dipped his head. "Greetings, Graywing," he meowed. "My name is Runningstorm of WindClan. This is Wolfheart"— he nodded to the elegant gray she-cat beside him—"and our leader, Smallstar."

The third cat, whose tiny frame was covered in sleek black-and-white fur, looked at Graywing. His blue eyes were friendly as he mewed, "We have traveled far to see you."

Graywing looked from one cat to the other. "I don't understand. Has something happened to Fallowstar?"

Smallstar shook his head. "Fallowstar is fine. We are the cats who would have been."

Graywing stared at them in horror. The image of three terrified bundles, falling one by one into the churning river, filled her eyes. "You are the kits who drowned," she whispered.

Wolfheart bent her head. "That is so. Come, we have something to show you."

CODE 12

She turned and led the way across the clearing toward the nursery. Graywing followed without having to tell her paws what to do; they seemed to be carrying her on their own.

Runningstorm nosed aside the bramble that was draped across the entrance to the nursery, protecting the precious cats inside. "Look," he urged Graywing.

Oh, StarClan, let our kits be all right, Graywing prayed as she poked her head inside. *Had the WindClan kits returned to punish her by hurting the youngest RiverClan cats?*

The den smelled warm and milky, and enough moonlight filtered through the branches for Graywing to see Hayberry curled around Wildkit and Minnowkit, who snuffled gently in their sleep. Hayberry's flank rose and fell in time with her kits' breathing, and although her eyelids flickered when Graywing looked at her, she didn't stir.

Graywing pulled her head out. "They're safe," she breathed.

Smallstar looked surprised. "Of course. Did you think we'd hurt one hair on their pelts? Kits are the most special part of a Clan. They are the warriors who will defend their Clanmates in moons to come, the hunters who will find food even in the coldest leaf-bare, the cats who will have kits of their own to pass on everything they have learned. A Clan that has no kits might as well be dead."

"And if one Clan dies, the survival of all the Clans is threatened," Runningstorm added. "We may be rivals, but we are linked by StarClan, stronger than rock, stronger than tree roots, stronger than the water in the river."

"I'm sorry." Graywing faced the shining warriors and bowed her head. "I should have let Brindleclaw try to save you. WindClan's loss is ours, too."

There was no reply. She lifted her head to see the three cats fading away, returning to their home in the stars.

Graywing blinked. She was lying in her nest, the moss and feathers underneath her looking as if a battle had been fought there the night before. Graywing hauled herself up and stretched one hind leg at a time. Why did she feel as if she hadn't slept at all?

The dream!

She raced out of the den and went straight to Ivystar. "I have to take a patrol out," she panted.

Ivystar put her head to one side. "Do we need herbs so desperately? Has a cat fallen ill?"

"No, nothing like that. Please, let me take Brindleclaw and Foxwhisker. I'll explain everything later."

"Very well. But be careful. The river will still be flooded."

Graywing shot out of Ivystar's den and went to wake up Brindleclaw and Foxwhisker. The she-cat was still icy cold toward her, but Graywing didn't try to apologize or even tell the warriors what they were doing. They would understand soon enough. . . .

Graywing led them along the shore heading downriver, toward Sunningrocks. She slowed as they drew near the looming gray shapes and started to sniff carefully along the river's edge.

"Are you looking for something?" Foxwhisker asked.

Graywing looked up. "I want to find the kits who drowned yesterday," she mewed. "They should have lived to become warriors for their Clan. We need to take them back home."

Brindleclaw stared at her in shock. "But yesterday you said we couldn't have anything to do with them because they weren't RiverClan!"

Graywing nodded. "And I was wrong. Kits should be precious to all Clans. After we have taken these three back to WindClan, I will ask Ivystar to suggest an addition to the warrior code: that kits should be protected by every cat in the forest, regardless of which Clan they come from. All our futures depend on them."

"Over there," came a quiet meow. Foxwhisker was standing on the edge of the water, facing away from them. He jerked his muzzle toward the far bank, where a tangle of sodden fur had been washed up against a branch.

"Come on," murmured Graywing. She and her Clanmates

code
12

slipped into the water and paddled strongly through the current toward the branch. The swollen river tried to drag them away, and battered them with twigs and other debris washed down from the gorge, but they stretched their necks to keep their muzzles above the surface and churned with legs well used to swimming. Graywing reached the kits first. Through the filthy, water-dark fur, she could just make out patches of black and white in the shape nearest to her. It was Smallkit, who would have been leader of his Clan had he survived. Graywing picked him up and carried him back to the RiverClan shore. Foxwhisker followed with Runningkit, and Brindleclaw brought Wolfkit.

They laid their tiny burdens on the shore to get their breath back. Graywing touched each body with her muzzle. "Your Clan will honor you with a burial for the warriors that you would have been," she told them. "And you will live on in the law that makes every Clan responsible for the safety of kits, wherever they are born.

"Precious kits, walk safely among the stars."

A Kit in Trouble

No cat doubts that cats of all Clans must protect kits. But we know from bitter experience that not all kits grow up to honor the warrior code that once protected them. Every full-grown tyrant or murderer was once a tiny bundle of fluff that swelled a mother's heart with pride. If we could see into the future, would we protect each and every kit the same?

Brackenfoot curled his lip as he pushed through the broad, sticky plants that grew along the Thunderpath that bordered ShadowClan's territory. He didn't share his Clanmates' taste for monster-kill, and the stench and the noise coming from the strip of black stone made him blind and deaf to everything else. He waited for the roar of the monsters to fade, then bounded onto the narrow strip of foul-smelling grass.

Archeye was sniffing at some crumpled gray and white feathers lying on the edge of the Thunderpath. "Looks like we might be able to take some pigeon home," he commented.

It won't taste of pigeon, thought Brackenfoot. *It'll taste burned and bitter, like licking a monster's paw.*

To his relief, Hollyflower wrinkled her nose. "There's not enough meat left to bother with," she told Archeye.

The still, hot air was ruffled by the sound of a growl; Brackenfoot spun around, expecting to see a curious dog that had broken away from its Twoleg. But nothing stirred on ShadowClan's hunting grounds. Then Hollyflower yowled, "Fox!"

Brackenfoot stiffened. A red-brown creature with the familiar pointed snout was standing among the ferns on the far side of the Thunderpath, in ThunderClan's territory. The fox's

CODE 12

fur bristled along its back, and it held its head low.

"Is it stalking us?" Archeye whispered.

"Foxes don't hunt full-grown cats," Crowclaw whispered back. "Not unless they're starving."

Brackenfoot peered closer. There was something trembling on the very edge of the Thunderpath, directly across from them. "It's not interested in us," he hissed. "It's found some much easier prey." The lump of fluff looked like a young rabbit or perhaps a very fat vole.

"ThunderClan won't like having a fox stealing their fresh-kill," Archeye commented gleefully.

"That's not fresh-kill!" Hollyflower burst out. "That's a *kit*!" She sprang onto the Thunderpath before the other cats could stop her and raced across to stand over the tiny cat. "Get away!" she spat at the fox.

Archeye glanced sideways at Brackenfoot. "I suppose we'd better join in before she loses both her ears," he muttered.

Brackenfoot sighed. Yes, all kits had to be protected whichever Clan they came from, but this kit was still on its own territory! Couldn't they wait for a ThunderClan patrol to come to the rescue?

Clearly not. Hollyflower was advancing on the fox, putting herself between it and the kit. Protecting another Clan's kit was one thing; saving your denmate from being savaged was another.

Side by side, Brackenfoot and Archeye pelted across the hot black stone, screeching a battle cry. The fox jumped back and growled, baring long pointed fangs.

"You don't scare us!" Hollyflower yowled. She lashed out with her claws unsheathed and drew her paw back clogged with reddish hair. The fox snapped at her, its breath foul as crow-food.

Brackenfoot reared up onto his hind legs and swiped with both front paws, catching the fox on its ears. At the same time, Archeye ducked low and ran at its snout, striking as he shot past. The fox shook its head, scattering scarlet drops from its muzzle.

"Go, warriors, go!" squealed the ThunderClan kit. Brackenfoot had almost forgotten it was there. He aimed one more blow at the fox before dropping to all four paws and springing backward, out of range of the cracking jaws. The fox snarled once more, then turned tail and vanished into the undergrowth.

CODE
12

"Wow! You were great!" called the kit. "The way you sliced his nose! And swiped his ears! I wish I could fight like that!" the kit continued.

Brackenfoot padded forward. "What's your name?"

The kit gazed up at him with huge amber eyes. "Tigerkit," he mewed.

"Well, Tigerkit, one day you will be able to fight like us, if you listen to your mentor and train really hard. But you shouldn't even be out of your camp. What if we hadn't seen you? That fox would have made fresh-kill out of you!"

"But he didn't!" Tigerkit gloated, bouncing on his toes. "Because you saved me!"

Brackenfoot realized there was no talking sense to this mouse-brained tuft of fur. "Just be more careful from now on," he growled. Then, nodding to his Clanmates, he led them back across the Thunderpath.

The kit watched them go, stretching his neck to keep them in sight. "May StarClan walk your path!" he squeaked. "Thanks for rescuing me! ShadowClan will always be my friends! One day I'll help you, too!"

CODE THIRTEEN

*Not every article of the warrior code is born out of
wisdom, and it might seem that this one came from a dangerous
lapse of judgment in all Clan leaders. Even so, this piece of
code has survived unchallenged all these moons. Why? In reality,
leaders take advice from their medicine cat and senior
warriors—one cat alone rarely makes a decision. And the best
warriors have never been afraid to challenge their leader, even at
the risk of breaking the code. But come what may, the leader
has to bear responsibility for what happens, and such a heavy
burden deserves our respect. The code guarantees it.*

Darkstar's Law

Raincloud held her breath as Darkstar heaved himself onto the Great Rock. The SkyClan leader was nearing the end of his ninth life and looked painfully frail as he scrabbled with his hind legs to boost himself up. Vinestar, the ThunderClan leader, came over and helped him by sinking his teeth into Darkstar's scruff and hauling him the last tail-length. Darkstar was too breathless to thank him, and lay on his side, panting, while the fifth leader, Yellowstar of ShadowClan, jumped up.

The SkyClan leader had been a strong and well-respected warrior for all his lives. Raincloud had been his deputy for many moons and dreaded the day she would have to watch him slip away from his Clan forever.

She stood with the other deputies at the base of the Great Rock and faced the cats who had come to the Gathering.

The RiverClan leader, Talonstar, began with a report of Twolegs staying in the fields on the far side of their territory; they came every greenleaf and didn't even seem to know the cats were there, but this time some of them had brought dogs, which had come dangerously close to the camp. Talonstar assured the other Clans that his warriors had chased them off with their tails between their legs.

Birchstar of WindClan announced a new litter of kits and two new warriors, then Yellowstar described an old, mangy fox that had been causing trouble on the edge of ShadowClan's territory because it didn't seem to be afraid of anything. Then Vinestar took his place on the edge of the rock.

"We have three new litters of kits and four new warriors," he announced with a flick of his long gray tail. "We thank StarClan for making the prey in ThunderClan run well this season, and we hope we can continue to feed ourselves in leaf-fall and leaf-bare."

He glanced sideways at Darkstar, whose head was hanging down with his eyes closed. Raincloud wondered if he had missed the thorn-sharp edge to Vinestar's report. ThunderClan patrols had been spotted more and more frequently on the boundary that they shared with SkyClan: not just border patrols, but hunting patrols, too. Raincloud suspected that, with so many new mouths to feed, they were starting to look beyond their territory for sources of fresh-kill.

Talonstar nudged Darkstar and the old tom's head jerked upright. Darkstar padded to the edge of the Great Rock. His milky yellow eyes gazed down at the cats in the hollow.

"Cats of all Clans," Darkstar began in a voice as thin as a whisker; the cats in the hollow fell silent, and Raincloud relaxed. "I, too, have an announcement. I wish to give part of SkyClan's territory to ThunderClan, to feed their new kits."

Raincloud stared at her Clan leader in disbelief. All along the line of SkyClan cats, fur bristled and cats whispered to one another in alarm. Raincloud glanced at Twigtail, the medicine cat, who shook his head and looked as stunned as she felt.

Darkstar raised his head and, outlined in moonlight, it was suddenly possible to see him as the great warrior he had once been. "ThunderClan may have the stretch of territory on our border as far as the silver birch on the riverbank on one side and the yellow Twoleg nest on the other. May these hunting grounds be as good to them as they have been to us!"

Raincloud jumped to her feet. She couldn't listen in silence any longer. "Darkstar, are you sure?" she pleaded. She hated that all the other Clans would see her challenge her own leader, but she didn't know what else she could do. Darkstar was handing nearly a quarter of SkyClan to their neighbors! Was he so terrified of conflict that he wanted to make peace with Vinestar before the borders were threatened?

Raincloud felt all the eyes from the watching cats burn into her pelt. Ignoring the gasps of shock, she jumped onto the rock

code
13

and put her face close to Darkstar's. "What are you doing?" she hissed. "Don't you trust your warriors to defend our territory? No Clan has ever given away part of its hunting grounds before!"

Darkstar pulled away from her, his mouth set in a stubborn line. "ThunderClan has more mouths to feed than we do. SkyClan can always extend on its other boundaries."

"No, we can't!" Raincloud twitched her tail in exasperation. "Twoleg nests block us on one side and the treecutplace on the other. And the warrior code says that we must protect our borders at all times!"

Darkstar looked at her, and she was unnerved by the strength in his yellow gaze. He stood up, and the cats below fell silent as if they were waiting for the next lightning strike he would drop among them.

"Forgive my insolent deputy," he rasped. "She does not understand what it means to be truly loyal to her Clan. Vinestar, the land is yours. My warriors will set new border marks tomorrow."

Vinestar dipped his head. His eyes were narrowed and full of questions, but he didn't challenge the generous offer.

Raincloud looked desperately up at the sky. Was StarClan really going to let this happen? But the full moon floated on, a perfect shining disk. There wasn't a single cloud in the sky. Their warrior ancestors could not have made it clearer that Darkstar could do as he wished with the territory that belonged to his Clan.

Her tail drooping, Raincloud turned to leave the Great Rock. It would be up to her to send out patrols to change the boundaries and shrink SkyClan's hunting grounds.

"Wait!" Darkstar ordered. Raincloud stopped and looked around.

"I want you to be my witness to a new law for the warrior code," the SkyClan leader rasped. His eyes were gleaming now but not

quite focused. Raincloud felt her pelt stand on end. Had her leader gone mad, right in the middle of a Gathering?

"No other leader should have to face such insubordination in front of the other Clans," Darkstar announced. "I propose a law that the word of a leader is the warrior code. What we say must never be challenged. StarClan gave us the power to lead; StarClan would wish it to be so."

Oh, no. That can't be made part of the warrior code. Leaders are cats, first and foremost, good and bad or a mixture of both. Raincloud realized her mouth had dropped open and she was shaking her head. She forced herself to stay still, and closed her mouth in case she said something that made Darkstar even angrier. She didn't care about being punished herself, but it suddenly felt as if she was all her Clan had left.

"I support the new law!" Vinestar declared.

There's a surprise. Raincloud waited for one of the leaders to point out how ridiculous this was, that there was more than one cat in each Clan with a worthwhile opinion, but the other three cats stepped forward in turn to agree with Vinestar. Yellowstar's eyes were troubled, and Talonstar's deputy stared hard at the RiverClan leader as if challenging the wisdom of his decision, but the law was accepted. The word of a Clan leader was now to be treated as if it was part of the warrior code.

As if sensing that several cats in the hollow were about to protest, Vinestar quickly announced that the Gathering was over and leaped down from the Great Rock. His Clanmates swarmed around him as he led them up the slope and out of the hollow. The other leaders followed, leaving Darkstar to dismount last of all, his stiff joints creaking. He paused as he went past Raincloud, who was still sitting in the shadows at the edge of the rock.

"You may continue to serve as my deputy," he croaked. "But never challenge me like that again. The borders will change at dawn."

He sprang down to the ground and beckoned the SkyClan cats with his tail. They headed out of the hollow, still muttering to one another. One or two glanced anxiously back at Raincloud, as if they thought she might have been exiled for arguing with Darkstar at the Gathering. *No. Just humiliated.* But Raincloud knew she wouldn't leave. SkyClan deserved better than that. Better than Darkstar, even.

She stayed on the rock until the shadows had stopped rustling with departing cats. She stared up at the moon, still expressionless and cloud-free. *Did you really want this, StarClan?* she wailed silently. *What happens when a leader comes who wants to change everything? Turn the Clans against one another, wipe out all the values we have ever lived by?*

What will you do then?

An Empty Prayer: Cloudstar Speaks

Few cats know of the fifth Clan that once lived in the forest.
SkyClan cats were the highest jumpers and lived among the tall trees
where they snatched birds from the branches. But long ago, SkyClan
was driven out of its territory by Twoleg monsters, and then driven
out of the forest by the remaining four Clans, erased from Clan
memory by a legacy of guilt. Come with me, to SkyClan in its new
territory, under new skies, far from the forest.

The gorge is so quiet when night falls. It makes my Clan uneasy; they are used to hearing the rustle of branches and the call of birds above them—not just endless sky splashed with stars, more than I ever imagined there would be when we lived in the forest. I wonder if any of our warrior ancestors can see us. And if they could, would they listen? I know those cold fragments of light in the sky are not my warrior ancestors. StarClan stopped watching over us long ago, as soon as the Twolegs attacked our territory with tree-eating monsters, churning up the ground to build their nests of hard red stone.

My poor Clan. Was I right to bring them here, so far from their home? Perhaps we should have fought to stay in the forest, mustered the last remains of our strength to take on ThunderClan or WindClan and steal some of their territory. Not ShadowClan or RiverClan, though: We would never have developed a taste for frogs or fish, however hungry we were.

We traveled far to come here, and I want this to be a home

CODE
13

to us as much as the forest was for all those countless moons. We have caves for shelter, fresh water to drink, and there's prey enough if we are patient and learn to stalk in the open rather than through branches high above the ground. Yesterday Buzzardtail and Mousefang brought back a squirrel,

so there must be trees close by. Maybe tomorrow I will explore beyond the cliffs. I have to: My Clan should not know more about our new territory than I do.

But I am so tired. I ask only for a place to sleep that is sheltered from the wind and rain, and a mouthful of prey. Maybe not even that: Do I really want to live for moons in this strange place carved out of sand? Everything is different without Birdflight. When I sleep, my dreams are dark and empty, and whatever I eat tastes of nothing.

I brought my Clan to a place where I thought they could live, but it seems that isn't enough. These stars are as unfamiliar to them as they are to me, so I am their only link to the way we used to live. *The word of the Clan leader is the warrior code.* So they watch me and wait for me to tell them that everything will be all right, that SkyClan will rise once more to be strong and proud, rulers of their territory.

But this is not our territory. This is an empty gorge, a tunnel through orange rock with the sky for its roof. Our ancestors are no longer with us—if they ever were at all. Our fresh-kill pile used to whisper with the sound of plump, thick-feathered birds; now we eat mice and rabbits, when we are swift enough to catch them.

I hear my cats wailing like kits in the dead of night, wishing they could go back to the forest. But there is nothing left for us there. This is our home now. We will learn to catch prey and defend our borders against whatever other cats live near here. We do not need our warrior ancestors, or the other Clans, to tell us what to do. My cats trusted me enough to follow me here; I cannot let them down. Birdflight would never have wanted that.

As long as I am here, SkyClan will survive.

The word of the Clan leader *is* the warrior code.

CODE
13

CODE FOURTEEN

AN HONORABLE WARRIOR DOES NOT NEED TO KILL OTHER CATS TO WIN HIS OR HER BATTLES, UNLESS THEY ARE OUTSIDE THE WARRIOR CODE OR IT IS NECESSARY FOR SELF-DEFENSE.

I know you kittypets think we are fierce, bloodthirsty creatures who line our nests with the fur of our enemies, but we are not. Battles with cats who do not live in Clans are far more likely to result in death, because those cats often have no sense of the honor in a victory without bloodshed. Now you are about to discover what bitter experience taught—that the way of the warrior does not have to be steeped in blood.

The Medicine Cats Decide

Mossheart finished chewing the marigold leaves to a pulp and spat them carefully onto a leaf. "These should help the infection," she told the mottled gray tom lying awkwardly on his side. The jagged cut smelled of crow-food and looked yellow around the edges, and the skin surrounding it was tender and inflamed.

"If I ever catch that mangy WindClan cat who did it, I'll rip out his throat," Smoketalon muttered through clenched teeth.

Mossheart shook her head. "Then his Clan will lose a warrior and swear vengeance on ShadowClan, and it will go on forever. Back and forth, shedding blood on one side of the border or the other, until the stars grow old."

"We have to defend our boundaries!" Smoketalon hissed. "The warrior code says so."

Mossheart sighed. The border skirmishes between ShadowClan and its neighbor WindClan had grown more and more violent in recent moons, with warriors from both sides darting across the Thunderpath on raids. Neither Clan was short of food, and it wasn't as if WindClan had developed a taste for frogs or ShadowClan had gained the swiftness needed to catch rabbits. It was nothing but mouse-brained pride that made each Clan refuse to be the first to stop. A WindClan warrior had died last moon, and a ShadowClan she-cat had been lamed and would never be able to hunt or fight for her Clan again.

Mossheart finished packing the wound with juicy green pulp and laid cobwebs on top in an attempt to hold the edges of the cut together and keep the poultice in place. "Don't move until I tell you," she warned Smoketalon. She pushed some dry moss under his head to make him more comfortable, then padded out of her den to clear her head of the bitter marigold scent.

Several of her Clanmates were standing on the far side of the clearing, staring into the trees with their ears pricked. A white she-cat, her belly round with kits, turned to look at Mossheart. "They're fighting again," she meowed. "Listen."

Oh, StarClan, no!

Mossheart padded forward to stand beside Lilyfur. Mossheart's pelt felt strangely hot and sticky, and there was a sour scent in her nose. She looked down. Her dark tortoiseshell fur was drenched in scarlet blood that ran down her legs and dripped onto the ground.

code
14

Mossheart opened her mouth to cry out and choked on a thick, salty clot. Retching, she spat it out.

"Mossheart? Are you all right?"

Mossheart opened her eyes. Lilyfur was bending over her, and Mossheart's fur was healthy and clean.

"Have you got a furball stuck in your throat?"

"No. I . . ." Mossheart straightened up. The only taste in her mouth was marigold juice. Faint sounds of battle drifted on the breeze: yowls and thuds as cats hit the ground, the rip of claws through fur. *So much blood . . .*

Mossheart bolted toward the noise.

"Wait!" Lilyfur called. "Where are you going?"

"We have to stop the battle!" Mossheart screeched without slowing down. Her vision must have been a message from StarClan that the cats in the forest were in danger of drowning in bloodshed.

Paws thudded behind her, and she realized Lilyfur was following. "Go back!" she panted. "Your kits . . ."

"My kits will be fine," Lilyfur wheezed. "I've watched you enough times to be useful." She risked a glance sideways at Mossheart. "It's going to be bad, isn't it? I mean, worse than before."

Mossheart nodded.

The two cats burst out of the trees into a clear patch of ground not far from the Thunderpath. The air tasted of monsters and the bushes at the edge were black and shriveled from the creatures' foul breath. A tangle of bleeding, screeching cats wrestled in the center of the clearing. Mossheart narrowed her eyes. Two large patrols, from the look of it, each containing several apprentices as well as warriors.

"Stop!" came a screech from the far side of the clearing, and a

small gray face appeared from the blackened bushes. "Stop right now!" he yowled again.

"It's Swiftfoot!" Mossheart mewed, recognizing the WindClan medicine cat from Gatherings.

The gray tom stepped around the motionless body of one of his Clanmates with a rueful glance and marched up to the nearest tussle. "Enough!" he ordered. "There is nothing to be won here!"

The two cats paused and stared at him. They stepped back and Swiftfoot gave the WindClan warrior a shove with his nose. "Go home!" he hissed. To Mossheart's astonishment, the cat spun around and ran into the bushes that separated the clearing from the Thunderpath. The ShadowClan warrior, a dark brown tabby called Logfur, bunched his haunches, ready to leap back into battle, but Mossheart hurtled up to him and planted herself in her way.

"You heard what Swiftfoot said! Go home!"

"There's a battle to be fought," Logfur growled.

"Not anymore," Mossheart replied.

Logfur glared at her, then slunk away, leaving a thin trail of blood from a cut on his tail.

CODE
14

"What in the name of StarClan are you doing?" demanded a voice.

Mossheart spun around. Silvermask stood behind her, the gray stripe on his face stained with blood. "Do you want us to lose?" he growled.

"No. I want you to *live*," Mossheart spat. "Are you going to keep fighting until there are no warriors left at all?" She flicked her tail at the bodies that lay slumped on the ground. "Three more cats dead? How is this going to help?"

"Because two of them are WindClan, which means two fewer enemies for us." Silvermask curled his lip in triumph.

Mossheart shook her head. "You are more mouse-brained than I thought," she mewed sadly.

Behind them, the warriors were staggering apart, stumbling into the undergrowth in the direction of their own territories. Silvermask eyed them in disgust. "Are you happy now, Mossheart? We could have won that battle."

"No, you couldn't. Every battle is a loss."

With a hiss, the deputy limped away. Mossheart decided she'd wait a while before telling him his wounds needed to be treated with goldenrod. Lilyfur padded up. "Is there anything I can do to help?" she offered.

Mossheart gazed around the clearing. Two WindClan cats wouldn't be making their own way back to their camp, and neither would a ShadowClan apprentice, Spottedpaw. Mossheart gulped as she looked at his little brown body. A warm breeze stirred the fur on his flank, making it look as if he were breathing. But the scent of death hung over him, and his bright blue eyes were glazed and milky.

Swiftfoot glanced up at Mossheart. "I am sorry for your loss," he meowed.

"And I for yours," Mossheart replied dully.

"This has to stop!" Swiftfoot hissed, startling Mossheart. "If we lose any more warriors, our Clans will starve when leaf-bare comes. How can StarClan let this happen?"

"Have you been to the Moonstone to speak with them about it?" Mossheart asked.

"No. Have you?"

Mossheart shook her head.

"Then we should go. You and me, and all the other medicine cats. If we all show up, perhaps StarClan will be forced to listen."

Mossheart stared at him. She'd met the other medicine cats at Gatherings but never alone, without other Clanmates around them. "How can we tell them what we want to do?"

"I'll visit them. I'll go on my own so it's obvious I'm not a threat, and I'll bring them all to the moor. Meet us by the pointed stone next sunrise."

Mossheart knew that Swiftfoot was right. The medicine cats needed to unite. They had the power to heal their Clans—perhaps this meant they could stop battles before they started.

"I'll be there," she promised.

Swiftfoot popped his head around the corner of the gorse as Mossheart approached the pointed stone the next morning. "I thought you'd decided not to come," he greeted her.

Kinktail, the RiverClan medicine cat whose tail had been crushed by a monster when she was a tiny kit, appeared behind Swiftfoot. Her eyes were shining. "I can't believe we're doing this!" she breathed. "All five of us, going to share tongues with StarClan at the same time."

CODE
14

"Maybe we should have done it before," muttered Swiftfoot. "Come on, we have a long way to go before sunset."

He led them across the moor, padding confidently in the

blazing sun. Mossheart walked beside Quailfeather of SkyClan, not envying her long, thick coat. Kinktail followed with Prickleface, the ThunderClan medicine cat with a temper to match his name. Mossheart waited for him to make a sour remark about what they were doing, but they traveled mostly in silence, speaking only when they needed to stop and find water. Above them, the sky was tinged purple as the sun slid behind the ridge, and a crisp half-moon appeared. Mossheart gasped.

"It's red!"

The moon was washed with scarlet, darker around the edge. Mossheart had never seen it look like that before.

"It's the color of blood," Quailfeather pointed out quietly.

Perhaps StarClan is already waiting for us, Mossheart thought.

Prickleface took the lead as they entered Mothermouth and began the long, echoey walk into darkness. Suddenly the blackness up ahead faded and a watery pink light started to filter along the stone walls. Prickleface quickened his pace, and soon they were running along the tunnel and exploding into the chamber where the Moonstone stood. The crystal reflected the scarlet moon tonight, giving off a reddish gleam that shone in the cats' eyes.

Swiftfoot nodded to the Moonstone. "You know what to do," he told his companions. "We have to ask StarClan if there is a way to stop the fighting."

Mossheart lay down and pressed her muzzle against the base of the stone. It was ice-cold and she winced, but gradually it grew warm and she felt it begin to throb gently, as if she were curled against the belly of her mother. She was safe here, safe and loved. No blood would ever be shed in the Moonstone chamber. . . .

"ShadowClan! Attack!" Mossheart jumped as Silvermask yowled right next to her ear. She looked around and realized she was back in the clearing by the Thunderpath, surrounded by a ShadowClan patrol rushing to hurl themselves on WindClan cats running toward them. She was watching yesterday's battle from the very start.

"You can't stop them, you know."

Mossheart looked down. A small brown tom stood beside her, his brown coat flecked with ginger. "Spottedpaw! You're not fighting!"

The apprentice looked up at her. "How can I? I'm dead, remember?"

"But this is yesterday!" Mossheart protested.

"No it's not. It's *every* day," Spottedpaw mewed. "This battle, and battles like it, will happen over and over, for all the moons to come, and there's nothing you can do to change that. We fight to protect our territories, our kits, our reputation among the other Clans. It's what warriors do."

"But you died because of it!"

Spottedpaw looked sad. "Yes. I wish I hadn't. I wanted to be the best warrior ShadowClan had ever seen."

Mossheart touched her muzzle to his fluffy ear. "I'm sorry, little one," she murmured.

Spottedpaw was beginning to fade. "You can't stop the fighting," he repeated. "But maybe you can stop the dying. That WindClan warrior didn't need to kill me. I knew I was beaten. If he'd let go of me, I'd have run away. He didn't have to keep biting me, harder and harder. . . . "

His blue eyes glowed for a moment after his body vanished, then they went out like setting suns. Mossheart closed her eyes as grief swept over her. What a bitter, bitter waste.

When she opened her eyes, she was back in the chamber, lying by the Moonstone. Her body was cold and cramped, so she stood up and stretched each leg in turn, arching her back and kinking her tail right over her ears.

"Well?" prompted Swiftfoot, who was sitting in the shadows with the other medicine cats. With a shock, Mossheart realized she was the last to wake up.

"I . . . I dreamed of Spottedpaw, the ShadowClan apprentice who died yesterday," she began. She stopped when she saw the other cats nodding to one another.

"We all dreamed of fallen Clanmates," meowed Quailfeather. "Each one said the same: that we could never stop battles from happening, but that they knew they had lost their fight before they were killed. They didn't have to die for the other cat to win."

"Victory without death," murmured Prickleface. "Do you think the Clans would accept it?"

"They have to," meowed Swiftfoot. "StarClan has told us all the same thing: that a warrior does not have to kill to be victorious."

"What if he is fighting for his life?" put in Kinktail, looking worried. "Against a fox or a rogue?"

Swiftfoot nodded. "There will be exceptions," Swiftfoot determined, "because some battles can only end in death. But for Clans fighting Clans, killing is not the answer."

"When should we tell our leaders about this?" Mossheart asked.

"Why don't we wait until the next Gathering?" Quailfeather suggested. "It's only a quarter-moon away. We can tell them about our dreams and suggest a new law for the warrior code. The leaders can't disagree with all five of us."

"That's right," Swiftfoot meowed. "And from now on, I think we should meet every half-moon to share tongues with StarClan together. None of us wants to see our Clanmates die, and all of us would be happy never to treat a battle wound again. Perhaps boundaries don't exist for medicine cats the way they do for our Clanmates. We should work together whenever we can, to preserve the peace and health of all the Clans."

He led them back into the tunnel that led to the ridge and fresh air and starlight. When they emerged, the moon had cleared and shone as white as ever. The cats began to head down the slope, their paws whispering over the short grass. Mossheart was convinced she could hear another set of paws close by, even though she wasn't near any of the other cats. Then she caught a trace of scent and knew who was running beside her.

Thank you, Spottedpaw whispered. *Your law will save the lives of many, many cats. StarClan will honor all of you forever.*

CODE
14

CODE FIFTEEN

A WARRIOR REJECTS THE SOFT LIFE
OF A KITTYPET.

*The life of the Clans is as far from the life of a kittypet as
you could imagine. We hunt for our food, choose our own boundaries
and fight to defend them, and raise our kits to follow traditions
laid down by cats long since faded from our memories. Many Clan
cats would say this makes us better than you; I would not necessarily
claim that. There are good and bad cats everywhere—and good
and bad within every cat. If every Clan cat was pure of heart and
unfailingly loyal, we wouldn't need the warrior code at all.*

Pinestar's Secret

"**h**ey, Lionpaw! Have you seen Pinestar?"

Lionpaw looked up from grooming his pelt. "I thought Pinestar went out with a hunting patrol," he told his mentor.

Sunfall narrowed his eyes. "I thought so, too, but the hunting patrol's just come back and Pinestar's not with them."

Lionpaw gave up on his tufty fur and padded over to the bright orange warrior. "Would you like me to look for him?" he offered.

Sunfall shook his head. "I want you to come with me on a patrol to check the border along the river," he explained. "The dawn patrol picked up some RiverClan scents as far in as the trees."

Lionpaw felt the hair along his spine bristle. Those mangy RiverClan cats! Why couldn't they stick to their own territory?

But when they went on patrol they found only the faintest hint of RiverClan scent under the trees, which could have been blown there by the wind, so they left their neighbors alone. When they returned to the camp, Pinestar was back. He greeted his deputy as soon as the patrol pushed its way through the gorse tunnel.

"Sunfall, is all quiet on the borders?"

"Yes," Sunfall replied. "Did the prey run well for you?"

Pinestar nodded. "StarClan was good to me."

Lionpaw was surprised. Pinestar didn't smell of fresh-kill, just flowers and crushed grass. Sunfall had told him he'd done well on the patrol today; Lionpaw hoped Pinestar would invite him on a patrol soon so he could show the leader how much he had learned. But Pinestar rarely went out with other cats; he preferred to patrol alone, he said, so he could hear and scent more clearly. Lionpaw was very frustrated. How would Pinestar know the best warrior name for him if he never saw him hunt or fight? He would only be an apprentice for two more moons, so there wasn't much time.

Lionpaw woke early the following morning, before any of his denmates. Outside the den, the air was clear and cold, with a hint of mustiness that suggested leaf-fall was on its way. The clearing was empty but the gorse tunnel was quivering as if a cat had just gone through. Lionpaw pushed his way in, wondering if whoever it was would like some company.

A reddish brown shape was just reaching the top of the ravine. Pinestar! Perhaps this was Lionpaw's chance to show off some of his skills. He bounded up the rocks behind him, intending to call out when he reached the top, but by the time he got there, Pinestar

CODE
15

had vanished. Lionpaw looked around. A fern was bobbing more strongly than the breeze was blowing, and the ThunderClan leader's scent drifted just above the dewy grass. Lionpaw put his nose down and followed the trail. He decided to see how far he could track Pinestar without being spotted. That would be a great way to show how good he was at stalking!

Staying far enough back to be out of sight and treading as softly as he could, Lionpaw followed Pinestar across the territory, past the treecutplace, and into the thinner trees. It was harder to track through the pine trees without being seen; Lionpaw had to rush between fallen branches and sparse clumps of bracken, hoping Pinestar didn't look back. He was so busy concentrating on not stepping on any crackly twigs that he didn't realize where he was until he looked over the bracken and saw Twoleg fences in front of him. They were right at the edge of the forest! But where was Pinestar? Lionpaw stretched his neck out from his hiding place and sniffed. The trail was still there—and it led straight out of the forest.

Had Pinestar chased a kittypet out of ThunderClan's territory? Lionpaw was sure he would have heard something like that. He crept through the long grass that grew under the outermost trees and sniffed the bottom of a wooden Twoleg fence. Pinestar had definitely climbed up here—there were scratchmarks on the wood. It looked as if this was a regular climbing place.

Lionpaw clawed his way up the wooden fence and looked down into the little square of Twoleg territory. Short green grass was edged with strong-smelling flowers, and a strange, leafless tree stood in the center holding bright-colored Twoleg pelts. Just past the leafless tree, the grass turned into flat white stone, where two spindly wooden objects stood on skinny legs. They each had a flat ledge at the top of the legs, and on one of the ledges a red-brown shape was curled, with a tail hanging over the edge. Lionpaw nearly fell off the fence.

What was Pinestar doing in the Twoleg territory?

Lionpaw was about to jump down and call to him when a flap in the Twoleg nest swung open and a Twoleg appeared. Lionpaw ducked behind some flowers, trying not to sneeze as the pollen tickled his nose. The Twoleg made some noises, and to Lionpaw's astonishment, Pinestar replied.

"Oh, thank you, I love it when you rub my ears! Could you do my back as well? That's perfect!"

Lionpaw peered around a leaf. The Twoleg was bent over the spindly object, stroking Pinestar's fur with one pink, hairless paw. If Pinestar hadn't been purring, Lionpaw would have thought he was being attacked. But he was *enjoying* it.

Pinestar rolled onto his back so that his hind legs dangled over the edge of the ledge. His head tipped back and Lionpaw caught a glimpse of his eyes, closed in delight. Suddenly afraid of being seen, Lionpaw scrambled back over the fence and dived into the long grass. He wanted to run all the way back to the camp and forget what he had seen, but he knew he couldn't do that. He had to ask Pinestar what he was doing.

"Lionpaw! What are you doing here?"

Pinestar was standing on top of the fence, looking down at him.

"I . . . er . . ." Lionpaw stammered.

Pinestar sprang down and looked closely at him. "Did you follow me?"

CODE
15

"Yes," Lionpaw admitted. "I wanted to show you my stalking skills."

"Well, I didn't notice you, so they must be good! Now, I expect you're wondering what I was doing with that Twoleg."

Lionpaw nodded. Every hair on his pelt seemed to be on fire.

Pinestar began walking back into the trees, and Lionpaw trotted to catch up. "The kittypet that lives there has been causing trouble for the last moon," Pinestar explained. "Straying into the forest, scaring our prey—not that he catches any, of course. But I decided to see how he liked it when I went onto his territory—and I wanted to give him a warning to stay away for good."

Lionpaw felt a little knot inside his belly relax. He had guessed this was the reason Pinestar had gone over the fence!

"He wasn't there, just my luck," Pinestar went on. "Then I heard the Twoleg coming, so I jumped on that ledge and pretended to be another kittypet so she didn't get suspicious. It was hard work, I can tell you!"

Lionpaw nodded. His leader was so brave and clever! Lionpaw would never have thought of pretending to be a kittypet!

"You won't say anything to the others, will you?" Pinestar checked. "I don't want any other warriors trying this. It's far too dangerous."

Lionpaw shook his head. "Oh, no. I won't say a word," he promised. His tail bristled with excitement. Pinestar must trust him as much as a warrior! Maybe his name would be Liontrust, or Lionloyal, because of the great secret they shared.

"I knew it!" Sunfall hissed. Keeping low so that his orange pelt was hidden by ferns, he looked back at Lionpaw. "Go back to the camp and tell Pinestar we're being invaded! Those RiverClan warriors have deliberately crossed the border. We can't let them get away with it. Pinestar needs to send a fighting patrol here at once."

Lionpaw nodded and whipped around. He squeezed past Bluefur and Tawnyspots and pelted back along the trail that led to the ravine. He jumped down the rocks in one giant leap and burst through the tunnel. "RiverClan is attacking us!" he yowled.

Several heads appeared around the clearing. "Where's Pinestar?" Lionpaw panted. "He needs to send a warrior patrol."

"I thought he was with you," meowed Thrushpelt. "I'll take the patrol to Sunningrocks; you go find Pinestar and tell him what's going on."

Lionpaw spun around and raced out of the camp. He could guess where Pinestar was: defending their territory against that pesky kittypet! Well, he'd have to focus on RiverClan right now, before those fish-faces took over all of ThunderClan. Lionpaw ran through the pine trees and threw himself at the wooden fence. He slithered down the other side, unable to stop on the top, and landed in a heap among the flowers. Shaking earth off his fur, he looked out.

Pinestar was standing on the white stone, eating a pile of brown pellets. The Twoleg was standing over him, showing its teeth and making soft, friendly noises. Pinestar swiped his tongue around his jaws and looked up at the Twoleg, curling his body around its hind legs. "That was delicious!" he meowed. "Is there any more?"

"Pinestar! What are you doing?"

The ThunderClan leader froze and looked straight at Lionpaw. A flash of horror appeared in his eyes; then he ran across the lawn. "You shouldn't be here!" he hissed. "What if that kittypet comes back?"

"RiverClan is invading!" Lionpaw told him. "You have to come!"

CODE
15

Pinestar looked down at his paws. "I can't."

"Why not? Did the kittypet hurt you?" Lionpaw peered at him but couldn't see any blood.

"There is no other kittypet," Pinestar mumbled. "Only me."

Lionpaw shook his head, confused. "You're just pretending to be a kittypet. So the Twoleg doesn't chase you away."

Pinestar glanced over his shoulder. The Twoleg was standing on the stone watching them. "She won't chase me away," he mewed. "She likes me."

Lionpaw stared at him in disbelief. "But you're our Clan leader! You can't be friends with Twolegs!"

"Then I can't be your leader anymore," Pinestar whispered. "I'm sorry, Lionpaw. I can't keep the Clan safe. I'm too old, too scared of losing any more battles. Sunfall will make a better leader than me. Tell ThunderClan that I am dead."

Lionpaw felt a surge of anger. "No! I will not lie for you! You might not want to be our leader anymore, but you could at least be brave enough to tell the Clan yourself. They deserve to know the truth, that you are leaving to become a *kittypet*."

He whirled around and scrabbled back over the fence. He heard Pinestar following, and the Twoleg call out in a high-pitched voice. "I'll come back, I promise!" Pinestar meowed from the top of the fence, before jumping down after Lionpaw.

They ran back through the forest. With a jolt, Lionpaw wondered what had happened by Sunningrocks. Had Thrushpelt's patrol been enough to drive out the RiverClan invaders? Would Pinestar be forced to fight for his Clan one last time? They reached the ravine and jumped down. The gorse tunnel was trembling as if several cats had just burst through it. The clearing was crowded with warriors and apprentices circling, some of them bleeding from scratches, others limping. Featherwhisker, the apprentice medicine cat, was chasing Rosepaw around with a mouthful of marigold leaves.

"If you just keep still long enough for me to put these on your cut," the medicine cat puffed, his voice muffled through the herbs, "I'll be able to treat the other cats."

"Treat them first!" Rosepaw protested. "That stuff stings!"

The cats fell silent one by one as they spotted Pinestar. When they were all quiet, Sunfall stepped out, bleeding from a torn ear.

"Where were you, Pinestar?" he asked.

Pinestar didn't answer at once. "Did you win?"

Sunfall nodded. "We chased those fish-faces back as far as the river. They still have Sunningrocks—that is a battle for another day—but they won't set foot across the border for a while."

"Good," Pinestar meowed. He padded across the clearing and jumped onto Highrock. "Let all cats old enough to catch their own prey gather to hear what I have to tell you!" he yowled.

Most of the Clan were in the clearing already, but they turned to face Highrock and settled down. Lionpaw joined Rosepaw and Bluefur, who was licking one of her claws. "I nearly tore it out on a RiverClan warrior!" she whispered proudly.

Lionpaw looked up at Pinestar. It felt so strange, knowing what he was going to say. The blood roared in his ears, and he didn't hear the start of the Clan leader's announcement, just the gasps of shock around him. Sunfall said something; then Pinestar spoke again.

"I have been honored to serve you for eight of my lives. My ninth will be spent as a kittypet, where I have no battles to fight, no lives depending on me for food and safety. Sunfall will lead you well, and StarClan will understand."

"The other Clans might not," Sunfall warned. "You won't be

CODE
15

able to come back to the forest, you know."

Pinestar let out an amused huff. "Oh, I can imagine the names they'll call me. I wouldn't be surprised if one of the leaders suggests an addition to the warrior code, that all true warriors scorn the easy life of a kittypet. But you'll make ThunderClan as strong as it ever was, Sunfall. My last act as leader is to entrust my Clan to you, and I do it confidently."

Sunfall dipped his head. "I am honored, Pinestar. I promise I will do my best."

Pinestar jumped down from Highrock and wove among his Clanmates for the last time.

A sleek black she-cat stepped forward. "Pinestar, what about our kits? Won't you stay to watch them grow up?" She nodded to the three tiny cats beside her. Two were weak and sickly-looking, slumped on the ground with glazed eyes, but the third, Tigerkit, was a sturdy dark brown tabby, who pounced on his father's tail. Pinestar gently pulled it away.

"They'll be fine with you, Leopardfoot. I'm not a father they could be proud of, but I will always be proud of them. Especially you,

little warrior," he added, bending down to touch his muzzle to the dark tabby's ears. Tigerkit gazed up at him with huge amber eyes and growled, showing thorn-sharp teeth.

"Be strong, my precious son," Pinestar murmured. "Serve your Clan well."

He straightened up and continued across the clearing. He paused once more beside Lionpaw. "Thank you," he meowed. "You were right. I had to tell my Clan myself. You have a good spirit, young one. When it is time for you to receive your warrior name, tell Sunfall I would have called you Lionheart."

He nodded, then padded softly into the gorse tunnel and disappeared. Lionpaw watched until the gorse stopped shaking.

May StarClan walk your path, always, he murmured to the old leader. *And may I be worthy of my warrior name.*

Lionheart.

❈

A Change of Heart: Sandstorm Speaks

If Fireheart was just a kittypet, would he have gone to Tallstar behind Bluestar's back and arranged to stop the battle before it began? Would he have risked Bluestar's trust because he believed what he was doing was best for the Clan? Would so many of his Clanmates have supported him, even Whitestorm and Goldenflower?

Dustpelt tells me over and over that Fireheart can never be a true Clan warrior because he wasn't born in the forest. He belonged to Twolegs, who fed him that muck that looks like rabbit droppings, and made him wear a *collar*! He was such a show-off when he first came to ThunderClan. He always had to be best in training, or catch the most prey, and be the most solemn when we went to Gatherings. Dustpelt and I could never figure out why Graystripe was friends with him; he didn't seem to know what fun was.

And he was always causing trouble! Like taking Ravenpaw

away—Fireheart said he didn't
know what happened when
Ravenpaw vanished, but I
saw them sneaking out of the
camp. He always seemed to
be doing something to annoy
Tigerclaw. But now it looks as
if he was right, and Tigerclaw
was our biggest enemy all along.
Would a kittypet have been able to
figure that out? Not even Bluestar realized until Tigerclaw tried
to kill her.

Maybe it's *because* Fireheart was a kittypet. He doesn't just
accept the warrior code; he thinks about it and figures out how
it's supposed to work. And when it doesn't, like when he should
have obeyed his leader who ordered him to attack WindClan, he
challenges it and does something different. Is that a weakness in
Clan cats, that we do what we're told just because that's what our
ancestors did?

Dustpelt insists that Fireheart doesn't belong in ThunderClan
because the code says we have to reject kittypets. But we have to
reject their *life*, not the cats themselves. And Fireheart has done
that, hasn't he? He started out as a kittypet and chose to leave it
all behind to join ThunderClan.

If I had to choose between Dustpelt and Fireheart to lead the
Clan, who would I pick? Dustpelt is so loyal to the warrior code,
he'd never dream of breaking it. The other Clans would respect
him for that, which might make them more peaceful toward us.
Fireheart would argue with any cat, in ThunderClan or outside,
if he didn't think they were doing the right thing. I don't want to
live in a Clan that is always at war.

But Fireheart won't fight a battle that he doesn't believe in. That's why he talked to Tallstar, persuaded him not to let his warriors fight when Bluestar led the attack on his border. Which means Tallstar must respect Fireheart and trust him, because he's always been friendly with Bluestar before now.

Maybe a kittypet can know us better than we know ourselves. Maybe it takes an outsider looking in to see the truth—like Fireheart knew the truth about Tigerclaw. I wonder if he'll ever see the truth in my own heart: that, whatever Dustpelt says, however much Fireheart breaks the warrior code, I love him more than I could imagine loving any other cat.

And if Fireheart knew, would he love me, too?

CODE
15

Rules That Did Not Become Part of the Code: Leafpool Speaks

Not every rule that was suggested was accepted by all the Clans—and it was always understood, without having to be made part of the code, that every Clan had to agree.

Did you know it was once suggested that only cats of pure forest blood could be Clan members? Kittypets, rogues, and loners would be barred from Clan life—and those already living in the Clans would be expected to leave. I can tell you assume it was a ShadowClan leader that put this forward, but actually it was Featherstar of WindClan. After a hard leaf-bare, when only the swiftest warriors could catch any of the fleet-footed prey on the moor, she blamed her Clan's hunger on those cats who hadn't been born with the ability to run rabbit-fast. She saw the other Clans struggling to catch enough fresh-kill and was convinced that only Clanborn cats could look after themselves and their Clanmates.

Owlstar of ThunderClan argued most strongly against her—it was rumored afterward that he had kittypets among his ancestors, but he didn't. He just saw that all the Clans would be weakened if they had to purge their members of non-forestborn cats. Loyalty to Clanmates has always lain at the core of the warrior code, and what Featherstar was proposing would let Clanmates turn on one another and claim superiority for something they had no control over. As long as cats were loyal to their Clan, Owlstar insisted, then they deserved to stay.

Not long after that, Hawkstar's successor, Robinstar, put forward that Clans should eat only the prey they were most suited to hunting: fish for RiverClan, birds for SkyClan, rabbits for WindClan, and so on. This was shouted down by all the Clans. It was unlikely that all the birds in SkyClan's hunting grounds would ever get sick and die, even during the coldest leaf-bare, but fish, rabbits, and ThunderClan's squirrels had all been known to suffer from an illness that either spread to cats or reduced the numbers of prey drastically. Besides, every Clan welcomes a chance to taste a different kind of fresh-kill when it strays into their territory— though RiverClan are welcome to keep all their slimy fish!

It was Dovestar of RiverClan who wanted to make it law that every Clan cat had to acknowledge that StarClan controlled Clan life; to deny the existence and power of the warrior ancestors would be to break the code. Does it surprise you that this is not one of our laws?

Being a Clan cat is not about being forced to believe something. We are allowed to think for ourselves, you know! It is not law that you have to stay in a Clan—cats may leave any time they wish if they no longer feel true to the warrior code or loyal to their Clanmates. As long as we believe in StarClan and the influence it has over our lives, accepting the warrior code is easy and loyalty comes as natural as breathing. You cannot force a cat to be faithful. That would be far worse than letting them be honest enough to choose a different path through life.

epilogue

Y ou've now heard the history of the warrior code. Stretch your legs; you've been sitting a long time. I'll walk with you to the edge of our territory. I could use some fresh air.

Thank you for listening. Perhaps you understand our way of life a little better now. As you've heard, we're not always perfect, but we have a great deal of faith in our warrior ancestors. The code lives in us in our heartbeat, the blood pulsing beneath our fur. When we die, the code carries on in our kits, and their kits, for all the moons to come. StarClan willing, the code of the Clans will live forever, until the forest and the lake have turned to dust and our hunting grounds are no more.

TURN THE PAGE FOR
A SNEAK PEEK AT **ERIN HUNTER'S**
BRAND-NEW SERIES!

SURVIVORS

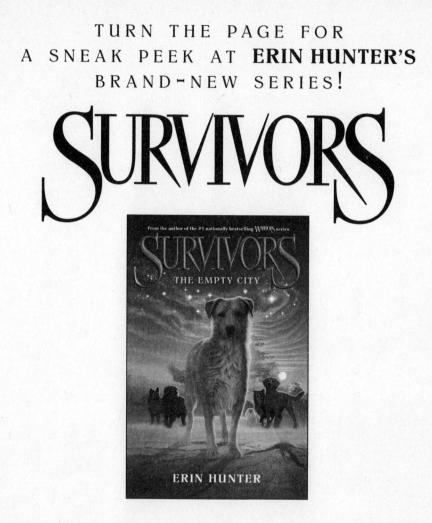

Lucky is a golden-haired mutt with a nose for survival. Other dogs have Packs, but Lucky stands on his own . . . until the Big Growl strikes. Suddenly, the ground splits wide-open. The longpaws disappear. And enemies threaten Lucky at every turn. For the first time in his life, Lucky needs to rely on other dogs to survive. But can he ever be a true Pack dog?

THE TIME HAS COME
FOR DOGS TO RULE THE WILD.

PROLOGUE

Yap wriggled, yawning, and gave a small excited whimper. His littermates were a jumble of warmth against him, all paws and muzzles and small fast heartbeats. Clambering over him, Squeak stuck a paw in his eye; Yap shook his head and rolled over, making her fall off. She squeaked with indignation as always, so he licked her nose to show there were no hard feelings.

The Mother-Dog stood over them, nuzzling them into order and licking their faces clean, treading her ritual circle before curling around them, ready for sleep.

"Wake up, Yap! Mother's going to tell us a story." That was Squeak again, bossy and demanding as ever. Their Mother-Dog washed her affectionately with her tongue, muffling her yelps.

"Would you like to hear about the Storm of Dogs?"

A thrill of excitement ran down Yap's spine, and he whimpered eagerly. "Yes!"

"*Again?*" whined Squeak.

But the others tumbled over her, drowning her protests. "Yes,

Mother! The Storm of Dogs!"

The Mother-Dog settled around their small bodies, her tail thumping. Her voice grew low and solemn. "This is the story of Lightning, the swiftest of the dog warriors. The Sky-Dogs watched over him, and protected him. . . . But the Earth-Dog was jealous of Lightning. She thought Lightning had lived too long, and that it was time for him to die so that she could take his life force. But Lightning's speed was so great that he could outrun the Earth-Dog's terrible Growls—he could outrun death itself!"

"I want to be like Lightning," murmured Yowl sleepily. "I could run that fast; I bet I could."

"Shush!" said Squeak, squashing his nose with a golden-furred paw. In spite of her protest, Yap knew that she was caught up in the story like the rest of them.

"Then came the first great battle," the Mother-Dog went on, her voice hushed. "The terrible Storm of Dogs, when all the dogs of the world fought to see who would rule over the territories of the world. Many stories are told of those terrible days, and many heroes were made and lost in the battle.

"At last, the Earth-Dog thought, Lightning's life force would be freed and she would take his body, as was her right. But Lightning was cunning, and he was sure that with his speed he could dodge his death once more, so the Earth-Dog laid a trap for him."

Yip's ears flattened against her head. "That's so mean!"

Their mother nuzzled her. "No, it isn't, Yip. Earth-Dog was right to claim Lightning. That's the way things should be. When your Sire-Dog died, his body fed the earth too."

Suddenly solemn, all of the pups listened in silence.

"Lightning tried to escape the Storm of Dogs with his speed. He ran so fast between the warring dogs that none of them could see him to tear his body apart with their teeth and claws. He was almost clear, almost free, when the Earth-Dog sent a Big Growl to open the ground in front of him."

Even though he'd heard the story so many times, Yap held his breath and huddled close to his littermates, imagining that this time Lightning would fall and be eaten by the terrible rip in the earth. . . .

"Lightning saw the ground open up to swallow him, but he was speeding so fast that he couldn't stop. He feared that the Earth-Dog had him at last. But the Sky-Dogs loved Lightning.

"Just as Lightning started to plummet to his death, the Sky-Dogs sent a great wind that spun so fast and so strong, it caught Lightning as he fell, lifted him up, and whirled him into the sky. And there he remains, with the Sky-Dogs, to this very day."

The pups snuggled more tightly against her side, gazing up at her.

"Will he always be there?" asked Yowl.

"Always. When you see fire flashing in the sky, when the Sky-

Dogs howl, that's Lightning running down to the earth, teasing Earth-Dog, knowing that she will never catch him." She licked Yap's sleepy face. He could barely keep his eyes open. "I've heard dogs say that one day, there will be another great battle, when a dog displeases the Earth-Dog. Then, dog will fight against dog, and great heroes will rise and fall. The Storm of Dogs will come again."

Yowl gave a great yawn, floppy with tiredness. "But not for a long time, right?"

"Ah, we don't know. It might come soon; it might not. We must always watch out for the signs. They say that when the world is turned upside down and broken open, the Storm of Dogs will come and we'll have to fight to survive once again."

Yap let his eyelids droop. He loved to fall asleep to his mother's stories. This was how it would always be, he knew: her voice, fading as sleep overwhelmed him and his littermates. The Mother-Dog, curled protectively around him, the end of the story the last thing he heard. It ended the same way each time. . . .

"Watch out, little ones. Watch out for the Storm of Dogs . . ."

CHAPTER ONE

Lucky startled awake, fear prickling in his bones and fur. He leaped to his feet, growling.

For an instant he'd thought he was tiny once more, safe in his pup-Pack and protected, but the comforting dream had already vanished. The air shivered with menace, tingling Lucky's skin. If only he could see what was coming, he could face it down—but the monster was invisible, scentless. He whined in terror. This was no sleep-time story: This fear was *real.*

The urge to run was almost unbearable; but he could only scrabble, snarl, and scratch in panic. There was nowhere to go: The wire of his cage hemmed him in on every side. His muzzle hurt when he tried to shove it through the gaps; when he backed away, snarling, the same wire bit into his haunches.

Others were close . . . familiar bodies, familiar scents. They were enclosed in this terrible place just as he was. Lucky raised his head and barked, over and over, high and desperate, but it was clear no dog could help him. His voice was drowned out by the chorus of frantic calls.

They were all *trapped.*

Dark panic overwhelmed him. His claws scrabbled at the earth floor, even though he knew it was hopeless.

He could smell the female swift-dog in the next cage, a friendly, comforting scent, overlaid now with the bitter tang of danger and fear. Yipping, he pressed closer to her, feeling the shivers in her muscles—but the wire still separated them.

"Sweet? Sweet, something's on its way. Something bad!"

"Yes, I feel it! What's happening?"

The longpaws—where were they? The longpaws held them captive in this Trap House but they had always seemed to care about the dogs. They brought food and water, they laid bedding, cleared the mess . . .

Surely the longpaws would come for them now.

The others barked and howled as one, and Lucky raised his voice with theirs.

Longpaws! Longpaws, it's COMING . . .

Something shifted beneath him, making his cage tremble. In a sudden, terrible silence, Lucky crouched, frozen with horror.

Then, around and above him, chaos erupted.

The unseen monster was here . . . and its paws were right on the Trap House.

Lucky was flung back against the wire as the world heaved and tilted. For agonizing moments he didn't know which way was up or down. The monster tumbled him around, deafening him with the racket of falling rock and shattering clear-stone. His vision went dark as clouds of filth blinded him. The screaming, yelping howls of terrified dogs seemed to fill his skull. A great chunk of wall crashed off the wire in front of his nose, and Lucky leaped back. Was it the Earth-Dog, trying to take him?

Then, just as suddenly as the monster had come, it disappeared. One more wall crashed down in a cloud of choking dust. Torn wire screeched as a high cage toppled, then plummeted to the earth.

There was only silence and a dank metal scent.

Blood! thought Lucky. *Death . . .*

Panic stirred inside his belly again. He was lying on his side, the wire cage crumpled against him, and he thrashed his strong legs, trying to right himself. The cage rattled and rocked, but he couldn't get up. *No!* he thought. *I'm trapped!*

"Lucky! Lucky, are you all right?"

"Sweet? Where are you?"

Her long face pushed at his through the mangled wire. "My cage door—it broke when it fell! I thought I was dead. Lucky, I'm free—but you—"

"Help me, Sweet!"

The other faint whimpers had stopped. Did that mean the other dogs were . . . ? No. Lucky could not let himself think about that. He howled just to break the silence.

"I think I can pull the cage out a bit," said Sweet. "Your door's loose, too. We might be able to get it open." Seizing the wire with her teeth, she tugged.

Lucky fought to keep himself calm. All he wanted to do was fling himself against the cage until it broke. His hind legs kicked out wildly and he craned his head around, snapping at the wire. Sweet was gradually pulling the cage forward, stopping occasionally to scrabble at fallen stones with her paws.

"There. It's looser now. Wait while I—"

But Lucky could wait no longer. The cage door was torn at the upper corner, and he twisted until he could bite and claw at it. He worked his paw into the gap and pulled, hard.

The wire gave with a screech, just as Lucky felt a piercing stab in his paw pad—but the door now hung at an awkward angle. Wriggling and squirming, he pulled himself free and stood upright at last.

His tail was tight between his legs as tremors bolted through his skin and muscles. He and Sweet stared at the carnage and chaos around them. There were broken cages—and broken bodies. A small, smooth-coated dog lay on the ground nearby, lifeless, eyes dull. Beneath the last wall that had fallen, nothing stirred, but a limp paw poked out from between stones. The scent of death was already spreading through the Trap House air.

Sweet began to whimper with grief. "What was that? What *happened?*"

"I think—" Lucky's voice shook, and he tried again. "It was a Growl. I used to—my Mother-Dog used to tell me stories about the Earth-Dog, and the Growls she sent. I think the monster was a Big Growl. . . ."

"We have to get away from here!" There was terror in Sweet's whine.

"Yes." Lucky backed slowly away, shaking his head to dispel the death-smell. But it followed him, clinging to his nostrils.

He glanced around, desperate. Where the wall had tumbled onto the other dog cages, the broken blocks had collapsed into a pile, and light shone bright through the haze of brick dust and smoke.

"There, Sweet, where the stones have crumbled in. Come on!"

She needed no more urging, leaping up over the rubble. Aware of his wounded paw, Lucky picked his way more carefully, nervously glancing around for longpaws. Surely they'd race in when they saw the destruction? Wouldn't they come and drag them back to the Trap House?

He shuddered and quickened his pace, but even when he sprang down onto the street outside, following Sweet's lead, there was no sign of any longpaws.

Bewildered, he paused, and sniffed the air. It smelled so strange. . . .

"Let's get away from the Trap House," he told Sweet in a low voice. "I don't know what's happened, but we should go far away in case the longpaws come back."

Sweet gave a sharp whine as her head drooped. "Lucky, I don't think there are any longpaws left."

Their journey was slow and silent. A sense of threat grew in Lucky's belly; so many of the roads and alleys he knew were blocked. Still he persevered, nosing his way around the broken buildings through tangled, snaking coils torn from the ground. Despite what Sweet thought, Lucky was sure that the longpaws would return soon. He wanted to be far away from the destroyed Trap House when they did.

The sky was darkening by the time he felt they were far enough from the Trap House to rest; Lucky sensed anyway that Sweet couldn't go much farther. Maybe swift-dogs weren't as good at long journeys as they were at quick dashes. He gazed back the way they'd come, shadows lengthening across the ground, hiding spaces emerging in dark corners. Lucky shivered—which other animals might be out there, scared and hungry?

But they were both exhausted from escaping the Big Growl. Sweet barely managed to tread her ritual sleep-circle before she slumped to the ground, laid her head on her forepaws, and closed her troubled eyes. Lucky pressed himself close against her flank for warmth and comfort. *I'll stay awake for a while,* he thought, *Keep watch . . . yes . . .*

* * *

He woke with a start, shivering, his heart racing.

He'd slept no-sun away. His dreams were full of the distant rumbling of the Big Growl and an endless line of longpaws running away from him and loudcages whining and beeping. There was no sign of others here now. The city seemed abandoned.

Beneath the thorny scrub, Sweet slept on, the flanks of her sleek body gently rising and falling with each breath. Lucky stretched life back into his limbs.

Something about Sweet's deep sleep was comforting, but suddenly he needed more than the scented warmth of her sleeping body; he needed her awake and alert. He nuzzled Sweet's long face, licking her ears until she responded with a happy murmuring growl. She got to her feet, sniffing and licking him in return.

"How's that paw, Lucky?"

Her words instantly brought the sting back. Remembering the wound, he sniffed at his paw pad. An angry red mark scored the flesh, pulsing with pain. He licked it gently. It was closed, but only just, and he didn't want to make it bleed again.

"It's better, I think," he said, more hopefully than he felt; then, as they both slunk out from beneath the dense branches, his spirits slumped.

The road before them was broken, wildly tilted, and cracked. Water sprayed high into the air from a long tube exposed by crumbling earth, making rainbows in the air. And it wasn't just here; in the sloping city streets, as far as Lucky could see, the light of the rising Sun-Dog glinted on tangled metal. A slick of water lay where he remembered that there had once been gardens, and the longpaw homes that used to seem tall and indestructible were now crumpled and slumped as if pummeled by a giant longpaw fist. The distant wail of broken loudcages went unanswered.

"The Big Growl," murmured Sweet, awestruck and afraid. "Look what it's done."

Lucky shivered. "You were right about the longpaws. There were packs and packs of them. Now I don't see a single one." He cocked his ears and tasted the air with his tongue: dust and an under-earth stink. No fresh scents. "Even the loudcages aren't moving."

Lucky tilted his head toward one of them, tipped onto its side, its snout half-buried in a collapsed wall. Light gleamed from its metal flanks but there was no roar and grumble; it seemed dead.

Sweet looked startled. "I always wondered what those were for. What did you call it?"

Lucky gave her a doubtful look. She didn't know what a loudcage was?

"Loudcages. You know—longpaws use them to get around. They can't run as fast as we can."

He couldn't believe she didn't know this most basic detail about the longpaws. It gave him a bad feeling about setting out with her. Sweet's naïveté wouldn't be much help when they were trying to survive.

Lucky sniffed the air again. The city's new smell made him uneasy. There was a rottenness, a lingering whiff of death and danger. *It doesn't smell like a home for dogs anymore,* he thought.

He padded over to where water sprayed from a wound in the earth. In the sunken hole was an oily lake, its surface shimmering with rainbow colors. It gave off an odd smell that Lucky didn't like, but he was too thirsty to care, and lapped the water greedily, doing his best to ignore the foul taste. Beside him he saw Sweet's reflection as she also drank.

She was the first to lift her dripping muzzle, licking her pointed chops. "It's too quiet," she murmured. "We need to get out of this longpaw town." Sweet's fur lifted. "We should go to the hills. Find a wild place."

"We're as safe here as anywhere else," said Lucky. "We can use the old longpaw houses—maybe find food. And there are plenty of hiding places, believe me."

"Plenty of places for *other* things to hide," she retorted, bristling. "I don't like it."

"What do you have to be scared of?" Her legs looked long enough to race through high grasses and her frame was slender and light. "I bet you can run faster than anything!"

"Not around corners, I can't." She glanced nervously to left and right. "And a city has lots of corners. I need space to run. That's where I can pick up speed."

Lucky scanned the area, too. She was right—the buildings crowded in on them. Maybe she had good reason to be edgy. "Let's at least keep moving. Some of those longpaws might still be close by, whether we can see them or not. I don't want to go back to the Trap House."

"Me neither," Sweet agreed, her lip curling to show her strong white teeth. "We should start looking for more dogs. We need a good, strong Pack!"

Lucky's muzzle wrinkled in doubt. He was not a Pack Dog. He had never understood what there was to like about living with a big mob of dogs, all dependent on one another, and having to submit to an Alpha. He didn't need anyone's help, and the last thing he wanted was someone who needed his. Just the thought of relying on other dogs made his skin prickle.

Obviously that isn't how Sweet feels, he thought. She was enthusiastic now, rattling off stories. "You would have loved my Pack! We ran together, and hunted together, catching rabbits and chasing rats . . ." She became more subdued, and looked longingly toward the outskirts of the wrecked town. "Then the longpaws came and spoiled everything."

Lucky couldn't help responding to the sadness in her voice. "What happened?"

Sweet shook herself. "They rounded us up. So many of them, and all in the same brown fur! Staying together, that's what got us trapped, but"—her growl grew fierce—"we wouldn't leave a single dog behind. That's Pack law. We stuck together, in good times and . . . bad." Sweet paused, her dark eyes distant, unable to repress an unhappy whimper.

"Your Pack was with you in the Trap House," murmured Lucky sympathetically.

"Yes." She came to an abrupt halt. "Wait, Lucky, we have to go back!"

He darted in front of her as she spun around, blocking her way. "No, Sweet!"

"We *have* to!" Lucky scrambled sideways to stop her from slipping past him. "They're my Packmates. I can't leave until I find out what's happened to them! If any of them are still—"

"No, Sweet!" Lucky barked. "You saw how it was in that place!"

"But we might have missed—"

"*Sweet.*" He tried a gentler tone, tentatively licking her unhappy face. "Back there, it's ruined. They're all dead, gone to the Earth-Dog. And we can't hang around here—the longpaws might come back. . . ."

That seemed to convince her. Sweet glanced over her shoulder once more, then turned away again. With a deep sigh she began to walk on.

Lucky tried not to show his relief. He walked close beside her, their flanks brushing with every second step.

"Did you have friends in the Trap House too?" Sweet asked.

"Me?" said Lucky lightly, trying to cheer her up. "No thanks. I'm a Lone Dog."

Sweet gave him an odd glance. "There's no such thing. Every dog needs a Pack!"

"Not me. I *like* being on my own. I mean, I'm sure a Pack's best for some dogs," he added hurriedly to spare her feelings, "but I've walked alone since I left my pup-Pack." He couldn't repress the proud lift of his head. "I can look after myself. There's no better place for a dog than the city. I'll show you! There's food for the finding, and warm crannies to sleep in, and shelter from the rain—"

But is that still true?

For a moment he hesitated, letting his eyes rove over the smashed streets, the shattered walls and broken clear-stones, the tilting roads and abandoned loudcages. *This isn't safe,* Lucky thought. *We need to get out of here as soon as we can.*

But he wasn't going to share that fear with Sweet, not when she was already so anxious. If only there were some distraction—

There!

Lucky gave a high bark of excitement. They'd turned a corner, and right in the road was another wreck. Lucky scented—*food!*

He broke into a run, leaping in delight onto the side of the huge overturned metal box. He'd seen longpaws throwing things they didn't want into these, locking them afterward so that Lucky was never able to feast on the unwanted food. But now the box was on its side, the half-rotten contents spilled out across the ground. Black crows were hopping and jabbing around the piles. Lucky held his head high and barked as loud as he could. The crows cawed, alarmed, as they half-fluttered away.

"Come on!" he yelled, springing into the stinking pile. Sweet followed, barking happily.

As Lucky nosed his way through the mound of scraps, he heard the dull fluttering of wings as the crows descended again. He leaped and snapped his jaws at an indignant bird and it darted into the air, its wings beating strongly.

Lucky sent a final snarl after the departing crow as he landed back on the ground, his paws skidding in the dirt. Immediately, his wounded paw howled with pain. It was like the fangs of the most vicious dog, biting all the way up his leg. He couldn't hold back his whimper of distress.

As Sweet dashed through the cloud of crows, chasing them clear, Lucky sat down and licked the pain away. He eagerly sniffed the air, enjoying the scent coming off the piles of discarded items that had spilled out across the ground. Contentment began to settle over him again, and he was distracted from his pain.

For a while the happy mood lingered as Lucky and Sweet snuffed out the delicacies the crows had left. Sweet pulled chicken bones from a cardboard bucket, and Lucky found a crust of bread, but the pickings were poor, especially after they'd worked up such an appetite.

"We're going to starve in this city." Sweet whined, licking an empty box that had once held some food. She pinned it down with one paw as she poked her nose inside.

"I promise we won't. It's not all scavenging." Lucky's mind was flooded with an image of a place he used to visit. He nudged Sweet's flank affectionately. "I'll take you somewhere where we'll eat like Leashed Dogs."

Sweet's ears pricked up. "Really?"

"Really. This place will change your mind about cities."

Lucky trotted confidently down the road, his mouth already watering at the prospect of food. Sweet was right behind him. It was strange how happy he was with her company, how much he liked being able to help her. Usually by now, he'd be itching for solitude, but . . . he wasn't.

Maybe the Big Growl had changed more than just the city.

CHAPTER TWO

Sweet pressed close to Lucky's side as they walked through the deserted streets.

He had expected to see other dogs by now, and certainly a few longpaws. But the city was empty, and far too quiet. At least they had found a few stale scent-marks; that was reassuring. He stopped to sniff at an upturned bench that had been marked by a male Fierce Dog.

"They can't be far." Sweet interrupted his thoughts. She bent her muzzle to the scent, ears lifting. "This is a strong message. And there are others! Can't you smell them?"

The fur on Lucky's shoulders bristled: Why was Sweet so determined to find a Pack? Wasn't his company enough?

"These dogs must be long gone now," he said, backing away from the bench. "We won't catch up any time soon."

Sweet raised her nose in the air. "They smell nearby to *me*."

"But this only smells strong because it was their territory. They marked it over and over. I'm telling you, Sweet, they're far away already. I can pick out their scent in the distance."

"Really?" Sweet sounded doubtful again. "But *I* could catch up with them. I can catch *anything*."

Why don't I just let her? Lucky wondered. *If she's so desperate to find a Pack, I should just tell her to run away as fast as she likes.*

Instead, he found himself rumbling a warning growl. "No, Sweet, you can't. *Shouldn't*, I mean," he added quickly as she bristled. "You don't know the city; you could get lost."

Frustrated, Sweet cast her nose around in the air, then barked angrily. "Why did this happen, Lucky? I was fine before. My *Pack* was fine! We were so happy in the open country, and we didn't do any harm to the longpaws. If they'd only left us alone, if they hadn't rounded us up into that awful Trap House—"

She'd come to a miserable halt, and Lucky sat down beside her, wishing he could think of something to say. But he wasn't used to being responsible for another dog. Already it gave him an ache in his heart that he would rather live without.

He opened his jaws to try to reason with her some more, but stopped, gaping as a gang of fierce, furious creatures tumbled, yowling and squealing, into the street right in front of them.

Lucky felt fear tear through his hackles as his back stiffened. At first, he thought the fighting bundles of fur and teeth were sharpclaws, but then he realized they were different—very different.

These animals were round and bushy-tailed—and they didn't hiss. They weren't dogs, and they weren't huge rats. Lucky gave an alarmed yelp, but the creatures didn't respond—they were too busy squabbling over a carcass that was so ripped and torn, he couldn't tell what it had once been.

Next to him, Sweet stood alertly, her eyes on the other animals. She took a moment to nuzzle his neck. "Don't worry about them; they won't hurt us."

"Are you sure?" asked Lucky. He'd caught sight of the face of one of them, a sinister black mask that seemed full of vicious little teeth.

"They're raccoons," Sweet replied. "We'll be fine if we give them a wide berth. Try not to show too much interest and they won't feel threatened. I bet they're as hungry as we are."

Lucky followed Sweet's lead to the far sidewalk. She shot the raccoons a fierce bristling glare as she went. Lucky copied her, feeling prickles of anxiety in the roots of his fur.

We're not the only ones looking to fill our bellies, he realized. With everything torn from the ground and lying in ruins, easy pickings were a thing of the past. This was about survival now. He picked up his pace, keen to put as much space as he could between themselves and the raccoons.

A few streets beyond, Lucky tasted familiar air and gave a happy bark. It was the alley he'd been looking for! He ran forward a few paces, then sat down and scratched at his ear with a hindpaw, enjoying the moment, anticipating Sweet's delight. The delicious smell of food was getting stronger. Here, at least, he could guarantee a meal.

"Come on!" he yipped. "I promise, you won't regret this."

She padded up behind him and cocked her head quizzically. "What is this place?"

He nodded at the panes of clear stone. There were long tubes there. Normally, they breathed chicken-scented steam into the air— but not today. Still, this was definitely the right place. Excited, he turned a couple of circles, tail wagging quickly.

"It's a Food House. A place where longpaws give food to other longpaws!"

"But we're not longpaws," she pointed out. "Who's going to give food to us?"

"Just you watch." Lucky jumped forward mischievously, dodging around tumbled trash cans and a small heap of rubble. He tried not to think about how ruined everything was, or that they hadn't seen a single longpaw walking the streets. "We'll do what Old Hunter does. He's the expert!"

Sweet brightened. "Old Hunter? Is he a Packmate of yours?"

"I told you, I don't have a Pack. Old Hunter is just a *friend*. Even Lone Dogs can find huntingmates, you know! Watch this. Copy what I do. . . ."

It was such an easy method of getting food, and it took no time to learn—Lucky was pleased to be able to teach Sweet something. He sat back on his haunches, tilted his head, and let his tongue loll out.

Sweet slowly slinked around him, studying the posture. Her head cocked. "I don't understand," she whined.

"Just trust me," Lucky growled.

Sweet whined again, then turned to sit down beside Lucky as she did her best to copy him.

"That's it!" Lucky barked. "Now, lift one ear a little higher. Like this, see? And a friendly mouth—look hungry but hopeful! You got it!"

Lucky wagged his tail as he gave Sweet an affectionate nudge with his muzzle. Then he turned his attention back to the Food House door, and waited. A longpaw would spot them soon. Slow moments passed and Lucky's tail began to wag more and more slowly until it came to rest in the dust. The door stayed resolutely shut, so Lucky padded over to scratch at it. Still no reply. He gave a small respectful whine.

"How long do we stay like this? It's a bit—undignified," said Sweet. She licked her chops, then let her tongue hang out again.

"I don't understand. . . ." Lucky's tail drooped in embarrassment. Where was his friendly longpaw? Surely *he* hadn't run from the Big Growl. Lucky scratched at the door again, but still there was no reply.

Sweet's nose was back in the air. "I don't think it's working."

"The longpaws must be busy, that's all," Lucky grumbled. "This is an important place for them. They wouldn't have just *left*." He tried not to notice how high and anxious his voice had become. He trotted around to the back of some bins and spoil-boxes and scratched his way through to a side door. Up on his hind legs, he put his paws against the wood, and felt it sag and creak.

"Look! The Food House is broken." He tugged at a sagging hinge with his teeth. "That's why the longpaws are busy. Come on!"

The Food House smells must have been enticing enough to make Sweet forget her doubts, because she helped him nose and pull and tug at the broken door until it cracked open. Lucky wriggled through ahead of her, his tail thrashing in anticipation of scrumptious food.

He slowed, glancing from side to side. This room was a strange place that he hadn't seen before, lined with huge metal boxes. There were snaking, shiny lengths of what looked like long worms. Lucky knew that these usually hummed with the longpaws' invisible energy. But nothing hummed now. Above him, water dripped from the collapsed roof, and broad cracks ran along the walls.

There was a blurred reflection of himself and Sweet in the big steel boxes. A shudder passed over him to see how distorted their faces were. The food smell was strong now, but old, and Lucky felt prickles of uncertainty.

"I don't like this," said Sweet in a low voice.

Lucky whined his agreement. "This isn't the way it normally is. But it should be fine. It's probably just a little bit of damage from the Big Growl." Tentatively Lucky pushed on through the rubble and mess. Sweet watched him, her muzzle wrinkling with uncertainty. "Don't look like that," he told her. "Come on!"

She lifted her slender paws high as she moved around broken, splintered shards of white stone that covered the floor.

There was another door, but it was easy to push open—almost too easy, because it swung wildly back and forth, practically bumping Sweet's roving nose and making her jump. As it grew still again, Lucky sniffed the air.

The chaos was even worse in here, beyond the room of metal boxes; longpaw stuff was flung in heaps, sitting-boxes broken and listing together, thick dust falling from the broken walls to cover everything. Shivers rippled through Lucky's fur.

Abruptly he stopped, drawing his lips back from his teeth. *What's that smell? I know it, but . . .* He couldn't repress a frightened growl. Something moved in the corner.

Lucky took a few hesitant paces, crouching low to the ground. The scent felt strong inside his nose. He bounded forward and pawed at the fallen roof beams. There was someone here!

White dust stirred and swirled; Lucky heard a groan, and a

breathless rasping of longpaw words. He recognized only one. "Lucky . . ."

The voice was weak, but it was familiar. Whimpering, Lucky sank his teeth into one of the huge broken beams and leaned his weight back on his paws, heaving. His whole body trembled with the effort, and he could feel his teeth being pulled from his jaws. It was no good! He released his bite and fell back, panting with the effort. The longpaw lay still and unmoving beneath the beam, a trickle of dried blood tracking down his face.

Lucky drew closer, ignoring his instincts, which were telling him to run away as fast as he could. Behind him, he could hear Sweet pacing with anxiety. Lucky lowered his head over the longpaw's body. One arm was free of the rubble, twisted at an unnatural angle. The longpaw's face was pale as snow, his lips a horribly unnatural blue, but they curved in a smile as his eyes met Lucky's.

He's alive! Lucky licked at his nose and cheeks, gently clearing some of the coating of dust. If Lucky could just clean the longpaw up, he'd look much healthier—just like his old self. But as Lucky stepped back, he saw that the skin beneath the dust was gray. The longpaw's ragged breath was the faintest of whispers, barely stirring the fur on Lucky's muzzle.

The longpaw's eyes flickered open, and with a groan of pain he lifted his trembling free hand to pat Lucky's head. Lucky nuzzled and licked him again, but the hand fell away, and the eyes closed once more.

"Wake up, longpaw," Lucky whined softly, his tongue lashing the cold, pale face. "Wake up. . . ."

Lucky waited. But the lips were still and cold.

The whisper of breath was gone.

CHAPTER THREE

A yelp of despair shattered the silence. Turning hurriedly away from the dead longpaw, Lucky stared at Sweet. Every hair on her sleek coat seemed to bristle with fear. Stiff-legged, she backed away, tail tight between her legs.

"I don't want your city!" she whined. "There's death and danger *everywhere*. I can't stand it!"

She let loose a howl of disgust and sprinted, making the door swing wildly once again as she shot through it. Lucky scrambled after her, knowing he had no hope of catching a swift-dog.

But Sweet's speed did her no favors in the close quarters of the steel room. She was hemmed in, dashing desperately from reflection to distorted reflection, crashing wildly into the metal boxes, and skidding on the slick floor. When she slammed into a wall in her terror, Lucky lunged forward and pinned her to the ground.

She squirmed beneath him, panicking, but Lucky kept his forepaws firmly on her sweating flank, his eyes fixed on hers. "Calm down! You're going to hurt yourself."

"I can't stay. . . ."

As Sweet's barks fell away to anxious pants, Lucky let his weight gently flop down on her. "It's nothing to be scared of, Sweet. He's only dead." He repeated what he was sure she already knew, hoping to calm her. "It's a natural smell: the longpaw's life force. Just like when we die—our selves leave our bodies, become part of the world."

Lucky had been taught ever since he was a pup that that was the way of life and death. When a dog met his end and his body went to the Earth-Dog, his self floated up to meet all the scents of the air, to mingle with them and become part of the whole world. That's what was happening to the longpaw now, Lucky was certain.

Sweet's flanks stopped heaving as her panting breaths subsided. Lucky could still see the whites of her wide, fearful eyes. He cautiously released her and she climbed to her feet. "I know that," she growled. "But I don't want to be anywhere near escaping longpaw spirits. I want to find as many dogs as we can. We need to track down other survivors, and get us all out of here *right now!*"

"But there's nothing we need to get away from—nothing will hurt us now, Sweet. The Food House fell on the longpaw in the Big Growl, that's all. . . ." Lucky needed Sweet to trust him. If he could reassure her, perhaps all of this would make sense to Lucky too.

"Where are the other longpaws?" Sweet barked, tossing her head. "They've either run away or they're dead, Lucky! I'm leaving this city, and I'm going to find a Pack. So should you!"

Lucky opened his mouth to speak, but the words dried up in his throat. He could only stare at her sadly. Sweet half-turned to leave, then froze with one paw raised and all her muscles tensed, eager to flee. She gazed at Lucky for a long moment, licking her lips uncertainly. "Aren't you coming with me?"

Lucky hesitated. The idea of a Pack didn't appeal to him one bit, but—for some reason—he didn't want Sweet to leave. He liked having her around. For the first time, he felt himself tremble at the prospect of being alone. And she was waiting for him, ears pricked, eyes hopeful. . . .

He shook himself. He'd spent his whole life on these streets. That's what he was—a Lone Dog.

"I can't."

"But you can't stay here!" Sweet howled.

"I told you: I'm not a Pack dog. I never will be."

She gave a sharp bark of exasperation. "Dogs aren't meant to be alone!"

Lucky gave her a regretful look. "I am."

Sweet sighed, and padded back to him. Fondly she licked his face. Lucky nuzzled her in response, fighting down a mournful whine that wanted to erupt from his belly.

"I'll miss you," she said quietly. Then she turned to wriggle through the door.

Lucky padded forward. "You don't have to . . ." But with a flash of her tail, she was gone. Lucky found himself staring at an empty space.

For a while, Lucky didn't feel like moving. He settled down on his belly, chin resting on his forepaws as he listened to the click of Sweet's claws on the ground, fading into the ruined emptiness of the streets. Even when he could hear her no longer, her scent still clung to the air. He wished it would vanish—and take this terrible pang of loneliness with it.

Lucky shut his eyes and tried to focus his mind on other things.

But that just left the hunger.

It was like a set of sharp teeth, gnawing and chewing at his stomach. Lucky was almost relieved to feel the pain—at least it took his mind off Sweet. *That's why I don't let myself get close to other dogs,* he thought.

Back in the room with the dead longpaw, Lucky sniffed and scratched in every corner, licking at crumbs and grease. Some of the broken things on the floor held smears of food, so he lapped at them, trying not to cut his tongue; then he leaped onto one of the untoppled tables to find small scraps to nibble on. There was so little, and the tantalizing taste of it only made his stomach growl louder, the teeth bite harder. He didn't go near the longpaw, forced himself not to look.

I'm on my own now. That's the way it should be.

The steel room would have food, he was sure—that was what must be in the metal boxes lined up around the walls. But when he scratched at them, they refused to open. Whimpering in hunger, he tugged and bit at the metal doors. They stuck firm. He flung his body against them. Nothing. It was no use: He was going to have to wander farther, see what else he could find.

At least he'd be in the open air again, he thought: free and easy, the way he used to be. He had looked after himself just fine until now—and he would keep on doing that.

Lucky headed back out into the alleyway. It seemed so much emptier than before, and he found himself scampering as fast as he could across the rubble, until he reached the broad open space beyond. Surely he'd find something here? It had always been such a bustle of noise and energy, full of longpaws and their loudcages.

There were plenty of loudcages, sure enough, but none of them were moving and there was still not a longpaw in sight, friendly or otherwise. Some of the loudcages had fallen onto their flanks—a big long one had crashed its blunt snout into an empty space in the wall of a building, shattered pieces of clear-stone glittering. Picking his way carefully through the shards, Lucky felt his hackles rise. The scent of longpaw was back in the air, but it was not comforting: It was the scent that had settled on the Food House owner when he had grown still. The silence was oppressive, punctuated only by the steady drip and trickle of water.

Above him the Sun-Dog, which had been so high and bright, was casting long shadows from the buildings that had withstood the Big Growl. Each time he passed through one of the pools of darkness, Lucky shivered and hurried back into the light. He kept moving, the patches of light growing steadily smaller, the shadows longer, and the ache of hunger in his belly sharper.

Maybe I should have gone with Sweet . . .

No. There was no point thinking that way. He was a Lone Dog again, and that was *good.*

He turned and trotted determinedly down another alley. This was his city! There was *always* food and comfort to be had here. Even if he had to dig deep for the leftovers in Food House spoil-boxes, or find another overturned smell-box in the road, there would be something the crows and the rats hadn't found. He was self-reliant, independent Lucky.

He was not going to starve.

Lucky drew to a stop as he got his bearings. This alley wasn't as damaged by the Big Growl as other places, but there was one deep, vicious crack running up the middle of it, and two spoil-boxes had been knocked flying. There might be a real feast there, if he rummaged. Lucky bounded up to the nearest one—then froze, nerves crackling beneath his fur. The scent was sharp and strong, and he knew it well.

Enemy!

Lips peeling back from his teeth, he sniffed the air to pinpoint the creature. Above him was a set of slender steps going up a wall, and his instincts pulled his eyes, ears, and nose toward it: That was the kind of place where this enemy liked to lurk, ready to pounce, needle-claws raking.

There it was: striped fur bristling, pointed ears laid flat, and tiny glinting fangs bared. Its low, threatening growl was punctuated by vicious hissing as it crouched, every muscle taut for its attack.

Sharpclaw!

KEEP WATCH FOR

SUPER EDITION

WARRIORS

YELLOWFANG'S SECRET

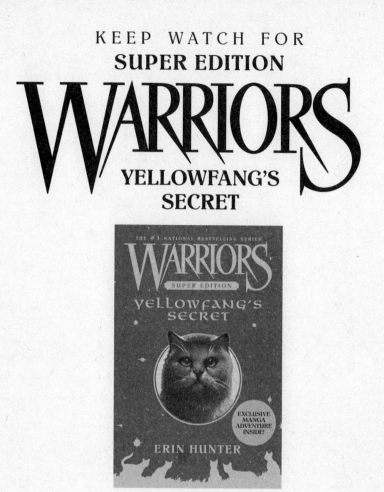

Yellowfang has dedicated her life to ShadowClan. She is a loyal medicine cat, ready and willing to do anything to protect her Clanmates and keep them safe. But a dark secret haunts her, threatening her life and the lives of every cat around her. . . .

PROLOGUE

Starlight shone down into a large cavern through a ragged hole in the roof. The faint silver sheen was just enough to show a tall rock jutting from the floor in the center of the cave, flanked by soaring rock walls, and at one side the dark, gaping hole of a tunnel entrance. The shadows in the mouth of the tunnel thickened, and six cats emerged into the cavern. Their leader, a speckled gray tom with clumped, untidy fur, padded up to the rock and turned to face the others.

"Sagewhisker, Hawkheart, Troutfin," he began, nodding to each cat as he named them, "we, the medicine cats of the four Clans, are here to carry out one of our most important ceremonies: the creation of a new medicine cat apprentice."

Two more cats lingered by the tunnel entrance, their eyes huge in the half-light. One of them shuffled his paws as if they had frozen to the cold stone.

"For StarClan's sake, Goosefeather, get on with it," Hawkheart muttered with an impatient twitch of her tail.

Goosefeather glared at her, then turned to the two young cats by the tunnel. "Featherpaw, are you ready?" he asked.

The bigger of the two, a silver-pelted tom, gave a nervous nod. "I guess so," he mewed.

"Then come here and stand before the Moonstone," Goosefeather directed. "Soon it will be time to share tongues with StarClan."

Featherpaw hesitated. "But I . . . I don't know what to say when I meet our ancestors."

"You'll know," the other young cat told him. Her white pelt glimmered as she touched his shoulder with her muzzle. "It'll be awesome, you'll see. Just as it was when I became Troutfin's apprentice!"

"Thanks, Bramblepaw," Featherpaw murmured.

He padded up to Goosefeather, while Sagewhisker, Troutfin, and Hawkheart sat a couple of tail-lengths away. Bramblepaw took her place at her mentor's side.

Suddenly the moon appeared through the hole in the roof, shedding a dazzling white light into the cave. Featherpaw halted and blinked in astonishment as the Moonstone woke into glittering life, blazing with silver.

Goosefeather stepped forward to stand over him. "Featherpaw," he meowed, "is it your wish to share the deepest knowledge of StarClan as a ThunderClan medicine cat?"

Featherpaw nodded. "Yes," he replied, his voice coming out as a breathless croak. He cleared his throat and tried again. "It is."

"Then follow me."

Goosefeather turned, beckoning with his tail, and took the few paces that brought him close to the Moonstone. His pale blue eyes shone like twin moons as he spoke. "Warriors of StarClan, I present to you this apprentice. He has chosen the path of a medicine cat. Grant him your wisdom and insight so that he may understand your ways and heal his Clan in accordance with your will." Flicking his tail at Featherpaw, he whispered, "Lie down here, and press your nose against the stone."

Quickly Featherpaw obeyed, settling himself close to the stone and reaching out to touch its glimmering surface with his nose. The other medicine cats moved up beside him, taking similar positions all around the stone. In the silence and the brilliant light, the new medicine cat apprentice closed his eyes.

Featherpaw's eyes blinked open and he sprang to his paws. He was standing chest-deep in lush grass, in a clearing of a sunlit forest. Above his head, the trees rustled in the warm breeze. The air was laden with the scent of prey and damp fern.

"Hi, Featherpaw!"

The young tom spun around. Approaching him through the grass was a tabby and white she-cat with blue eyes; she gave him a friendly flick with her tail as she drew closer.

Featherpaw stared at her. "M-Mallowfur!" he gasped. "I've missed you so much!"

"I may be a warrior of StarClan now, but I am always with you, my dear," Mallowfur purred. "It's good to see you here, Featherpaw. I hope it's the first time of many."

"I hope so, too," Featherpaw responded.

Mallowfur kept walking, brushing through the grass until she joined a ginger tom at the edge of the trees; together the two StarClan cats vanished into the undergrowth. Close to the spot where they had disappeared, another StarClan warrior crouched beside a small pool, lapping at the water. Heartbeats later, a squirrel dashed across the clearing and swarmed up the trunk of an oak tree, with two more of Featherpaw's starry ancestors hard on its tail.

Featherpaw heard his name being called again. "Hey, Featherpaw! Over here!"

Featherpaw glanced around the clearing. His gaze fell on a black tom, almost hidden in the shadows under a holly bush. He was small and skinny, his muzzle gray with age.

The dark-furred cat beckoned with his tail. "Over here!" he repeated, his voice low and urgent. "Are your paws stuck to the ground?"

Featherpaw shouldered his way through the long grasses until he stood in front of the tom. "Who are you? What do you want?"

"My name is Molepelt," the cat replied. "I have a message for you."

Featherpaw's eyes stretched wide. "A message from StarClan, my first time here?" he breathed out. "Wow, that's so great."

Molepelt let out an irritable grunt. "You might not think so, when you've heard what it is."

"Go on."

Molepelt fixed him with an icy green gaze. "A dark force is on its way," he rasped, "with the power to pierce deep into the heart of ThunderClan. And it will be brought by a ShadowClan medicine cat."

"What?" Featherpaw's voice rose to a high-pitched squeak. "That can't be right. Medicine cats have no enemies, and they don't cause trouble for other Clans."

Molepelt ignored his protest. "A long time ago, I was the ShadowClan medicine cat," he went on. "My Clanmates and I did a great wrong to another Clan—a Clan that belonged in the forest as much as any of us, but that was driven out through our selfishness and hardheartedness. I knew then that what we did was wrong, and I have waited, my heart filled with dread, for the Clans to be punished."

"Punished? How?" Featherpaw asked hoarsely.

"The time has come!" Now Molepelt's green eyes were wide, and he seemed to be gazing into the far distance. "A poison will spring from the heart of ShadowClan, and spread to all the other Clans." His voice became a soft, eerie wailing. "A storm of blood and fire will sweep the forest!"

Featherpaw gazed at the old cat in horror. Before he could speak, a powerful black-and-white tom pushed his way through a clump of ferns and padded up to the holly bush.

"Molepelt, what are you doing?" he demanded. "Why are you spilling all this out to a ThunderClan apprentice? You don't know that this is the time!"

Molepelt snorted. "You were once my apprentice, Hollowbelly, and don't you forget it! I *know* I'm right."

Hollowbelly glanced at Featherpaw, then back at Molepelt. "Things are different now," he meowed.

"What do you mean? What's going to happen?" Featherpaw asked, his voice shaking.

Hollowbelly ignored him. "There's no reason to punish ShadowClan," he went on to Molepelt. "What happened was too long ago. The medicine cat code will keep the Clans safe."

"You're a fool, Hollowbelly," Molepelt growled. "The medicine cat code can do *nothing* to save the Clans."

"You don't know that for sure!" When Molepelt did not respond, Hollowbelly turned to Featherpaw. "Please, say nothing about this," he meowed. "There is no need to spread alarm, not when the future is lost in mist even to StarClan. Promise me that you won't tell any of your Clanmates. Promise on the lives of your ancestors!"

Featherpaw blinked. "I promise," he whispered.

Hollowbelly nodded. "Thank you, Featherpaw. Go well." Nudging Molepelt to his paws, he led the old medicine cat away into the trees.

Featherpaw gazed after them. After a few heartbeats he scrambled out from underneath the holly bush and staggered into the sunlit clearing. "Even if Molepelt was telling the truth, it makes no sense!" he meowed out loud. "How can ThunderClan be threatened by a ShadowClan medicine cat?"

CHAPTER 1

❧

"**S**hadowClan warriors, attack!"

Yellowkit burst out of the nursery and hurtled across the ShadowClan camp. Her littermates Nutkit and Rowankit scurried after her.

Nutkit pounced onto a pine cone that lay among the debris at the foot of one of the trees overhanging the camp. "It's a WindClan warrior!" he squealed, batting at it with tiny brown paws. "Get out of our territory!"

"Rabbit-chasers!" Rowankit flexed her claws. "Prey-stealers!"

Yellowkit leaped at a straying tendril from the bramble barrier that encircled the camp; her paws got tangled in it and she lost her balance, rolling over in a flurry of waving legs and tail. Scrambling to her feet, she crouched in front of the bramble, her teeth bared in a growl. "Trip me over, would you?" she squeaked, raking her claws across its leaves. "Take that!"

Nutkit straightened up and began to scan the camp, peering around with narrowed amber eyes. "Can you see any more WindClan warriors on our territory?" he asked.

Yellowkit spotted a group of elders sharing tongues in a shaft of sunlight. "Yes! Over there!" she yowled.

Nutkit and Rowankit followed her as she raced across the camp and skidded to a halt in front of the elders.

"WindClan warriors!" Yellowkit began, trying to sound as dignified as her Clan leader Cedarstar. "Do you agree that

ShadowClan is the best of all the Clans? Or do you need to feel our claws in your fur to persuade you?"

Littlebird, her ginger pelt glowing in the warm light, sat up, giving the other elders an amused glance. "No, you're far too fierce for us," she meowed. "We don't want to fight."

"Do you promise to let our warriors cross your territory whenever they want?" Rowankit growled.

"We promise." Silverflame, the mother of Yellowkit's mother, Brightflower, flattened herself to the ground and blinked fearfully up at the kits.

Mistfang cringed away from the three kits, shuffling his skinny brown limbs. "ShadowClan is much stronger than us."

"Yes!" Yellowkit bounced up in the air. "ShadowClan is the best!" In her excitement she leaped on top of Nutkit, rolling over and over with him in a knot of gray and brown fur.

I'm going to be the best warrior in the best Clan in the forest! she thought happily.

She broke away from Nutkit and scrambled to her paws. "You be a WindClan warrior now," she urged. "I know some awesome battle moves!"

"Battle moves?" a scornful voice broke in. "You? You're only a kit!"

Yellowkit spun around to see Raggedkit and his littermate Scorchkit standing a couple of tail-lengths away.

"And what are you?" she demanded, facing up to the big dark tabby tom. "You and Scorchkit were still kits last time I looked."

"But we'll be apprentices soon," Raggedkit retorted. "It'll be moons and moons before you start training."

"Yeah." Scorchkit licked one ginger paw and drew it over his ear. "We'll be *warriors* by then."

"In your dreams!" Rowankit bounded up to stand next to Yellowkit, while Nutkit flanked her on her other side. "There are *rabbits* who'd make better warriors than you two."

Scorchkit crouched down, his muscles tensed to leap at her, but Raggedkit blocked him with his tail. "They're not worth it," he mewed loftily. "Come on, runts, watch us and we'll show you some *real* battle moves."

"You're not our mentors!" Nutkit snapped. "All you know how to do is mess up our game."

"Your game!" Raggedkit rolled his eyes. "Like you wouldn't go squealing into the nursery if WindClan really attacked our camp."

"Would not!" Rowankit exclaimed.

Raggedkit and Scorchkit ignored her, turning their backs on the younger kits. "You attack me first," Scorchkit ordered. Raggedkit dashed past his littermate, aiming a blow at Scorchkit's ear. Scorchkit swung away and pounced on Raggedkit's tail. Raggedkit rolled over onto his back, all four paws ready to defend himself.

Annoyed as she was, Yellowkit couldn't help admiring the older toms. Her paws itched to practice their battle moves, but she knew that she and her littermates would only get sneered at if they tried.

"Come on!" Nutkit nudged her. "Let's go and see if there are any mice in the brambles."

"You won't catch any, even if there are," Raggedkit meowed, rising to his paws and shaking debris from his fur.

"I wasn't talking to you." Nutkit's fur bristled and he bared tiny, needle-sharp teeth. "Kittypet!"

For a moment all five kittens froze. Yellowkit could feel her heart pounding. Like her littermates, she had heard the elders gossiping, wondering who had fathered Raggedkit and Scorchkit, asking each other whether it could be true that Featherstorm's mate had been a kittypet. The young she-cat had often strayed into Twolegplace, and she'd never been obviously close to any of the toms in the Clan. But Yellowkit knew that it was something you should never, never say out loud.

Raggedkit took a pace closer to Nutkit, stiff-legged with fury. "*What* did you call me?" he snarled, his voice dangerously quiet.

Nutkit's eyes were wide and scared, but he didn't back down. "Kittypet!" he repeated.

A low growl came from Raggedkit's throat. Scorchkit's eyes narrowed and he flexed his claws. Neither of them looked one bit like a soft, fluffy kittypet. Yellowkit braced herself to defend her littermate.

"Nutkit!"

Yellowkit turned at the sound of her mother's voice. Brightflower was standing beside the thornbush that shielded the nursery hollow. Her orange tabby tail was twitching in annoyance.

"Nutkit, if you can't play sensibly, then you'd better come back here. You too, Yellowkit and Rowankit. I won't have you fighting. Come on."

"Not fair," Nutkit muttered as all three littermates began trailing back toward the nursery. He scuffed his paws through the pine needles on the floor of the camp. "They started it."

"They're just stupid kittypets," Rowankit whispered.

Yellowkit couldn't resist glancing over her shoulder as she reached the thornbush. Raggedkit and Scorchkit stood in the middle of the clearing, glaring after them. The force of Raggedkit's anger scared her and fascinated her at the same time. Behind it she could sense something else: a black space that echoed with fearful questioning. She thought of her own father, Brackenfoot, who told stories of patrols and hunting and Gatherings at Fourtrees, who let his kits scramble all over him and pretended to be a fox so they could attack him. Yellowkit loved him and wanted to be like him.

What must it be like, not to know who your father is? she asked herself. *Especially if every cat thinks he was a kittypet?*

Then Yellowkit realized that Raggedkit's gaze had locked with hers. He knew that she was staring at him. With a squeak of alarm she ducked underneath the thorn branches and tumbled down into the nursery after her littermates.

ERIN HUNTER is inspired by a love of cats and a fascination with the ferocity of the natural world. As well as having great respect for nature in all its forms, Erin enjoys creating rich mythical explanations for animal behavior. She is also the author of the bestselling Seekers series and the forthcoming Survivors series.

Download the free Warriors app and chat on Warriors message boards at www.warriorcats.com.

For exclusive information on your favorite authors and artists, visit www.authortracker.com.

ENTER THE WORLD OF
WARRIORS

Warriors

Sinister perils threaten the four warrior Clans. Into the midst of this turmoil comes Rusty, an ordinary housecat, who may just be the bravest of them all.

Download the free Warriors app at www.warriorcats.com

Warriors: The New Prophecy

Follow the next generation of heroic cats as they set off on a quest to save the Clans from destruction.

All Warriors and Seekers books are available as ebooks from HarperCollins.

🎧 Also available unabridged from HarperChildren's*Audio*

HARPER
An Imprint of HarperCollinsPublishers

Delve Deeper into the Clans

Warrior Cats Come to Life in Manga!

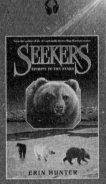
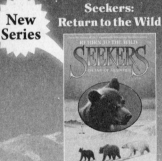